NEVER

LOOK

DOWN

NEVER

LOOK

DOWN

Warren C. Easley

W✷RLDWIDE ®

TORONTO • NEW YORK • LONDON
AMSTERDAM • PARIS • SYDNEY • HAMBURG
STOCKHOLM • ATHENS • TOKYO • MILAN
MADRID • WARSAW • BUDAPEST • AUCKLAND

To Jackson, Virginia, and Joaquin,
the hope of the future.

Recycling programs
for this product may
not exist in your area.

Never Look Down

A Worldwide Mystery/June 2017

First published by Poisoned Pen Press

ISBN-13: 978-0-373-28411-5

Copyright © 2015 by Warren C. Easley

Printed in U.S.A.

Acknowledgments

Very little that I write sees the light of day without first passing through my wife, Marge Easley. This manuscript was no exception. I'm not sure which is more beneficial, her unwavering encouragement or her skillful proofreading.

Once again, my editor, Barbara Peters, provided guidance that significantly strengthened this work, and the upbeat staff at Poisoned Pen Press gave strong, cheerful support. As always, much credit goes to my amazing critique group, Alison Jaekel, Debby Dodds, Janice Maxson, LeeAnn McLennan, Kate Scott, and Lisa Alber—writers of the first order, all. They keep me honest while making writing even more enjoyable. Thanks to Karen Bassett for insight into how federal re-entry centers work. A special shout-out to Guy Donzey, alpine guide extraordinaire, who introduced me to the joys of mountaineering back in the day.

Finally, I wish to extend my thanks and admiration to the teaching staff at New Avenues for Youth for their steadfast commitment to homeless youth, and to their courageous students, who are a continuing source of hope and inspiration to the author.

People say graffiti is ugly, irresponsible, and childish…but that's only if it's done properly.
—*Banksy*

The city is many things to many people, but for me, right now, it is a total revelation. It is a newly discovered mountain range.
—*Alain Robert*

ONE

Cal

IT'S HARD TO pinpoint when a story begins. Who knows when that butterfly flapped its wings, churning up the atmosphere enough to send a new tangle of events careening your way? If I had to choose, I'd say this story started early last fall when, for some reason, I woke up feeling unusually good. Not that I normally wake up feeling depressed. As a matter of fact, I've learned to keep myself in a fairly tight band—not too low, not too high—and take each day as it comes, and above all, not look for trouble.

But that particular morning there was something about the light suffusing my bedroom and the happy chatter of a gang of unruly crows out in the Doug firs. Or it could have been that the Trail Blazers had dismantled the Lakers in a home basketball game the night before. I'm from LA, but when I moved up here to Oregon, I left my allegiances behind. Better for a clean start, I figured. As I stretched myself awake, Archie, my Australian shepherd, eyed me from his mat in the corner, his soft whimpers a not-so-subtle request for me to get out of bed, and his big, coppery eyes promising a good day. Of course, for Arch, every day was good.

After feeding him, I ground some coffee beans and

loaded my espresso machine. I drew a double shot, added milk I'd steamed to a froth, and carried the cappuccino out to the side porch. The sun was bloodred through the firs and already busy dispatching the last tendrils of fog lurking in the valley. The sky promised that dazzling clarity peculiar to cloudless days in the Northwest, and the outlines and contours out on the horizon were already turning from violet to blues and greens.

It was a Thursday and I was heading to Caffeine Central, which is what I called my law office in the Old Town section of Portland, because it used to house a coffee shop by that name. I spent some Thursdays and most Fridays there giving legal advice to the down-and-out. It was a far cry and a welcome diversion from my one-man law practice here in Dundee, a town of eight thousand that lies twenty-five miles south of Portland in the heart of the Oregon wine country.

Normally my office was a forty-five-minute commute from Dundee, but traffic on the I-5 suddenly congealed on the edge of Portland, affording me a leisurely view of Mt. Hood to the east. Floating on a low cloud bank, the massive white cone was beautiful, to be sure. But it seemed to wink at me that morning, as if to say, "I'm an active volcano, too, a Trojan horse less than seventy miles from the heart of your city."

It wasn't until I parked in my designated slot that I noticed the graffiti two stories up on the Caffeine Central building, on the side that faces a vacant lot. Stenciled in large black letters, the words *ZERO TOLERANCE* were enclosed in a red circle. A red diagonal line cut across the words, the universal symbol of rejection. Below the image the tagger had stenciled *K209* in red letters against a black diamond, a nickname or moniker of some kind.

The image sat at least fifteen feet off the ground, suggesting the tagger had either used a ladder or managed to hang down from the roof somehow. I walked around to the back of the building, but of course there was no sign of a ladder. Nothing of value is left sitting around in the city. The other side of the building was jammed against an equally old six-story structure that had once been a tannery and now housed luxury loft apartments. The gap between the two walls was too narrow for anyone to have used it to work their way up to the roof.

K209 must stand for human fly, I decided.

I stood back, looked at the piece again, and chuckled. I was no fan of spray can vandalism, and judging from the dearth of graffiti around town, Portland's strict zero tolerance policy on graffiti seemed to be working. But I had to admit that the kid who did this had verve—to say nothing of athletic ability.

I walked away wondering how he'd managed it.

I had a light schedule that day and had just wrapped up my last appointment when Hernando Mendoza called. A friend and business associate, Nando also owned the building that housed Caffeine Central. That wasn't an altogether easy arrangement, since he was notoriously tight with a buck, but he made up for it by being the best friend a person could have.

"Calvin," he began, "how was the do-gooder business today?"

"Just great, but it got kind of chilly this afternoon. I thought you were going to send someone over to look at the furnace? It hasn't figured out how to fix itself yet."

He gave me his patented *basso profondo* laugh. "Actually, I did send someone over, and we are, uh, awaiting parts."

"By raft from China? It's been a month, Nando."

"Okay. I will check on it. Tell you what, why don't you join me for dinner tonight? It will be my treat."

Nando was tightfisted in his business dealings but generous in his personal life, and he didn't skimp on food…or clothes, or cars, or jewelry, come to think of it. I accepted his offer, and we met at a Cuban restaurant in Northeast called Pambiche. It was housed in a turn-of-the-century Victorian landmark, painted canary yellow and turquoise with fuchsia trim and a swirling, eye-popping three story mural on a side wall. Hardly what the Victorians had in mind, but very much in line with buildings in Havana, or so Nando had told me. He arrived shortly after me, but it took him a good five minutes to work his way through the outside and inside tables before reaching me. The Cuban community in Portland was small and tight-knit, and Nando knew them all. The man could work a crowd.

An imposing figure at six feet four with thick shoulders and an ample girth, Nando wore a long-sleeved black silk shirt buttoned at the neck, cream-colored slacks, and hand-tooled Italian loafers with woven tops. But what people remembered most about my Cuban friend was his incandescent smile and thick, arching brows that moved up and down above a set of dark, expressive eyes.

He greeted me and crunched my hand. "Ah, the

smells in this place remind me of home. I am so hungry I could eat two horses."

After advising me on what to order, Nando started off by complaining about problems with his janitorial business and the low billable hours at his private detective agency. An avowed capitalist, he had rowed a boat of his own making from Cuba to the Florida Keys when he was a young man. His PI firm tended to cut corners and play fast and loose with the law, which didn't sit well with the Portland Police Bureau. That's where I frequently came in, and my legal work on Nando's behalf hadn't won me many friends among Portland's finest, either. It was a bit of a Faustian bargain on my part.

When I told him about the graffiti on the building, he said, "Ah, those punks with their cans of paint. American kids have no respect for private property. I will find someone to remove it."

I shrugged. "Might be pricey."

His eyebrows dipped and a couple of vertical creases appeared on his forehead. "Then I will leave it there."

"The city won't like that. You could get fined for not removing it."

"Fined? Surely you are joking, Calvin. It is *my* property."

"It may be, but once the graffiti has been reported, you'll have ten days to remove it, or they'll issue you a ticket."

Nando rolled his eyes and shook his head. "*Es loco.* Always the hand in my pocket. Okay, okay, I will take care of it."

Our dinners arrived, and Nando speared a jumbo

prawn in the mojo sauce on his plate, took a bite. "*Madre mía. Qué rico.*" He closed his eyes. "These *camarones* could have been cooked by my grandmother." I could only nod in agreement since I was chewing a bite of red snapper bathed in a piquant sauce done up with West Indian spices.

Nando opened his eyes and smiled broadly. "I have something to tell you, Calvin."

That phrase usually signaled an incoming financial zinger. "I can't afford another rent increase," I shot back preemptively.

He laughed, and his eyes lit up. "No, no. This isn't about money. I have *met* someone."

I rested my fork on my plate and leaned forward. After all, despite Nando's reputation as a ladies' man, he was the prototype of a confirmed bachelor. "You have?"

"Yes. Her name is Claudia Borrego. I met her at a salsa club." He paused for a moment as if savoring the memory. "At first it was just her dancing. She is a magnificent salsa dancer. But then I got to know her." He shook his head in reverence. "She is wonderful." He fished a photo from his shirt pocket and handed it to me. Caught in a dramatic salsa move, she and Nando faced each other, their eyes locked together. Claudia's back was arched with an arm and leg extended behind her in dramatic fashion. Framed in flowing black hair, her head was tilted up, exposing a finely sculpted face, large almond-shaped eyes, and voluptuous lips.

"She's beautiful, Nando. How long has this been going on?"

He smiled so broadly I swear it increased the light

in the room. "Oh, a month or so. Long enough to know she is the love of my heart. We have already begun to talk about the engagement. I am shopping for a suitable diamond ring."

I sat back and looked at my friend. Hyperbole was his stock in trade, and I loved him for it, but it was clear he was genuinely smitten by this Claudia Borrego. "I can't wait to meet her." I told him. And I meant it. The woman who could reel in Hernando Mendoza must be some woman, indeed.

Later that night I took Archie for a walk along the Willamette River, which divides the city east from west. The river caught the light of the buildings and the bridges in perfect reflection until a breeze kicked up. I zipped up my jacket and pulled my hood up as the lights on the water began to tremble. I kept thinking about that starstruck look in Nando's eyes as he talked about Claudia. I was happy that he'd finally found someone, and Claudia sounded like a jewel. At the same time, a fragment of concern nagged at me like a splinter under my fingernail. I knew Nando would fall in love the way he did everything else—with total commitment and reckless abandon.

Claudia Borrego now held my friend's heart in her hands. I hoped she'd treat it with care.

TWO

Kelly

Three weeks later
Old Town, Portland

KELLY SPENCE SAT in the shadows of the alleyway. The wind had apparently shifted because she could smell the Dumpster down the alley now. The smell nudged her out of a light sleep. She thumbed her cell phone to life and checked the time. 1:05 a.m. From the side pocket of her backpack she extracted a dog-eared, paperback copy of Camus's *The Stranger* and began reading by the light of her phone. It was slow going but better than just waiting in the dark. She was half-way through the book and had decided to give it one more chance. But after twenty pages more she put it back in her pack, knowing she would never finish it. That guy Meursault just made her mad. *Why so frigging passive, dude? I mean, get a life.*

She wasn't like Meursault. She was angry and had stuff she wanted to say.

After she played a couple dozen games of Osmos on her cell, it was 2:20. Time to start. She was hungry but glad she hadn't brought anything to eat. You climb best on an empty stomach, her dad always told her. She never really understood why that would be the case, and he never explained his reasoning. When it came to climbing, whatever her dad said was gospel.

She wondered what he would think of her now, if he'd approve. He never said much about anything except climbing, but he'd lived his life on his own terms, for sure. She was trying to do that now, and you know, make a difference somehow, or at least stick it to the man, which was the same thing, wasn't it?

Kelly missed her dad, and that empty space he'd left in her heart began to ache.

She took her climbing harness out of her pack, pulled it over her jeans, and cinched it up. She still felt guilty about having boosted it, but she was broke at the time and had outgrown the last harness her dad had given her. She took inventory of the contents of her backpack one more time—two neatly folded stencils, nine spray cans—four black, two blue, two red, and a white—spray caps, duct tape, fifty feet of climbing rope, and a black scarf she always used as a mask. Since she'd be changing spray caps to go from broad to fine work, she moved them from her pack to a small haul sack attached to her harness.

Her objective was to tag the wall of a six-story turn-of-the-century warehouse that was now an office complex in Portland's Old Town. The blank wall beckoned to her like an immense, empty canvas, but it would be no easy task to gain access to the roof where she could launch her assault.

A gap of maybe three feet separated the six-story building from an adjacent four-story structure that was more accessible. She put on her backpack and moved down the unlit alleyway to the corner of the lower building, where a vertical course of wide, rough-hewn granite cornerstones promised a tough but manageable fifty-foot line up to the roof. Cool to the touch, the cornerstone seams were reasonably spaced and, most importantly, dry. Kelly stretched her arms up, found a seam with her fingertips, and lifted off—the soft soles of her climbing shoes sticking firmly to the granite. Holding herself with her right hand, she slowly extended her legs and found the next seam with her left hand, then reversed the process. Like a crawling insect, she reached the top of the building and pulled herself over the low retaining wall onto the flat roof in a matter of minutes.

With her back against the wall, Kelly rested for a couple of moments, breathing in the cool night air. The city was silent, as if someone had hit the mute button, and the stars, which she noticed for the first time that night, seemed particularly close and bright. Staying low, she moved over to where the two buildings joined. Gaining the next two stories to the roof of the higher building would be the toughest part of the climb and where she was most likely to be seen by a passerby. But the bars were closed, and NW Third showed no signs of car or foot traffic.

Her ascent would follow a single line of decorative brick on the side of the higher building. The line started where she stood and slanted up the side of the building to the roof, where it joined another from the other side to form a peak. A narrow ledge of maybe four inches, the route demanded she stay absolutely flat against the building *without* the counterweight of her backpack. She took her pack off and tied one end of her climbing rope to it and the other to her harness. After checking the street below one more time, she worked herself out on the ledge, facing the wall, seventy-five feet above an empty parking lot.

She could hear her dad's familiar chant in her head, "Stay focused, Kelly. You can do this." Of course, she was always belayed when climbing with her dad. He would've never let her free climb like this. But, hey, if a little French dude named Alain Robert could scale the Sears Tower without a belay, surely she could manage this brick face.

With the rope trailing behind her, she used the gaps between the century-old bricks for fingerholds as she worked her way across and up the face of the building, one sideways step after another. Finally, her left hand grasped the ledge of the roof, then her right, and she was up. Wasting no time, she used the rope to retrieve her backpack, then looped the rope around the stout vent pipe she'd spotted from the street the day she settled on this project. She threaded the rope through the figure-eight attached to her belay hook, and after checking the street again, rappelled effortlessly down the face of the building.

Piece of cake.

Twenty-five feet down, she tied off using a mule knot, her dad's voice going off again in her head. "Tie off properly, Kelly. Screw it up, and you'll splat like a bug."

Extended out from the wall with her back to Third Street, she hung above the dimly lit parking lot for a few moments battling the fear of exposure she always felt at the beginning. You're just a shadow against a dark wall, she told herself. *Calm down.* She closed her eyes, picturing the image and the steps required to execute it. *Don't rush. Feel it. Let it flow.* She exhaled a deep breath, removed the first half of the stencil and the duct tape from her backpack, and set to work.

She finished the image and was stenciling in the letters below it when a car entered the parking lot. She froze in place. *People don't look up,* she reminded herself. When she heard the second car, she turned her head to watch over her right shoulder. She caught a glimpse of long hair as the figure got out of the first car. A woman. She wasn't much more than a shadow in a dark coat and slacks. Someone got out of the second car and walked toward the woman—a man, judging from his size and manner of walking.

Kelly exhaled and snickered a little—john meets hooker. She had just turned her head back to the wall when she heard a female voice say something like, "Where's man—" but the voice was cut off by two dull reports—*chuck, chuck*—like a hammer striking lead. Kelly looked back over her shoulder as the woman collapsed in a motionless heap. The man put a pistol with a long barrel in his coat and stood over the body.

Stunned and not believing what she'd just seen, Kelly turned back toward the wall as if the act would make her invisible. But the motion knocked the spray cap from her hand. *You asshat!* she screamed to herself. She was climbing hand-over-hand back up the wall before the cap even hit the pavement.

She'd nearly reached the top when she heard more muffled shots—*chuck chuck, chuck chuck chuck.* Like angry hornets, the bullets tore into the bricks around her, scattering a hail of fragments. She felt a searing pain in her right calf but managed to clear the ledge, tear the bandanna from her face, and step out of her harness.

The thought of being trapped on the roof, either by the killer or the cops, shot a bolt of panic through her. *Forget the harness. Forget the rope. Forget the pain. Just get off this friggin' roof.*

She ran across the roof to an old iron fire escape that clung to the back of the building. It led down to the alleyway where she had waited earlier that night. One end of the alley was blocked with a high wrought-iron fence, the other was open to Everett, the cross street. Fighting back tears and wincing in pain, she took the ladder two rungs at a time while watching for the killer from the entrance to the alley.

The fire escape landing was a good fifteen feet above the alley. The swing-down ladder had been removed when the fire escape was decommissioned long ago. Without hesitating, Kelly ripped off her backpack and, hoping to create a diversion, smashed open a window adjacent to the landing with her pack, then tossed it, spray cans and all, through the jagged opening. She hung off the platform and dropped, barely managing to muffle a scream of pain as she landed hard, twisting an ankle and banging an elbow. She hobbled toward the iron fence but stopped abruptly. A tough climb healthy. Not a chance now.

Her throat constricted in terror. *You idiot. You should've stayed on the roof!* But it was too late. She was trapped.

Or was she? Prying open the heavy lid to the Dumpster across the alley, she squeezed in and began to burrow into the debris and rotting garbage like a mole, or more accurately, she had to admit, like a maggot. She was still working her way toward the bottom when she caught the sound of a car rolling up next to the Dumpster.

She held her breath, suspended there in a cocoon of muck. A car door clicked open. The scuffing of footsteps, then silence. More footsteps. Finally, a door slammed, followed by the sound of a car in reverse, but not before a man said, *"You little bastard,"* in a voice ringing with rage and frustration.

THREE

_____

Kelly

KELLY LOST TRACK of time. Her leg and her elbow were throbbing in a bass drum duet, and Dumpster juices were soaking through her clothes. She had heard the killer's car pull out from the alley onto Everett before the sound quickly faded into the night. Did he really leave? Or was he out there somewhere waiting for her? It didn't matter. She had to get out of the Dumpster.

But it was easier said than done. Dumpster diving, it turned out, was a lot easier than Dumpster surfacing. When she finally made it to the top of the debris and pushed on the heavy lid, it hardly budged. That's when she realized how weak she was, how utterly spent, and she couldn't muffle her cry of pain this time, when the lid scraped her wounded leg as she wriggled free and dropped, arms extended, to the alleyway.

There was only one way out of the alley, and it was half lit by a street light. More than anything in the world Kelly wanted to run for it. But what about the woman lying on the other side of the building? What if she were still alive? She couldn't just leave her there.

She moved along the alley, staying in the shadows, and when she turned the corner of the building, crawled on her hands and knees to the base of an ornamental tree. From there, in deep shadow, she could see maybe a half block in either direction. The street looked deserted. She watched for a long time. Nothing stirred. She wondered if the killer would dare hang around and decided he probably wouldn't chance it.

Kelly hobbled around the building. Maybe the woman's not there, she told herself. But she was. You have to know how to check your pulse, her dad had told her, so you can pace yourself when you're climbing. The woman lay on her back, her right arm thrust out like she was waving to someone, her left curled across her chest. Kelly kept her eyes averted from the dark patch surrounding the woman's head as she grasped the underside of her limp wrist between a thumb and two fingers. No pulse. Holding her breath as her heart battered her ribs, she moved in and checked for a pulse in the woman's neck. Nothing.

She stood up too fast and fought off a wave of vertigo. Where to go? She couldn't go home. Too far. Rupert. She had to find her friend, Rupert. He'd know what to do.

She started down Everett toward the river. Everything about Rupert was shrouded in mystery and whacky rumors, but one thing was certain—the kids on the street knew they could trust him. That was saying a lot because trusted adults were in short supply with the kids Kelly hung out with. One rumor had it that Rupert was a wanted fugitive who was using homelessness as cover. In another story, he'd been banished from the Umatilla Reservation for some terrible crime. Kelly figured it was the latter, since Rupert, with his fierce eyes, leathery skin, and shoulder-length silver hair, reminded her of the picture of a chief—Geronimo, maybe—she'd seen in a history book. But when Kelly had asked him about this, he'd just smiled and shook his head.

She found Rupert under the Burnside Bridge, propped against a wall, reading a paperback with a flashlight. He shined the beam on her as she approached. "Kelly? Is that you, child? Are you okay?"

"No. I'm not, Rupert." Then Kelly did something she hadn't done for a very long time. She sat down and cried.

Rupert let her go for a while before saying, "Let's have a look at that leg." He cut her jeans off halfway up her calf with a knife that appeared out of nowhere, washed the wound with a handkerchief wetted with bottled water, and applied a bandage he took from a pouch on his backpack. "It's nasty, but not a bullet wound. I think I got all the brick chips out. You don't need stitches. I haven't got any antiseptic, so put some on it when you get home, hear?" Of course, he didn't ask her what happened. Rupert never would. But after she got hold of herself, Kelly told him everything.

When she finished he sat quietly for a long time before saying, "Did he get a look at you?"

"Nah. It was dark and I had a bandanna covering my face. I always cover up when I'm spraying."

"What about your hair? He saw your long hair didn't he? He'll know you're a girl."

Kelly laughed. "No he won't. Lots of dudes have long hair, Rupert."

He nodded. "Uh huh. So, how much you leave up there?"

"I wasn't finished, man."

"You sign it?"

"No, not quite."

Rupert met her eyes. "Good. How many of your friends know you're this crazy K209 tagger?"

Kelly smiled. "Everyone thinks it's some *guy* doing the tagging."

"Portland's Banksy, huh?"

"Something like that. But Banksy doesn't climb."

Rupert held her eyes. "What about that climbing gym you work at? Has anyone put two and two together?"

"Nah. I don't talk about the job much, and when it comes up, I just say I sweep up around there. I only climb after hours."

"So, you're sure nobody else knows?"

Kelly shrugged. "I worry about Kiyana. We learned to stencil together at school, but she doesn't know I can climb. I never talk about my dad, just that he got killed in an accident. The woman I live with, Veronica, should know I'm up to something, but she's pretty clueless. When I make stencils in our back bedroom, I tell her it's for a school project."

"What about that tall boy I see you with?"

"Zook? Nah, he doesn't spend any time thinking about me."

"Good. Keep your mouth shut about this, Kel. The killer's gonna be lookin' for you. You need to stop the spray can crap and stay away from that place." He glared at her with his fierce eyes. "Leave it unfinished, Kelly."

Kelly nodded. "Don't worry. I'm not going near that building. What about the cops? What should I do?"

"What you saw might help them catch this guy."

Kelly shook her head. "No way. I'm not talking to them. I can't get busted again. Besides, it was dark. I didn't see anything."

"You should at least phone in what you saw." He exhaled a deep breath and shook his head. "But it wouldn't be smart to let 'em hear your voice. Get me a burner phone from Henny Duzan. I'll make the call for you. Make sure it doesn't have a GPS chip, and don't pay more than twenty bucks for it."

Huddled on a thin mat next to Rupert, Kelly slept fitfully until dawn, which broke clear and still. Kelly felt naked without her backpack, and frighteningly conspicuous because of her slashed jeans and the bandage on her leg, which was now soaked through with blood. She caught the first TriMet bus across the Burnside Bridge to the apartment she shared with Veronica.

Their third-floor apartment above a shop that sold used audio components was accessed by a street-level door opening to a small vestibule and a steep, narrow staircase up two flights. It really wasn't home to Kelly but better than the street. Having run away from her foster home in Eugene, she had been on the street better than nine months when Veronica showed up in Portland sporting a new last name. Twelve years younger than her dad, Veronica had been his girlfriend when he died. She told Kelly she wanted to take her in, see if the two of them could make a go of it. It was only after Veronica had too much to drink one night that she admitted she was wanted on a drug charge down in California.

Since Kelly had vowed never to go back to foster care, no matter what, and life on the street had gone from an adventure to a grind, the decision to throw in with Veronica was an easy one. It was working okay, Kelly conceded, at least when Veronica was sober and not fawning over some new boyfriend.

Veronica was asleep in the recliner, head back, mouth agape. She'd apparently fallen asleep waiting for Kelly to come home. In sleep she looked softer somehow, even with her mouth open. Her thick blond hair—her best asset, she always said—was splayed out on the recliner, her eyes seemingly glued shut with a thick layer of mascara. The apartment smelled of cigarettes, rancid cooking oil, and something that had been fried the night before, probably hamburger. Veronica's dog was curled up on her lap, a sharp-nosed little mutt named Spencer. The dog growled when he saw Kelly. Veronica stirred, closed her mouth, but didn't awaken.

Kelly tiptoed through the living room and down the short hallway to her bedroom. She went straight to her battered chest of drawers and fished out the pair of wool socks she never wore. Sitting down on her unmade bed, she separated them and shook the bills and change out of the toe of the inner sock and counted sixty-eight dollars and thirty-six cents. Her stash— what her dad used to call mad money. Maybe enough to buy a new backpack and a burner cell phone.

She fell back on the bed as the horror of what had happened crushed in on her again—the bullets snapping into the bricks, the limp feel of that dead woman's arm, the dark halo of blood around her head. Kelly prided herself on being tough. She knew about street violence. She even saw a dead guy once, an overdose under the Morrison Bridge. But the viciousness of the act she'd witnessed had shattered her tough-girl confidence. She felt cut off now, adrift in a dangerous sea, and very much alone.

She kept asking herself over and over again, *What kind of monster could do something like that?* She curled into a fetal ball and rocked on the bed. One sob, two, three. Then she pulled herself back up and dried her cheeks with her fists. *This is no time to lose it, girl*, she told herself.

In the bathroom Kelly managed to find a nearly empty tube of antiseptic cream and a tin holding six small bandages. The tube yielded a couple of drops, and the bandages just barely covered her wound, which had begun throbbing again. She pointed her elbow at the mirror for a look. It was swollen and discolored like the twisted ankle below her wounded calf.

She slipped off her climbing shoes and put on a clean pair of jeans, a black hooded sweatshirt, and a pair of beat-up sneakers. After gathering up and pocketing the money, she slipped out of the apartment as the mutt's beady little eyes followed her.

It was a clear, bright Portland morning, and she had important things to do. Trouble was, aside from buying a throw away phone for Rupert, she wasn't too sure what they were.

FOUR

Cal

IT'S NEVER EASY to schedule my pro bono clients at Caffeine Central, so I work on a first-come, first-served basis. Three clients were already queued up when I came downstairs from the little apartment above my office. The graffiti on the outside of the building was still intact, although three weeks had elapsed since I first noticed it. When I asked Nando about it, he said, "I have heard nothing from the city, and the cost of removal is robbery, simple and pure."

"Well, it's not bothering me," I told him, "but if the city contacts you, you better get it scrubbed."

First up in my office that morning was a feisty, elderly woman with hair that looked like a pewter helmet. Her name was Thelma McCharles, and she had just received a notice of foreclosure on her house. She was angry and confused since she was also in the middle of negotiations to modify her mortgage with the same bank. "It's a pretty common occurrence," I told her, "the right hand not knowing what the left is doing." I collected Thelma's information and told her I'd contact the bank on her behalf.

A thirtysomething man with a bad case of meth-induced jitters was up next. His face was scabbed and blotchy, his teeth so crusted I couldn't look at them.

The cops had planted a quantity of crystal meth in his backpack, he told me. I explained that I didn't do criminal defense, that he should contact the Public Defender's office. He groaned. "The Public Pretender? No, thanks. I've been there, done that."

I handed him a card. "Here's a list of treatment centers. Your biggest problem isn't this bust, it's your habit, man." I looked him in the eye. "You need to clean yourself up, or that stuff's going to kill you." He left but not before giving me a look that said that wasn't what he wanted to hear.

After dealing with the next client, I locked up, hung the "Back in 15" sign on the door, and took Arch for a walk. He pulled at his leash and sniffed the crisp fall air, as if he were smelling the river on the shifting breeze. We were down by the Lan Su Chinese Garden when my cell went off. "Cal? This is Esperanza." Esperanza Oliva was the secretary at Nando's detective agency. Her strained voice caused me to tense up. "Something terrible has happened."

"What?"

She sobbed once and caught herself. "Cal, it's Claudia, Nando's fiancée. She's…she's dead."

"My God! No! What happened?"

"She was found dead early this morning. That's all I know."

"Where's Nando?"

"He's here. In his office. Can you come, Cal?"

"I'll be right there."

Located in Lents, a diverse, blue-collar neighborhood in Southeast Portland, the Sharp Eye Detective Agency was just off Powell Boulevard, on Ninety-second. Nando's building once housed an independent pharmacy that had stubbornly survived into the third millennium owing to strong neighborhood support. But when a huge chain pharmacy opened a block away, the octogenarian owner, who was also the druggist, sold the building to Nando.

A sign reading Closed hung in the storefront window, and the blinds were down. I rapped on the door and Esperanza let me in. Petite, competent, and always fashionably dressed, her eyes were puffy and red as she offered herself up for a hug. "Oh, Cal, I'm glad you're here. He's in his office. He won't talk to me."

I knocked softly, and when Nando didn't respond, let myself in. My friend was sitting at his desk, shoulders slumped, head down. He looked up when I entered, a dazed expression on his face. "I'm going to have to call my mother in Cuba, tell her the wedding is off. I told her Claudia and I would marry there, in Havana. She was so excited. How can I tell her about this?"

"I'm so sorry, Nando. What the hell happened?"

He propped an elbow on his desk, closed his eyes and began massaging his forehead like someone with a migraine. "The police came to my place at six forty-five this morning. They said the body of a woman had been found in Old Town, on Third Avenue, and that my phone number was in her recent call log. They wanted me to come with them to help identify the body. Lots of women have my number, so I was more curious than worried." He stopped for a moment, as if the next words were stuck in his throat. "It was Claudia. She was just lying there. In a parking lot." He looked up in utter bewilderment as tears filled his eyes. "She had been shot twice in the head. Executed, Calvin. How could this happen?"

I shook my head, feeling like he needed some kind of answer. But there's just no explaining this kind of inhumanity. "Who found her?"

"Some woman who pushes her belongings around in a shopping cart. She was still there when I arrived." Nando kneaded his brow some more with his thick fingers. "Of course, the police have the hard-on for me. You know, the boyfriend is always the first suspect. They have requested a second interview." He glanced at his Rolex. "I have to leave in a few minutes."

"Do you have an alibi?"

He shrugged. "I believe so, but it depends on the time of death. I was up most of the night watching Real Madrid play Barcelona with my crazy soccer friends. I returned home about four thirty and went to bed."

"Who caught the case?"

"Scott and some new detective. A guy I don't know named Ludlow."

I nodded. "Good." Nando and I had been involved in a murder investigation with Harmon Scott a couple of years ago. He was a good detective and a decent man. "What'd you tell Scott?"

"I told him to pick up Anthony Cardenas."

"Who's he?"

"Claudia's ex-husband. He still has the thing for her. A very jealous man. Not Cuban. Mexican."

"You didn't tell me Claudia had been married."

Nando gave a half shrug. "She didn't tell me until recently. It is something she is not proud of. Cardenas is a lowlife, a gambler. He is known as Tony the Card at the casinos and poker clubs."

"You think he did this?"

Nando looked at me without answering, his eyes smoldering like hot coals. We sat there for a while with only the noise from Ninety-second Street filtering in. Finally, he said, "I have to go, my friend. Thank you for coming."

I followed him out, and when he got into his car, I said, "You're not going to do anything stupid about Cardenas, are you?"

He shut the car door without answering, which was an answer of sorts and not the one I was looking for.

FIVE

Cal

I LEFT NANDO'S office and drove back over the Willamette to Caffeine Central, the death of Claudia Borrego hanging heavily over me. Nando's heart, as big as the island of Cuba, had been shattered, and I worried about what my friend might do if he caught up with Claudia's ex-husband, Anthony Cardenas. My wife's suicide down in LA had taught me all too well what a blow like that could do to a person. Nando wasn't a violent man, but on the other hand, he was big and strong and volatile.

Since I'd closed for the day, I leashed up Archie and walked over to the crime scene, only a few blocks away. The body had been removed, but yellow crime tape still cordoned off a large section of the parking lot, where a couple of techs in white coats were milling around. A cherry picker had been brought in, the kind used to trim high trees. Fifty feet up in the basket, another tech examined the brick wall at close range. An image with large red letters below it covered an upper section of the six-story wall.

I stood there, taking in the scene. The tech in the basket seemed very interested in what looked like divots in the brick. He examined them, photographed them, then took several samples of something by

gouging the divots with a tool. I walked around to
get a better look at the image, which was partially
obscured by the cherry picker. It was a blue sphere
against a black background, the iconic "blue marble"
image of Earth as seen from space, except that it had
wavy red lines rising off it, a suggestion of radiating heat. Below the image, the tagger had sprayed
"THERE IS NO PLA" in large red letters.

The hair on my neck tingled a little. It was the
scale, boldness, and difficult placement of the image
that struck me. "Huh," I said aloud, causing Arch to
look up at me, "that's gotta be by the same guy who
did Caffeine Central." I paused to think of the moniker. "K209, that was it, right, Arch?" My dog looked
up at me and wagged his stump of a tail in apparent
agreement.

Judging from the uncompleted text and the absence
of a signature, it looked like the tagger had been interrupted. And those divots were caused by bullets,
I was sure of it. The divots were vertically elongated,
suggesting the shooter fired up from the parking lot.

Arch and I walked around the building where more
crime tape blocked off the narrow alley between it
and another structure. A technician, crouched up on
the landing of an old fire escape no longer in use, was
busy dusting for prints at a broken window. Shading
my eyes, I looked up into the bright morning. High
above the alley a black iron ladder connected the roof
of the building with the landing. The shooter was on
the ground, so it must have been K209 who broke into
the building on his way down. Maybe he was trying
to evade the shooter. If so, did he make it? If he did
take refuge in the building, the cops might have him

now. Or maybe he somehow got away clean. I wondered which it was.

On the way back to Caffeine Central, I called Nando, but he didn't pick up. I beat back a twinge of anxiety. It was only an hour and a half since I'd seen him, so no cause for alarm. The grilling from Scott and his partner could run well into the afternoon. Murder interviews had a way of doing that. To be on the safe side, I called Esperanza and told her to call me the minute she saw or heard from Nando.

I could have left it there, but I wanted to know more about the tagger who called himself K209. I called a young man who might be able to shed some light on the matter. His name was Danny Baxter, but everyone called him Picasso, a street name that reflected his considerable artistic prowess. I'd helped him solve his mom's cold-case murder, an effort that nearly got us both killed but bonded us forever. We agreed to meet at the Black Rooster, a little coffee shop on South West Tenth. When Archie saw Picasso sitting at an outdoor table, he squealed and strained at his leash. Picasso was one of Archie's favorite people.

Picasso got up as we approached and dropped to one knee to embrace Arch in a bear hug before rising again to shake my hand. He was tall with an angular face and dark, liquid eyes, not unlike those of his namesake. A black turtleneck covered the vivid tattoo of a coral snake on his neck, a relic of his life as a homeless teen. His shirt choice could have been a nod to his new, straighter life as the manager of a hip art gallery in the Pearl, but I doubted it. The tattoo craze in Portland showed no signs of waning, particularly among the creative set. We ordered at the counter—

a green tea for him, a double cap for me—and with drinks in hand went back outside, where it was bracingly cool but sunny.

"How's the art biz?"

He blew on his tea, then frowned before taking a sip. "Slow, man. My mural commissions are keeping us afloat. People aren't buying much hanging art." Then he looked at me more closely. "What's the matter, Cal? You don't look so good."

I sighed and shook my head. "Nando's fiancée was murdered last night."

"*No.* I didn't even know he was engaged. What happened?"

Picasso listened as I unpacked the whole story of the graffiti at Caffeine Central, the murder of Claudia Borrego, and the unfinished words left behind on the building on Everett. When I finished, I said, "You ever hear of a tagger in Portland using the name K209?"

Picasso shook his head. "Don't know the moniker, but I don't keep up with the street art as much as I used to. Dude sounds interesting, though, mixing tagging with a little buildering."

"Buildering?"

"You know, like bouldering, but on buildings. Urban climbers. Why go all the way to Smith Rock or Half Dome when there's plenty of climbs right here in the city?"

I nodded. "Is there a Portland buildering group of some kind?"

Picasso chuckled. "Nothing official, but I know some dudes. I'll ask around. By the way, some graffiti artists would call this guy a writer, not a tagger."

"What's the difference?"

"Taggers are less evolved, you know, haven't proved themselves yet. Writers have skills and props. You gotta earn it."

"What's this guy, then?"

Picasso shrugged. "Still a tagger, I'd say, since I haven't heard of the dude. Of course, the distinction only matters with the people into this on the street. He could be the next Shakespeare or da Vinci, but if he does a wall in this town, he's condemned as a tagger by the powers that be. A paid-for ad on the side of a building is no problem, but put something up without permission, and they send in the flying monkeys." He sipped his tea and looked at me over the cup. "So, this guy saw the shooting go down?"

"Yeah, it looks that way. If the shooter didn't get him—and I haven't heard anything to suggest that— then the cops are probably looking for him as we speak, but you know as well as I do that he won't be easy to find, especially for the cops. I was thinking maybe you could connect me."

Picasso sat back in his chair. "If I find this guy, there's still a problem. No way he'll want to come forward. He runs the risk of being busted for the graffiti. And if he's trying to stay anonymous, it'll blow his cover."

I nodded. "I realize that. But we're talking about the murder of an innocent woman here."

Picasso tugged absently on the silver ring piercing his eyebrow for a moment. "You're one of the few people in town he might trust, Cal. Everybody on the street knows about Caffeine Central. If he came to you, could you shield him somehow?"

I shook my head. "Not his identity. If he witnessed a murder, he needs to come forward." I paused for a moment. "Tell him I'll try to trade his cooperation for any legal problems with the graffiti he's left around town. Best I can do."

"Okay. I'll have a look at the piece on Everett and compare it with the one on Caffeine Central. If I agree K209 did them both, I'll see if I can find him."

"Fair enough."

Picasso shook his head and smiled. "Listen to us. K209 could be a *her*, you know."

I feigned a forehead slap and laughed. "You're right. My daughter would kill me for making that assumption."

SIX

Cal

ARCHIE AND I were walking back to Caffeine Central when my cell chirped. "Cal? It's Esperanza. Nando came back to the office, then left again, in a hurry."

"What did he say?"

"He had me look up the address of someone named, uh, Anthony Cardenas. I gave it to him, and he took off without saying anything else. Cal, he…the way he looked at me…it frightened me. What does he want with this man?"

I had Espinoza read me Cardenas's address and took off in a dead run. When I reached my building, I put Archie inside and left in my car. Cardenas's place was in Northeast, near Wilshire Park, on Thirty-third. I took the Burnside Bridge and was there in under ten minutes. As I approached his block, I saw a patrol car sitting up ahead in my lane with its blue strobe pulsing. My own pulse ramped up. "Oh, crap." I parked a block away and hurried up the street. A uniformed cop stood behind the double-parked patrol car.

That's when I saw him. Nando was standing with his arms folded across his chest in the shade of a dogwood across the street from the duplex bearing Cardenas's address. I exhaled and walked over to join him.

"I arrived a bit too late," he said, keeping his eyes trained on the duplex. "The police were already here."

"What were you going to do?"

He pulled a large pearl-handled switchblade from his pocket and turned it over in his hand. "I was thinking along the lines of cutting his balls off after beating him senseless."

I knew my friend well but didn't know whether to laugh or take him seriously. "Probably not the best idea you've ever had."

He didn't laugh, but instead puffed out a derisive breath and shook his head. "*Eso cabrón mató mi Claudia.*"

"How are you so sure this guy killed her?"

He shrugged and continued looking straight ahead. At that point, the door to the duplex opened and a tall man in a dark, elegantly tailored suit and narrow tie appeared first, followed by Lieutenant Harmon Scott and another detective I didn't recognize. The man had black, swept-back hair and sharp features and was doing his best to look cool and unconcerned.

"That's him," Nando said. "That's Tony the Card. They are taking him in for questioning."

"Looks like a banker, not a card shark," I remarked.

Scott marched the man to an unmarked patrol car and put him in. As Scott was rounding the car, he saw us, said something to his partner, and shambled across the street, stopping short of the curb in front of us. He'd packed on some weight since the last time I saw him, and his heavily furrowed forehead glistened with a sheen of sweat. "Gentlemen, can I help you?"

Nando shifted his feet but didn't speak. I said, "Hello, Harmon. We're just, uh, watching the wheels of justice turn. We want to see Claudia's Borrego's killer put away fast." Nando grunted at my last sentence.

"Well, so do we." He narrowed his eyes, swinging his gaze from me to Nando, then back to me. "We don't need any help, either. Are we clear on that?" He held my eyes until I nodded, then turned and headed back across the street.

"I think I know the moniker of the tagger who witnessed the shooting," I said to his back.

He whirled around, *"What?"*

I stepped into the street and Nando joined me. I could feel the heat of Nando's questioning glare on the side of my face. "A tagger put some graffiti on our building on Couch a couple of weeks ago. Signed it K209. I was over at the murder scene this morning. Looks like the same person who did the piece above the parking lot, only he didn't sign it because he got interrupted."

Scott put his hands on his hips. "You sure about that?"

"Not completely. But the styles look very similar."

Grimacing, Scott took a ballpoint and a small notebook from his shirt pocket. "You know who the hell this K209 is?"

"No, but I've got some feelers out."

Scott made a couple of quick notes and closed the pad. "Good. Stay in touch on that. And keep this on the down low, would you, gentlemen? I don't want it to get out that we know about the witness."

As Scott walked away, I turned to Nando. "Sorry, man. I didn't have a chance to fill you in." I went on to explain what I'd seen, my conclusions, and the fact

that I'd asked Picasso to see if he could find K209.
It didn't matter to me who found the tagger first, Picasso or the police.

I followed Nando back to his office in Lents. Esperanza was sitting at her desk, her face showing a flicker of relief when her boss walked in ahead of me. She started to speak but apparently thought better of it. What do you say, after all?

Nando glanced at his watch. "Please cancel any appointments, Esperanza, and take the rest of the day off."

We went into his office, where Nando extracted a bottle of Havana Club Gran Reserva rum and two glasses from a wall cabinet and placed them on his desk. I pulled up a chair and sat down across from him. It occurred to me that the last time we shared a drink like this was the day, some twenty-odd months ago, that Picasso was sprung from jail and murder charges against him were dropped. It was a case Nando and I had worked together. Good liquor can go either way, I observed—either a means of celebration or a balm in the face of unspeakable tragedy.

Nando poured without speaking, neat, no ice. His face was drawn tight, eyes dull as lampblack, his body somehow shrunken in grief. He let out a deep sigh. "I waited my whole life for Claudia. Other women? Oh, they were nice enough. But when I met Claudia…" He shook his head slowly, his voice tailing away as his eyes filled.

I knew from experience that shedding grief is a marathon, not a sprint, and that talking is the best first step. We drank and I let my friend talk until he'd poured out the contents of his heart. Well into our second glass, the room fell silent except for the hum of traffic out on Ninety-second and the occasional shard of a guitar chord from a busker playing on the corner. I finally spoke into the silence. "So, I got the impression Scott likes Cardenas for this more than he likes you."

"Well, I am sure they checked my whereabouts last night. If the killing took place before four thirty a.m., then I am cleared. If not the boyfriend, then the ex-husband. It is only logical. Besides, I told them he threatened Claudia."

"Had he?"

He shrugged. "She said she was not afraid of him. Those words imply a threat, do they not?"

"Sometimes. What else did Claudia say about him?"

"She didn't say anything until a couple of weeks ago. Apparently the ball of slime had moved back to Portland from Las Vegas, where he had supposedly made a great deal of money."

"Doing what, exactly?"

"Poker, I am told. I don't understand this American obsession with gambling. A stupid way to use your money, unless you are the house, of course. Anyway, he came back to Portland and pledged to Claudia that he was finished with the gambling. He expected her to come crawling back to him. When she told him about me, he flew into a rage."

"Did you confront him?"

"I wanted to, I should have, but Claudia insisted on handling it herself. That's when she told me she was not afraid of him." Shaking his head, he stared past me, mumbling, *"No debí haber escuchado a ella."*

"Any idea why she would meet him, or anyone, for that matter, in a vacant lot in Old Town in the middle of the night?"

Nando sighed and ran a hand through his thick, black hair. "Maybe she was killed somewhere else."

I shook my head. "Not likely."

"If she did go there to meet someone, I am missing the clues, Calvin. He must have tricked her somehow. It seems very strange to me."

"Strange, for sure," I said, shifting in my seat.

The room fell silent again. A Clapton-esque fragment drifted in from the guitar player. Nando drained his glass and wiped his lips with the back of his hand. "It was Cardenas who killed my Claudia, Calvin. I can feel it in my body."

I nodded. Not in agreement, but simply to acknowledge his comment. I wasn't there yet but knew better than to say so.

SEVEN

Kelly

To keep things looking normal to the outside world, Kelly decided she'd better go to class before buying the phone for Rupert. She took the bus back across the river and despite the pain in her ankle and calf, gritted her teeth and walked without a limp. The first thing she heard after being buzzed into New Directions Alternative High School was, "You're late, Sprout."

"So what, Zook?" she shot back. "And my name's not Sprout, you retard."

The kid answering to "Zook" loosed a goofy, lop-sided grin and raised his arms in mock surrender. "My name's James Bradford, not Zook, but do I get all pissy? Nooo."

Zook was a tall kid with a thatch of dirty blond hair, inquisitive eyes, and a pair of arms giving new meaning to the term rangy. Under her breath she said, "Jesus, Zook, it's not even nine thirty and you're baked. What's up with that?"

He shrugged and flashed the off-kilter grin again. "A little weed to take the edge off. No big deal."

"Idiot," she hissed before stomping off to join a knot of students across the room. They were huddled around a printing frame, where a local artist was demonstrating the fundamentals of silk-screen printing.

It was the part of the week when the school brought in volunteers to turn the kids on to the arts, a break from the grind of juggling academics with their lives on the street.

A year earlier a local artist had taught the class the basics of stencil art. That's when the idea hit Kelly—maybe she could combine climbing and stenciling to leave graffiti in places that would really piss the city off and make them wonder how she'd gotten there in the first place. She hadn't tagged since she got busted, and the terms of her probation forbade it. But this was too sweet. A step up from being a scribble monkey. And a challenge. Rupert had told her the idea was reckless and a waste of her energy, but she didn't care. Putting a sharp stick in the Man's eye would feel good.

Her first pieces were modest and tentative, and she hid her identity more out of fear of being ridiculed than anything else. But as her confidence grew so did her resolve to stay anonymous. Her best friend, Kiyana, had her suspicions, but the rest of the world assumed K209 was a guy. This gave her good cover and provided a ton of motivation, too.

"Leave some of that energy for the part of the day that counts toward your diploma," one of her instructors chided Kelly after she complained about having to wrap up her first stencil project to begin studying math. The academic subjects left her, if not cold, certainly cool. But that was more out of interest than ability. Kelly was a voracious reader, a whiz in math, and on track to graduate from high school early.

But that morning the art of silk-screening held no interest for Kelly. Her calf, ankle, and elbow ached,

and her anxiety about postponing the cell phone purchase built like steam in a pressure cooker. She'd seen
enough cop shows to know the first twenty-four hours
of a murder investigation were critical, and although
what she had to tell the cops seemed inconsequential,
she wanted to help put away the monster who'd shot
that poor woman.

Kiyana caught her chewing her lip. Six feet tall
with broad shoulders and lustrous, dark skin, she had
intimidating eyes and a set of dreads that gave her a
badass look. "What's with you, baby girl?" She nodded at Kelly's elbow. "What'd you do to your arm?"

This was dangerous territory. It was hard to keep
anything from Kiyana. "I tripped getting off the bus,
and I feel a little whoozy." Kelly forced a smile. "Just
call me Grace." Might as well go for all of it, she
thought. "And I, uh, took my backpack off when I
sat down to check out my leg. I looked around and
the pack was gone. Some A-hole just picked it up
and walked off with it. In all the confusion, I didn't
see a thing."

Kiyana's eyes got huge. "No! They ripped off your
backpack? What's the matter with people? That really sucks. Well, get outta here then. You ain't gonna
miss nothin'."

Around ten thirty, Kelly took Kiyana's advice, telling the instructor she had cramps and had to leave.

She had to ask around and finally found Henny
Duzan over by the Salmon Fountain talking to two
hipster dudes straddling their bicycles. Kelly backed
off, waiting until goods and cash were exchanged before approaching Duzan. A short man with a shaved

head and little snake eyes, he wore a long coat too heavy for the weather.

"Rupert told me you have cell phones."

Avoiding eye contact, he said, "I got smartphones. Eighty bucks."

"I want a burner. No GPS chip."

"I got a TracFone. Fifty."

"I'll give you ten."

He barked a short, derisive laugh. "Beat it, kid."

"Fine." Kelly turned to leave, saying over her shoulder, "See you around."

She hadn't taken more than three steps when Duzan answered. "Twenty."

Kelly turned to face him. "Fifteen."

Duzan blew a breath and shook his head. "Okay. Fifteen. *Sheeze.*"

She found Rupert in Tom McCall Park, near the battleship monument. He was sitting on a bench facing the river, eyes closed, lips moving, the breeze off the water gently stirring his silver hair. She knew better than to disturb him when he was meditating, so she sat down cross-legged on the grass next to him. Workers on their lunch hours were starting to filter into the park, and the walkway along the river was already thrumming with walkers, joggers, and people on non-motorized conveyances of every possible description.

"Why aren't you in school, Kelly?" The sun warm on her face, Rupert's voice brought her out of a drowse that was sliding into deep sleep. She wondered how long she'd been dozing there.

"Um, I wanted to give you the phone. It's cool. I have an excuse." She handed him the TracFone and a piece of notepaper folded into quarters. "I wrote down everything I saw. It's hardly anything, but maybe it'll help."

Rupert opened the folded paper and read the notes she'd written. "You told me the other night that you didn't think you could recognize this man if you saw him again. Do you still feel that way?"

Kelly hesitated, pursed her lips, and nodded slowly. "Yeah. He was facing away from me most of the time."

"Okay. This man wore a jacket, a ball cap, and boots. What kind of boots?"

Kelly hesitated for a moment. "Uh, you know, cowboy boots, sort of pointy-toed."

"How big was he?"

Kelly shrugged.

"Taller than the woman?"

She shook her head. "Yeah. Kind of a medium build. It was hard to tell from where I was."

"What else? Did he have a limp? A hump back?"

Kelly didn't laugh because Rupert jogged something, a vivid impression. "When he got out of the car, he had this strut, you know? Like he thought he was some kind of macho dude or something." The memory caused her to shudder visibly. Rupert waited while she recovered. "Uh, there's something else. The woman started to say something just before she got shot, 'Where's man,' or something like that."

"Man?"

Kelly shrugged. "That's all I heard."

Rupert nodded. "Good, Kelly. Anything on the cap or the jacket?"

"No. Nothing I could see."

"Okay. What about the gun. In his right hand or left?"

She closed her eyes again. "I didn't see him shoot her, but when I looked back, he held the gun in his right hand, I'm sure. The gun had a really long barrel. I think he used a silencer, Rupert. The gun shots didn't sound loud, you know? Just a kind of *chuck, chuck.*"

Rupert nodded. "Good, Kel. What about his car?"

"Like I said in the note—big, dark color. I didn't see the plates. It happened so fast."

"Squared-off in the back like an SUV?"

Kelly tapped her forehead with the heel of her hand and smiled sheepishly. "Yeah, now that you mention it, maybe it was an SUV. Wow, I saw more than I thought. Were you a cop, Rupert?"

He laughed. "Let's just say I have experience with the criminal justice system. Now, how's the leg?"

"Okay. I put some antiseptic on the cut and rebandaged it like you told me."

"Good. Let me see that elbow."

She gingerly slid the sleeve of her sweatshirt up and turned the elbow toward him. "It's sore is all."

He took her arm in his big, rough hands and gently flexed it. "Hurt?"

"No," she lied, and just for an instant she yearned for her dad with such intensity she thought it might burst her chest. She fought off an urge to crumple into Rupert's arms and cry.

"Okay. Now go on about your business like nothin' has happened, Kelly. I'll let you know how the call goes."

Class was over, so Kelly ambled along the river toward the Skidmore Fountain in Ankeny Plaza, gossip central for the kids who hung out in Old Town. When she saw a group gathered at the fountain, some sitting, some standing, but all with backpacks, she was suddenly reminded of the loss of hers. She might as well have lost a limb. She wondered what she could get with the fifty-three bucks she had left. Probably not much.

They were talking about the murder and hardly noticed when Kelly walked up.

"...yeah, so me and Mickey walked over there this morning to check it out, you know," a tall kid everyone called Twig was saying. "The body was gone but the cops had one of those bucket trucks up alongside the building. Looked like they were checking out some piece a tagger had done."

"Hey, I heard about that," a girl named Mellow chimed in. "Heard some dudes were asking around about who painted that."

"Some guy asked me, man," a young man using his backpack as a pillow piped in. "He acted like he didn't believe me when I said I didn't know. Like I go around studying all the graffiti in this town."

Kelly's stomach dove like a roller coaster. "Was he a cop?" she managed to ask.

The young man smiled. "Doubt it, man. He said he'd hook me up if I would tell him. Anything I wanted."

Kelly's stomach kept diving. The cops were bad enough, but the thought of the killer looking for her was like a stab in the heart with an icicle. She listened for a while longer, taking some solace in the fact that the moniker K209 wasn't mentioned. Maybe the killer, and the cops for that matter, won't make the connection between the piece she left unsigned and her other work. That would mean they'd be looking for other taggers, too.

Then an even worse thought occurred to her, if that was possible. *What if the killer mistakes some other tagger in Portland for her?* There was no doubt in her mind what would happen in that case, just like there was no doubt what would happen if the killer caught up with her.

She slunk away from the group without being noticed, fear and anxiety weighing on her every step. Suddenly Old Town seemed like a dangerous place, and she wanted to go home in the worst way. But she had her weekly appointment with her case manager at three. *You better show*, she told herself. Like Rupert said, act like nothing's happened.

Monica Sayles looked up and smiled as Kelly entered her office at New Directions. Kelly was assigned to Monica when she came to the school eighteen months earlier as a runaway and "habitual truant" with one tagging bust. Monica was demanding at first, but at least she cared. Except for the tagging, Kelly had straightened out, but even with Monica's influence, she still felt angry and defiant for reasons that were difficult for her to understand, let alone explain. But this much she knew—some girls cut themselves, others threw up, starved themselves, or took drugs. Kelly climbed and tagged.

"Are you limping?" Monica asked as Kelly sat down.

Crap, Kelly thought, *didn't think she'd notice.* "Not really. Just banged up my ankle a little."

"Your elbow, too. Did you fall?"

She notices everything. "I, uh, tripped getting off the bus, but it's fine."

Monica drew her face into a familiar look of concern. "My goodness. Maybe you should go to the infirmary."

Sheeze. The last thing I need is some nurse poking around. "Nah. It's okay." Kelly forced a smile. "Really."

In the middle of their chat, which was what Monica always called their discussions, Kelly almost blew it. Monica leaned back and seemed to trap Kelly with her eyes. "Are you sure everything's okay?" She asked. "You seem upset. Are things okay at the apartment?"

An urge to tell Monica everything crashed over her like a sneaker wave. Telling Rupert had helped, but telling Monica would mean she could put the burden down completely. Kelly opened her mouth to speak but resisted the urge. Stubborn like her dad. "I, I, uh, I'm okay. Everything's good, Monica."

She could tell Monica didn't buy it, but it got her out of there unscathed.

Kelly took the TriMet bus across the river and found a used backpack for forty bucks at a consignment shop on Sandy. It wasn't identical to the one she'd lost, but it was dark blue, matching the color. She stopped next at a food cart where she wolfed down two pieces of pizza before heading home. Veronica was out, which was a relief. Kelly dutifully fed the ungrateful mutt and made a beeline for her bed.

She managed to get both some math homework and an essay done before Veronica came home and stuck her head in to say good-night, something she very seldom did. Kelly wondered what was up with her. After showering and putting on the last of the bandages and antiseptic, she slipped beneath the covers. But sleep didn't come, so she put on her sweatshirt, jeans, and climbing shoes, slid her window open, and used the drainpipe to climb down into the dark alley. She walked three blocks to a turn of the century, four-story brick building with cornerstones like the ones she encountered the night before.

The southeast corner of the building stood in deep shadow. Her ankle and elbow screamed out, but the exhilaration of a sixty-foot free-climb was worth the pain. It was a climb she'd done many times before. An old friend. A refuge.

At the top she sat on the edge of the flat roof, hung her legs over, and breathed in the night air. As the sweat cooled her body she watched the traffic down on Sandy and began to relax.

Trouble waited for her down there on the street, but up in her domain Kelly ruled.

EIGHT

Cal

I LOVE THE city of Portland, but I always look forward to getting back to my Aerie in Dundee. Except for the crows, the odd coyote, and the wind in the Doug firs, it's quiet up there, and after a couple of hectic days in the city I'm ready for quiet. But that Friday night I stayed at Caffeine Central as a show of support for Nando. We were both anxiously awaiting news from Picasso. If he could tell me who K209 was, maybe we had a shot at helping find Claudia's murderer.

I changed into my jogging gear, leashed up Archie, and had nearly reached Johns Landing along the river when my phone went off. I managed a "Hello" as I struggled to catch my breath. I'd set a fast pace to clear my pipes.

"Cal? It's Picasso. You okay?"

"Yeah. I'm jogging, man. What's up?"

"I took a look at the piece over on Everett and compared it with the one on your building signed by K209. No question they were both done by the same person."

"Good." I waited and when he didn't continue, added, "Still no idea who it is?"

"No, not yet. Nobody I talked to knows, but they know the work. Some of the tags are pretty funny, and they're all in tough-to-reach places. My guess is you're looking for a teen—smart, angry, and a damn good climber."

"That's got to narrow the field some. So he's a tagger, not a writer, huh?"

"Oh, he's no scribble monkey, that's for sure, but, you know, he has to produce a body of work to earn a writer designation." Picasso chuckled. "K209's working on it. A red middle finger up on the Portland Police Bureau building, a big thumbs-up below the word graffiti about eight stories up on a brick wall near Powell's, a rifle with its barrel tied in a knot over near the Lloyd Center. That one's beautiful. I think Caffeine Central got tagged because of your reputation, Cal. You were being sent a message."

"I like the kid's spirit, but I'm no fan of defacing public buildings."

"Yeah, well, these kids don't have any options. Everything's off limits in Portland, man. San Francisco, Seattle, Tacoma—they all have free walls where kids can express themselves without getting arrested."

"I doubt some free wall in Portland would've stopped that middle finger from going up. The location was the whole point."

Picasso chuckled. "Probably, but it's hard to say."

I sighed. Already suffering from outrage fatigue, I had no interest in another cause. "Okay, so the Portland taggers and writers are being persecuted. But right now, I want to focus on one thing—finding this kid."

After promising to call immediately if he heard anything, Picasso rang off. When Archie and I got back to Caffeine Central I gave him his dinner, and it dawned on me how hungry I was. So I showered and we headed over to Fong Chong for some dim sum, the best in the city. The streets of Old Town bustled with energy that night, the result of the crisp, clear, and decidedly dry fall weather. It was as if the entire city was saying, "Enjoy it now, the rains will come soon enough."

Archie was in full city-dog mode, lying next to my chair at the outside table we'd scored, showing casual indifference to the goings-on, including a parade of his fellow beings and the admiration of several human passersby. I'm biased, for sure, but it's hard to beat the looks of an Aussie tricolor.

Nando called just as I finished eating. "Has Picasso located the graffiti witness?"

I sensed the strain in his voice, like he was trying to sound all business. "Not yet. But he's sure it's the same person who wrote on the wall at Caffeine Central."

"I see. I just learned the police cut Cardenas loose." The voice was especially deep, the words thickened by the Havana Club.

"How do you know?"

"Sources. I am told a woman came forward who claims she spent the night with him."

I groaned. "Let me guess. Rent an alibi?"

"Indeed. I am working on getting her name."

"And?"

"I will make an independent assessment of whether or not she can be believed. Of course, Cardenas could have hired someone to make the hit. Another avenue of inquiry. One way or the other, I will put the nail in the bastard."

"What I keep wondering is why Claudia ever

agreed to meet whoever this person is in the first place? Maybe that's another way into this thing."

We both fell silent for a few moments. "Calvin, I appreciate your help in locating the graffiti tagger. Perhaps it would be best if you also looked at this question?" His voice broke a little. "It would be too painful for me to delve into Claudia's life right now, and maybe there are things I do not want to know."

A small warning flag popped up in my head at this point. After all, I had a habit of agreeing to things before I really knew what I was getting myself into. But what could I say? This was for Nando, my friend.

"I'll see what I can find out," I told him.

We spent the rest of the phone call discussing Claudia Borrego. I learned she had a mother and brother in Miami, where she earned bachelor's and master's degrees in sociology. She moved from Miami to Portland seven years earlier to take a job as a counselor at some kind of halfway house for federal prisoners.

When I asked how she was viewed in the Latino community, Nando replied, "Everyone loved her. She sang in the church choir, campaigned for the immigration bill, and the salsa dancing—" his voice broke "—ah, I was honored just to step on the same dance floor with her."

What emerged from my friend was the portrait of a beautiful, committed human being who loved life. It's a pity life hadn't loved her back.

It was still light when I got off the phone, so Archie and I walked over to the scene of Claudia's murder, which was eerily close to Fong Chong. The cops were gone, the crime tape down. I walked into the pitted parking lot and found the chalk outline that marked where the body had lain. I looked up at the unfinished graffiti. To the right I could just make out the divots in the brick that marched up the wall, five of them. If the shooter hadn't missed, another body would have been found there. A young kid, probably. I stiffened at the thought.

The message—THERE IS NO PLA—was obviously incomplete. I was pretty sure what the finished message would have been and filled in the missing letters in my head—THERE IS NO PLANET B.

I was thankful K209 had apparently gotten away and wondered just how much the young tagger had seen that night. Could he identify the shooter, or his car perhaps? I stood there wondering about these questions, but what nagged at me most was the thought of this young person witnessing such a brutal act.

NINE

Kelly

KELLY AWAKENED THE next morning and lay staring up at the cratered, yellowed ceiling in her bedroom as she mulled over her options. She had slept fitfully and awakened feeling agitated and weighed down, as if someone had stacked a load of bricks on her chest. She could hide out in the apartment until the cops either caught the killer she'd dubbed Macho Dude or he gave up looking for her. Her sudden absence from the Old Town street scene on a Saturday would look suspicious.

It was a no-brainer. Like Rupert had advised, she would go about her business as if nothing had happened. Of course, that was a joke. Too much had happened, and she felt like she'd never be the same now.

She forced herself up and into the bathroom, which was free because Veronica had already left for the little diner on Sandy Boulevard. Veronica worked there as a waitress, but to hear her tell it she ran the place. But Kelly knew she only made minimum wage and the tips, well, they didn't amount to much, either.

Kelly stood in front of the mirror, ran a comb through her shoulder-length hair, and sighed. She hauled a dirty sheet out of the laundry basket and dragged it to the bathroom, where she spread it on the floor. Then she took a pair of scissors from the bureau and began cutting her hair, the auburn strands falling onto the sheet in thick clumps. Midway through the haircut she threw down the scissors in frustration. *"Oh, this really sucks!"*

She ran to her bedroom, Googled "Riot Grrrl" on her ancient laptop, and began scrolling through the rock bands until she found a hairstyle on some obscure bass guitarist she thought she might be able to duplicate. She carried the computer into the bathroom to use the image as a guide. Twenty minutes later she had something between a pixie and a buzz cut she could live with. To her surprise, she kind of liked the look.

Emboldened by her new look, Kelly decided to go to Old Town. She would check out the latest rumors on the street and then look up Rupert. In a gesture that surprised Kelly, Veronica had replenished their supply of bandages and antiseptic cream. To Kelly's relief she seemed to have bought the bus accident story. Kelly changed her bandages and topped up the dog's water dish on the way out. She got a growl from him for her effort.

On the way to the bus stop on Burnside, she slipped into a coffeehouse to check out *The Oregonian*. An account of the murder was in the left-hand column of the front page. Kelly's chest tightened as she read the article. If the reality of the horror she'd witnessed had receded somewhat overnight, it came back in full force. The victim now had a name, Claudia Borrego, and worst of all, a face, a beautiful face, that had been full of life and hope.

The article made no reference to a witness or a suspect. She was sure Rupert had phoned in the information. The cops didn't want Macho Dude to know all the details of what she'd seen, she decided. Then it hit her—it wouldn't just be this person looking for her. The cops would be, too. She dropped the paper and stepped back into the street. *This is really messed up*, she told herself.

An east wind from the Gorge joined the sun that morning, buffeting the bus as it crossed the river on the Burnside Bridge. She looked downriver, past the Steel and Broadway bridges, catching a fleeting glimpse of the rainbow arch of the Fremont Bridge, taunting her, it seemed. A bridge just begging to be climbed. She pushed the thought down, smiled grimly, and said under her breath, "You'll get your chance."

The outdoor market that erupted every Saturday and Sunday along the river was booming. Tents and stalls spilled across Ankeny Plaza like multicolored islands in a sea of humanity, but Kelly saw no one she knew at the fountain. She made her way farther down the parkway to the Battleship Monument, where she saw Zook and Kiyana standing off to the side of a ragged circle of kids lounging on the grass. The thick, oily aroma of burning marijuana drifted on the breeze. Her friends were talking to a kid Kelly guessed to be a new arrival. He was bent by the weight of a huge backpack, carried a gnarled walking stick, and looked way past down-and-out, or as Rupert said, broken on the wheel of life.

The kid walked away as Kelly approached. Kiyana's eyes enlarged when she saw her friend. "What'd you do to your hair, girl?"

Kelly shrugged. "It was either this or dreads."

Kiyana laughed. "You in dreads? *Sure*. Seriously, I like it. Shows off those pretty eyes of yours."

Zook, who held a basketball on his hip nodded in agreement. "Cool. The Angry Fem look. Very Portland."

Kelly shot him a look, then decided he wasn't being sarcastic. At least he noticed. "Low maintenance," she said, and nodded at Zook's ever-present basketball. "Shoot-around today?"

"Yeah. One of the assistant coaches at Portland State invited me to come to their practice. An informal thing. I think they want to get a look at me."

Zook was a great basketball player, but lacked both a GED and the money that would allow him to go to PSU. And he needed to stay clean. "That's great, Zook," Kelly said, glancing at the circle of kids and waving her hand as if clearing smoke. "Um, you better stand clear of these fumes or you'll be too messed up to dribble."

They laughed and moved upwind of the smoke. Kelly let the small talk continue for a while before asking, "You hear anything more about that woman who got murdered?"

Zook switched the basketball to his other hip. "The cops were already here. They're looking for that tagger, too." He shook his head and whistled. "I wouldn't want to be that dude."

"Did anyone tell them about the other guy who's asking around?"

Zook and Kiyana laughed in unison. Kiyana said, "Are you serious? Nobody's gonna do that."

"Yeah, well, nobody seems to know anything about the tagger, anyway," Zook added.

Kelly shifted her weight to her other foot. "Have you seen Rupert?"

"Saw him doing his tai chi routine this morning," Zook answered, "But I'll bet he's gonna be hard to find."

"Why's that?"

Zook shook his head. "I heard Digger told the cops they should talk to Rupert, that he knows everything that goes down in Old Town. I gave the old man a heads-up, and he was pissed at what Digger told them. He wants nothing to do with the cops."

Struggling to keep her face calm, Kelly nodded. *Leave it to that douche Digger to shoot off his big mouth*, she thought to herself. If the cops were tipped to Rupert, could Macho Dude be far behind?

As Zook headed off to practice, Kelly said under her breath, "Can you believe it, Ki? He didn't call me Sprout."

Kiyana laughed. "I think he got the message. And I think he likes you, too."

Kelly pushed her friend, but she couldn't contain a grin. *"Shut up."*

The two friends hung out at the monument for a while, then headed upriver to watch the kids play in the Salmon Street Fountain. It was one of their favorite pastimes. Kids playing. Parents watching. Happy families. Halfway there, two men cut them off. The older man, who carried a folder in one hand, flashed a badge with the other and introduced himself as Harmon Scott. Kelly's heart and breath stopped simultaneously. *Don't freak out. They can't know who you are.*

Scott had sympathetic eyes and didn't look like a cop. His partner was younger and trimmer with short cropped sandy hair, wraparound shades that blocked any hint of his eyes, and a stiff bearing that said nothing but "cop."

Scott wiped his brow and smiled as a breeze ruffled his wispy hair. "You young ladies look like you know this part of town." He opened the folder to display two large photographs. "Have any idea who did this graffiti? The tagger uses the name K209."

Kelly struggled to find her breath as Kiyana leaned in to look at the photographs. Kiyana said, "Seen that one on Couch Street, but I don't know nothin' about who did it."

Scott's eyes swung to Kelly, suddenly not so friendly. "How about you?" His partner shuffled his feet but kept his face like stone.

Kelly willed a blank look and shook her head. "Nah. Sorry."

Scott looked disappointed. "We don't care whether the graffiti's legal or not. This is part of a murder investigation." He handed them each a business card. "If you hear anything related to this tagger, please give us a call."

As Scott and his partner strode off, the sweat that had formed in Kelly's armpits broke loose and snaked its way down her rib cage. Kiyana eyed Kelly skeptically. "You think Rupert knows who the tagger is? If we see him let's ask him."

Kelly forced a smile. "If he knows he won't tell us, Ki."

Rupert was nowhere to be seen that afternoon. But Kelly was pretty sure she knew where to find him, at least after it got dark. She needed reassurance, and Rupert was the only person on the planet who could give her that.

TEN

Cal

EARLY SATURDAY MORNING I was awakened out of a dead sleep by someone down on the street calling, "Harley, c'mere Harley." Archie raised his head and issued a half bark, half grumble over in the corner. Harley had to be a dog. I swung out of bed and moved down the short hall to the galley kitchen at Caffeine Central. Archie shadowed me, knowing he would get fed before I made my first cappuccino.

After he was fed and I was caffeinated, I took him for a short walk and then returned for my breakfast. I toasted two pieces of Dave's Killer Bread, fried up some red potatoes and onions, and scrambled three eggs into which I crumbled smoked salmon and some local blue cheese.

Not a bad way to start the day.

I plunked around on my computer and at nine called Tayshia Jefferson, one of Claudia's colleagues at work and her best friend. She was the first name on the contacts list Nando had given me. She was obviously distraught over her friend's death but agreed to meet me after an interview with the police. Around ten thirty, she said, at a coffee shop she knew called the Rain or Shine on SE Division. I was halfway through a cappuccino when she walked in. Tall and stately, she had short hair parted and combed to one side. Her eyes were wide-set, the color of dark honey, her skin like black tea with a dash of milk. Her eyes were rimmed in red.

I stood up and offered my hand. "Thanks for coming, Tayshia."

We sat. "It's Tay," she said, meeting my eyes, her face drawn up in a frank, no-nonsense expression.

"I want you to know how sorry I am for your loss, Tay."

Her face clouded over. "Thank you. I still can't believe Claudia's gone. Who would do something like this?" Her eyes filled but contained the tears.

"It's hard to believe, I know. I, uh, just wanted to ask you some questions about Claudia."

Her eyes shifted from sad to somewhere between questioning and skeptical. "I came because you're a friend of Nando's, but I don't get it. I just told the police everything I know. What's Nando doing, some kind of vigilante thing?"

I smiled and shook the question off. "No. Not at all. It's just that, well, you can imagine how he feels. He wants to make sure nothing gets missed. I'm just trying to help him out. I have a law enforcement background."

"I thought you were a lawyer from the wine country?"

That surprised me. I hadn't told her anything about myself. "I am, but I used to be a prosecutor for the city of Los Angeles. Old habits die hard. Look, Tay, I know you've been all through this. I just have a couple of questions."

She allowed herself the slightest smile. "Well,

whatever it takes to catch the person who did this. I'm glad to help any way I can." Her eyes filled again. "Claudia was the best."

I ordered up another cappuccino and got Tay a latte with a double shot. A woman after my own heart. "When did you last see Claudia?" I said as I sat back down and slid her cup across the table.

She winced and exhaled a breath. "Last Thursday at work. She left around five."

"How did she seem? Upset at anything? Nervous?"

"No. She seemed fine. Nothing out of the ordinary."

"What can you tell me about Anthony Cardenas?"

Her face hardened and her eyes narrowed down, revealing a toughness I already sensed might be there. "She didn't tell me much. Said he'd come back to Portland and was trying to get her back. She shut him down in no uncertain terms. Told him their marriage was the biggest mistake she ever made, that she didn't give a damn how much money he had."

"So they argued?"

She laughed, a gleam of white teeth. "A bunch. Mostly Claudia telling him to get lost."

"Did he ever threaten her?"

Her eyes flashed at me like brown lasers. "Oh, yeah. Plenty of times. Hell, he was practically stalking her. She told me he used to park near her place and wait for her to get home from work. She told me he said he was going to get her back no matter what it took."

"You told the police about that?"

"Of course I told them."

"Ever meet Cardenas?"

"No, never had the pleasure."

"So, you think he killed her."

She shot me an incredulous look. "Who else? Claudia didn't have an enemy on the planet. Everyone loved her."

A young couple sat down at the table next to us and immediately dropped their heads to study the tiny screens on their cell phones. I lowered my voice, anyway. "Tell me a little about work, Tay."

"I work at a Federal Reentry Center, a fancy name for a halfway house. Federal prisoners, men who have a release date six to twelve months out, come to the FRC. The residents—we don't call them inmates—come from federal prisons all over the country, but mainly the two in the Northwest, Lompoc and Sheridan. It takes good behavior to earn a slot at an FRC. It's a sweet deal because residents can leave prison six to twelve months early and look for work or go to school while they serve out their term."

"What do you do at the FRC?"

"I'm a mental health counselor. My job's to assess a resident's mental condition when he arrives at the site. If there are psychological issues—and there usually are—I work with him and make sure he's got a treatment strategy before he leaves us." She smiled. "It's my dream job."

"What about Claudia?"

"She's, uh, she *was* a caseworker. Caseworkers have overall responsibility for the residents, you know, making sure they have a reentry plan, helping them make contacts outside, write résumés, apply to college, that sort of thing."

"How did she go about this?"

"One-on-one counseling. Her residents met with her on a regular basis. She was very busy and damn good at her job."

"Did she have any conflicts with any of the residents, anyone who would want to hurt her?"

Tay took a sip of her latte, then stared into the cup. "There're always plenty of issues, but she never felt threatened by anyone as far as I know. The residents adored her."

"What kind of issues did she deal with?"

"Oh, God, you name it—hostile family members, prior criminal affiliations, problems finding work or qualifying for school, the gamut. A caseworker has to be a jack-of-all-trades."

"Would anything about Claudia's work lead her to meet someone in Old Town at three a.m.?"

Tay closed her eyes as if she'd asked herself that question a thousand times. "I can't imagine why she did that." A faint, wistful smile crossed her face and she shook her head. "But it was Claudia, you know? If she had one flaw it was that she could become emotionally attached to her clients. She was just *so* committed."

We finished our coffees and I thanked Tay, gave her my card, and told her to call if she thought of anything else. As we were leaving, she put a hand on my arm and rested her eyes on me. "Good luck, Cal. I hope you catch the bastard."

Like I needed any more motivation.

I drove back to Caffeine Central, leashed up Arch, and walked over to the food carts on Ninth for a quick bite. I was halfway through a fava bean falafel when Nando called. "How did it go with Tayshia?"

"Didn't get much. She's down on Cardenas like everyone else."

"Yes. Well, the name of his alibi provider is Sheri Daniels. She dances at the Lucky Dragon on Broadway and turns the tricks to augment her income. She has been seen with Cardenas, which gives his story some credibility. However, she would be easy to buy. She has a strong affinity for oxycodone, an expensive habit."

"You can bet Scott's going to look hard at her."

"No question. But another set of eyes cannot hurt. We are checking to see if she just happened to be with someone other than Cardenas last Thursday night."

"Tayshia told me Claudia wouldn't meet Cardenas anywhere at high noon let alone three in the morning. If Cardenas was the shooter, I'd like to know how he pulled it off."

Nando went silent so long I thought the call had dropped. Finally, he said, "*If* he was the shooter?"

I shook my head and smiled. I understood why he was so invested in Cardenas, but, damn it, Nando knew better than that. I settled for, "You're running on emotion, not evidence, right now, my friend."

Another silence. "Can I count on your support, Calvin?"

"Of course you can."

ELEVEN

Cal

I DROVE BACK to Caffeine Central with the intention of taking Archie for a jog along the river before spending the afternoon interviewing more of Claudia's friends. But a front moved in, and by the time I got back to the building rain was dancing on the streets. I'd left my rain gear at the Aerie, so the run was off, which was fine by Archie, who was no fan of water of any kind.

The first person on my afternoon list was Robert Vargas, executive director of a Portland immigration rights organization called Justicia. Claudia was a member of his board, which had met the previous Wednesday night. Vargas told me Claudia was her usual self, cheerful and full of energy, and hadn't mentioned anything out of the ordinary when he spoke to her briefly prior to the meeting. Anita Perez, with whom she had organized the popular salsa club, Salsa Libre, met with her the previous Thursday night to go over details of the Friday night dance. If Claudia was bothered about something or had something on her mind, she hadn't shown it, Perez told me. Another friend, a neighbor and mother of four, told me Claudia was at her apartment that Thursday evening. If she left early Friday morning to meet someone in Old Town, the friend hadn't heard it.

On my way out of Portland that evening I parked down from Claudia's apartment, an old, asbestos-sided duplex on SE Holgate, near Lents Park. Nando had called earlier to ask if I could stop there and pick up a photo album, explaining he couldn't bear to enter the apartment where his beloved Claudia had lived. "The album is a collection of pictures of us that I gave her," he explained. "I'm afraid it will become lost. I have secured permission for you to enter the apartment from the landlord, a friend of mine." He went on to describe where the apartment key would be hidden and where I might find the album.

"A crime scene notice might still be on the door," I warned.

"The album is of no evidential value, Calvin."

"I'm not going in if the notice is still up."

A long sigh. "Must you always be the Boy Scout?"

I swallowed a comeback as was often the case when talking with my friend. "I value my law practice, Nando. It's the only one I have."

The streetlights in Claudia's neighborhood came on as Arch and I sat in the car checking things out. Although I had permission to enter, I didn't particularly want anyone to see me. The last thing I needed was to have it get back to Harmon Scott and his partner that I was snooping around in their case. Cops are touchy like that.

The street was quiet, so after cracking the car windows for Arch, I approached the apartment. I brought along a penlight I kept in the glove compartment, which, remarkably, still had working batteries.

Scott and his partner had apparently finished with Claudia's apartment. I could see a few remnants of the fluorescent-orange crime-scene notice that had been stripped from the front door. I found the key and tried the lock, which was sticky but finally released with a loud click. The door creaked open into a small vestibule containing a brass umbrella stand next to an old church pew polished by years of use in another setting. A Calder print hung above the pew. I stopped to straighten it.

After locking the front door behind me, I moved into the living room and my heart rate ticked up a notch. I was legal, but there was something a bit unsettling about the mission I was on. The ambient light was low but still sufficient for me to navigate the space without the penlight. My nostrils balked at the musty air, and I heard nothing except a faint whir as the refrigerator compressor came on in the kitchen.

A compact leather couch and matching easy chair dominated the right side of the living room. When I glanced left I stopped. Papers and magazines were scattered around an antique desk that stood with its roll top up and its drawers emptied out. I used the penlight to quickly scan the papers, an uninteresting tangle of receipts, utility bills, and the like.

I moved quickly to the dining room, which sported a round mahogany table, an old china cabinet with doors inset with wavy glass, and an antique sideboard that spanned most of one wall. The top and bottom drawers of the sideboard were open, and a few papers littered the floor. Expensive-looking silverware and silver serving trays were visible within the sideboard. Maybe just a careless job of searching, I decided. My tax dollars at work.

A framed set of two photos of Claudia and Nando

salsa dancing lay face up on the sideboard. Nando hadn't mentioned the photos, so I set it back up and left it there.

The kitchen was small and painted a shade of yellow that appeared to match van Gogh's *Sunflowers*, a copy of which hung in a tiny breakfast nook. The kitchen looked more orderly except for a scattering of cookbooks on the countertop, which must have been stripped from a nearby shelf. I found the photo album among the cookbooks. "She kept the album in the kitchen, her favorite room," Nando had told me. "She loved to cook."

The album—a handsome tome bound in thick, expensive leather—was filled with pictures of the happy couple. The picture on page one was a selfie taken somewhere on the coast. Nando and Claudia smiled back at me, the thrill of new love so evident in their faces. I had to swallow a lump in my throat.

The bedroom was only a few steps down the hall. I was curious to see if it was left in disarray like the rest of the apartment. I tucked the album into the front of my pants to give myself a free hand and used the penlight to navigate down the dark hallway. The doors to the bathroom and hall closet were open, but the bedroom door was shut, which struck me as a bit odd. I stopped and listened. Nothing. I pushed the door open without stepping in. At this point, adrenaline began to trickle into my bloodstream.

Still nothing, so I entered the room.

A closet door to my left flew open and a figure rushed me. I dropped the penlight but not before seeing a glint of steel. I twisted instinctively, and the knife blade grazed the album tucked in my belt and snagged on my windbreaker. That gave me just enough time to grab the wrist of my attacker's gloved knife hand with both of my hands. Realizing I was defenseless, he swatted at me with his free fist.

We danced like that for several steps, him trying to punch me, me slipping his blows and forcing his knife hand up and away from my exposed body, and both of us grunting like hogs in a feed yard. Once I had his knife hand above my head, I pulled him closer. He responded by swinging wildly with his free hand, the blows ripping at my ear. When I finally worked him close enough that I could smell his breath—a thick fog of garlic and whiskey—I kneed him hard in the groin, once, twice. He groaned, his legs buckled, and I felt the strength go out of his right arm. I twisted his wrist with everything I had. The knife came loose, falling to the floor between us.

I let go of his wrist and dropped to the floor to retrieve the knife. But he recovered much quicker than I anticipated and kicked me hard in the ribs, knocking most of the air from my lungs and sending a shock wave of pain through my body. When he tried to kick me a second time, I grabbed his foot with both arms, folded my body around it, and twisted his leg with every ounce of my strength. He let out a guttural cry and fell backward through the open doorway into the dark hall. I rolled in the opposite direction with nothing but his smelly boot in my hands.

By the time I located his knife on the floor, I heard the back door in the kitchen slam shut.

I stayed down and took stock while my breathing came back to normal, my ribs screaming in pain.

"Damn," I said, forcing myself to my feet, "could have skipped the bedroom."

I went into the kitchen, locked the back door, and called the Portland Police Bureau. Scott and Ludlow had left for the day, but Scott called back in less than five minutes and told me to sit tight. I went out to check on Archie, carrying a butcher knife from the kitchen in case the one-booted cowboy was still in the neighborhood. Arch was okay but disappointed when I told him to stay in the car. I put the album in the trunk to prevent it from becoming part of the new crime scene and hobbled back to the apartment, every step greeting me with a fusillade of pain.

Scott arrived first. Wearing faded jeans and a knit shirt, his shoulder holster visible under a light jacket, he'd obviously come straight from home and wasn't happy about it. "Jesus Christ, Claxton, why the hell do you keep turning up in my crime scenes? You're like a piece of gum on my shoe."

"I'm a lawyer, not a gumshoe," I reminded him. My attempt at levity went unappreciated.

Then he noticed I was listing about twenty degrees to port. "You need an ambulance?"

I waved off the question and began detailing an account of what happened, which I had to begin again when his partner, Aaron Ludlow, arrived a couple of minutes later. When I finished, Scott said, "So, you really didn't get a look at the guy?"

I shook my head. "It was dark. He was my size, maybe a little shorter, with breath that could wilt flowers. That's about all I got, except for the knife and boot. You might find some prints, but he was wearing gloves."

Scott smiled thinly, but Ludlow continued to frown. With a square jaw and pale blue eyes below short-cropped hair, I figured Ludlow for ex-military based on the way he carried himself. He said, "Why were you in here, anyway?"

Best not to mention the album now residing in my car's trunk. I turned to the sideboard and pointed to the set of photos of the couple salsa dancing. "Mendoza wanted these pictures back. They're his."

"You just walked in?" Ludlow said.

"No. Nando cleared it with the landlord." I stopped for a moment, swung my gaze from Ludlow to Scott, and back to Ludlow. "Uh, I'm the victim of an attempted murder here, guys."

Scott nodded, but Ludlow continued as if he hadn't heard me. "Why didn't he get the pictures himself?"

I shrugged. "Sensitive, I guess."

We continued in that vein for a while, Ludlow asking more annoying questions and me trying to control my temper. By this time, a couple of crime scene techs had arrived and were busy dusting for prints, particularly around a broken bathroom window, clearly the point of entry. I gave the detectives the cowboy boot and the switchblade and then followed them downtown, where I made a formal statement. When they finally cut me loose, it appeared they'd concluded I'd barged in on a routine burglary. At least, that's where Ludlow seemed to be. "People read the newspapers, Claxton," he said at one point. "An unmarried woman is murdered. The bad guys figure that once the cops leave, her place is easy pickings." I wasn't so sure about Scott. He was an old pro not likely to jump to conclusions.

As I was leaving, Scott followed me into the hall of the nearly deserted building. He took off his glasses, polished them on his shirt, and put them back on. His forehead looked like a ploughed field. "You hear from your artist friend about that tagger?"

"Yeah, but he hasn't come up with a name. Still has some feelers out. You're probably looking for a teen who's pretty athletic. Ever hear of buildering?"

Scott's forehead grew a few more furrows. "What the hell's that?" I explained what Picasso had told me, then added, "So, that red middle finger way up on the Police Bureau building—that was K209's work."

"Damn, we hadn't made that connection." He chuckled despite himself. "The powers that be got that finger scrubbed off in a hurry." He let out a long breath and shook his head. "Thanks for the tip, Cal. We probably shouldn't expect a lot of cooperation from this K209. Uh, you'll stay close to Picasso on this, right?"

I nodded. There was another reason Scott wanted to keep me between him and Picasso. I won't say there was bad blood between them, but the truth was Scott had arrested Picasso in an incident that nearly cost Picasso his life. "If Picasso comes up with a name, you'll be the first to know," I told him.

"Thanks." I turned to leave, and he added, "Look, Claxton, I know Mendoza's a friend of yours, but we both know he's a loose cannon. Don't let him do anything stupid, okay?"

Without looking back, I wagged a raised index finger to let him know I'd heard him.

After letting Arch stretch his legs for a couple of minutes, I retrieved the photo album from the trunk.

It was only then that I noticed that the thick leather cover had been nearly slashed in two by the attacker's knife. A vision of what that blade, undeflected, would have done to me flashed in my mind like a crime scene photo, and a cold shiver rattled through me. A random burglary? I doubted it, but the only way to know for sure was to find the one-boot cowboy with bad breath. That would be a worthy goal, I decided. I owed him.

TWELVE

Kelly

ALTHOUGH A CLOUD of dread shadowed Kelly that Saturday afternoon, she was trying hard not to show it. If Kiyana sensed something was wrong, Kelly worried that she might crack under the grilling her perceptive friend would give her. Kiyana had run away from her abusive, drug-addicted parents in Eugene and had spent three years on the streets of Portland before getting her own apartment, subsidized by the alternative school, and a part-time job. She wasn't just a friend, she was a rock—proud, strong, and fearless. Everything Kelly wanted to be.

When Zook joined them later that afternoon, Kelly felt relieved. She'd pulled off the deception so far. They hung out at the Ankeny Fountain, and then Zook announced he was taking them to dinner. "Well," he went on to explain with his big, crooked grin, "it's actually at the Sisters of the Road Cafe. The assistant coach at PSU gave me a handful of meal vouchers."

"Oh, man, I'm not up for a meal with a bunch of homeless people," Kiyana shot back.

Kelly burst out laughing, and Zook said, "Hey, *I'm* homeless, girl, and so were you three months ago."

Kiyana went along with it, and they ate what turned out to be a fine meal at one of the few spots in Port-

land that turns no one away. At nine thirty, Kelly said
her goodbyes and headed for the bus stop, but when
Kiyana and Zook were out of sight, she doubled back
down the stairs on the Burnside Bridge and headed
downriver on Naito Parkway.

A half-moon had worked its way above the trees
lining the parkway, and a light breeze carried a faint
hint of the river. Pedestrian and car traffic thinned out
along the corridor into the riverfront industrial area.
Kelly passed under the Steel and Broadway bridges
and was nearly to the Fremont when a huge, abandoned building seemed to materialize out of the shadows. Lit by low-wattage security lights and covering a
full block, the complex was a mishmash of brick and
corrugated iron. A rusted water tower balanced on
one of its multiple roofs and four massive silos scal-
loped into a section of wall. "Albertson's Milling" was
painted in faded blue on white at the top of the silos.

Rupert called this place his penthouse, although
he'd settled in on the fifth floor of the eight-story
complex. He'd filed a key to fit one of the ground-level
doors and arranged a comfortable spot in one of the
abandoned offices. Kelly made her way through the
deserted parking lot on the south side of the building
to a metal door adjacent to a long loading dock. A
single bulb on a spindly arm cast a dim pool of light
in front of the door. She looked around to make sure
nobody was coming by out on the road, then knelt
down and worked a loose brick out of the corner of
the loading dock and put her hand in the cavity.

"Crap. Where's the key?" she said out loud.

She stood up feeling disappointed. She was sure
she'd find Rupert there. He always came to the pent-

house when he wanted to get away from people. Maybe she was early. But where was the key? Rupert always put it back, and as far as she knew, she was one of just a few kids who knew about it. The deal was, use it only in an emergency, and don't disturb Rupert on the fifth floor unless you have a damn good reason.

She stepped back and looked up at the roofline. A corner window on the seventh floor was broken out. An intact drainpipe ran down from the roof along the corner of the building to the ground. The drainpipe was stout copper and the grout between the bricks worn and grooved, affording manageable finger and toeholds. *Why not?* Kelly asked herself. It was too late to be heading home, and she really wanted to talk to Rupert. Surely he would show up.

Left hand on the drainpipe, right hand fingers jammed in the grout cracks. She wasn't wearing her climbing shoes, but her sneakers, which she retied as tightly as possible, gave her ample purchase. Push with the legs, slide the hands up. Find new holds and do it again. Flat against the wall. Breathe evenly. Focus.

Halfway up, she rested. The breeze cooled the sweat on her brow and carried off most of the anxiety she'd felt that day. She thought of her dad. Not one to show his emotions, he beamed that first time she reached the top of the Zebra Seam at Smith Rock. "You've become quite the little climber, young lady," she remembered him telling her. "Another year, you'll be ready for Beacon Rock." Kelly allowed a moment of emotion before reminding herself that she was forty feet off the ground without a belay.

Once inside the building on the seventh floor, Kelly could scarcely see her hand in front of her face. As she waited for her eyes to adjust she heard the exterior metal door below her open, the sound drifting up in the still night.

She turned back to the broken window and looked down on the parking lot. A figure was standing next to the loading dock, just outside the ring of light cast by the overhead security light. It was a man, but she knew it wasn't Rupert. A second man emerged from the doorway and stood in the pale light. The man in the shadows shifted nervously and said, "Oh, Christ," in a guttural hiss.

The second man, the one in the light, said, "We did what we had to do, man. Deal with it," and disappeared into the darkness along the building.

"At least take that damn jacket off before you walk out of here, you idiot," the first man called after him.

The second man walked under the next security light and stopped to remove his jacket. His profile from the back looked familiar, but the way his body rocked from side to side as he walked, a kind of exaggerated swagger, was unmistakable. Kelly gasped so loud she ducked down for fear they'd heard her. She would know that walk anywhere. It was the killer, Macho Dude. She was sure of it.

As her heart pummeled her rib cage, Kelly eased back up and watched as the two figures disappeared into the night. She waited there, watching and listening until she heard a single car start up and head south on Naito Parkway toward Old Town.

Kelly let herself out of the office and groped her way to the stairwell, which she knew was located at the left end of the narrow hall. The air seemed viscous and laden with the smell of mildew, motor oil, and an almost overpowering smell of something akin to stale bread.

Rupert's "penthouse" was the center office on the fifth floor. She worked her way down two flights of stairs and into the hallway. The center office door was closed. She opened it and called softly. "Rupert? Are you in there?" She waited, hearing nothing but the blood pounding in her ears. Weak light from a window cast the room in deep shadow. As she entered she nearly fell over Rupert's backpack. She fumbled through the pockets and found his flashlight, the only object left in it. She snapped the light on and gasped audibly, the sound quickly dying in the dead air. The place had been trashed. His battered suitcase—the one with rollers—was lying open and empty, his few toiletries and tattered clothes scattered across the floor.

She swung the beam to the corner of the room and saw him. He sat on the floor, slumped against the wall, his head lolled to one side, chin on chest, wet blood glistening in the light beam. "Rupert!" she called as she went to him.

It was no use. The blank-eyed stare told her that. Beaten to death, his arms crisscrossed with purple welts, his head gashed and misshapen by repeated blows. The heavy, bloodied pipe used to torture and kill him lay next to his body. Kelly's heart stopped as fear, anger, and sorrow crushed down on her. She knelt next to her friend and gently closed his eyes, then turned her head and in a single, violent heave, emptied the contents of her stomach. She forced herself up and wobbled as the room took a half turn.

Oh, Rupert. No, no, no.

No tears came, only an overwhelming desire to get out of that god-awful place. But first she pushed a wooden box—the only furniture in the room—over to a corner. She stood on it, moved an acoustic ceiling tile to one side, and removed a flat, gray box and the TracFone, the one she bought the day before.

She knew about this hiding place because Rupert had gone to it the one time she ventured up to the penthouse. She needed a loan of forty bucks for a pair of climbing shoes they were practically giving away at US Outdoor. Rupert gave her the money, no questions asked. "Now get out of here, I need my privacy," he'd said with a gruffness she knew he didn't mean. She left that day, basking in the knowledge that he trusted her and vowing to pay him back if it was the last thing she ever did.

She put the box in her backpack and made her way down the stairs and out of the complex, leaving the ground floor door ajar. When she nearly reached Burnside, she called 911 and told the operator she'd heard a man screaming inside Albertson's Mill as she was cutting through the parking lot. She didn't dare mention the connection to Claudia Borrego's murder because that would tip the cops that K209 was a girl. Then she tossed the TracFone in the river, all the while moving as if in a dream. But she knew this was no dream.

And she knew something else, too, something deep in her heart. No matter how much they tortured him, her friend Rupert had not given her up.

THIRTEEN

Kelly

KELLY SAT VERY still admiring the moon, a perfect hemisphere with a vertical edge so sharp and clean it looked like someone had sliced it with a razor blade. The moon seemed to levitate above the sparsely lit outline of the US Bank Tower. Called the Big Pink by Portlanders on account of its rose-tinted marble facade, it dominated the buildings on the west side of the river like Mount Hood dominated the horizon to the east. From her vantage point, she could also see the twinkling contours of the Burnside Bridge and a thin strip of river on either side that reflected the city lights like a polished mirror.

She was thinking about the people out there, thousands of them with not a care in the world, going about their business, most getting ready for bed by now. She almost laughed at the thought of bed and sleep. These weren't options for her. Every time she closed her eyes, all she could see was Rupert's battered face staring back at her. So instead of going home after riding the bus back to the east side, she climbed to the top of her four-story refuge to try to collect herself.

Okay, she cried some, too. A lot, actually. With Rupert gone, she felt alone, abandoned. The cops were out. She was violating the key term of her probation—no tagging of any kind—and that would bring the cops down on both her and Veronica.

Worst of all was the guilt. After all, Rupert had probably been tortured and killed because of her.

What about Ki and Zook? Are they in danger, too, just because they hang out with me?

She cried some more until the tears simply wouldn't flow anymore. She thought about her dad that last day. His diary was recovered after the fall, and she'd committed to memory most of what he'd written that day. He talked about finding the strength for a final push to the summit, despite being sick and frostbitten. He'd mentioned her, too. His exact words were, "Thinking of Kel this morning. Want to get back to my darling girl." The words brought her strength. They always did.

Kelly forced herself to revisit the scene back at the mill. The first man she saw from that broken window was deep in shadow. The only thing she could say about him was how his voice sounded. It was commanding, like he was in charge. She focused in on the other man, the man she knew had shot Claudia Borrego. She only saw his back, but the cocky way he moved was burned into her memory. There was something else, too. He wore a jacket with something on the back. She saw the image before he took it off under the second light. She closed her eyes and tried to pull up the image. Most of his back was in shadow, but she'd seen what looked like flames on the fraction that was illuminated. That's what caught her eye initially. But there was something else—letters. They arched above the flames, part of an insignia or logo.

She closed her eyes again, took a deep breath, and let it out slowly. She could see him walking away with that swagger that made her want to puke. The letters, the ones she could see, came back to her. They spelled out *B-R-I-D-G-E-T-O*. Yes, that was it!

It was all she could come up with, but it was a start—the first clues to finding the two men, Macho Dude and the Voice.

Kelly eased herself down from her eighty-foot perch. The granite was cool and comforting to the touch, and the seams between the cornerstones were like the rungs of a ladder. When she let herself into the apartment Veronica was waiting for her. A cigarette smoldered in an ashtray next to the recliner, where she sat with the mutt on her lap. The mutt growled and Veronica said, "Where have you been, Kelly? I've been worried about you."

"I was over in Old Town. Lost track of time. Sorry."

"How's your leg?"

"It's okay."

"I've been thinking, Kelly, when you fell getting off the bus, was it their fault? Maybe you need to see a doctor?"

Kelly blew a breath out. "No, Veronica. Sorry, but no grounds for a lawsuit."

Veronica shifted in her seat, and the mutt jumped to the floor with a sharp bark. "I didn't mean it that way, Kel. It's just that, you know, without any insurance—"

Without looking back, Kelly went down the hall to her bedroom and slammed the door.

Kelly called her old Compaq laptop "The Glacier" for obvious reasons. While she waited for it to boot up, she extracted Rupert's gray metal box from her backpack. She'd almost forgotten about it and when she opened it, gasped out loud. It was filled with cash. It took her a couple of minutes to count it all, two thousand eight hundred fifty-nine dollars to be exact. Mostly in twenty- and fifty-dollar bills.

Buried under the bills was a birth certificate for Rupert Louis Youngblood, born at the Los Angeles General Hospital on January 8, 1960, at 1:52 a.m. Kelly's eyes filled when she realized the ink impression at the bottom of the certificate was Rupert's tiny footprint. Beneath the birth certificate was a single photograph of a handsome young woman with her arm around a young girl. The caption read, "Molly and Tanya, September 23, 1992." The last thing she found was a faded article cut from a newspaper. The headline read Mother and Daughter Killed in Freeway Crash." The short article described the accident. A drunk driver crossed the median strip and struck the car containing the Youngblood family head-on. Molly and Tanya Youngblood were killed instantly and Rupert Youngblood was left in critical condition.

Stunned, Kelly sat on the bed as memories of her friend flashed in her head. Now she knew why Rupert had chosen his path, and the sadness of it bit into her like sharp teeth. But she knew instinctively not to let the sadness cripple her. What mattered was doing something about it. She put everything back in the box, hid it in the back of her closet, and turned her attention back to her laptop.

When Google finally came up, she tapped in "BRIDGETO," and then to narrow the field, added "Portland." Two choices came up. The first was "Bridge to Brews," an annual ten-kilometer walk/

run that began and ended at the Widmer Brothers Brewing Company in Portland. Kelly quickly ruled it out. She was pretty sure she saw BRIDGETO as part of *one* word, and their logo had no flames on it, and was sold on T-shirts, not jackets.

The second choice to come up was "Bridgetown," a popular nickname for Portland. When she clicked on it over a dozen businesses incorporating the word in their name popped up, from Bridgetown Archery to Bridgetown Zumba. "Bummer," Kelly uttered as she fell back on her bed. She felt like crying again but forced herself back up. In a few minutes she narrowed the list down to four businesses she guessed might have jackets with logos on them: Bridgetown Archery, Bridgetown Street Bikes, Bridgetown Comedy Club, and Bridgetown Arsenal.

The archery shop sold everything, it seemed, related to the sport of archery except clothing. The bike shop and the comedy club had cool logos but not with flames in them.

Kelly knew an arsenal was a place where weapons were stored, and when the Bridgetown Arsenal site came up, she decided it was a bit of a stretch to apply the term to a retail gun store and indoor shooting range. But, she had to admit, they were totally into weapons there. You could take shooting classes, buy ammo reloading equipment, get your gun blued—whatever that meant—buy shooting attire, and for a bit of "nostalgia" you could even rent and fire an authentic Thompson submachine gun.

When she ran across a page of pistol silencers for sale—properly called suppressors, she noted—she almost got sick to her stomach. But when she came to the clothing section and looked at the windbreakers, the blood drained from her head and her heart nearly stopped.

One of the jackets—referred to as "Our Most Popular Range Jacket"—featured a logo on the back consisting of a fierce looking eagle with wings spread and the words *BRIDGETOWN ARSENAL* arched over the top.

She studied the picture, then closed her eyes and brought back the scene at the mill. *Holy crap*, she said to herself. *Those weren't flames I saw, they were freakin' eagle feathers. That's the jacket the dude was wearing.*

She fell back on her bed again, thrust her arms up, and let out a scream, more like a screech, of triumph, excitement, and fear, all wrapped into one.

"Are you okay in there?" Veronica called out.

"Oh, yeah," she answered. "I'm okay."

Then under her breath she added, "Now what?"

FOURTEEN

Cal

WHEN I FINALLY finished up that night in Portland
after my near disembowelment at Claudia's apartment, Arch and I headed for home—my real home.
When we reached the Aerie, I let Arch out at the mailbox, and he led me up the long drive to our gate, his
bob of a tail switching with excitement in the headlights. Sure, he loved being with me in Portland, but
the Aerie, all five acres of it, was his kingdom, and
he ruled over it like a proud lion. A bright half-moon
was straight up, the night air bracing, like a drink of
cold well water. From high up in one of the Doug firs
dotting the property, our old friend the barred owl announced his presence with his familiar "who cooks
for you, who cooks for youuuu?"

Arch was right—it was damn good to be home.

I dragged my body into the house, my battered
ribs protesting every step. I sorted through the mail,
a check from a client, a couple of bills, and a letter
from a woman I knew in Russia. I tucked the letter,
unopened, into my briefcase.

My bed upstairs sang a siren song, but I had a cowboy to chase down. I took a business card from my
shirt pocket and read what I'd written on the back:
"Timmons's Custom Boots, 33-3-10." The name was

branded into the sole of my attacker's boot, next to the heel. The numbers, some kind of product code, were on the inside of one of the boot's pull straps. I Googled the bootmaker. According to his website, Farnell Timmons made his custom boots near Estacada, Oregon, a small ranch and farming community southeast of Portland. These were boots for the serious, or at least the well-heeled, cowboy with a range of prices topping a thousand dollars.

I shrugged after jotting down some notes. Surely Scott and his partner, Ludlow, would be all over this. On the other hand, if they bought the random break-in view, then the boot I gave them could very well get ignored in the rush of the murder investigation.

No way I was going to ignore it. I rubbed my sore ribs and grimaced. This was personal.

I woke up that Sunday morning feeling like I'd been dropped from a three-story building. My left side looked like a target in shades of purple, and although I was breathing a little easier, I paid handsomely for even the slightest twist of my torso. On the bright side, the bruises on the side of my face weren't particularly deep or very sore. The most active thing I accomplished that day was a walk down to the mailbox to get the Sunday paper.

On Monday morning it took me twice as long as usual to shower, shave, and dress. After feeding Archie, I stood at the kitchen sink sipping a double cappuccino as an ugly mass of gray clouds boiled up the valley. By the time I finished my coffee and polished off some granola, we were being strafed with pea-sized hail. The storm front cleared just as Archie and

I left for a nine o'clock divorce hearing at the circuit court in McMinnville. He would wait in the car without a fuss. He was just glad to be making the trip.

After the hearing, I sat in the echoing hallway of the courthouse and used my cell phone and laptop to clear my schedule in Dundee for the next two days. My billable hours were down, so it wasn't exactly a task I relished. I called ahead to Farnell Timmons's Custom Boot Shop but only to confirm that it was open. I figured my best shot at finding the owner of my souvenir boot was to make a personal appearance.

It rained steadily until I turned off I-205 at Route 224, which parallels the Clackamas River. Halfway to Estacada the sun broke through, and the river answered by turning from slate gray to turquoise blue in the blink of an eye. Across the river, second growth Doug firs and cedars crowded the banks, their rich green canopies broken here and there by maples, oaks, and alders whose leaves burned with the colors of fall. I rolled the windows down so Arch and I could drink in the smell of the trees and the river.

Timmons's place sat off a two-lane road past Estacada in an unincorporated section of Clackamas County. A small sign next to his mailbox said, "Timmons's Custom Boots," and below that in smaller letters, "Take the fork to the right." I drove down a narrow lane through a stand of firs, parked, and after leaving a window down for Arch, entered a low, cedar-sided building with a red metal roof.

The showroom smelled of leather, and a sign next to a set of swinging doors put me on notice that the proprietor could refuse me service if the spirit moved him. All manner of cowboy boots lined one wall, from the elegantly understated to fancier models with intricate, hand-tooled designs. There were leather gun cases and belt and shoulder holsters on display, as well. The biggest rebel flag I ever saw hung on the opposite wall. A couple of framed signs below the flag espoused pro-gun sentiments. One read, "The Second Amendment Is My Concealed Weapons Permit, Period," signed Ted Nugent; the second, "Free Men Do Not Ask Permission to Bear Arms."

Tell me how you really feel.

A young man battling acne came through the double doors. "Hi. I'm Wade. Can I help you?"

"Maybe you can, Wade. I'm a big fan of your boots. Great craftsmanship. I'm curious about that numerical code that you sew in, you know, inside, next to the pull strap?"

Wade nodded. "Yes sir?"

"Can you use it to tell who you made the boots for?"

"Sure. We keep records."

"If I give you a number, can you look up a name for me?"

Wade licked his lips and swallowed. "Uh, you'll have to ask Farnell about that."

"Is he here?"

"No, sir. He's at lunch. Won't be back til two or so."

After Wade gave me directions to where Timmons was eating, I said, "How will I know him?"

"He'll be in the back, at a table. Just ask for him."

A small bar and grill on the outskirts of Estacada, the Trail Away was dimly lit with the smells of deep-frying oil, beer, and the twang of a country song all vying for dominance. Once my eyes adjusted, I noticed everyone in the place had turned to look at me. I asked the bartender for Farnell Timmons, and he nodded in the direction of three men at a back table. "Timmons is in the middle."

I stopped in front of the table, introduced myself, and said, "Sorry to interrupt your lunch, gentlemen." Then, looking directly at Timmons went on, "I was just over at the boot shop, and Wade said you might be able to help me, Mr. Timmons."

He nodded, taking the measure of me. "Yeah, Wade just called. Said you wanted some information on a pair of my boots." He smiled but his heart wasn't in it. "You don't look like the type that wears my boots." The men on either side of him shifted in their seats, and one suppressed a laugh.

"I want to talk to the man who bought a pair of your boots."

Timmons took a long pull on his beer. "Why?"

"It's a confidential matter. The number in the boots is 33-3-10. I just want a name."

"Can't help you, partner. Even if I wanted to, which I don't, I couldn't give you a name. I made those boots four and a half years ago. I purge my tax records every three years."

"The IRS might frown on that."

The eyes flashed at me. "Screw the IRS. They're lucky I pay any taxes at all." He took another long pull on his beer and waved a meaty hand. "We're done here."

I nodded, and as I turned to leave I saw him tip his head in my direction. The two men at the table got up and followed me out the door. I could hear the crunch of their boots in the gravel as we crossed the parking lot, but I forced myself to walk without a limp and willed myself not to look back. I wasn't going to give them the satisfaction.

When I got to my car I turned around, an action that sent a stab of pain radiating out from my ribs. I hoped they didn't see me wince. "Gentlemen, is there something else that needs discussing?"

The taller of the two, dressed all in black like Johnny Cash, said, "We're just making sure you get to your car safely. Sometimes people get their asses kicked out here. Damnedest thing."

The other man was squat and despite his enormous belly looked powerful. He said, "Yeah. Happens all the time to people who don't mind their own business." He chuckled. "Judging from your face, looks like somebody already got after you."

I bit back a comment that would have undoubtedly escalated the situation. Instead, I opened the car door. Archie hopped out and sensing the threat immediately, positioned himself in front of me and dropped his ears. Now the sides were even. An eighty-pound dog will do that. Both men stepped back. The tall man shrugged and turned to leave. The short guy followed. I breathed a sigh of relief, clapped Arch on his broad back, and let us both in the car.

On my way to Portland I called Nando. He didn't pick up, so I left a voice mail telling him I'd failed to get the boot owner's name. Farnell Timmons had been uncooperative, I told him, and there was a good chance that even a subpoena from Scott and Ludlow wouldn't yield anything since Timmons said he'd purged the records.

A couple of minutes later my cell chirped. I was

hoping it was Nando, but it was Tay Jefferson instead. "Cal, something's come up I think you should know about." When I asked what it was, she said she'd rather talk in person and suggested we meet at a little deli she knew near the Federal Reentry Center.

"Does the place have outside tables?" I asked. "It looks like it might clear up."

"Yeah, I think they still have them out."

"Good. Grab one if you wouldn't mind. I've got my dog with me."

I found Tay sitting under a radiant heater in an outside table at Maureen's Deli on SE Eighty-second. She smiled and waved as Archie and I approached, but her smile faded when she saw my bruised face and the slow, deliberate way I sat down in front of her.

"What happened to you, Cal?"

When I told her I'd slipped on my porch steps, she kept her eyes on me for a couple beats before her mouth turned up slightly at one end, a half smile that was becoming familiar. She had no reason to doubt me and didn't press it, but it was clear you couldn't get much past Tay Jefferson.

Archie introduced himself by plopping his muzzle in Tay's lap and wagging his entire backside. He got a big hug for his trouble. That dog of mine's a shameless womanizer.

Tay wore calf-length leather boots, skinny jeans, and a blazer over a white oxford blouse. Her eyes had a slight Asian tilt that lent her an exotic look. They seemed even larger than I remembered. Her upper lip was shaped in a cupid's bow that the little cherub himself would have been proud of. "Thanks for coming, Cal. It's a little nippy, but we can talk in privacy out here. I've only got thirty minutes."

"Good. So what's up?"

"One of our residents at the FRC, a man named Manny Bonilla, was found dead in the Willamette yesterday, near Sauvie Island. I heard about it at work this morning. It was in the paper, too."

"I missed it. What happened to him?"

"Our director didn't know, and the paper didn't say. They'll do an autopsy, right?"

I nodded. "So why call me?"

A waitress appeared, and Tay continued after we ordered. "Claudia told me something about Bonilla in confidence." She hesitated and I waited. "He was, uh, the only son of a cousin of hers. Claudia wanted to recuse herself from being his caseworker, but her cousin begged her to work with him."

"So she did?"

"Yes."

"Would it make any difference one way or the other?"

Tay shrugged. "Not really, but there are strict rules against that kind of thing at the FRC. There can be no prior connection between a caseworker and a resident. The cousin pressured Claudia to get involved. It was a dilemma for Claudia—family versus job. She's Hispanic, Cal. Family comes first. She didn't have a choice."

I nodded. "You think Claudia's and Bonilla's deaths are related?"

Our coffees arrived. Tay waited until the waitress left before responding. "I don't know, but the timing's weird, right? Knowing Claudia, I'm sure she promised her cousin she'd do everything she could to help him."

"Have you told the police about this?"

Tay dropped her eyes to the table. "Uh, not yet. They need to know, right?"

"Yeah, they need to know right away. It could be very important."

Tay shifted in her seat and studied her latte. "Then I need some advice on how to handle this. I don't want, you know, any blowback." She looked up and met my eyes. "I like my job, Cal. A lot."

I nodded and sipped my cappuccino. "You could go to the police and ask that they not tell your employer, but I doubt they'd promise anything. It's understandable that you don't want to get involved. You could do it anonymously, I suppose. The key thing's the information, not the source."

Her face brightened. "How would I do that?"

"Nando Mendoza could handle it. I can probably arrange something, if you want."

She met my eyes. "That would be such a relief, Cal."

I nodded and then listened while she told me more about Manuel Diego Bonilla. He was twenty-eight years old, scheduled for release after serving time for a possession-with-intent-to-distribute charge. He'd been working in the kitchen of Jewel, a little bistro in the Pearl District. His dad got deported to Mexico when he was young, and his mother, Sophia Hidalgo, had remarried and was living in eastern Oregon.

I told Tay I would also try to talk to Hidalgo, and when her eyebrows went up, assured her that I wouldn't blow her cover. As Arch and I walked back to the car, I couldn't help feeling a little upbeat, at least mentally. And it wasn't just from having lunch with Tay Jefferson, although that had almost crossed the line from business to pleasure, at least for me. I'd pass her information on to Nando, who'd make sure Scott and Ludlow got it. But the death of Manny Bonilla intrigued me.

A random burglary and now a coincidental suicide? No way.

FIFTEEN

Cal

WHEN I GOT to Caffeine Central I found Nando out front talking to a man in paint-spattered white coveralls standing next to a beat-up, unmarked pickup. The conversation was heated, part English, part Spanish, and I caught enough of it to realize they were discussing the repair of my furnace. They finally came to some kind of agreement, but the man didn't look too happy when he left.

When Nando noticed me, he opened his big hands and said, *"What?"* in a decidedly defensive tone.

"That guy looked like a painter. Does he know anything about heating systems?"

Nando wrinkled his brow in feigned confusion. "He was the low-cost bidder, Calvin, and I got him to throw in removal of the graffiti at no extra charge."

"Of course. The low-cost bidder. That explains everything." Nando looked away, and I studied my friend for a moment. His chinos and long-sleeved shirt looked slept in, his face was a thicket of dark stubble, and his eyes were puffy and seriously bloodshot. "Come on," I said. "You look like you need a coffee."

He followed me to the back of the building and up the narrow staircase to my apartment. Nando sprawled on the sofa while I filled Archie's water bowl and set about grinding coffee beans to make him a cappuccino. Nando said, "You are walking crooked. How are the ribs?"

"Tender." As I readied his coffee, I gave him more details about my encounter with Farnell Timmons. When I finished he said, "So the bootmaker told you he had destroyed the records, but the young man at the shop said they had them."

I nodded. "Yeah, but the kid might've been referring to records for the past three years, which Timmons said he kept for tax purposes. In any case, Timmons made it clear he wasn't about to share anything with anybody. And he told me in no uncertain terms to mind my own business."

"Why would he feel it necessary to threaten you?"

"I don't know. Probably just a general dislike of outsiders. But it might make sense for you to get a line on this guy."

Nando nodded. "I will ask Esperanza to run a background check."

"What about Cardenas? Anything new on that front?"

"Yes. I have acquired a copy of the security tape from the Lucky Dragon the night of the shooting. Cardenas was indeed present, but so were a couple of other possible clients for Sheri Daniels, men she was seen talking to. Once I identify these men, I will have the chat with them."

"Make sure it's just a chat. I've been put on notice by Scott to keep you on a short leash. We're both on thin ice here."

Nando exhaled a long breath. "If the police would do their jobs, this would not be necessary, Calvin."

I rolled my eyes but didn't counter. "I have some other information, too." I went on to describe what Tay had told me about Manny Bonilla and the need to pass the information on to the Portland Police.

When I finished, Nando massaged his forehead, then rubbed his eyes and frowned deeply. "So Tayshia would like me to fix it so she doesn't have to say what she knows about Claudia and this Bonilla?"

"Can't blame her," I said. "She thinks it could cost her job. She's caught in the middle just like Claudia was."

He nodded. "This will reflect poorly on Claudia, you know."

"I won't be a party to withholding information from the cops. This needs to get done, Nando, and you know it."

He sighed. "Very well. I will make sure Harmon Scott gets this information anonymously." He turned to face me. "The photo album? You brought it?"

I got up, opened my briefcase and extracted the book. "Here."

He took it a bit tentatively. "Thank you. I can't look at the pictures. I just wanted it back." He flexed the slashed cover, looked up at me, and wrinkled his brow.

"Sorry about that," I said. "I, uh, had the book in my belt. The bastard's knife sliced it instead of my stomach."

Nando's eyes widened. "*Dios mio*," he uttered in a half whisper. "You didn't tell me it was so close, my friend."

I shrugged. "A miss is as good as a mile."

"Well, please accept my apology for calling you a Boy Scout. That was uncalled for."

I laughed and waved off his apology.

We fell silent for a long time. Finally Nando sipped some coffee, leaned back, and ran his hands through his hair. "I called my mother in Cuba and told her what happened." He paused as if to gather himself. "I broke her heart, Calvin. Again. The first time was when I left Cuba. She begged me to come home. She said America is a bad place. Too many guns. Too many violent people." He turned to face me, his eyes suddenly bright. "Maybe she is right."

"Americans probably aren't any more violent than other groups of people on this planet. My guess is the violence gene's spread pretty evenly." I shrugged. "But your mother has a point about the guns. We're swimming in them in this country. Maybe that's the difference."

Nando smiled bitterly. "You know I am fond of guns. I remember when I bought my first one, a Sig Sauer P226. It had a stainless steel body and a mahogany handle with a knurled inlay." He closed his eyes and smiled again, with pleasure this time. "It was beautiful, balanced in my hand perfectly, and shot like silk, hardly a recoil. I'd been here only a year or so, and, of course, I didn't need a gun. But this was America, right?" He shook his head. "I even bought a box of hollow-point bullets. More stopping power."

"Stopping power for what?"

"Precisely. For what? And I bought all of this out of the trunk of a car." He shook his head. "*¿En qué estaría tensando?*"

"You were young. The gun represented something you couldn't have in Cuba. It's understandable."

He studied the hardwood floor and continued like

he hadn't heard me. "So now, after seeing what those bullets did to my Claudia I'm not so sure about all this gun freedom." He looked up and met my eyes. "That beautiful Sig Sauer was made for one thing—killing people."

Our discussion was cut short by a call from Esperanza that sent Nando scurrying off. It was just as well. It was now the fourth day since Claudia was shot and no arrests had been made.

Philosophy was fine, but we both had work to do.

SIXTEEN

Cal

THE WEATHER WAS decent so I leashed up Archie and we headed off to Jewel, the bistro in the Pearl District where Manny Bonilla had worked. Arch tugged at his leash and stretched out in front of me like he owned the street. Once a seedy warehouse district just north of Old Town, the Pearl was now dotted with coveted loft apartments, tony shops, and upscale restaurants. Jewel was a small place with a menu promising "fine dishes from local ingredients and a full selection of Oregon microbrews." I left Arch leashed to a chair outside and went in. I didn't worry about leaving my dog on the sidewalk. He was friendly enough, but he was also eighty pounds of solid muscle and there was no way he'd let someone walk off with him.

The bistro was maybe a quarter full. The bartender called the manager, a thin, thirtysomething sporting a narrow mustache and an appropriately ironic gray fedora with a black band. Yes, Manny Bonilla had worked there, and yes, they had heard what happened and had been visited by the police already. And no, they didn't wish to talk to me about anything.

At least the walk was good exercise.

The weather was holding, and it was only a short hop over to the gallery where Picasso worked. I decided to pop in to see if I could catch him. Arch and I found him painting a large canvas in the back of the gallery—a geometric abstract in primary colors. He worked intently with his back to us. His art had broadened and matured, but it still had the punch and brashness of the outdoor murals he was well known for.

"I like it," I said. "And I'm sure I can't afford it." Picasso turned around, and Archie whimpered a couple of times and went to him, wagging his backside.

He set his brush and palette down, wiped his hands with a paint-stained cloth, and began petting Arch and talking to him in a low voice. When he looked up at me, he smiled. "You get the bro discount, Cal."

I laughed. "Still can't afford it. We were just passing through. Anything new on K209?"

He shook his head. "I'm stumped, man. Nobody seems to know who the dude is. The pieces only go back a year or so, so it's someone new on the scene."

"Any more thoughts on the profile?"

"Not really. A feisty, angry kid." He chuckled and shook his head. "Know the type. Used to be one."

I nodded. "You used to tag before you got into mural painting. What's the attraction, anyway?"

Picasso paused and tugged at his eyebrow ring for a couple of beats. "Rebellion, man. Telling a kid he can't tag a wall is like waving a red flag in front of a bull. Identity's huge, too. Most taggers don't have much, so their moniker becomes really important. You know, it's their mark on the world. If society condemns it, that's all the better. More recognition." He tugged some more on his ring. "For the hardcore types who become obsessed it goes a lot deeper. A crazy-strong artistic urge—like for me—or, you know, a protest about how screwed up things are, which is where K209 seems to fit in. I mean, look at our national politics. It's a wonder we have any blank walls left in this country."

I had to laugh. "Maybe these angry kids are paying more attention than we give them credit for."

"You read about it, Cal, they live it—abusive parents, underfunded schools, no jobs, no respect."

I nodded and chuckled. "I remember Claire's rebellious stage, all right. It left her mother and me cross-eyed."

"Sure. And your daughter eventually channeled all her frustration into getting a PhD in environmental science, which you're paying for, Cal. Most of the kids we're talking about won't get that chance, or they'll have to borrow a crippling amount of money to do it."

"Okay. I get it. But I still don't like it when I see graffiti on bridges and highway signs."

Picasso laughed. "Me neither, man."

I thanked Picasso and left feeling frustrated. If he couldn't find K209 then it was clear the tagger had pretty good cover. That wasn't all bad, I decided. The shooter was probably in this hunt, too, and I sure as hell didn't want him to find K209 first.

SEVENTEEN

Kelly

THE DAY AFTER finding Rupert's body was hell for Kelly. The morning broke clear, but then the sky grayed over and it started to rain, only to clear and start the cycle again. Just like the weather, Kelly swung between a desire to hide in her room and never come out again and a burning urge to see if she could somehow find out more about Macho Dude and The Voice. But then the image of them slipping away from the mill would pop into her head, melting away all her courage and resolve. They were out there now, she told herself, looking for me.

That afternoon, Veronica managed to coax Kelly out of her room. Standing with a cigarette smoldering between her fingers, she said, "I picked up some KFC. Thought we could have some dinner together."

The fear, the anxiety, the lack of sleep slammed together in Kelly like a perfect storm. "Fried chicken? *Really?* We're supposed to have vegetables, and, and, whole grains, and stuff like that, not friggin' *fried* foods. Have you been living under a rock or something?" She pointed at the cigarette in Veronica's hand. "And have you ever heard of secondhand smoke? *Sheeze*, Veronica."

What happened next took Kelly by surprise. The

expectant look on Veronica's face crumbled, she burst out crying and dashed to her bedroom, slamming the door. As Kelly stood there trying to process what just happened, it occurred to her that she hadn't seen Veronica with a drink in her hand in quite a while. And that had to be the first time Kelly ever made *her* cry. What's going on, she wondered? She felt awful about blowing up like that but couldn't bring herself to apologize. Veronica didn't deserve it, she told herself.

As Kelly made her way to school on Monday morning she felt jumpy and hollow inside, but she was determined to show up again like nothing had happened. Before catching the bus she scanned the paper in the coffee shop and found the article in the Metro section, just eight or ten lines with the headline Homeless Man Found Beaten to Death. The article concluded, "…the murder appears to have resulted from a dispute between Mr. Youngblood and possibly other homeless individuals squatting in the abandoned Albertson's Mill on NW Naito Parkway."

Kelly fought back tears, anger, and a wave of shame for having left Rupert in that awful place. Not now, she told herself. No more tears.

Later that morning Kelly sat at a computer terminal trying to concentrate on a set of algebra problems when the door connecting the education center with the rest of the complex swung open. She looked up as her case manager, Monica Sayles, came through the door followed by the tall, sandy-haired cop who, along with his partner, had stopped her and Kiyana in the park. He was carrying what she immediately recognized as her backpack, the one she ditched the night of the shooting. In all the excitement, she'd forgotten about it. Blood drained from Kelly's head so fast that she saw little black dots dancing in her field of vision like a swarm of gnats.

Chill, she told herself as she took a deep breath. She knew she hadn't left anything in the backpack that could be traced to her. She made that a strict rule when she tagged. But what if someone recognizes the pack itself?

"Hey, guys," Monica said in a cheery tone to the whole class, "this is Detective Ludlow from the Portland Police. He wants to take just a minute to show you something."

Ludlow stepped into the middle of the room and held up the backpack. It was a dark blue, low-cost REI model. Lots of kids at the school and on the street carried that model because the school distributed dozens at last year's Christmas party. That's where Kelly got hers.

"Good morning. Sorry to interrupt your studies, but I'm hoping you folks could help us locate the owner of this backpack. Now I want to stress that this person is not in any trouble. We just want to talk to the owner about a crime that occurred early last Friday morning over on NW Third between Davis and Everett."

Kelly figured Kiyana might recognize the backpack but knew she wouldn't say anything even if she did. When Kelly glanced Kiyana's way she saw that her friend's brows were knitted.

She was more worried about Zook. She glanced at him, and to her relief it was clear he wasn't paying the least bit of attention. *Boys. So unobservant.*

One of the students called out, "This is about that

woman that got shot, right?" The room started buzzing with conversation and nervous laughter.

Ludlow held up a hand for silence. "Yes. This involves a murder investigation." He rotated the pack slowly so everyone got a good look at it. Then he set it down, unzipped the top, and extracted a book. "This book was in the pack." He held it up. "It's called *The Stranger*, by Albert Camus." Ludlow scanned the students' faces expectantly, unaware that Camus was not pronounced *Cam-us*. "Ring any bells?"

I'm okay, Kelly thought. She bought the book at the used bookstore on Sandy the day before the shooting. The only person who might have seen her with it was Veronica.

A couple of kids giggled at the mispronunciation, but no one said anything. Kiyana shot Kelly a glance and smiled, but Kelly looked away. Her mouth was dry and she had difficulty swallowing.

Ludlow put the book down and pulled out a can of spray paint and Kelly's harness. Laughter and a couple of cheers rippled through the group. Ludlow held a deadly serious look. "There were a half dozen spray cans in the pack plus this climbing harness. We think the person owning this backpack is a tagger who uses the moniker K209. Now, we don't condone graffiti tagging in Portland, but that's not our interest here. If this person comes forward, there will be no questions asked about the tagging." No one moved or spoke.

Kelly scanned the faces of those in the group she could see without being obvious about it. Things looked cool until she got to Digger, the kid who'd shot his mouth off about Rupert. She should have known. Short, with a nasty attitude, Digger fancied himself a hardcore skater. But Kelly had seen his moves, and the truth was he had more bluster than skill.

He studied the backpack, glanced at Kelly, then back at the pack. He might have smiled. She wasn't sure. He was always hanging around Kelly. "Like a dog in heat," Ki had observed. Maybe he recognized something, like the frayed pocket on the left side. Kelly held her breath and prepared for the worst, but Digger didn't say anything.

Ludlow held up the backpack again. "Anyone?"

Kelly looked straight ahead. The room fell absolutely silent. The cops weren't a big favorite with this crowd. After what seemed an eternity to Kelly, Ludlow shrugged, thanked the group, and turned to leave with a should-have-known look on his face. Before he left, he pinned a photo of the backpack and one of his business cards on the bulletin board.

When class ended, Kelly, Kiyana, and Zook drifted off toward O'Bryant Square. When they were out of earshot of the rest of the students Kiyana whirled around to confront Kelly. "What the hell, girl? That was *your* backpack that cop had, wasn't it? How did that happen?"

Zook looked shocked. "No way? That was yours, Kel?"

Kelly waivered for a moment. She wanted to unburden herself to her friends in the worst way. But she'd gone to Rupert and look what happened to him. She shrugged. "I, uh, don't really know. If it was mine, looks like whoever ripped me off got tangled up in that murder. Thanks for not saying anything, Ki."

Kiyana smiled and nodded. "No problem." Then she locked onto Kelly's eyes and drew her face into that don't-bullshit-me look she was famous for. At the same time Kelly could feel Zook's eyes on the side of her face, boring into her like a laser. Ki said, "I don't know about that taggin' stuff, but that book by Camus, that's your kind of reading. You sure there's nothin' goin' on, Kel? This is serious."

You're telling me? Kelly wanted to blurt out. Instead, she dropped her eyes, swallowed and tried a smile, but it didn't take. "Hey, everything's cool. I just lost my backpack, that's all. Give me a break."

Kiyana left for work, but not before she made it clear she had her doubts about Kelly's story. Zook and Kelly sat for a while on the rock wall at the edge of the park. It was cold, and as they conversed their breath mingled to form a thin, gray cloud before vanishing a moment later. Zook ran a big hand through his hair, then rubbed the stubble—peach fuzz, really—on his cheek. "You seem upset, Kel." He grinned crookedly. "Did Veronica's dog die or something?"

Kelly folded her arms across her chest. "Very funny."

"Seriously, it's okay at home?"

"*Sheeze*, why does everybody ask me that?"

Zook leaned away from her. "*Excuse me* for breathing."

This only made Kelly madder. "I'm surprised you even noticed. You're so hammered most of the time."

Zook turned to face Kelly, his eyes wide with surprise that turned quickly to pain. He hopped down from the wall and stomped off, saying over his shoulder, "Fine then. See you around."

Kelly sat there blinking away the tears, but it was

no use. They flooded her face, mingling with the rain that had started up again.

She hadn't felt this alone and this afraid since her dad died.

EIGHTEEN

Kelly

KELLY SAT ON the rock wall in O'Bryant Park trying to stop crying. The events of the last few days had left her dazed and shaken, her plans blown to bits. If she had finished the piece on Everett, her next project was going to be the Fremont Bridge. She wasn't clear on what she might do beyond climbing it, but that high, arching span drew her like a magnet. That dream's over now, she told herself. Get a grip. You've got other priorities now.

She unzipped the pouch on her new backpack and pulled out a bulky, legal-sized envelope that was stamped and addressed to the Portland Rescue Mission on Burnside. Inside the envelope Kelly had stuffed two thousand dollars in cash and a note that read:

To whom it may concern,

I'm sure you know Rupert at the mission. He's been hanging out at the Burnside Bridge for a long time. His full name is Rupert Louis Young-blood and he was born in Los Angeles on Jan. 6, 1960. He told me once that you do good work at the mission. You probably heard that he got

murdered the other day. This money is to make
sure he has a nice funeral with lots of flowers.
I don't know where they took his body, but I
think you can find out. You can keep any money
left over.

A friend of Rupert's

Kelly dropped the envelope into a mailbox at the
corner of the park. Next she caught the #33 bus and,
once she found a seat, called Hanson's Granite Works,
where she worked two afternoons a week, sometimes
more. When the owner, Phil Hanson, answered, she
said, "Hey, Phil. I, uh, won't be able to come in until
Friday. I have too much homework, you know, GED
exams and stuff."

"Kind of short notice, Kel," Hanson answered in
a slightly irritated tone. Hanson was a climber who
knew Kelly's dad by reputation, which explained how
she got the job. He was a good man, and Kelly hated
herself for lying to him.

"I'm sorry, Phil. I'm, uh, kind of behind. Didn't
realize how much I have to do this week. I'll make
it up to you."

"Well, your studies come first, young lady." He
paused before adding, "Are you okay, kiddo? You
sound a little teary."

There's that question again, she said to herself, bit-
ing back an urge to scream. "I'm fine, Phil, and I'm
sorry. I'll see you Friday."

She got off the bus near the Hawthorne Bridge on
SE Water Street, a light industrial area that ran below
the I-5 freeway along the east side of the river. Housed

in a low, nondescript building, the Bridgetown Arsenal was a block and a half down Water, sandwiched between an old firebrick foundry and a sheet-metal fabricator. The Arsenal announced itself with a large circular sign bearing the screaming eagle logo. Kelly was on the opposite side of the street when she saw the sign, but she stopped dead and her stomach took a half turn. Suddenly she felt very conspicuous. After all, there weren't a lot of young kids in this neighborhood. In fact, there was hardly anyone on the street.

Resisting a strong urge to retreat, Kelly reminded herself that she came to scope the place out, see if there was any chance of identifying Macho Dude. She kept walking, repeating to herself mantra-like, *He doesn't know who I am. He doesn't know who I am.* A half-block past the Arsenal she came to a skeletal four-story structure, obviously under construction and abandoned. A five-foot chain-link fence surrounded the property.

She stepped off the sidewalk and followed the fence around to the back of the building, which faced a high brick wall, part of an adjacent property. The cover was excellent. With her heart pounding, she was over the chain-link fence in a couple of bounds, confident no one had seen her. Climbing the steel framework within the interior of the building was a snap, too. Soon she was lying on a girder on the fourth floor with a view of the Arsenal's entrance, the customer parking lot in front, and a loading dock and staff parking area on the north side of the building. She could spot customers coming and going as well as anyone working on the dock, which was perfect except that she wished she were a little closer.

The rain started an hour and a half later, but before then Kelly had watched an assortment of people come and go through the front entrance of the Arsenal. Most of the visitors were carrying long, narrow bags or small satchels. It finally dawned on her that the bags most certainly contained rifles and the satchels, handguns. Kelly tensed when a dark SUV, not unlike the one she saw that night in Old Town, parked in the lot between the Arsenal and the sheet-metal fabricator. But a man and woman got out with a little girl no more than five years old. The little girl took the hands of the adults, who both were carrying black satchels. A family outing, she decided.

She wondered whether the little girl would participate in the target shooting. The thought made her a little queasy.

Wet and cold, Kelly climbed down and started home as the light began to fade that afternoon. She should have been discouraged, but she wasn't. If Macho Dude was wearing a jacket from that place, he was bound to come around, wasn't he? And if she could get a license plate number or something, then she could turn him in to the police without getting involved.

This was better than getting busted, she told herself. How would Rupert and that woman Claudia feel about her not going directly to the police? She hoped they would've understood.

NINETEEN

Cal

ARCHIE AND I stopped at Whole Foods as we walked back from the Pearl District. I saw some fresh rockfish, which I bought along with tomatoes, jalapeños, a couple of limes, a handful of fresh cilantro, and a pack of tortillas. Back at Caffeine Central, I fed Arch and whisked up a marinade for the fish. I drank a Mirror Pond IPA and sifted through the day's emails while the fish marinated. But my thoughts kept flashing back to those divots in the brick wall above the scene of Claudia's murder. Did the tagger know how much danger he or she was in?

Not likely. The thought was unsettling.

After the best damn fish tacos I'd made in a long time, my thoughts turned back to Manny Bonilla, the only thing close to a lead I had left. I didn't want to bother his mother in her time of grief, but I was anxious to know what she could tell me about her son and his situation at the Federal Reentry Center. I decided to chance a call, hoping it wouldn't be too invasive.

Her husband, Robert Hidalgo, answered the phone and told me she was too upset to talk. When I explained I was a lawyer looking into the death of Claudia Borrego on behalf of her fiancé, he said, "We already talked to the Portland Police."

"I'm sure you have, Mr. Hidalgo. We're working in parallel with the police, you know, just making sure no stone's left unturned." It was a true statement as far as it went.

He surprised me by agreeing to talk. Some people need to talk in a time of grief, and Hidalgo was apparently one of those.

"Look, Mr. Claxton," he began after I expressed my condolences, "Manny didn't kill himself, I can tell you that. He was a good Catholic boy."

"Are the police saying he did?"

"Reading between the lines, yes. But they're not through with all the tests yet."

"What do *you* think happened?"

"I don't know. A crazy accident. A robbery. It was Portland, after all. We wanted him to come to eastern Oregon when he got out, but he wanted to stay there. Now look what's happened. Nothing good ever happens in that damn city."

"What plans did he have?"

Hidalgo exhaled a long breath, and when he spoke his voice broke a little. "He, uh, he was so excited. He had a decent job as a waiter in the Pearl District and was going to get his own apartment. Had a better job offer, too, but he turned it down."

"What was that?"

"He was going to be the driver and sort of all-around handyman for a wealthy family. It wasn't ideal but beat working in a kitchen. He was real mechanical, you know, and tried to get on as an apprentice in a machine shop, but with a record it was hard. Anyway, two days before his release he announced he wasn't taking the driver job."

"Did he give a reason?"

"Nope. Couldn't get a thing out of him."

"Do you happen to know the name of the family?"

"The Jenkins family. They own a bunch of gun shops. Real wealthy. He said he was going to work for the woman who owns it all. It was a good place to start, I guess. His lawyer got him the job."

"Manny had a lawyer?"

"Well, he's the lawyer who represented him at his trial. He stayed in touch with Manny when he was at Sheridan. Helped him get into that halfway house, too. He helps felons that way."

"What's the lawyer's name?"

"Jack Pfister. Has an office over in Oregon City."

When I finally worked up to the drug bust that had sent Manny away, Hidalgo didn't give me much. Apparently, Bonilla was caught driving a truck with a lot of drugs in it. According to Hidalgo, he was set up, something I hear a lot from loving parents with wayward kids. I took him through a few other questions but didn't learn anything else. I didn't bring up the connection between Bonilla and Claudia Borrego. I wasn't supposed to know about that. And Hidalgo didn't volunteer it. My guess was Claudia had sworn the Hidalgos to secrecy to protect her job.

After the phone call I did some online research. Rosalind Jenkins had to be the woman Manny was slated to drive for. She owned a string of "family friendly" gun ranges and shops headquartered in Portland and stretching from Seattle down to San Diego along the I-5 corridor. The headquarters— aptly named the Bridgetown Arsenal—was located along the river on SE Water Street. I'd vaguely heard of Rockin' Roz, a celebrity in Oregon's gun-friendly circles, who, if memory served, advocated lifting all restraints on gun ownership.

I found Jack Pfister's website next and jotted down his phone number and address in Oregon City. In addition to advertising his defense work, he billed himself as something called a Gun Trust Lawyer.

With not much else to go on, I decided the Arsenal/Jack Pfister connection was worth a closer look. I also made a mental note to ask Pfister, if and when I saw him, what the hell a gun trust lawyer did.

Before I turned in that night I removed an unopened letter from my briefcase, the one from Russia. I started to tear it open, then hesitated and leaned back in my swivel chair. The ceiling needed paint, and a wispy spider web had formed in a far corner. No sign of the spider.

I opened a desk drawer and pulled out a photo of the woman who'd written the letter. I'd snapped it on a trip we'd taken to Canada. A big steelhead had her rod bent double, but her face was turned toward me, grinning, radiant with childlike enthusiasm.

I tore open the envelope and read the letter through. She was settling in okay. She'd found a job teaching English. She understood that nothing else could be done legally. She missed me, wished me well, and signed it with love.

I propped the photo up on my desk and got up, the old roller chair creaking in protest. The most painful things in life, it seemed, were the things that might have been.

TWENTY

Cal

I SLEPT FITFULLY that night as a cavalcade of strange dreams and half-formed images marched through my head, dominated by the image of a shadowy young person stranded high on a sheer rock wall. I kept wondering if the figure was my daughter, Claire. I awoke the next morning with a vague sense of anxiety, so I called her at Berkeley. "Claire, it's Dad," I said. "Did I wake you?"

"No, Dad. What's up?"

"Oh, I just wanted to hear your voice. I, uh, I've been missing you." I apologized for not having told her about the death of Nando's fiancée. I just didn't want her to worry about it but realized now how ridiculous that was. She knew Nando and deserved to know. I gave her a brief rundown.

"That's terrible," she said when I finished. "Please give him my heartfelt condolences." The line went silent for several beats. I knew what was coming. "Are you involved in this in any way, Dad?"

"Well, I'm helping Nando chase down some loose ends, you know, routine stuff. He's keen to see the killer caught, as you can imagine."

"Uh huh," she said very slowly, her voice assuming a tinge of wariness. "Nothing risky, right?"

As if on cue I swear a rogue throb of pain radiated out from my bruised ribs. "No worries," I answered with faux casualness. *How did this happen?* I asked myself. I'd called Claire to ease my anxiety, and now I felt like a kid lying to a parent. My daughter had a way of doing that to me.

I got off the line without doing too much more damage. It was worth it, though, just to hear her voice. And I extracted a promise for her to come home for Christmas, too.

I fed Arch, had a double cappuccino, and after calling ahead for an appointment, drove to Jack Pfister's law office in Oregon City. The office was located in a four-story office building on High Street, near the museum. I figured Pfister would have a good view of the river and Willamette Falls, and I was right. After checking in with his receptionist, I went over to admire the view from a window facing west. The horseshoe-shaped falls cut a massive white gash in the river, which ran bluish gray in the cloud-filtered light.

"Great view, isn't it?" Jack Pfister stood in the doorway of his office, his close-set, avian eyes regarding me with unabashed curiosity.

"Uh, yeah, I've never seen the falls from this angle before. They're much larger than I thought. Amazing."

I introduced myself and followed him into his office, a study in Scandinavian austere, and took a seat in front of a teak desk with nothing on it except a thin stack of papers. I felt a twinge of envy at his tidiness. His black hair was pulled into a short ponytail, and he wore dark slacks, a briskly starched white shirt, and an understated, striped tie configured in a full

Windsor, a knot I never quite mastered back in my suit-wearing days.

"What can I do for you, Cal?"

"I, uh, have a small practice out in the valley. Dundee." I slid a business card onto the desk. "I'm doing a favor for a friend. His fiancée, a woman named Claudia Borrego, was murdered last week in Portland. You probably read about it."

Pfister's expression remained neutral. "Sorry to hear that. Your friend—anyone I know?"

"A PI out of Portland. Hernando Mendoza. Anyway, he isn't a fan of the Portland Police Bureau, so he's insisting on doing his own investigating."

Pfister gave a skeptical smile and shook his head.

I raised my hands and smiled back. "I know. I know. But, he's a friend. I couldn't say no."

"What's this have to do with me, Mr. Claxton?"

"Uh, we're wondering what you can tell us about Manny Bonilla?" He registered a couple of rapid blinks at my question. "I'm sure you heard about his death."

Pfister dropped his gaze, shook his head, and exhaled a breath. "Manny's death is a real tragedy. We had such high hopes for him." He brought his gaze back up. "But I'm not seeing the connection here."

"His body was found the day after Borrego was shot. She was his caseworker at the Federal Reentry Center. We're just wondering about, you know, the timing."

In a kind of slow-motion double take Pfister seemed to reappraise me, this time with more care. It was a reaction I got from a lot of people I questioned. "My God, come to think of it, I did read something about that shooting, but I didn't make the connection. Are you suggesting foul play was involved in Manny's death?"

"His stepdad says no way Manny killed himself."

"Huh. That's interesting. What are the police saying about it?"

I shrugged. "Not much at this juncture. Uh, Mr. Hidalgo also mentioned you arranged a job for Manny as a driver for the Jenkins family." I gave him what I hoped would pass for an admiring smile. "He had nothing but praise for your mentoring efforts."

A flash of white teeth. "Oh, we do what we can."

"Any idea why he turned the job down?"

Pfister furrowed his forehead in what looked like genuine exasperation, not at me for asking the question, but at Manny. "I don't really know. I think Manny made a big mistake, and I told him so."

"How does that work, you getting him a job?"

"Oh, it wasn't difficult in this case. I do legal work for the Jenkins family, and they said they needed someone. I told them Manny could not only drive but could take care of their cars, too. He was quite the mechanic. They were willing to give him a chance. It was pretty embarrassing when he changed his mind."

At this point Pfister glanced at his watch and announced he had a court appearance coming up. I thanked him and got up to leave. Pfister stood and took a card from a silver box on his back bar and handed it to me. "The link to the website of my foundation's on this card. It's called A Hand Up. Check it out, Cal. I'm always looking for new volunteers, especially lawyers."

I told him I'd do that, then at the door turned and

asked one more question. "What's a gun trust lawyer, anyway? Just curious."

Pfister leaned back in his chair and beamed a smile. "Gun trusts protect a critical asset in many estates—firearms. I help families plan for an orderly transition, you know, so they're passed on responsibly when an owner dies. Divorces can be a disaster, too. A good trust makes sure they stay in the right hands. Best of all, a trust can protect against the specter of future restrictions. After you die all your firearms will stay legal if you put them in a well-crafted trust."

I nodded approvingly. "How's business?"

"Couldn't be better. Gun sales in this country are booming, thanks to Obama. He's been a one-man stimulus package for the firearms industry. Look into it, Claxton. Plenty of gun owners out your way in the Willamette Valley."

"Sounds interesting. I think I'll check it out." I thanked him for the tip and left, feeling like there was a whole universe out there—the universe of guns— that I knew very little about. And I was also unsure what to make of the gun trust lawyer and mentor of young felons, Jack Pfister.

TWENTY-ONE

Cal

I TOOK THE 99E back into Portland and just before going over the Hawthorne Bridge turned into the industrial area that ran along the east side of the river. The Bridgetown Arsenal was housed on the ground floor of an old warehouse. After parking, I sat in the lot mulling over the pros and cons of popping in unannounced on Roz Jenkins. On the downside, if I showed up asking questions ahead of Scott and Ludlow, they'd take a dim view of it, to say the least. On the other hand, there was a fair chance they wouldn't even bother coming here to ask about Bonilla.

I decided to go for it.

The front door of the Arsenal opened into a brightly lit retail space. Aside from the sporadic, muffled reports of weapons being fired behind a back wall, the first thing I noticed was a play area in a corner, just inside the door. A flat-screen TV, a small, indoor slide, a couple of tables stocked with Legos, books, and jars of crayons stood at the ready. A cute little blond girl, maybe all of five, sat at one of the tables, deeply absorbed in a coloring book.

A perky female clerk with short, dark hair and designer jeans came from behind the glass case that lined an expansive wall. The case was filled with handguns, and the wall behind her arrayed with all kinds of rifles, most of which looked like military-issue with their hollow-frame stocks, ventilated barrels, and large, curved ammo clips. "Hi. I'm Jamie. Welcome to the Arsenal."

"I'm Cal. I'm, uh, just looking around." I was fascinated and maybe a little disturbed by the place and wanted time to browse. As an ex-prosecutor, I was familiar enough with guns—at least what they could do to people—but had never been inside a store devoted entirely to the sale of firearms and their accoutrements.

When she sauntered off I noticed how tight her jeans were. Sex sells, I reminded myself, even in the gun market.

Racks near the center of the store displayed all manner of shoulder holsters and clothing designed for concealing a carried weapon. Sport shirts with hand-entry slots and cargo pants and chinos with hidden pockets allowed someone packing heat to go casual. The pants styles designed to conceal a weapon were referred to as "covert" and "tactical," I noted.

I was checking out a rack of women's handbags when Jamie rejoined me. "Those make a nice gift for the wife."

"How do they work?"

She removed a sporty leather bag from the rack, placed the strap over her shoulder, and slid her hand into a side pocket. "There's a hidden compartment in here for a handgun." She removed her hand and tilted the bag so I could see the compartment inside. "If your wife's in the parking lot and a mugger or rapist shows up, she can access her weapon quickly and with complete stealth." Jamie slid her hand back into the side pocket, swung the bag to face me. "Bang, bang, you're dead."

"Incredible," I said. "How do they sell?"

She gave me a perky smile. "Like hot cakes. The holidays are right around the corner. Makes a great Christmas gift, or," she went on, "we have some really nice handguns for women, too. The pink Glock's my favorite. It's light and compact, but a .44-caliber round will stop a horse. Would you like to see one?"

She was good, no doubt about it. "Actually, I'm a little pressed for time, Jamie. I was hoping I could talk to your boss. Is Roz Jenkins around?" I removed a card from my shirt pocket and handed it to her. "Tell her I'm an acquaintance of Jack Pfister's." It wasn't a lie.

Jamie made a call and then showed me to a staircase. "Up the stairs, first door on your left." I knocked on the unmarked door, and a voice boomed out, "Door's open." Jenkins sat behind a massive desk in an equally large office with a window that looked out over Water Street and east toward Mount Hood, which was out there somewhere behind the cloud cover. She laid her reading glasses on the desk and stood to greet me. She was tall, close to six foot, and full-figured, with short, blond-going-to-gray hair atop a round, open face that was windblown and wrinkled, yet attractive at the same time. Her eyes were robin's-egg blue, wide and intense, almost unblinking. She met my eyes and smiled, disarmingly so. "You're a friend of Jack Pfister's?"

I introduced myself and said, "I practice law out in the north valley—Dundee. Jack's been, uh, advising me on becoming a gun trust lawyer. Sounds like a growth opportunity." When in Rome, speak Italian.

She nodded and smirked. "With all the goddamn laws and regulations out there today, people certainly need good legal advice about handling their firearms. Pfister's one of the best."

I nodded back. "But that's not why I'm here." I went on to explain my interest in Claudia Borrego's murder using the just-doing-an-old-friend-a-favor routine, which was working for me. Then I said, "I understand a young man named Manny Bonilla was set to be your driver."

Jenkins looked surprised. "Was that his name? Never met him. My son-in-law handles the hiring and firing around here."

I nodded. "He turned the job down at the last minute. I'm just trying to fill in some blanks, wondering if you recall anything about this? Jack Pfister helped him get the job."

"What, he wants the job after all?"

"No. Unfortunately, he was found dead shortly after Ms. Borrego's murder. The cause of death's still under investigation."

Jenkins made a face. "Damn, that's too bad. Bonilla, huh? Name rings a bell. That the fella they found in the river up by Sauvie Island? I remember reading about that."

"That's the one."

"He an ex-con? I know Jack's real active in helping them out."

"Yes. Bonilla did time at Sheridan and was in the federal reentry program here in Portland."

Roz popped up from behind her desk. "Come

on, let's go find my son-in-law, Arthur. I believe
he's down at the range." She walked fast in a pair of
pointy-toed boots with some handsome inlay work,
straight leg jeans, and a checkered shirt with pearl
buttons. A diamond-encrusted Rolex with a gold
band jounced on her wrist. At a door in the retail
space marked "Firing Range," she removed two sets
of molded plastic earmuffs and safety glasses from a
rack and handed me a set of each. "Here, put these on.
Arthur's demonstrating the Thompson right now." I
must have looked puzzled, because she laughed, the
sound coming from her belly. "You know, the Chi-
cago Typewriter, a vintage submachine like the Al
Capone days. Come on. You'll get a kick out of this."

The firing range was twenty stations deep, with
each station separated from its neighbor by insulat-
ing foam walls, the targets retrievable by the push of
a button and backed by a huge mound of what Roz
explained were ground-up tires. There were half a
dozen single shooters scattered along the range and
a group of four or five huddled toward the far end.
As we entered we heard a muffled *rat tat tat tat tat
tat* coming from the far end, followed by howls and
peels of nervous laughter.

Jenkins pointed in that direction and smiled
broadly. "That's the Thompson. Arthur collects guns
and loves to demonstrate them." We joined the group
where a man I took to be Arthur was adroitly reloading the straight clip with .45-caliber bullets that
looked like fat bumblebees. He was substantially
shorter than his mother-in-law, with thinning hair,
an angular face that tapered to a sharp chin, and eyes
the color of shallow water.

A twentysomething standing next to him held the Thompson, which had a gleaming blue-black barrel and a wood shoulder stock and matching, curved handgrip with finger grooves. The wood was burnished to a rich luster by years of use and meticulous care, giving the weapon the appeal of a fine antique. I could understand the desire to own such a gun. The rest of the group, including one man my age, was arguing about who was going to fire the Thompson next.

Jenkins and I waited through two more *rat tat tat* cycles before Arthur broke free of the group, submachine gun in hand. I gave him a gee-whiz look as Jenkins introduced me but watched his face carefully as she explained what I wanted.

"Manny Bonilla? Yeah, I seem to recall the name." He smiled affably enough, but the muscle along his jawline flexed a couple of times as the smile faded. He looked at Jenkins. "I really don't think our hiring practices are any of Mr. Claxton's business."

Jenkins straightened up. "Oh, hell, Arthur, tell the man what he wants to know. He's just trying to help a friend out, for Christ sake. This fella's turned up dead."

Arthur seemed unfazed by the news of Bonilla's passing. "He was going to be your driver. God knows you can't afford another accident, Roz."

Roz drew her face into a pout and waved a hand at him. "That last one could've happened to anyone."

Turning to Arthur, I said, "Uh, Bonilla turned down your offer so he could work at a minimum wage job at a little bistro over in the Pearl. Any idea why he did that?"

Arthur fixed me with his pale eyes and shrugged. "Beats me. We start our people at seventeen an hour—"

"With benefits," Jenkins interjected.

"—right, with benefits," Arthur said. "All I know is Pfister called and told me Bonilla wasn't coming. It was no big deal. There were five more in line for that job."

I said, "Was Bonilla upset about anything?"

Arthur shrugged again. "Dunno. He didn't bother to call me. Look, Mr. Claxton, I have over a hundred wage employees working for me up and down the coast. I don't get into the way their heads work."

"How did you feel about hiring a convicted felon?"

Arthur smirked at what he clearly considered an inappropriate question, and his jaw flexed again. "If Jack Pfister says a man's okay, that's good enough for me. Now if you'll excuse me, I've got work to do." He turned abruptly and sauntered off, the Thompson lolling at his side.

As Roz Jenkins was showing me out I said, "Looks like a great business here. You must be very proud."

She stopped, put her hands on her hips, and smiled broadly. "Sure am. We just opened our fifteenth store. For me, it's the family aspect. Folks can come here and spend an afternoon shooting, not out in the damn woods somewhere, like we did when I was a kid. Especially families in the city. They need a decent place to shoot."

I nodded. "I see your point. Arthur seems very knowledgeable."

She chuckled. "Oh, he's an expert on firearms. Has an MBA, too. Stanford. Wants us to be the Starbucks of gun shops and ranges. He runs the day-to-day operation now. Gives me more time to devote to my passion, gun rights." She paused then added, "Do you shoot, Cal?"

"Oh, I have a Glock up in the closet a friend gave me. But, I'm, uh, not very handy with it."

She flashed the broad smile again. "You come on back then. Bring the Glock. I'll teach you how to shoot it."

I told her I would, and as she turned to leave I nodded at her feet. "Nice boots. Who made them?"

She glanced down. "Oh, a custom shop out near Estacada. Bootmaker named Timmons."

TWENTY-TWO

Kelly

As KELLY HURRIED to class the next morning Digger rolled up next to her on his longboard, hopped off, and appraised her with beady eyes set deep and close on either side of his nose. "S'up, girl? You goin' to class today?"

Kelly kept up her brisk pace, trying not to look at his zit-ridden forehead. It was hard to do, like not looking at a car wreck. "What's it look like, Digger?"

"Why not cut? I've got a couple of blunts. We could hang out at my cousin's place. He's, uh, at work."

Kelly stopped and looked at him, her face drawn up in genuine amazement. "You're kidding, right?"

His smile slimed over. "No. I thought we could, you know, have some kicks."

Kelly felt her skin crawl. She knew she should probably not provoke him, but she had little skill in letting people down easy. She turned and faced him full on, her anger engulfing her. "Digger, I'd rather eat a bowl of maggots than go anywhere with you."

His face hardened, and his eyes seemed to recede into their sockets like burrowing animals. "Yeah, well, I thought we could talk about your backpack and that chick that got snuffed, too. You must know a lot about that."

Kelly deflected the comments without changing expression. "You don't know what you're talking about. That wasn't my backpack that cop had. Old Town's full of those blue bags and you know it."

"So where's yours, then?"

"It got ripped off at a bus stop, you dick wad."

"Sure it did."

"If you don't believe me, that's your problem. Now run along on your kiddie board."

Digger tried to smile, but it morphed into a sneer. "Okay, *bitch*, have it your way." He mounted his board and pushed off, but not before calling Kelly every ugly and abusive term he'd learned on the street.

Kelly stood there for a moment in shock. What would the little creep do now? Would he go to the cops, or worse, Macho Dude? Or maybe he bought her story. After all, she didn't cave in to his threats. That had to count for something, didn't it?

She must have been still visibly shaken, because when she ran into Kiyana and Zook at the park Ki said, "What's happened, baby girl? You're white as a sheet."

After Kelly described the encounter with Digger, Zook said, "That little turd. How 'bout I bust his long-board over his head?"

Kiyana laughed. "Don't do that unless I'm there to watch, Zook."

Kelly's heart swelled at Zook's words. *Maybe he did care, after all*. She wanted to hike up on her tip-toes and kiss him, but she resisted. The last thing she wanted was for Zook to add more fuel to the fire by confronting Digger. She said, "Hey, guys, let's just cool it, okay? I can take care of myself."

Maybe Digger was bluffing. She could hope, anyway.

TWENTY-THREE

Cal

I WAS PLANNING to swing by The Sharp Eye to talk to
Nando after I left the Arsenal, but Esperanza told me
he'd left for the day. I caught him by phone and by
the time I reached Caffeine Central had filled him in.
The tagger, K209, was still MIA. When I mentioned
the lawyer, Jack Pfister, Nando said, "Yes, I know of
this Pfister. His foundation helps ex-offenders find
employment. Two employees in my office cleaning
business were recommended by him."

"Yeah, well, Pfister arranged a pretty decent job for
Bonilla as a driver for a wealthy woman named Rosalind Jenkins. She owns a chain of gun shops on the
West Coast. The one in Portland's called Bridgetown
Arsenal. But Bonilla turned the job down at the last
minute with no explanation. That strikes me as a little
strange. I visited Pfister and the Arsenal today. All I
can tell you is that both Pfister and the guy who runs
the gun shop seemed to get a little heartburn when I
brought Bonilla's name up."

"Perhaps they are worried about the publicity."

"Could be. There's something else, too. I met the
woman who owns the chain. She had on a handsome
pair of cowboy boots. Guess who made the boots."

"Not the bootmaker from Estacada?"

"None other."

Nando paused several beats. "So all roads seem to lead to this gun shop."

"It would appear so. What about Bonilla's cause of death? Have you heard anything?"

"I checked this morning. There is a woman in the ME's office who I used to, uh, see. At the moment, the death is classified as suspicious on account of some unexplained bruises, but they have not ruled out suicide. He could have jumped off the Fremont Bridge."

"Good work, Nando. Maybe this thing's starting to give a little. Keep digging on Cardenas, and I'll keep working the Bonilla-gun shop angle. If there's a connection, we've got to find it."

"There's a connection, Calvin, I assure you."

I SPENT THE rest of the afternoon on the phone talking to clients and one judge with whom I was having a running dispute over a change of venue. I have to admit it felt good doing some real work—the kind that results in a check payable to me. When Archie got restless I took him out for a walk, and when I returned Tay Jefferson was standing in front of Caffeine Central.

"Hi," she said. Her honey-brown eyes looked darker in the weak autumn light, but her smile seemed to light the street. You can tell a lot from a smile, and Tay's seemed to derive from a kind of inner peace I could only envy. Archie made a beeline for her, and she knelt down, hugged his neck, and scratched him behind the ears. *"Oh,"* she said, as she ran her finger along the ridge of a whitish scar that peeked through his fur at the base of his right ear, "what happened to cause this?"

"He, uh, was hit with a tire iron. A friend of mine who's a vet saved him. The guy that hit him is serving a life term for murder."

When I finished the story she took Archie's head in both hands, looked him in the eye, and said, "Well, I'm not surprised you pulled through, big boy. You have a lot to live for." Then she smiled up at me. "Esperanza told me I might find you here, Cal. You weren't picking up, so I thought I'd drop by to see if I could catch you."

"Sorry. I was on the phone most of the afternoon. What's going on?"

She stood up and faced me. "I've done a little sleuthing myself. Thought maybe I could buy you a drink and tell you about it."

I looked down at Arch. "I've got to feed this guy. Tell you what, why don't you join us for dinner? You like pasta?"

She accepted my invitation and followed me up the stairs to the apartment. I poured us each a glass of wine and after confirming she liked spicy food, set to work chopping garlic, cloves, onions, red peppers, Kalamata black olives, and basil on a cutting board. I was curious to hear about her "sleuthing" but saw no need to rush the conversation and apparently neither did she. After a couple of sips of wine she closed her eyes. "Umm, this is a good white. Bone dry, just the way I like it."

I smiled and held up the bottle. "Sancerre. From the Loire Valley. They invented dry."

She nodded. "Where did you learn to cook?"

I put a pot of water on the stove for the penne. "Self-taught. Uh, after my wife passed away I had no choice. I'd grown accustomed to good food."

"Sorry to hear about your wife. Did that happen in LA when you were a DA?"

"Yeah." I poured some olive oil into a big skillet and began heating it. "I came up here after." I forced a smile. "You know, a new direction and all that. Where are you from?"

"I'm an LA refugee, too, South Central. I got a masters at UCLA and worked in counseling down there. Came up here eight years ago to take the FRC job."

"Family down there?"

"A younger brother. He's a high school teacher." She smiled a bit wistfully. "Our mother died of cancer when I was twelve. My brother and I wound up in foster care."

"Sorry to hear that."

She waved a hand. "Oh, it worked out okay. The foster parents turned out to be wonderful people. My brother and I are still very close to them."

I poured the penne into the boiling water and sautéed the spices in hot olive oil. I then added red wine, a pinch of brown sugar, and crushed tomatoes to the sauté and let the sauce begin to simmer.

Soon the kitchen was filled with a tangy tomato aroma. Tay got up and used a spoon to taste it. "*Yum*. What do you call this concoction?"

"Arrabbiata. It's about as spicy as it gets in Italy." While the penne cooked and the sauce simmered, I made a quick salad, sliced-up half a baguette, and opened a bottle of Sokol Blosser pinot that I'd stashed away for an undefined special occasion. A dinner with this interesting woman seemed to fit the bill.

When we were finally eating, I said, "So, tell me about this sleuthing."

She finished chewing a bite before answering. "Well, there's been a lot of talk at the center about both Claudia and Manny, as you can imagine."

"Is anyone connecting the two deaths?"

She shook her head. "No. I haven't heard anything like that. The police have been back asking more questions, though. Thanks to you and Nando, I'm not involved in that discussion. But I was talking to a Hispanic resident yesterday, and he let something slip."

I stopped my fork halfway to my mouth and waited for her to continue.

"He said he wasn't surprised Manny's dead. He said when Manny was inside he was seen mixing with some bad dudes."

"Did he give you any names?"

"One. A guy named Javier Acedo. He's known as Javi, a local banger with mucho cartel connections. Runs a lot of bad stuff from inside Sheridan."

"How was Manny involved?"

"Don't know. My source shut up after that, like he'd already said too much. Whatever it was it wasn't obvious. He never would have gotten into the FRC program if that came to light. I have some good contacts at Sheridan. I'll do some more digging."

I nodded. "Good."

"There's more. Manny had another contact you should know about—a graduate student at Portland State named Brent Gunderson. He conducted a batch of interviews with some of our residents at the FRC for a project he was working on, but it seemed like he spent most of his time with Manny. I noticed it and so did Claudia."

"What kind of interviews?"

"Oh, something about correlating elements in offenders' backgrounds with their offenses. I don't know much more than that. Gunderson's working on a master's degree, I think."

"Any idea why he zeroed in on Manny?"

"No clue. But he might be willing to talk to you."

I jotted the name down. Tay said, "Did I hear you right? Manny was going to be the driver for some woman who owns a bunch of gun shops?"

"Yeah, it's a chain. Bills itself as family friendly. They want to be the Starbucks of gun shops. One on every corner, I guess."

Tay groaned. "I hate guns. South Central LA is an armed camp." She smiled bitterly. "I think drive-by shootings were invented there." Her face clouded over. "A friend of my brother's got hit. He wasn't a gang-banger or anything. He was just walking down Alameda Street after school." She closed her eyes, shook her head, and grimaced. "He, uh, the shooter used some kind of assault rifle, an AK-47 or something. James took three bullets in the neck." She looked at me, her eyes bright in the overhead light. "It, uh, nearly decapitated him."

"Jesus, Tay. I'm sorry."

Her look turned angry. "A military weapon, Cal. How does a kid on the street get a military weapon? Why can't we stop that?"

I shook my head, because I didn't have a lot of answers. "Yeah, it seems like a slippery slope to me.

The more we arm in this country, the more we feel we need to arm. That can only be good for the gun industry."

The bitter smile again. Her eyes had gone from warm honey to molten rock. "Maybe that explains why the NRA stonewalls every sensible curb on ownership. Market share."

I nodded. "Full disclosure here. I own a gun. A Glock that Nando gave me when I felt like I needed some protection. But I barely know how to load the damn thing."

"A Glock's a handgun, right? I have no problem with someone owning a handgun. That's not the issue. Never has been as far as I'm concerned."

We sat in silence for a long time, but it didn't seem uncomfortable. Finally, I said, "No significant other?"

"There was, but it's over now." She gazed at the space between us for a couple of beats then looked up with an expression that made it clear the subject was closed. "What about you? Family?"

"A daughter, Claire. She's in graduate school down in the Bay Area."

Tay raised an eyebrow. "Stanford?"

I laughed. "I won't take that personally. No. Berkeley."

"Of course. What was I thinking? You must be very proud of her."

"Yes, I am. She's an amazing young woman."

Tay gave me a teasing look. "Significant other?"

"Nah, not really. I was dating a woman living in Seattle, but she, uh, it turned out she was here illegally and got deported to Russia."

"Deported? My God, what happened?"

I waved a hand, shaking the question off. "It's a long story. Too long."

I made us both shots of espresso and served them with squares of dark chocolate. We sipped, nibbled on the chocolate, and talked a while longer. When I walked her to her car and she turned to face me, I offered my hand. "Thanks for joining me for dinner, Tay, and thanks for the information. Keep your ear to the ground at the FRC."

She took my hand, thanked me, then smiled and leaned forward. Her kiss was warm on my cheek. "It was my pleasure, Cal."

TWENTY-FOUR

Kelly

KELLY RETURNED TO her perch in the building down and across from the Bridgetown Arsenal later that week, armed with a pair of cheap binoculars she'd bought at the army surplus store on Grand. A brisk east wind sifted through the building's exposed girders, making low whistling sounds as it twirled a sputtering mist in the gray light. She was cold and wet and for the first time began to question why she was doing this. The two previous afternoons, she saw nothing familiar except the family in the dark SUV with the little blond girl. They were apparently intent on honing their familial shooting skills.

As the afternoon light faded, Kelly began to work her way down the steel framing. Halfway down she saw a flash of headlights and stopped to watch as two unmarked panel trucks came down the street, pulled into the gun shop driveway, and stopped at the loading dock. She worked her way forward on a crossbeam, found a gap in the cladding that had been left unfinished, and focused her binoculars. Two men got out of the first truck, climbed the loading dock, and disappeared into the building. Two other men got out of the second truck. One came around to the back of the truck, leaned against it, and lit up a cigarette.

The other followed the first two into the building. Kelly watched him walk up the stairs at the loading dock. Her breath stopped and her spinal column began to hum like a high-voltage line. The man wasn't wearing a Bridgetown Arsenal jacket, but there was *something* about that swagger. Was it him? Was it Macho Dude? She was pretty damn sure. She waited anxiously for him to reappear.

The other three men loaded the two trucks with boxes, and the man with the swagger didn't reappear until they were done. But it was too dark by then. All Kelly saw was a shadowy figure descend the steps and get into one of the vans. *Damn, damn, damn.*

After both vans pulled out, she climbed the rest of the way down and slipped away. *Was it him?* She must have asked herself that a thousand times as she sat slouched on the bus. She wasn't sure, but how else could she explain her reaction when she saw him?

WHEN KELLY ARRIVED back at the apartment Veronica called out, "That you, Kel? I'm in here." Kelly was shocked to smell something good, something that reminded her that she hadn't eaten anything since breakfast. She followed the smells into the tiny kitchen. Veronica was turning meat in a frying pan as a pot on the stove belched steam. The mutt was curled up in a corner and when Kelly entered opened its eyes and yawned.

"Wow, smells good. What's the occasion?"

Over her shoulder Veronica said, "No occasion. I got to thinking about what you said the other day, you know, about the way we eat around here." She turned around and smiled. "I'm frying a couple of chops and, get this, steaming some broccoli. I—"

"Look V, I'm sorry I blew up the other day," Kelly cut in. "I was having a crappy day."

Veronica's thick hair was pulled back and tied off, and she looked younger without her usual overdone makeup. She met Kelly's eyes. "Are you okay? Ever since that night you didn't come home, you've been a little off. I don't mean just your arm and leg, Kel."

Kelly dropped her eyes. "I'm fine. Really."

Veronica laid the spatula down and exhaled a breath. "Look, Kel. I hope you're not in some kind of trouble. I mean, if you bring the cops around here, we're both screwed. Don't do that to us, okay?"

"Don't worry. That's not going to happen. It's all good, V."

The pork was a little dry and the broccoli a bit on the limp side, but they both ate with pleasure and lingered at the table afterward to talk. By this time the mutt had climbed into Veronica's lap. Kelly had to make up stories to explain why she'd been getting home so late the last several days. Finally Veronica brought up what was on both their minds. She said, "Know what day tomorrow is?"

Kelly nodded. "October twenty-fourth. The day Dad was supposed to summit."

Veronica grimaced and shook her head. "God, I had a bad feeling about that mountain. Damn climbers, they just keep trying until they find something they can't handle, something that kills them."

Kelly winced. "I figured he was invincible. Never dreamed he wouldn't come back."

Veronica stroked the mutt's head. "Yeah, well,

you were, what, eleven?" She sighed. "Look, Kel, I'm sorry about the way I handled the whole thing." She studied the scratched surface of the table for a while. "I never should have taken off like that. I...I just fell apart."

"You ran away with a tweeker, V. That's what you did."

Veronica dropped her eyes this time. "I know. Can you ever forgive me?"

Kelly's mind flashed back to her foster home—that old bastard coming into her room that night. "I'm trying," she said, tears welling up in her eyes. She willed the tears back. "I just wish Dad were here and it was like it used to be. You know, the three of us."

Veronica couldn't hold her tears back. "I know, Kel. I know."

Kelly lay in her bed later that night with ten thousand thoughts and emotions careening around in her head like bumper cars. It was still drizzling outside, so a trip to her refuge was out. Veronica seemed to be trying a lot harder, she told herself, but could she trust her? She wanted to, but V ran out on her before. She could do it again. And what about the mess she found herself in? Veronica could get busted, which would mean Kelly would wind up back in foster care. *You can't let that happen, no matter what.*

Her mind kept coming back to the Arsenal and the man she saw that afternoon. Had she really recognized Macho Dude, or was she kidding herself because she wanted so badly to find him? And the crazy thing was, she'd only be able to recognize him from behind, when he was walking. She imagined a police lineup, where each subject was instructed to walk away from her. She giggled at that, despite herself.

She had no answers yet and more reasons to feel afraid than optimistic. But when she finally fell asleep that night, Kelly Spence dreamed she was off somewhere in a vast expanse of snowcapped mountains, climbing with her father.

TWENTY-FIVE

Cal

AFTER TAY LEFT that night, I busied myself cleaning up. I could mess up the kitchen counters just boiling an egg, so a pasta dinner for two had catastrophic consequences. But I didn't mind so much because I had plenty to think about. And apparently so did Archie, as he lay under the table in the dining area with his chin on his paws, watching me intently. "No, there aren't any table scraps tonight, big boy," I told him. "And you're lucky you've got paws, not hands. Otherwise, you'd be drying these dishes."

He lifted his head and wagged his stump of a tail in response.

I can't say a pattern began to form in my head, but something started to jell, something with Manny Bonilla and the Bridgetown Arsenal in it. And I had a new lead to chase down—a young sociology student named Brent Gunderson. What could he tell me about Bonilla? I was anxious to talk to him, but it would have to wait. I was booked solid for the next two days at my office in Dundee. The bills have to be paid, after all. I was restless, so I packed up and drove back to the Aerie that night instead of waiting until morning.

Nando called me at my office in Dundee on Thursday with an edge of excitement in his voice. "I have some news on the witness-front," he began. "One of the men in the security tape talking to Cardenas's supposed alibi, Sheri Daniels, is Kyle Kirkpatrick. He's an administrative assistant to the mayor. The tape only showed his back and partial side, but an associate of mine knew him well enough to pick him out. Kirkpatrick was talking to Daniels just before closing."

"Does Scott know about this?"

"I don't know, but he and his partner have the original copy of the tape. In any case, I talked to Kirkpatrick last night. He was up very tight, not wishing to become involved for obvious reasons."

"What did you tell him?"

"I told him that being with a prostitute was a forgivable offense, but if he lies about it in a murder case and is caught he can kiss his job and his career goodbye."

"How did he respond?"

Nando chuckled. "He told me to go to hell, but his upper lip had broken out in little pimples of sweat. I am sure he is thinking it over."

On Friday of that week, I headed back to Portland. As I pulled into my space at Caffeine Central, I could see a half dozen people already lined up at the front door. The only thing typical about my clients was that there wasn't anything typical about them. The first three that morning were the indomitable Thelma McCharles, the elderly woman trying to refinance her mortgage; a young man from Michigan who wanted to fight a ticket he got for camping in Forest Park; and a sixteen-year-old girl who wanted help in becoming emancipated from her crack-addled parents.

I had good news for Thelma. The bank agreed to a meeting. I told the kid from Michigan to clean himself up before he went to court and to tell the judge he'd pay the fine after he found a job. Chances are the judge would waive it.

The girl's name was Kiyana Howard. She was nearly my height with a kind of regal yet unpretentious bearing, like some African princess set down in the middle of Portland. She had an open countenance, big, intelligent eyes, and dreadlocks that looked like they'd been woven by a master weaver. Yes, she could prove a history of neglect by her parents, she told me, and yes, she had an apartment and was supporting herself.

"Okay, Kiyana," I said after we went through the details of her story, "I think we've got a shot here." The look on her face made my week.

Arch and I took a midmorning break when the waiting room finally emptied out. When we returned, there were still no customers waiting for us. I used the lull to answer some mail, but it wasn't long before the buzzer on the front door announced a new arrival. I looked up through the half-open door to my office to see a man in an elegantly tailored suit enter. He looked familiar, but I had only gotten a fleeting look at him. I got up and swung the office door open. "Can I help you?"

He turned to face me. "Uh, yeah. You Cal Claxton?"

I nodded. The swept-back hair and hard-featured

face most women would consider handsome rang a bell.

"I'm Anthony Cardenas," he said. "We need to talk."

I invited him into my office and closed the door. He was dressed like a banker with good taste—a pinstriped navy-blue suit, paisley tie with matching handkerchief in the breast pocket, and a bit of light blue shirt cuff showing at the sleeve. He took a seat in front of my desk, hunched forward, and shook his head resolutely. "I didn't kill Claudia, man."

I leaned back. "I didn't say you did."

"Yeah, but your buddy Mendoza's saying that. He and his Cuban buddies are all over Portland trying to put a wire up my ass. I've got enough trouble with the cops. I don't need him making things worse."

"As I understand it, you've got an alibi. You were with Sheri Daniels the night of the killing, right?"

He leaned back and opened his hands. "Yeah, right." He exhaled another long breath. "But you're a lawyer. You know she's, uh, got some issues that don't make her the most reliable witness. And Mendoza's out there trying to turn her against me. The cops would like nothing better than to hang this on me. You know, the ex-husband's always suspect number one."

"What about Manny Bonilla's death? Know anything about that?"

He opened his hands and shrugged. "I saw that, man. The dude's her cousin. I mean, what the hell's going on?" A faint, wistful smile. "He was a good kid, crazy about Claudia. We used to hang out sometimes. I taught him how to play Texas Hold'em and, man, did that piss Claudia off."

I sat back and looked at him. "Why are you telling me this? I'm sure you've got a lawyer, and he's not going to be happy about this visit."

Cardenas closed his eyes for a couple of beats as if fighting off a wave of emotion. I flashed back to Nando doing the same thing. "Damn straight I've got a lawyer. But I call the shots. Look, man, I hear you might have some influence on that crazy Cuban. He needs to back off. I didn't kill Claudia." He opened his hands again and looked me full in the face. "I *loved* that woman just like he did. I wouldn't touch a hair on her head." His gaze was direct and unflinching. "That's the truth, man."

I nodded. There wasn't much I could say and even less I could do. Even if I believed him, controlling Nando would be like trying to redirect a hurricane. I settled for, "I'll give him the message."

He leaned forward again and pulled his face into a sneer. "Don't just give him the message. I'm asking for your help, man. Convince him."

I met his eyes. "Are you asking me or threatening me?"

"I'm asking you, man. I didn't kill Claudia Borrego. Tell Mendoza to back off."

I stood up. "I got the message. If you didn't do it, you don't have anything to worry about."

His sneer morphed into a sarcastic smile. "Oh, sure. Our justice system's such a model of fairness." When I didn't reply, he got up abruptly. At the door he turned and pointed a finger at me. "And tell Mendoza that I'm going to the funeral tomorrow to pay my respects. Tell him I won't be looking for any trouble and he shouldn't be, either."

I sat there for a few minutes trying to process what just happened. Obviously, Cardenas was worried the alibi provided by Sheri Daniels wasn't going to hold up. I didn't blame him for being nervous. I wouldn't want Nando Mendoza breathing down my neck. I was glad for one thing—the heads-up on the funeral. I would remind Nando that Cardenas had a right to attend and that an ugly scene would serve nobody's interest, particularly the deceased's.

TWENTY-SIX

Kelly

Earlier that same Friday

A BIG DROP of sweat broke loose from Kelly's forehead, seeped through an eyebrow, and blurred her vision. The next handhold's a bitch, she told herself. If you don't make it, you're coming off. Just as she stretched out, a voice boomed up from below, "Hey, get the hell off there." The tips of her fingers caught the block, but without enough purchase to arrest her fall. Her dad's favorite saying—*gravity never sleeps*—flashed through her head as she plunged downward.

The belay caught her about six feet off the gym floor with a jarring snap that made Phil Hanson laugh. Hanson owned the climbing gym from whose wall— the one for advanced climbers—Kelly had just fallen. "Good timing," he said, still chuckling. "Now get to work, young lady. We open in an hour, and the floor needs sweeping." Kelly did odd jobs around the gym for minimum wage and climbing privileges off-hours, which helped her stay sharp.

"Damn eager beavers," she mumbled, as someone began rapping on the front door. She unlocked the door and prepared to tell the person that the gym didn't open until eight thirty. But instead of an early climber, Kelly stood looking at one of the cops who'd stopped her and Kiyanna in Tom McCall Park. He was the older one with the friendly eyes, although they weren't so friendly now. Kelly fought to quell the blood rushing from her head. *Stay cool, girl*, she told herself.

The cop held his badge up. "I'm Lieutenant Harmon Scott of the Portland Police. Is your boss in?"

Kelly tried to smile, but her face turned to granite. "Uh, yeah, he's, uh, in the back, in his office."

"Can you take me to him, please?"

As they were walking through the gym, Kelly in the lead, Scott said, "You look familiar, have we met?"

Without turning, Kelly said, "Maybe, but I've been told I have a familiar-looking face." Lying to this cop didn't seem like a smart thing to do.

He didn't respond, and when they reached Hanson's office at the back of the gym, Kelly knocked twice before opening the door and announcing Scott. As he entered the office Scott took another, more careful, look at her.

Kelly went back to her sweeping, pushing the broom as fast as she could. *Get the hell out of here*, she told herself. But before she could finish Hanson yelled out, "Hey, Kel, come on back here for a minute."

She had an urge to bolt, but she knew that would be stupid. When she entered the office and closed the door behind her, both men eyed her with interest. Hanson said, "The lieutenant here is looking for a witness to a crime over in Old Town. A woman got shot early last Friday morning." Kelly nodded, and although she kept her eyes on Hanson she could feel the pressure of Scott's gaze. "He thinks the witness is a teenage boy or young man who likes to tag and knows how to climb, too. You know anyone fits a profile like that?"

She shifted her eyes to Scott, then quickly back to Hanson. "No." That was the truth. She didn't, but even if she did, no way she'd set the cops after him, even if it meant less heat on her.

"You sure?" Hanson persisted. "What about that Davidson kid, the one who's always challenging you on the wall?" Out of the corner of her eye she saw Scott lean forward slightly.

She forced a smile. "Him? He's an okay climber, but he's no tagger. I think he's an Eagle Scout or something."

"What about that skinny blond kid's been coming in the last month or so? What's his name?"

"Charles something. I don't know his last name. He, uh, can't even do the beginners' wall yet."

Hanson tossed out a couple more possibilities, and Kelly managed to find fault with each of them. Scott took a few names down but didn't seem particularly interested. Finally Kelly said, "Can I go now? I'm going to be late for school."

Scott said, "Hasn't school already started?"

"I go to an alternative school. The academic program doesn't start till ten."

Scott snapped his fingers and pointed at her. "That's where I saw you. Out on the parkway last Saturday. You were with a tall black girl."

"Oh, yeah," Kelly said, feigning recollection, "I remember now."

Scott handed Kelly another card, his eyes linger-ing on her longer than she would have liked. "Thanks for the help, Kelly. If you think of anything else, any-thing at all, give me a call. We want this killer off the street."

Kelly's pulse didn't come back to normal until she was on the bus heading over the river. All Scott had to do was check her juvenile record and he'd know that she fit the "profile." But the thought, unsettling as it was, caused her to smile. She could tell that de-tective couldn't imagine a girl doing K209's tags. Hanson couldn't either, for that matter. *Men. They're so clueless.*

Kelly arrived at school, where she found Zook standing outside the entrance puffing a cigarette. "That stuff'll kill you," Kelly said as she walked up.

He took a deep drag and flicked the smoldering butt into the gutter. "I thought it was demon weed gonna do that?"

"Both. What's up at PSU?"

Zook's face brightened, and his mouth stretched into that lopsided grin of his. "They love me, man. Want me on the practice squad. When I can get my GED, I've got a shot at a scholarship next year."

Kelly's face broke into a radiant smile. "That's great! Uh, they gonna make you pee in a cup?"

"Yeah, I think so, one of these days."

Kelly met his eyes and frowned. "How's that going to work?"

Zook looked aside and ran a big paw through his hair. "No worries. Three days clears it."

Kelly shook her head. "Not the way you use."

Zook forced a grin. "Hey, I got this." He reached in

his pocket, pulled out a small plastic vial containing a yellowish liquid and held it up. "I just got this from Billy Porter. He hasn't smoked in a year."

Kelly made a face. "Ew, how disgusting. They aren't stupid, Zook. You're gonna get caught. Why don't you just quit?"

He showed the grin again. "I got it covered, Kel."

The scare at the climbing gym left Kelly uneasy, but fortunately Zook needed help with his math. Helping him was never a chore—it was how their relationship began—and that day it was a welcome distraction, as well. Zook was a bright kid who could read and write at a high level, but he cowered in fear at the very mention of the word *algebra*. "Look, Zook," Kelly said at one point, "using the quadratic equation is pretty simple. Just lay the problem out, determine the constants, plug them into the equation, and do the arithmetic to get X."

He ran a big hand through his hair, scratched his head, and scowled. "Simple for you, maybe." He turned to face her. "Why did they have to make the GED math test even harder, man? I mean, I had a shot at passing the old test, but not now. Wasn't putting it online enough? Did they have to make it harder, too? I'm screwed, Kel."

"No, you're not screwed," she told him. "Now shut up and do the next problem." He dropped his eyes back to the math book, but she could tell his heart wasn't in it.

That afternoon, after Zook went off to practice at PSU and Kiyana to work, Kelly walked over to the library on SW Tenth Street to get her homework done. But it was hard to concentrate. That cop's last words

bore down on her—*We want this killer off the street.*
Was she a bad person for not coming forward? A now
familiar feeling of indecision settled on her like an
itchy blanket. It would be such a relief to put the burden down, a small voice in her head suggested. Let
someone else handle this. *You're in over your head,
Kelly Spence.*

Then she thought about Veronica, the desperate
look in her eyes when she pleaded for Kelly to stay out
of trouble. What would happen to Veronica? And foster care? *You'll be back in the system in a heartbeat,*
she reminded herself. That thought made her shudder.

No, she wasn't about to come forward. But that
didn't mean she was going to quit, either.

Late that afternoon, Kelly was back at her perch
across from the Arsenal. It was a cold, gray day, and
even though it wasn't raining she could smell damp-
ness in the stiff breeze coming off the river. The shadowy image of the man she saw at the Arsenal the other
day was seared into her memory. She needed another
look at closer range. She figured she could spot that
walk either coming or going.

In any case, if he showed again she had a plan,
sort of.

Hastened by the thickening cloud cover, night was
coming on when a lone panel truck turned in the drive
and parked at the loading dock. Kelly watched as
two men got out. The one she could see best—short
and borderline obese—opened the back doors of the
truck and walked into the building. The other man
stood next to the car, frustratingly shielded from Kelly's view.

She scrambled down the girders, and was over the

back fence and out on the street a few moments later. She stood there in the gathering darkness and took a deep, trembling breath. *They don't know me,* she repeated to herself several times and then, after stashing her binoculars in her backpack, started across the street.

She followed the sidewalk and turned at the driveway along the side of the Arsenal. With any luck, she might get a better look at the man shielded by the truck. The other man suddenly emerged from the building carrying a large, rectangular box. He stopped abruptly when he saw her. "What the hell do you want, kid?"

She was ready for the question. "Uh, Tyler Tea?" She knew it was up the street. "You know where their building is? It's around here somewhere, on Water Street."

His hands full, he nodded in the direction of Water Street. "Up about six blocks on the right. Now beat it."

The man behind the truck didn't move or say a word. *Just my friggin' luck,* Kelly told herself. *The other guy's standing there like a statue, and I can't even see him. What a dumb-ass plan.* The man holding the box kept glaring at her. "Thanks, mister," she said as she began to retreat. A car suddenly swung into the driveway, bathing her in harsh light. She moved aside, flattening herself against the building. Gravel popped beneath the tires as the car moved slowly past her. She saw the dark, indistinct shape of the driver from behind heavily tinted glass, his head turned to appraise her. For reasons she couldn't explain, an involuntary shiver passed through her at the sight of that man's outline.

The car pulled to a stop, and she heard the car window retract. Kelly turned and began walking toward the street. From behind her she heard the man call out, "What's taking so long? You need to get your ass out of here."

Her breath caught in her throat, and she stopped dead for a moment. *That voice. I've heard that voice before!* The realization hit like a slap to the face— that's the man she saw with Macho Dude the night Rupert was killed, the man in the shadows. What had he said? "…at least take that damn jacket off, you idiot." The words reverberated in her head with a tone and texture that meshed perfectly with what she'd just heard. *That's The Voice. I'm sure of it.*

She stole a quick glance back at the car, but it was dark and The Voice didn't get out. With rubbery legs she kept walking toward the street while repeating her mantra—*They don't know me, they don't know me*— which was the only thing keeping her from breaking into a dead run.

She walked for three blocks before stopping again. In her panic to get out of there, she hadn't gotten the plate number of either the van or the car. If you go back now, she told herself, you might have a shot.

But that option closed when The Voice's car, followed by the truck, pulled out and headed south on Water, away from her. As Kelly walked toward the bus stop, she fought back a stiff wave of disappointment. *What a joke*, she told herself—a shooter you can only recognize by his walk and a voice you can't put a face to. *You've got nothing.*

But she was pretty sure of one thing—she wasn't wasting her time. The gun shop she'd been watching seemed to be at the center of something...

TWENTY-SEVEN

Cal

CLAUDIA BORREGO'S FUNERAL service was held the next day at St. Mary's Cathedral in Northwest Portland. I found a seat on the aisle toward the back of the church where I could keep an eye on things. Nando had been asked to sit in the front with Claudia's family. Anthony Cardenas filed past me and took a seat three rows behind him. I'd warned Nando about Cardenas but got no indication of how my friend might react to the ex-husband's presence. I figured Cardenas would keep his cool, and I could only hope Nando would, as well.

The cathedral was filling up fast when Tay Jefferson walked by me looking for a seat. Realizing there were none closer in, she turned, and I pointed to the space next to me. Her eyes widened in recognition, but her face continued to register nothing but pain. When she slid in beside me, she rolled her eyes and exhaled a long breath. "Thanks, Cal. God, I hate funerals."

I nodded, knowing exactly what she meant and how she felt. "Me, too."

I don't remember much about the service, except when the priest talked about what a giving person Claudia was. To make the point he asked, "How many people in this room feel they were a special friend of Claudia's?" Tay and half the room of well over a hundred people raised their hands. Enough said. Oh, and the casket was closed. Two bullets in the head will spoil even the prettiest face.

Tay and I were toward the front of the long line that had formed after the service to offer condolences to Nando and the family, who were gathered outside the church. A private burial was to follow at Riverview Cemetery on the Willamette River. Nando's face was taut, like a drum skin, and watching him there I realized it was the longest I'd ever seen my friend go without smiling when surrounded with people. Cardenas left the cathedral by a side exit rather than filing out the front. I exhaled. Confrontation avoided.

Tay and I found ourselves walking together as the crowd dispersed. There's something therapeutic about walking, and we both needed therapy after that service. Neither of us said anything for several blocks. It seemed natural, walking with Tay. Finally, she said, "That was too close to home. My brother's friend's casket was closed, too. Now this." She sighed. "Oh, Claudia, I miss you already."

The comment broke loose a flood of memories for me, none of them pleasant. I said, "My wife's casket wasn't closed, but I wished it were." Then I caught myself. I wasn't going down that well of self-pity, no matter what the excuse. I glanced up. Tufts of cottony clouds drifted against a cobalt sky like boats without rudders. "The pain never completely leaves, but it gets bearable somehow."

She nodded and we walked some more in silence. We stopped at a little bar and grill on Twenty-first and got drinks, a Mirror Pond for me and a glass of sauvignon blanc for her. A new convert to Sancere wine, she was miffed that the bar didn't stock the label and told them so. We took a table near the back of the place and talked about nothing in particular. We were at a lull in the conversation when she said, "Have you talked to Brent Gunderson?"

I chuckled. "It's on my to-do list for later today, as a matter of fact." She was pushing me. I liked that. "Anything on Bonilla's prison contacts?"

She frowned and sipped her wine, her eyes dark in the low light. "I got a call yesterday, but I didn't get much. Nobody seemed to know what was up between them, business of some kind or, uh, something more intimate."

I nodded. "Okay. So maybe business or maybe sex."

She laughed. "Or both. Anyway, my source is still digging."

"That's good. But, listen, Tay, make sure your name doesn't get used. That could be dangerous."

She met my eyes, and for a moment hers softened as if touched by my concern. Then they narrowed back down and her lips compressed into a straight line. "Don't worry. I know what I'm doing. I owe this to Claudia."

We finished our drinks, and I walked Tay back to her car. As if it was the most natural thing in the world we hugged each other before she got in. It was the kind of hug that two friends give each other as a show of strong support.

TWENTY-EIGHT

Cal

I took Arch for a well-deserved walk that afternoon. When we returned he gave me a baleful look and whimpered a couple of times when it was clear I was leaving again without him. "Guard the castle, big boy," I told him.

Brent Gunderson lived near the Portland State campus, close enough that I decided to walk. I crossed Burnside and made my way to the South Park Blocks, a twelve-block strip of green that cuts through downtown and terminates at the PSU campus. The sky had cleared to a deep blue, and the elms, maples, and oaks lining the greenway were lit with fall colors. Half the city, it seemed, had found an excuse to congregate there.

Gunderson's apartment was on SW Seventeenth, just off Columbia Street, in a once-proud, now shabby, Victorian two-story. Gunderson lived on the first floor, according to a hand-scrawled note tacked to the wall next to the mailboxes in the entry. I rang his bell, a charming three-note chime that must have been the original doorbell. He buzzed me in.

An inner door opened, and a young man peered out at me, backlit by a table lamp. A bit on the plump side, he had short, neatly parted black hair and clean-shaven cheeks that glowed healthily. "Oh, God, you're not selling something, are you?"

I chuckled. "No. If you're Brent I just want to talk to you."

The smile faded. "About what?"

"I'm Cal Claxton." I handed him a card, which he took without glancing down at it. "I was wondering if we could chat a few minutes about Manny Bonilla?"

His cherub face hardened. "Oh," was all he said before shutting the door in my face.

"Crap," I uttered under my breath. "That was a long walk for nothing." I knocked on the door again and said in a louder voice, "Brent, I just want to talk, that's all. Open the door, please." But all I heard on the other side was the sliding of a deadbolt and his receding footsteps.

I was halfway across the 405 overpass when I glanced back at the Victorian mansion and noticed a metallic gray Chevy Malibu maybe a block and a half behind me. I'd seen a similar car on the way over. The only reason I noticed the Malibu was because my neighbor and accountant, Gertrude Johnson, owned a similar model. Coincidence. The car, which contained a single, male driver behind tinted glass, drove by and continued on SW Columbia.

It was a pleasant evening, so when I got back to the South Park Blocks, I took a seat on a bench next to a rousing bronze statue of Teddy Roosevelt leading the charge at San Juan Hill. I was in the middle of trying to think of how to re-approach Gunderson when there he was, striding toward me with a backpack on. He hadn't seen me yet, so I got up and put the statue between him and me. When he passed, I followed him to a coffeehouse on Market.

I loitered outside, and after he bought a coffee and took a seat in the back, I entered and slid into the chair across from him. He looked up with surprise. I said, "I'm sorry to bother you, Brent, but I've got to talk to you about Manny Bonilla. I'm a lawyer. Whatever you tell me will be held in strictest confidence." Okay, that wasn't necessarily a true statement, but I needed this guy to talk to me.

A ripple of emotion crossed his face, a mixture of sadness and fear, but he kept his seat. "I, uh, just heard about his death three days ago. I don't know anything. Why are you involved, anyway?"

"I'm investigating the death of his caseworker, a woman named Claudia Borrego."

"She's dead, too?" His hand went to his face, which had gone a shade paler. "She helped set up my interviews at the FRC. I don't keep up with the local news. What happened?"

"She was shot to death not far from here a week ago. Manny drowned a short time later. His death has been ruled suspicious. The crimes might be related."

He took a sip of coffee as if to calm himself, rattling the cup against the saucer when he replaced it. "Oh, my God. They're both dead," he said, half to himself. "Manny, he, uh…"

When he didn't finish his sentence, I said, "Go on, Brent, tell me what you know about this."

"Nothing," he snapped. "I don't know a thing."

I leaned in. His blue eyes betrayed his anxiety. "Look, Brent, you'll feel a lot better if you get this off your chest."

His eyes welled up, and a single tear broke loose and followed the arc of his cheek. "We became friends after I interviewed him for a project I'm working on. We were, um, talking about him moving in with me when he was released. He told me he was going to come into some money when he got out and that he had a great job lined up. I didn't care about the money."

"Where was the money coming from?"

"He didn't say." Gunderson paused, and I waited. "Then, like last Thursday, Manny calls me and says that he has to leave town for a while, that he's *not* taking the money, and can't afford to move in with me. I told him it didn't matter, that we'd work something out." Gunderson dried his eyes and took a sip of coffee. "Then he says something like, 'I'm involved in some bad shit, Brent, and I'm trying to get out of it. You need to forget you ever knew me.' I told him I'd help him, but he said, no, it was too dangerous, and that if anything happens to him, I shouldn't get involved. You know, like he was trying to protect me or something."

"Did he say anything about Claudia Borrego?"

"Yeah, he did. He said she was helping him do the right thing."

"Have you told anyone about this?"

Gunderson dropped his eyes. "No. I'm such a coward." He looked back up and forced a smile. "I, um, I'm only out here in Portland. I'm from Utah, and the rest of my family doesn't know I'm gay. I figured this might blow it, and, besides, Manny scared the crap out of me." His gaze dropped back to the table. "Now he's dead."

We talked over a second cup, a decaf for me. I didn't get anything else. By this time Gunderson was visibly relieved, as if he'd just shucked off a huge weight. I gave him Harmon Scott's number, and he promised to call him as soon as I left. As I stood to leave he smiled and shook my hand. "Who knows?" he said. "Since I'm making phone calls, maybe I'll call home, too. I've got some things that need saying."

It was dark as I walked back to Caffeine Central, but that damn gray Malibu was still back there. I spotted it in the streetlights on Tenth, a block behind me in the left-hand lane. I crossed the one-way street and stepped behind a covered Trimet bus stop. When the Malibu pulled up to the stoplight I stepped out and rapped sharply on the driver's side window.

The window rolled down, and a man looked up at me with a very annoyed look on his face. "Hi," I said, "I'm Cal Claxon. What can I do for you?"

TWENTY-NINE

Cal

THE MAN IN the car shook his head and smiled, seemingly in spite of himself, then reached into an inside breast pocket and produced a badge. "Special Agent Truax, ATF. Since you made me, you might as well climb in. And hurry. The light's about to change." The badge looked legitimate, so I took him up on the offer.

Truax was my size with thick forearms covered with wiry black hair and large hands with no jewelry except for a plain wedding band. His face bristled from a two-day growth, and he had deep-set eyes the color of good bourbon. The funny thing was he looked vaguely familiar.

"Where are we going?" I asked him.

"Well, hell, I might as well just take you home. You've had a long walk tonight."

"I wouldn't have noticed you, but you're driving the same car as my bookkeeper."

Truax shrugged. "Just my luck. Surveilling someone who's on foot's a bitch in the best of situations."

"Are you going to tell me why you've been following me?"

He gave me a pained "oh, please" look and then turned his attention back to the street. "You've been busy lately, Claxton. What's the deal?"

"Deal?"

"Oh, come on. I'm a federal agent. What the hell are you up to?"

I shrugged. "I suppose you're referring to the Claudia Borrego murder. She was my best friend's fiancée. He's a PI here in Portland—Hernando Mendoza." Truax nodded, suggesting he knew about Nando or at least the name. "He's understandably upset about her death. I've been helping him run down some potential leads, you know, trying to help the investigation."

Truax barked a laugh. "I'm sure Portland PD's just thrilled about that. And…?"

"And what?"

"What've you learned?"

I laughed. "Very little. Look, I'm just going through the motions here, trying to help a friend cope with his loss." Since Truax wasn't sharing anything with me, I saw little reason to open up to him.

After driving in silence for several blocks he pulled up to the curb in front of Caffeine Central and left the engine running. "That apartment you just visited on Columbia—who did you talk to?"

"Oh, that was on an unrelated matter. Turned out I had the wrong address." I didn't want to drag Gunderson into this after he bared his soul to me.

Truax looked at me and held his gaze for several beats. "Look, Claxton, I'm sure you and your buddy Mendoza mean well, but you need to cut this crap."

"What crap? We're not breaking any laws, and anything we learn will go straight to the team investigating the murder."

He exhaled a breath and shook his head. "You're mucking around in something you know nothing about. Maybe there's more here than meets the eye. You get my drift?"

"No, I don't. Maybe you should give me a little more information."

Truax placed both hands on the steering wheel and stared straight ahead. His knuckles shown white through tufts of dark hair. "Goddamn it, Claxton. Maybe you're going to find your ass between a rock and a very hard place, too."

I smiled, nodded, and clicked the car door open. "I'll keep that in mind." After I got out I leaned back in and said, "I finally figured out why you look familiar. You're Richie Truax, aren't you? You were a linebacker at USC back in the Ted Tollner era."

A smile got loose on his face and faded just as fast. "That was a long time ago. Talk to Mendoza, Claxton. Tell him what I said. Rein it in, cowboy."

After the Malibu pulled away I stood there feeling uneasy. What had Nando and I been up to over the past week that would worry the Bureau of Alcohol, Tobacco, and Firearms? Whatever it was, Truax wasn't about to tell me. Maybe I should have leveled with him, but hell, I didn't have anything, anyway.

One thing was certain, though—the investigation that Nando and I were carrying out seemed to be upsetting an awful lot of people.

THIRTY

Cal

THE WEEK FOLLOWING Claudia Borrego's funeral did not go well for her ex-husband, Anthony Cardenas. I was back at the Aerie on Tuesday when Nando phoned. "Calvin," he began, "I have good news. Kyle Kirkpatrick has admitted that he was with Sheri Daniels the night of Claudia's murder."

"So, Cardenas's alibi's busted? That's great, Nando. Did you have a hand in this?"

He chuckled. "Yes. I convinced him Sheri Daniels was about to crack. To his credit I think he wanted to come forward all along. He is a man of conscience."

"What about Daniels?"

"I told her and her lawyer the police were more likely to believe Kirkpatrick than her, and that if she cooperated she could probably work a deal. If not, she was looking at serious jail time." He chuckled again. "Addicts are not fond of jail time."

The development made *The Oregonian* under the headline Witness Retracts Statement in Murder Case.

Archie and I came back to Portland on Thursday of that week, and as I was opening up Caffeine Central, a Portland unmarked pulled up in the yellow zone in front of the building. Harmon Scott got out and glanced at the half dozen people already queued up. He looked tired and annoyed. "Mind if I jump the line, Claxton?"

I turned to my waiting clients. "Uh, this gentleman's a police officer. I'm going to speak to him first this morning. There are plenty of seats in the waiting room. I'll get to you just as soon as I can."

Scott followed me into my office, slumped in a chair, and began polishing his glasses on his shirt-sleeve. I closed the door and looked at him. His skin was pale, even for an Oregonian, and the hollows under his eyes seemed deeper and a shade darker. "You look overworked, Harmon. Don't you ever take a break?"

He puffed a derisive breath and shook his head. "I've got the caseload from hell. I'll take a break when I'm dead."

I flashed back to my days in LA when I carried a similar attitude like a badge of honor, but I knew better than to say anything to this proud, hard-working cop. "Congrats on breaking Cardenas's alibi."

His laugh had a trace of bitterness. "You know full well who I have to thank for that."

I flashed an innocent smile. "Who might that be?"

He rolled his eyes. "Just tell Mendoza he's done enough, okay? You both have."

I nodded. "Are you close to an arrest?"

He chuckled without any mirth. "The case sucks. We think that tagger K209 saw the shooting. I need the kid to close this thing."

I opened both hands. "I've tried, Harmon. He's elusive. Either that or the killer caught up with him, and the body hasn't turned up yet."

Scott shook his head. "No reports of missing teens,

but I guess we can't rule that out. You, uh, asked Picasso, right? Told him how important this is?"

"Yeah. He's checked *all* his sources. Nothing. Do you have anything else?"

He shrugged. "We got an intact .22-caliber round from the murder weapon. Brain tissue, it turns out, has a lot of stopping power. But we got no weapon to go with it. It's probably rusting somewhere in the Willamette."

"What about the kid from the Federal Reentry Center, Manny Bonilla? Is he tied into this thing?"

Scott met my eyes and his narrowed slightly, giving me the impression he knew I'd been snooping around. "Just find K209 for us, okay Claxton? We can handle the rest."

I HAD A series of court appearances in McMinnville the following week that kept me at the Aerie with my head down, busy doing the kind of work that allows one to pay the bills. It was just as well because I was out of ideas and, to be honest, out of enthusiasm, as well. It looked like Scott and Ludlow were closing in on Cardenas and whatever the hell was going on at the Bridgetown Arsenal, and how Manny Bonilla figured in might be better left to Richie Truax and the ATF. Sure, I still had a score to settle with the one-boot cowboy, but my bruised ribs were starting to heal. As for K209—it would be great to find him and seal the case against Cardenas, but maybe the kid didn't need rescuing. Maybe he had good reasons to stay hidden, reasons I didn't understand.

On the Thursday of that week Arch and I walked down to the mailbox to get the paper. It was a crisp, cool autumn morning, and the breeze off the valley smelled sweet and clear. The article was on the front page:

Suspect arrested in Old Town murder

In a dramatic development a police spokesman announced today that Anthony Cardenas of Portland was arrested for the murder of Claudia Borrego, also of Portland. Borrego's body was found on SW Everett St. near 3rd Ave. early on October 17. She had been shot in the head twice with a handgun.

Borrego had been employed as a counselor at the Federal Reentry Center in Southeast Portland. Cardenas lists his occupation as professional gambler and is the ex-husband of Borrego. The police stated that physical evidence found at the crime scene has been linked directly to Cardenas but declined to provide details. Cardenas's attorney, Melvin Steinberg, said his client vehemently denies any involvement in the crime and looks forward to presenting his side of the story.

I PUT THE paper under my arm and called Nando immediately, but the call went to voice mail. When I finished up a hearing later that day in McMinnville, I swung back by the Aerie for Archie and headed for Portland. I still hadn't connected with Nando, so I drove directly to his detective agency. Looking sharp in a silk blouse, pencil skirt, and spike heels, Esperanza flashed a brilliant smile. "Hello, Cal. You heard the news?"

I gave a thumbs-up. "Sure did." She told me to go on in. Nando was at his computer with his back to me, centered between two pictures up on the wall—one of President Obama and the other of Raul Castro. I said, "So, Cardenas is in jail."

Nando spun around and flashed a smile that made Esperanza's look dim by comparison. "Yes, we got the bastard." He was clean-shaven and wore sharply creased wool slacks with an expensive-looking pearl-colored V-neck sweater.

I sat down and faced him across the desk. "What broke it?"

"The science of ballistics, Calvin."

"You mean they found the murder weapon?"

"No. Not exactly. Let me explain. A tip came in some while ago stating that Cardenas owned a second car, a vintage Thunderbird, which he kept in a garage farther down on NE Thirty-third. Cardenas, it seems, had failed to mention this to the police, an unintentional oversight according to his attorney. A search warrant was executed, and a subsequent search of the rented space turned up a Sparrow silencer threaded to fit a Walther P-22. The silencer was stashed in the wheel well of the T-Bird. It was known, of course, that a .22 was used to kill Claudia. The search and what it turned up were kept quiet. Not even I had heard about it until the news broke today."

"They found a silencer but no gun?"

Nando smiled and nodded. "Yes, that is what my source told me."

"A silencer can't leave a ballistics signature, can it? Even I know it's bored-out to a larger diameter than the gun barrel so it doesn't touch the bullet."

Nando smiled again. It was clear he was enjoying this. "What you say is true, but this particular silencer has a defect. It was made slightly out-of-round, which leads to the bullet touching the silencer as it leaves the gun. The scientific term is baffle strike."

"So this baffle strike leaves a unique mark on the bullet?"

"Yes. And the ballistic work showed that the strike pattern exactly matched the one on the bullet that killed Claudia. The silencer found in Cardenas's garage was the one used in the murder of Claudia, Calvin. It is a proven fact."

"So the actual gun's superfluous?"

"In this case, yes."

I leaned back in my chair and frowned. "Why would Cardenas toss the gun but not the silencer?"

Nando's eyes flashed impatience. "Because he had no idea whatsoever it could incriminate him, that's why. It took a ballistics expert to do that. And silencers are not that easy to come by these days, even for criminals. Perhaps he wanted to hang on to it. It is understandable."

"Stupid is more like it."

"Any man who gambles for a living is stupid, Calvin."

I sat back in my chair. "Well, that's absolutely incredible. What a break! And from an anonymous tip."

Nando sat back, as well. "Yes. I am pleased with this outcome." He ran a hand through his hair and his face clouded over momentarily. "But it doesn't bring my Claudia back."

That night I joined Nando for dinner at Pambiche. As usual, I got there first and had to wait as he made his customary entrance and worked his way through the tables. The going was particularly slow because everyone wanted to discuss the recent turn of events and hear Nando's take on them. After all, this was what they all wanted. Justice. Closure. Hands were shaken, cheeks were kissed, and even though the news was good, there was hardly a dry eye in the place. Such was the love that the Cuban community felt for my friend and for the woman who was to have been his wife.

It was late when I got back to Caffeine Central, but I wasn't sleepy. I leashed up Arch and started off toward the river. We hadn't gone more than a block when a light rain began to fall. As I pulled my hood up, Arch turned his head and gave me a look. "You've got a thick coat, big boy," I told him. "You can do this." He turned and plodded on ahead of me. At the river, a thin mist had formed, and the city lights were a smear on the water like an abstract painting.

I stopped at the Morrison Bridge and tried to clear my head. I should have felt some closure, too, but I didn't. The case against Cardenas wasn't that impressive. He had a motive and threatened the victim, had lied about his whereabouts, and at least a *part* of the weapon used to kill his ex-wife was found in his possession. As a prosecutor I would have preferred the gun, of course. But from what Nando told me, the silencer was strong physical evidence—enough for an indictment, for sure—but no slam dunk for a conviction because nothing put him at the scene. No surprise that Scott was still interested in the only apparent witness to the shooting—the tagger, K209.

But the tagger was nowhere to be found. *Let it go*, I told myself. If it's good enough for Nando and for the Portland Police it should be good enough for you.

But there were enough loose ends in this case to weave a rug. And I hated loose ends.

THIRTY-ONE

Kelly

KELLY FOUND OUT about the arrest of Anthony Cardenas as she rode the bus on the way to Granite Works. Someone had left a newspaper on the seat, and there it was—a headline: Suspect Arrested in Old Town Murder. She was numb for a few moments, then felt an overwhelming sense of relief. She must have made some kind of squealing noise because a man and woman sitting across the aisle both looked at her with concern. Kelly turned away to hide her eyes, which were brimming with tears. She soaked up every detail of the article and studied the head shot of Cardenas. His long, angular face was a bit unsettling for reasons she couldn't quite explain. *Don't be stupid*, she told herself, you never saw Macho Dude's face.

But her relief was short-lived when she realized there was no mention of Rupert's murder or of a second suspect. Macho Dude acted alone in Claudia Borrego's murder, but Kelly knew that a second person—the one she'd dubbed The Voice—was involved in Rupert's death. Give it some time, she told herself. Maybe this guy, Cardenas, will finger The Voice. If that didn't happen, she knew she'd have to find a way to come forward, some way that wouldn't screw everything up. She owed that to Rupert.

Despite the uncertainty Kelly whizzed through her work at the gym that morning and walked into school feeling better than she had in a long time. Class hadn't started yet, and Kelly spotted Kiyana in a corner of the room talking to the pretty Roma girl named Jaelle, who was clutching her violin case and crying. "Look, Jaelle," Kiyana was saying, "they can't just kick you out. You have rights, girl."

Jaelle caught a tear with her index finger. "They said we have to be out in seven days."

Kiyana stiffened. "That's bullshit. You signed a lease, right?"

The girl, who had an olive complexion and long, flowing hair Kelly could only dream of, nodded.

"You need to go over to Caffeine Central and get some legal help," Kiyana continued. "Dude over there named Claxton helps people like us and doesn't charge much, if anything." When Jaelle looked hesitant Kiyana said, "Hey, I know about this guy. Trust me." A look of pride flickered across her face. "He's helping me divorce my parents, man. Caffeine Central. It's over on Couch."

The sun managed a showing that day just as break time came around. Kelly and Kiyana wandered over to O'Bryant Square for something to do. An old dude with long gray hair stood in the center of the square playing classical music on an acoustic guitar as an admiring crowd began to gather. Kelly said, "So you're going to do it, the divorce thing?" Kiyana had told her about her plans, but Kelly hadn't taken it too seriously. *I mean, divorce your parents?*

"Yeah. The lawyer says I have a shot. It just

means they can't boss me around anymore or take my money."

Kelly knew Caffeine Central had street cred. After all, she'd tagged the building a few weeks earlier, figuring the lawyer there might get the message about the city's stupid zero-tolerance policy on graffiti. "Uh, this guy Claxton, he's cool?"

"Seems like it. We'll see."

As they were heading back Kelly glanced around hoping to see Zook coming to class, late as usual. But he didn't show. "Know where Zook is?" she finally asked her friend.

Kiyana shook her head, and her face seemed to cloud over. "I heard he's been hanging with Sprague and those jerkwads. Thought he was playin' ball at PSU?"

"He is," Kelly shot back as Kiyana's words gripped her heart like a cold hand. A known black-tar dealer who bragged about rolling spangers and newcomers just for the fun of it, Johnny Sprague was bad news in every possible way. Digger was in and out of that group, too. Kelly pursed her lips and shook her head. "No way he's hanging out with Sprague and his wannabes. That can't be!"

Kiyana gave her a look but didn't comment. Shortly after that, as if on cue, Digger cruised past on his longboard. He didn't say anything either, but Kelly found the look he shot her unnerving. It was the kind of look a snake might give a cornered mouse, or so it seemed to Kelly at the time.

Zook didn't show at school that day. A driving rain pocked the river as the bus carried Kelly back across the Burnside Bridge that afternoon. *Well, at least I don't have to worry about watching that damn gun shop anymore*, she told herself. *They've got one of the killers now. Surely they'll get the second one.*

She wanted to believe that about as much as she wanted to believe that Digger's look didn't mean anything and that Zook hadn't fallen in with the wrong people.

Things had to start looking up, didn't they?

THIRTY-TWO

Cal

ANTHONY CARDENAS WAS immediately arraigned for the murder of Claudia Borrego. He entered a plea of not guilty and was remanded to custody at the Multnomah County Jail. Bail was denied, which was typical for a murder charge, particularly when the defendant was a rich, itinerant gambler. The chess game between the prosecution and the defense would now begin.

Nando went to the arraignment and called me afterward with a blow-by-blow description of the brief proceedings. You'd have thought it was the actual trial the way he carried on. It seemed my friend had regained his footing, although I worried that perhaps he was trying too hard. Grief is a tricky emotion. It has to run its course. I wasn't sure my friend understood that yet. He wanted it done with. Now.

Tay Jefferson called me shortly after the news broke. "So, that bastard Cardenas did it, huh?"

"Looks that way, yeah." I described the case against Claudia's ex-husband and answered her questions as best I could.

"What about Manny Bonilla?" she asked when I finished. "Did Cardenas kill him, too?"

"I don't really know. I'm sure Scott and Ludlow

are trying to link the two deaths. Having Cardenas in custody should help."

"What about you? What are you going to do now?"

The question caught me off-balance. I paused. "Nando's happy. I guess I need to move on."

She didn't respond, giving me the impression she was somehow expecting more from me, but I left it at that. After the call ended I sat there thinking about what I just said. I wanted to move on, but the fact that I hadn't found the tagger or understood what really happened to Manny Bonilla still nagged at me. I decided to do what I normally do to clear my head—go fly fishing. Steelhead weren't running in the coastal rivers, so Archie and I packed up the next day and headed for the McKenzie River, whose upper reaches abounded in wild rainbow trout year-round.

I knew a stretch of river high in the Cascades between mileposts 13 and 16 on the McKenzie River Highway that alternated between roiling whitewater and the pools and eddies preferred by the feisty native rainbows. Framed by steep hillsides of old growth Douglas fir and western hemlock, the McKenzie ran a deep turquoise in the autumn sun that day. The first sight of the river always got to me, and I had to swallow to relieve the catch in my throat. It was the same catch I got from certain riffs by Coltrane or an achingly pure soprano note from Callas or Baez. Closer in there was the sound of the river, too—the happy noise of water striking rock that never failed to relax me.

Trout or no trout I would've fished the McKenzie that day just for the beauty of the river.

The caddis fly hatch I expected to see that afternoon didn't materialize, and the fish I hoped to coax up from the bottom of the river stayed put. I switched over to a fly called a Chubby Chernobyl— a big, leggy-looking bug tied by a fly designer with a sense of humor—and immediately hooked into a half dozen nice fish. This turn of events delighted Archie, who was shadowing me along the bank. He barked and spun in circles every time I hooked a fish. And, of course, I had to show him each fish before I released it.

I was just releasing an eighteen-incher when my cell pinged with an incoming text. Surprised that there was any reception at all, I waded back to the bank and retrieved my phone from the waterproof pouch in my waders. A single signal dot showed on the phone, apparently enough for the text to make it through. It read: "Hello, Mr. Claxton. You're not picking up, so I decided to try a text. Could you please call me? It's important. Brent Gunderson."

I stood there weighing my options. *You came here to fish*, I reminded myself. The man said important, not urgent. I tried calling and texting him back, but both attempts failed. I fished until it was nearly dark and tried Gunderson when we got back to our camp-site downriver, where the cell signal was much stronger.

He answered the first ring. "I, uh, found some things today that Manny left behind," he began after we exchanged greetings.

"What kind of things?"

"A gun. And some other stuff."

I pressed the phone tighter to my ear. "A gun?"

"Yeah. It was in a bucket in the window seat along with a brush and some rubber gloves. Those were mine. The gun was wrapped in a T-shirt. There was a box of bullets and some diagrams of some kind, too." I thought he chuckled. "I guess Manny figured I'd never look in a bucket filled with cleaning supplies. He knew I hated housework. But my sister's coming. I had to clean up."

"Did you touch the gun or any of the rest of it?"

"God, no. When I saw what it was I just recoiled, you know?"

"You said diagrams—of what?"

"Uh, they were of rifles, you know, showing how all the parts go together. They looked like instructions, maybe. Probably something to do with the job he was going to take."

"Okay. Look, Brent, leave everything right where you found it and call the police and tell them about this."

He paused for several beats. "Yeah, well, last time you told me to call the police, they sent some homophobe named Ludlow to interview me. Turns out he's Mormon, like me. Let's just say he made no effort to hide his contempt for my sexual orientation. That's why I called you. Any way you could help me handle this?"

That little voice—the one I should listen to but hardly ever do—told me to say no. But it was too late. My curiosity had already trumped my sense of caution. I heaved a long sigh. "Tell you what… I'm up in the Cascades right now. Sit tight. I'll be there around nine. We'll get this sorted out."

Damn, I thought as I began taking down my tent. *Tomorrow morning was going to be primo fishing.*

But I was as hooked as some of those rainbows I caught earlier.

I fed Arch before we broke camp but I didn't bother to eat. Hunger finally got the better of me, and I pulled off the I-5 at the Carmen Drive exit for a black bean burger and sweet potato fries at a Burgerville. I called Gunderson to tell him I was running late. "No problem," he told me. "I have to go to class tonight. If I'm not back when you get here, just go on in. There's a pair of keys under a ceramic frog on the left side of the front steps."

I found a parking space directly in front of his apartment building at a little after ten. His lights were on, but no one answered the doorbell. I found the hidden set of keys and let myself in. The apartment was done in primary colors with black leather and chrome furniture and plush Oriental rugs. The only problem was it had been thoroughly tossed. A couch in the living room was stripped of its cushions, an end table lay on its side, and I could see a rifled desk in the next room. I stopped dead in the doorframe and called out for Gunderson. Nothing. I listened intently for couple of seconds. Not a sound. "I've seen this movie," I said as I backed out of there.

Keeping to the shadows, I moved quickly to the back of the building to see if I'd flushed anyone. The back door was ajar and a side window smashed, but no one came out. After calling 911, I returned to the front of the building and breathed a sigh of relief when I saw Gunderson walking across the 405 overpass toward me.

A patrol car arrived next, and it took an hour and a half for them to complete an investigation. You guessed it—the bucket in the window seat was gone, along with the items belonging to Manny Bonilla. Nothing else in the apartment had been taken. I put a call into Harmon Scott's cell phone and left a message. Gunderson looked pretty shaken, so I offered to put him up at my place.

Later that night we sat at the kitchen table going over what had happened. Sensing a certain vulnerability in Gunderson, Arch curled up at his feet as a show of support. My dog was like that. Gunderson's cherub cheeks were darkened by a day's growth, and he looked tired, so I made him a cup of Darjeeling tea I kept around for guests. I was having a Rémy Martin that I kept around for me. No, he hadn't noticed anyone watching his apartment, and no, he hadn't told anyone else about the items he found. There didn't seem to be any explanation for the timing of the break-in, either. Gunderson discovered the items in the bucket that morning, and the burglary occurred that night. His phone or mine could have been tapped, but that seemed highly improbable. A lucky coincidence for the intruder, and unlucky for me, I decided.

"I know you didn't get a good look at the gun or the box of shells, but what about the drawings?" I probed. "What else do you remember about them?"

He sipped his tea and wrinkled his forehead. "Like I told the police, they looked like some kind of engineering drawings, you know, exploded views, showing how the parts of rifles go together."

"Which parts?"

He paused and stroked his chin. "The triggers and the thingies that hold the bullets."

"Ammunition clips."

"Yeah, those and the trigger mechanisms mostly."

I probed some more, but that's all he could remember. "That's it? Nothing else in the bucket, right?"

Gunderson dropped his eyes and studied the nicked surface of the table for a while, then sighed deeply. "Well, there was something else, something I didn't mention."

I almost spilled my Rémy. "What the hell was it?"

He brought his eyes back up but evaded my gaze. "There was a notebook, too, but I, um, took it out after I called you."

By this time I was standing. *"Why?"* Archie got up, too.

Gunderson's cheeks burned red through his dark beard. "Manny had written some mushy stuff in it about us. I, I didn't want it to get out, you know, be part of evidence that's made public or something." He rolled his eyes. "I could just imagine that cretin Ludlow's reaction."

"What did you do with it?"

"That's why I called you instead." He reached down and extracted a small spiral notebook from his backpack and slid it across the table. "Here."

Oh, great, I thought. There's nothing like being given evidence that's been tampered with.

THIRTY-THREE

Cal

I LET THE notebook lie there on the table between us. "Is there anything else in this besides the mushy stuff?"

"Yeah, some notes and dates and weird stuff I really didn't understand." He smiled and nodded toward the notebook. "Manny's handwriting's almost indecipherable. I spent most of the time on the entry to me. It was, um, a draft, I think, of a note he was going to send to me." Gunderson's eyes filled but he held back the tears. "He didn't finish it."

"You realize you're going to have to turn this over to the police."

"Do I have to give them *everything*?"

"Yes." I sighed and drained my Rémy. "But let me read it. All of it."

He was right about the handwriting—it looked like the scratchings of a drunken chicken. I skipped over the other entries and went straight to the unfinished love letter. With Gunderson's help I finally got through what turned out to be a sweet, almost poignant declaration of love, which included some details that no one would want made public. I could certainly understand his reluctance to part with it. When I finished, he eyed me expectantly. I exhaled a long breath and ran a hand through my hair. "To-morrow, you need to call Harmon Scott and tell him you found the notebook when you were straighten-ing up. I advise you to give him everything, but if a couple of pages are torn out, I can't control that and don't want to know anything about it."

Exhausted but obviously much relieved, Gunder-son slept on my threadbare couch that night. After taking Arch for a quick walk, I used my cell phone to photograph everything in the notebook except for the unfinished love letter. But any attempt to deci-pher what Bonilla had written would have to wait. I was exhausted, too.

The next morning I made us a six-egg omelet with some black morels I had stashed away along with Tillamook cheddar, green onions, and fresh garlic. I sent Gunderson off a well-fed man, although he was rightly concerned about his safety. I told him to start carrying his house keys or find a better hiding place, and if he couldn't get his smashed window repaired that day, he could stay with me until he did.

Later that morning, my favorite police detective called. "Goddamn it, Claxton," Harmon Scott said the moment I answered, "I thought you were out of my life."

"Good morning to you, too, Harmon."

"I know you had something to do with Gunder-son coming forward in the first place, and I'm grate-ful for that—"

"Always a pleasure to serve."

"—but how in hell did you turn up as a witness in that break-in last night?"

"Blame your partner, Ludlow. He and Gunderson

share the same religion but not the same beliefs about sexual orientation. Gunderson didn't want to deal with him, so he called me for advice. It screwed up a good fishing trip, if you really want to know." I answered some more of Scott's questions, and he told me Bonilla's death was still classified as "suspicious" and that they'd found absolutely no link between his death and Claudia Borrego's other than their blood relationship.

When I asked about the assault on me and if he'd followed up with Timmons the bootmaker out in Estacada, he replied, "Sorry. Dead end. The guy's paranoid about Big Brother, purges his tax records religiously, and couldn't remember anything that far back."

"No search warrant?"

"Nah, you know how it goes. Money's tight. Searches ain't cheap. No reason to doubt him."

"What if he's covering for a friend?"

When Scott didn't respond, I let it ride. I did know how it goes. We signed off after I extracted a promise that Scott would have a patrol car watch Gunderson's apartment for a couple of nights.

I thought about taking a run before looking at the material I'd photographed in Bonilla's notebook, but a front had moved in, and it was pelting rain. I fixed myself another cappuccino instead, and after emailing myself the photos and saving them in a file, set to work at my computer. Reading the love letter the night before prepared me somewhat for the mangled, torturously cramped combination of cursive and print letters and atrocious spelling that characterized Bonilla's handwriting. But, it was still slow going. The notebook served as a kind of do-it-yourself day minder and catch-all for the young man.

The first dozen or so pages were notes from meetings, sequentially dated from the latter half of August through September. Several entries were headed "Meeting with CB," and were followed by brief notes, mostly tips on interviewing and résumés. I assumed these referred to meetings with his case manager, Claudia Borrego. Nothing in the notes caught my eye. There were also a couple of "TJ Meeting" entries, probably sessions with Tay Jefferson, his psychological counselor. No notes were recorded.

On September 12, Bonilla had scribbled "Interview— Sept. 19." I assumed this referred to his interview for the driving job. An entry dated September 19 read: "Training Sept. 23, 26, 30 at 9 a.m."

"Three days training for a driving job?" I said loud enough to cause Archie to lift his head in the corner. I couldn't read the first letter following the 9, but surely it was an *a* and not a *p*. I mean, why begin training at nine at night?

There were three pages titled simply "Notes" with no dates. The pages contained odd jottings and crude three-dimensional sketches of a block of some kind showing a curved appendage that jutted from the bottom and what appeared to be a lever arm on the top. A few dimensions were noted and lots of arrows with the tagline, "See Diagram." I wondered if this referred to the drawings Gunderson had described that disappeared along with the gun and ammunition.

There were three even more puzzling entries on the next page. The first read,

Oct. 23—two trucks/100 units.
ECA-25
MGC-30
BRC-45

The second,
Oct. 24—one truck. 45 mods-SDGC

The third,
Nov. 19—two trucks/80
ECGR-35
RBRR-45

And the fourth,
Nov. 23—one truck SDGC—40

On October 12, just five days before he died, Manny Bonilla wrote a final entry in the notebook, right below the heading for a ten o'clock meeting with Claudia Borrego. It read,

I am not a product of my circumstances.
I am a product of my decisions.

I pushed myself away from my desk, leaned back, and clasped my hands behind my head. Certainly the quote on the last page suggested Manny was having a change of heart, but I already knew that. His nearly incomprehensible sketches suggested a link to the diagrams stolen from Gunderson's apartment, but only that. I would need help to decipher the sketches. The entries referring to the training were interesting, but, again, only suggestive of a link, this time to the Arsenal.

I considered the missing gun again. He must have known the possession of such a weapon jeopardized his release from federal prison. Did he acquire it for self-protection, or did he have a darker use in mind?

The alphabet soup meant something, too, but I didn't have a clue. Units of what? Mods? What the hell did these refer to?

Finally, I wondered what that old fox, Harmon Scott, would make of all this. I smiled just thinking about it and knew, even though neither of us would ever admit it, there was kind of a competition going on between us.

The rain had dwindled to a light mist, so I put on my Asics and Gore-Tex, leashed up Arch and headed for the river. Arch gave me a couple of irritated looks but fell into a brisk trot beside me. We went past the Salmon Fountain and all the way to McCormick and Schmick's before turning around. My lungs were burning when we finally came to the steps at the Burnside Bridge, but I forced myself to take them without slowing down and kicked it all the way back to Caffeine Central. Frustration neutralized, at least for the moment, and next steps decided.

After a shower, I made two phone calls. First, I called Jack Pfister and invited him to lunch. He accepted.

Next, I called Roz Jenkins at the Bridgetown Armory. I was told she was tied up, but she called me back a few minutes later. We made a date to meet at the Bridgetown Arsenal the next morning.

Just like that I was back in it.

THIRTY-FOUR

Cal

THE NEXT DAY I took down a shoebox containing my
Glock 17 from the closet of the tiny bedroom apartment in Caffeine Central. Nando gave it to me after
the place was been broken into. I had never shot the
gun, and the one time I carried it for self-protection,
I wound up being kidnapped and nearly killed. So
much for my skills with a handgun. I removed the gun
from the box and held it in my hand, marveling, as I
always did, at how well it seemed to fit my hand and
how substantial it felt. A means of projecting power, a
guarantor of personal safety, a murderous instrument,
a brilliantly engineered machine—it said all of that
and a lot more. I pulled the slide back to make sure
the chamber was empty, then slid the clip from the
handle and removed the cartridges, ten of them. The
clip held seventeen, but somehow that many bullets
seemed excessive. I put the shells back in a cartridge
box and tucked it and the Glock into the briefcase I
used for court appearances. After all, I couldn't just
walk into the Arsenal carrying the damn gun, could I?

It was a ringingly clear day, but an arctic air mass
from the north had brought an early, light frost that
vanished by midmorning. I left a clearly disappointed
Archie inside Caffeine Central on guard dog duty

and crossed the Willamette by way of the Hawthorne Bridge. The Arsenal looked busy with better than half the parking lot full. I reached the entry just as Roz Jenkins was seeing off a group of about a dozen women, mostly middle-aged and well-groomed. "Hello, Calvin," she greeted me from inside the building. I smiled, nodded, and made way past the women. "That's my Tea and Targets group," she explained as I entered the Arsenal. "We get together every week to have coffee and tea, to chat, and to shoot."

"Oh, they all shoot pink Glocks, I suppose."

She chuckled and shook her head. "Some do. It's a damn fine gun but a bit prissy for my taste, and spendy, too." She turned and said over her shoulder, "Come on. Let's get started."

I followed her through the showroom. The young saleswoman with the tight jeans was showing some kind of assault rifle to three admiring young men. I couldn't tell which they admired the most, the gun or the girl.

As we walked by I thought I recognized the boots the young girl wore.

After we both donned ear and eye protection, Roz led me to a firing lane midway down the range and watched as I loaded the clip with seventeen 9x19mm Parabellum cartridges and set the trigger safety. "Good," she said. "Now, remember, unless you're aiming at the target, keep the barrel down." After demonstrating the proper two-handed grip, she said, "Keep the barrel level when you aim, and put the front sight blade in the center of the rear notch; equal light on both sides." She handed me the Glock. "The target's set at thirty-five feet. Let's see what you've got."

She watched as I fired off several rounds, the sharp recoil a vivid reminder of the energy being unleashed. She smiled broadly. "Not bad, Cal. Widen your stance a bit. Relax, aim using both sights, and *squeeze* off the shots." The pattern on the target got a little tighter.

As I reloaded the clip for the third time, Roz Jenkins beamed. "Don't you just love that Glock?"

I nodded, admittedly flushed by the display of the gun's power and precision, but I was yet to feel any romantic involvement.

She laughed, full throated, sensing my hesitation. "Listen to me. God, I'm such a zealot. That gun's not evil, you know. It's just a block of steel. It takes a human being to misuse it."

I wanted to say it's more complicated than that but thought better of it. I was considering a more neutral reply when I saw Arthur striding toward us. He gave me what passed for a smile. "Mr. Claxton, welcome to the Arsenal."

"Thanks." I finished loading the clip and snapped it in place. "Roz here is a good instructor." I squared up and fired off a half dozen shots that ripped the target in a reasonably tight pattern around the bull's eye.

Roz whooped. "Look at that! He's a natural, Arthur."

Arthur said, "Not bad. Put the target at fifty feet, see how he does." I did okay at fifty feet, then reloaded and offered the Glock to Arthur, barrel down. He proceeded to quickly and efficiently obliterate any trace of the bull's eye.

Roz whooped again. "Nice shootin', Arthur!" She turned to me. "Whataya think of that, Cal?"

"Impressive." And it was.

Arthur handed the Glock back to me. "Jack Pfister tells me you're looking at becoming a gun trust lawyer."

"Yeah. I checked it out. Looks like a nice growth opportunity. If you've got some time, I'd love to pick your brain, you know, about the business."

He looked at his watch and frowned. "I don't know. I'm kind of jammed."

"Oh, come on, Arthur. You're not that busy." Roz to my rescue once again. "The movement needs good lawyers."

The movement?

I thanked Roz and followed Arthur to his office, just down from his mother-in-law's. He took a call, so I checked out his gun collection. The Thompson submachine gun hung in a glass case surrounded by an array of other weapons, a hulking World War I era Browning Automatic Rifle, a Kalashnikov AK-47 with its familiar forward-curved ammo clip, an M-16 assault rifle used in Vietnam, to name three. The opposite wall sported a collection of old flintlock pistols, tiny derringers, and long-barreled six shooters.

"Some collection," I said when he punched off.

He flicked a wrist indifferently. "Oh, thanks. I enjoy collecting."

"I didn't know a derringer could be so small."

Arthur smiled indulgently. "Yes, small but deadly. One shot's all you need if your aim's good."

"You ever shoot one of these little guys?"

He nodded. "I've shot all the guns in my collection. They're all in perfect working order." He sat ramrod straight in his chair and regarded me with pale, almost colorless eyes. "I read in the paper that they arrested a man for that shooting you were investigating."

I smiled brightly. "Yes. The ex-husband. Surprise, surprise."

"What about that kid who was going to drive for Roz?"

"Manny Bonilla?" I shrugged. "I don't really know. Suicide, maybe. Who knows?"

He leaned back in his chair, steepled his fingers, and looked as if he wasn't sure what to say next. I didn't help him. "So," he finally ventured, "a gun trust lawyer, huh?"

I smiled modestly. "Oh, you know, I have a small practice, so every little bit helps. I'm interested in your take on the business."

Arthur suddenly became animated, and as if reading from an invisible PowerPoint script began dazzling me with facts and figures about the growing gun market. He even made a little joke about his "bullet proof" business plan before going through it in mind-numbing detail. He capped it all off by telling me how the gun business was a shining example of the capitalist system and a boon for the American way of life. I took on a gee-whiz air and popped in enough questions and comments to demonstrate the sincerity of my interest.

The bottom line—if I were smart I'd develop a business plan of my own and get in on the gravy train.

As the conversation began to wind down I said, "I understand you have a workshop here at the Arsenal where you do gun repairs and recycle ammo, that sort of thing. I'd love to see your operation."

Arthur smiled, but his eyes didn't. He straightened back up in his chair. "Sorry, Cal, but we only allow our workers in the shop area. That's a strict rule. Safety, you know."

I smiled back. "Of course." This was the opening I was looking for. I wasn't quite sure how to play it, so I just barged ahead. "That reminds me. Did Bonilla receive some kind of training here at the Arsenal?" It never hurts to ask.

Arthur's smile withered, and his eyes went as flat as a couple of nickels. "Of course not. He can't work here. He's a felon."

I smiled. "Oops. Shows you how much I have to learn."

"Where did you hear that?"

I paused and furrowed my brow. "I think his step-father mentioned something," I lied. I left it at that and waited for a response.

Arthur gripped two fingers of his left hand in his right palm and twisted, as if that would force a smile. It didn't. "Well, he never worked for us, period." Then he forced his hands apart and flattened them on the surface of the desk. "Look, uh, Cal, I'm a busy man. I wish you all the luck in your law practice."

I gave him my best sheepish smile. "Well, there I go, asking too many questions. Bad habit of mine." I popped up and offered my hand. "Thanks for your time, Arthur, and good luck with that business plan."

On my way out I stopped at Roz Jenkins's office and stuck my head in. "Thanks again for the shooting lesson, Roz. Am I good to go on the range now?"

She looked up from a desk spread with papers and smiled. "You bet. Keep it up and I'll be after you for our shooting team."

I gave her an aw-shucks laugh. "Arthur gave me some great insights. Tried to get a tour of your shop, but he was too busy."

"Don't feel bad. He's tight as a tick about security and safety." She laughed. "Even with me."

I nodded agreement. "Say, did your salesgirl out there on the floor have on a pair of those custom boots, the ones you were wearing the other day?"

"Probably. They're popular around here. It works both ways, too. The bootmaker and his crowd are regular customers at the Arsenal."

"You don't say. Uh, that would be Farnell Timmons, right?"

"Right." Then she added, "There's a pro-gun rally this Sunday down on the river, Tom McCall Park." Her face lit up with a bright smile. "I'm gonna speak. You should come, Cal. Three o'clock."

I told her I would and left the Arsenal that day feeling drained. That much acting in one day will do that to you.

But at the same time I knew I was on to something, something I would have to see through no matter where it led me. It wasn't a particularly comforting thought.

THIRTY-FIVE

Kelly

KELLY SPENT THE next week watching the newspaper, hoping to see the Anthony Cardenas's arrest lead to the arrest of the other man involved in Rupert Young-blood's murder. Each day without any news ratcheted up her anxiety until she felt like a rocket on a launch pad in the middle of a countdown. What should she do? Going to the cops would wreck everything that she and Veronica had managed to put together. She even caught herself worrying about what would become of the mutt if they got busted. Spencer was ugly and ill-mannered, but at least he wasn't yappy. That would have been too much.

The situation with Zook wasn't any better. On Thursday of that week, when he still hadn't shown at the alternative school, Kelly and Kiyana went looking for him over in north Portland at an abandoned house. The house, they were told, was being squatted by Johnny Sprague and some of his friends. Zook had been seen there. They found him a half block down from the house, talking to a skinny kid with bleached hair. The kid sauntered off as they approached, and Zook put something in his jeans.

"S'up, Zook?" Kelly said. "Haven't seen you around at school."

Zook, whose blond stubble was maybe three days old, wore grimy jeans and a stained, too-small fleece jacket Kelly had never seen before. His ever-present basketball was nowhere to be seen. He dropped his eyes, then brought them back up. "What are you two doing here?"

"No, Zook," Kiyana shot back, "what are *you* doing here?"

"Yeah," Kelly added, "I mean hanging with a dirt-bag like Sprague. Are you kidding me?"

Zook raised his hands and uncurled his long fingers in mock surrender. "Hey, no worries. Everything's cool."

"What about basketball practice?" Kelly said.

"Uh, I've missed a few, but it's no problem. They still love me there."

"And school? You've missed a few there, too."

He tried to give his boyish smile, but it came out strained. "Yeah, well, I'm taking a sabbatical."

That did it. Anger, frustration, and worry collided in Kelly's head in a critical mass so strong she completely lost it. "You idiot," she screamed as she began pounding on Zook's chest with both fists. "You had a good plan and you're just throwing it all away. How can you be so stupid?" Her face flushed red, tears welled up and streamed down her cheeks, and her nose began to run.

"Whoa." Zook took a step back, his eyes wide with surprise.

Kiyana stepped in, grabbed Kelly by both shoulders, and pulled her back. "Hey, baby girl, chill out." Kelly dropped her hands, turned to Kiyana and continued to cry uncontrollably. Kiyana embraced her friend and held her until the sobbing ceased. When she looked up, Zook was gone.

Kiyana stepped back but continued to hold her friend at arm's length. "Okay, talk to me. What's wrong, besides Zook being an idiot?"

Kelly tried to speak, but the sobs kicked back in. Finally, she managed to choke out, "*Everything's* wrong, that's what. Now Zook thinks I'm crazy, too."

Kiyana shook her head. "Look, Kel, if Zook makes bad decisions, it's *not* on you. You can't stop him from screwing his life up. Nobody can do that but Zook."

Kelly sniffed hard and wiped her cheeks on her sleeve. "I know that."

Kiyana met Kelly's eyes. "It's more than just Zook, isn't it?"

The desire to confide in her friend washed over Kelly stronger than ever. But the image of Rupert's lifeless body filled her head, and she held back.

When she didn't respond, Kiyana shrugged but was unable to hide the disappointment in her eyes. "Okay, you don't want to tell me, I can respect that. But remember, Kel, I'm here for you, no matter what."

LATE THAT FRIDAY afternoon Kelly finally made up her mind. She walked over to the Multnomah County Library on SW Tenth and queued up for a computer console. The line was long, so she tried a couple of games of Osmos on her phone. But she was too nervous to concentrate. *Was she doing the right thing? Or was it just too late?*

She went back and forth with herself, but thirty minutes later when a slot opened up she logged in to a website called Hide My Ass!, opened an anonymous account, and wrote an email to that attorney over at Caffeine Central, the one Kiyana told her about.

Kelly sat there for a long time reading the message over and over. When she finally hit the send button she felt tears coming on. *Sheeze*, she told herself, *no more crying.* But her eyes welled up and spilled over before she could stop them. The sense of relief was overwhelming.

She dabbed her eyes quickly and straightened up in her chair. *Maybe he's there at Caffeine Central right now*, she told herself. *Maybe he'll answer me.*

The library was so quiet it seemed deafening. She waited.

THIRTY-SIX

Cal

That same Friday

As COLDER WEATHER sets in in Portland some of the homeless find their way to warmer climes. The ones that stay become more desperate, and the potential for bad things to happen goes up sharply, and so does my caseload at Caffeine Central. It was the day after my visit to Bridgetown Arsenal, and I was so swamped I skipped Arch's midmorning walk. At noon I taped a hastily written "Back at 2" sign on the door, took Arch on a quick trek around the block, and then headed for a lunch date with Jack Pfister.

"No, you can't go," I explained to a clearly disappointed Archie before I left. "The restaurant doesn't allow dogs, and it's too cold to sit outside." Reasoning with your dog is always a good idea.

I suggested the lunch, but Pfister picked the venue, a trendy little joint in Northeast called Toro Bravo. That was fine with me, because it was a short drive, although I worried I'd have to pick up the bill. You can't eat cheap at that tapas restaurant despite the small serving sizes. Wearing a conservative blue suit and understated striped tie, he smiled when I approached his table, but his hawk eyes held reserve.

"So," I said as I sat down, "I expected you to pick a place in Oregon City."

He raised one corner of his mouth and shook his head. "Culinary wasteland. Actually, I'd move my practice to Portland in a heartbeat, but my client base tends to be outside the city."

I nodded. "More gun owners, huh?"

"Right. And folks who are a lot more passionate about the Second Amendment." He gave me a conspiratorial smile. "Rednecks love their guns, and I love my rednecks."

I bit my tongue and smiled back. The waiter came and we ordered a selection of tapas and a bottle of Rioja. I managed to deflect some of his sales pitch on his foundation, A Hand Up, explaining that I was already doing pro bono work in the inner city. He took it well, considering this was probably the only reason he agreed to see me. What he did say left me with the impression that he viewed his mentoring work like some kind of merit badge, an effort that would be good for business and perhaps guarantee a happy afterlife. *Don't judge*, I told myself. *Consider the actions, not the motives.*

When I nudged the conversation around to my budding interest in gun trusting, Pfister launched into a recitation on the financial benefits with a kind of evangelical fervor. I learned how my practice in Dundee was ideally positioned to serve the Willamette Valley, how the valley was replete with gun owners anxious about their Second Amendment rights, and what sections of the law I'd have to brush up on.

It was a familiar message—the market was up,

and the gravy train was moving down the tracks. All I needed to do was hitch on.

Thank God for the Rioja. I drank two glasses before he finished.

When the waiter brought our tapas I changed the subject. "You're probably curious about the Manny Bonilla situation." I was surprised he hadn't brought the subject up.

Pfister took a bite of empanada with chorizo and slid from his lawyer persona back to his mentor persona without missing a beat. "Oh, yes. I read about the arrest. What's the latest?" I gave him the Bonilla-probably-killed-himself version. When I finished, he said, "I don't buy that. He didn't seem despondent."

"When did you see him last?"

He drank some wine. "Oh, maybe two weeks before he died."

I swallowed a bite of seared scallop, and without seeming to press casually asked a couple of questions about the job he'd gotten Manny with Roz Jenkins. That didn't earn me any new information, so I tried a different tack. "I guess as his mentor you must have visited Manny at Sheridan, you know, to help get him into the Reentry program."

"Well, I handled his case, so it was no problem getting in to see him."

"Were you aware that he was known to be associating with a man named Javier Acedo, an inmate with hard-core cartel connections?"

A good lawyer knows how to control his facial expressions. Pfister's face stayed neutral, but his eyes flared for just an instant. Was he surprised I knew about Acedo or just the implications of the question? No verdict.

"Who told you that?"

"Oh, something I picked up from Claudia Borrego's fiancé, the private eye. He has sources inside Sheridan." There I go, lying again.

Pfister laughed. "Well, that's absurd. I would've heard about it. I've got sources, too. And I would've never placed him if that were true."

I nodded. "Did Manny get any training for his new job, you know, from Arthur?"

"Not that I heard."

"Nothing at the Bridgetown Arsenal?"

His laugh was laced with incredulity. "Are you kidding me? As a felon he's not allowed to set foot inside the building. He'd be breaking a federal statute."

"Arthur wouldn't bend that rule? Maybe Manny had a needed skill set, you know, he had a good mechanical aptitude."

"Look, even if Arthur wanted to train him for some bizarre reason, Roz would never allow it on the premises. She knows the law."

"Roz isn't at the Arsenal all that much these days."

He smiled and shook his head. "Look, we're talking about Arthur here. If Roz or that ugly daughter of hers says, 'Shit,' Arthur says, 'What color?' Where'd you get such a crazy idea, anyway?"

I laughed and waved a hand. "Don't mind me. I ask too many questions."

Jack Pfister didn't show it, but I'm sure I left him wondering about me that day. He thought he came to recruit a volunteer but wound up getting the third degree. Or he was up to his neck in something and now he knew I was nibbling around the edges. I wasn't sure which. In any case the guy was a piece of work. *But we're all bundles of contradictions*, I reminded myself.

One plus-mark in Pfister's column—the tapas and Rioja were damn good, and he insisted on picking up the check.

On the way back to Caffeine Central I idly wondered why the car behind me—a dark sedan, a Ford Taurus, I think—made sure he stayed on my tail by bolting through a yellow-turning-red light I'd just sailed through. I thought of ATF special agent Richie Truax. Maybe he got himself a new car. But then the sedan turned off. *Don't get paranoid*, I told myself.

I let myself into the office, left a voice mail for Tay Jefferson, and was attacking some long-overdue paperwork when someone rapped on the front door. I was officially closed, so, grumbling about people not reading the posted hours, I got up and answered the door. Tay stood smiling at me in spandex, a fleece jacket, and jogging shoes, a sheen of sweat on her face. Archie went around me to greet her. She dropped to one knee, hugged him, and then looked up at me. "Got your message. I had the afternoon off and was running the river. Thought I'd see if I could catch you." She laughed. "I love the graffiti outside. I'm surprised it's still up there."

She was referring to the anti-zero-tolerance piece K209 had left on the side wall of the building. I chuckled. "Yeah, that piece was considered evidence at one point. I think it got lost in the system."

"You never found the tagger, huh?"

"Nope. It's a shame, too. He's the only witness to Claudia's murder."

Tay lifted a teasing half smile. *"He?"*

I smiled back a bit sheepishly and shook my head. "Okay. I don't know for sure. What pronoun do you want me to use, *it*?" I went on to tell her about Brent Gunderson's burglary, my visit to the Arsenal, and my lunch with Jack Pfister. I left out the part about my having a copy of Bonilla's notebook. I trusted Tay, but she didn't need to know that.

When I finished, she said, "So Manny was involved in something illegal at this gun shop, and you think that got him killed. Do the police know about this?"

"They have the same information I have."

"Then what's the connection between his murder and Claudia's?"

"I still don't know. I think Claudia got caught in the middle. Probably tried to help him or knew too much."

Tay shook her head and blew a breath in disgust. "No good deed goes unpunished."

"Something like that."

Still frowning she asked, "How does this connect to Anthony Cardenas?"

"You asked me that before. I still don't know."

Her eyes narrowed, and she shot me a skeptical look. "Are you suggesting he didn't do it?"

I shrugged. Nobody wanted to hear that. "That ship has sailed. I'm just focused on what happened to Bonilla. Which reminds me, have you heard anything more about his relationship with Javier Acedo?"

"No. The line went dead on that."

"Any chance you can get me the visitation records

for Bonilla when he was at Sheridan?" She gave me a quizzical look. "If he was some kind of conduit between Acedo and the outside, I'd like to know who was calling the shots. I know Pfister visited him, but who else?"

We were wrapping up when, out of habit I guess, I glanced at my computer screen, which was open to my email inbox. A new message with the subject line "Rupert Youngblood Murder" had come in from someone using the name "Witness." Needless to say, those words caught my eye. I asked Tay to excuse me while I opened the message.

I know some stuff about the murder of Rupert Young-blood. I want to help but I can't use my name. A friend said you might be able to help. If you are interested, reply to this email. It can't be traced so don't even try.

"Huh," I said. "Take a look at this."

Tay got up, came around the desk, and bent over my shoulder to read the email. "Who's Rupert Young-blood, anyway?"

"I don't know."

"Hang on, I'll check." She took her phone from her jacket and a few beats later said, "Found it in *The Oregonian*. He was a homeless man…found beaten to death at a deserted granary on Naito Parkway… on October 18."

"Let's see if the sender's still online." I hit reply and sent the following message:

I am interested in helping you. What do you know about this murder?

A minute later this came through:

The guy who shot Claudia Borrego also killed Rupert
with the help of another man.

"Whoa!" I said to Tay, "Look at this."
She leaned into the screen. "Oh, my God. Do you
think it's a prank?"
"I don't know. Let's see what else comes through."

How do you know this?

I saw the guy shoot Claudia Borrego. I saw the same
guy leave the granary with another dude right after
Rupert was killed. Rupert was killed because he
wouldn't give me up. They tortured him.

Tay squeezed my shoulder with her hand and
leaned in closer to the screen. My pulse rate ramped
up.

Tell me something that wasn't in the newspapers.

After an agonizing pause, this came back:

I was tagging the building when he shot the woman.
He shot at me, too. Five or six times. I got away by hiding in the Dumpster in the alley behind the building.

I pictured the alley behind the building where
Claudia was shot. Yes, there was a Dumpster there. I
looked around at Tay, my mouth agape. "My God, I
think I'm talking to K209."

THIRTY-SEVEN

Kelly

KELLY'S HANDS HAD trembled as she typed the messages to Cal Claxton, messages that essentially revealed she was K209, her closest-kept secret. She knew it was necessary, but it made her panicky, like she was somehow losing control. She gnawed at the cuticle on her right thumb and stared at the computer screen, waiting for a reply. Finally it came:

You must be K209. If you are, I'm advising you to come forward and tell the police what you know. If you're worried about the tagging violations, I'll be glad to help you deal with the police.

Kelly's heart sank with the feeling she'd made a horrible mistake. *Come forward? Are you kidding me? I should have known*, she told herself. It wouldn't be so simple. Nothing ever is. She sat there for the longest time trying to decide how to respond. Finally, she squared up at the keyboard and wrote:

I thought attorneys had to keep stuff confidential. I can't come forward. If you tell the police, I swear I will disappear. I want to make sure that Rupert's murder isn't just forgotten about because he was homeless. That's why I'm asking for your help.

An equally long time elapsed before Claxton's reply appeared on her screen:

Okay. I agree to do what I can to help you and keep this confidential. Who are you and what else can you tell me about both murders?

A warning came up on her screen saying she had seven minutes of screen-time left. She sent a hasty final note to Claxton telling him she would be in touch the next day around the same time. She felt relieved that she'd timed out. She needed time to think about the next session. A stupid mistake could give too much away.

It was still light out when Kelly descended the expansive front steps of the Central Library and joined the afternoon rush hour. By the time she caught the bus the streetlights were on, and tentative reflections began playing on the river. Kelly caught sight of the shadowy form of a lone kayaker moving upriver and felt an immediate kinship. She was fighting to stay upright, too, and the going was against the current.

A sign in the window of the audio components shop on the first floor of Kelly's building greeted her: CLOSED UNTIL FURTHER NOTICE. Now she remembered that Veronica had said something about the owner being busted for selling stolen equipment from the shop. Kelly checked the mailbox in the narrow vestibule and headed up the creaking stairs to the landing on the second floor. She heard a noise, glanced up, and froze. A man was standing on the third floor facing her apartment door. He turned and smiled at her. "Hi. You must be Kelly."

"Uh, yeah. Who are you?"

"I'm a friend of Veronica's. Larry." He had dark, shaggy hair, a three-day growth and both arms sleeved in ink.

Just then Veronica appeared, all smiles. "Come up and say hi, Kel." When Kelly reached the third floor, Veronica said, "Go on in, Larry. There's cold beer in the fridge." When he did Veronica turned to Kelly and said in a low, urgent voice, "I invited him to dinner, Kel. I like him a lot." She thrust out her hand, a pleading look in her eye. "Here's twenty. Go out and get yourself a nice dinner and take in a movie or something."

Kelly pushed her hand away. "Keep your money. I'll see you later." As she started down the stairs, she added over her shoulder, "Don't let him sleep over, Veronica. It's the first date."

Kelly went back out on the street. It was clear, but nightfall had sharply chilled the air. She fished a light fleece jacket from her backpack, put it on, and walked around the building to the alleyway. Three blocks down, she had to duck into the shadows to let a giggling young couple pass by. Then she was up and away, her hands and feet welcoming the cold, dry touch of the granite cornerstones of her refuge. As she climbed the cares of that day began to melt away.

She summited a couple of minutes later, her breath smooth and deep and her mind clear, although she was still pissed at Veronica. As she sat watching the Friday night traffic on Sandy Boulevard, she thought about the contact she'd made with the lawyer, Claxton, and began planning what she would tell him the next day. The more she thought about the exchange, the better she felt. Kiyana was probably right. She could trust the lawyer, but there was no way she was giving him her name. *That's not going to happen*, she vowed, *no matter what he promises*.

Her thoughts turned to Zook, and she began to feel anxious. She needed to find him and apologize for her outburst. Maybe it's not as bad as you think, she told herself. Maybe he's just working his way through a rough patch. When she did find him, she would invite him over for dinner. And Veronica could clear out and go to a damn movie. Yeah, that's what she'd do.

THIRTY-EIGHT

Cal

AFTER THE K209 messages went silent, Tay and I sat in my office reading back through the email string. Tay gave me a now familiar skeptical look when we finished. "You know, you didn't get all that much proof that that was K209."

I nodded. "Yeah, now that the excitement's wearing off, I see your point. The only new thing I learned about Claudia's shooting was the fact that the tagger got away by hiding in the Dumpster behind the building. There's a Dumpster back there, all right, but that's no secret."

Tay smiled, a vestige of skepticism still visible. "I hope somebody's not laughing up their sleeve at you."

"I doubt it. The connection to Youngblood's murder is pretty compelling. I mean, why would someone lie about that?"

"Good point. I wonder how Youngblood got mixed up in this?"

"That'll have to wait until tomorrow. See if anything else comes in."

She straightened up in her chair. "Mind if I sit in?"

I figured that question was coming. I shifted in my seat and leaned forward. "I'm, uh, in an awkward legal position here, Tay. Even a lawyer's required to come forward in this situation. My out is that I don't know whether this is legit or not."

"And you promised the kid you wouldn't reveal anything."

"I said I'd do what I can to keep it confidential."

She fixed me with those honey-brown eyes of hers. "You can trust me, Cal. And I've got some skin in this game, too, you know."

I told Tay to come back the next day and we would see what happens. I knew I could trust her. That wasn't the reason for my hesitancy. I had a sense this thing could get dangerous, and I didn't want her to become more exposed. But there was no way I could say no to this strong, willful woman, and frankly I was glad she was in my corner.

After seeing Tay off I followed Archie up the stairs to the apartment. He was hungry, and come to think of it, so was I. I fed him and then cut up some carrots, new potatoes, sweet onions, and red bell pepper, slathered them with olive oil to which I added rosemary, garlic, and salt and pepper, and tossed them into a hot oven. Twenty minutes later I seared a small steak in a cast-iron skillet and served it up with the veggies and a glass of Carabella pinot noir. Dinner.

I took Archie out afterward, and, of course, he headed straight for the river, his favorite place in the city. The air was crisp and still, and the river held the reflections of the city lights with such clarity it was impossible to tell where the city left off and the river began. Just as we reached Caffeine Central on the way back, a black Ford Taurus like the one I saw earlier that day pulled up to the curb. A passenger-side window slid down and ATF Special Agent Richie Truax nodded to me.

I turned and leaned into his window. "Like your new ride."

He cracked a minute smile. "Well, you know how the government is. The budget money just flows in abundance. Why don't you park your dog and get in?"

I dropped Archie's leash and told him to sit and stay, and got in the Taurus. Truax wore gray slacks and a blue blazer he'd outgrown fifteen pounds ago. His deep-set eyes regarded me with perhaps a little less hostility than our last encounter. The minute smile showed again. "I saw that Portland made an arrest in the Borrego murder. You and your Cuban buddy must be pleased."

I smiled. "A fine example of our tax dollars at work."

His brow grew a few creases. "So, it's all good, right? No more mucking around?"

I nodded emphatically. "Right." I had a good idea what he was driving at, so I added. "One good thing has come out of this. I've discovered that the firearms market offers a real business opportunity for me. I'm planning to add gun trusting to my practice out in Dundee. Working up a business plan right now."

Truax shook his head. "Oh, wonderful, just what we need—another gun trust lawyer in the world." When I gave him a questioning look, he said, "The federal regs have a huge loophole that allows gun nuts to buy restricted weapons through a trust. You didn't know that, Claxton?"

I shrugged. "I'm, uh, still doing my due diligence."

He shook his head. "Well, it's a real pain in the ass

for us. Dealers aren't even required to do background checks on representatives of a trust when they buy firearms. It's insane."

I let Truax vent, and we tossed a few questions back and forth. Finally, he handed me a card. "Look, Claxton, you see anything weird going on out there, just call me at this number, okay?"

I said I would, and as I got out turned back to him and said, "I remember the California-USC game in eighty-five. You must have made sixteen, eighteen tackles that day."

He smiled ruefully. "Yeah, well, we still lost that game. Don't tell me you're a Berkeley grad."

"Boalt Law School."

He laughed, a sharp clap. "That explains a lot." Then he drove off.

"Well, big guy," I said to Arch, "do you think he bought it?" Maybe I should have told Truax everything I knew at that juncture, but I didn't have anything conclusive. And something in my gut told me to hold back until I had a better picture of what the hell was going on at the Bridgetown Arsenal.

TAY STROLLED INTO my office the next day wearing jeans, a black turtleneck sweater, and a bright smile. Tough and sexy looking without even trying. "Well, do you think K209 will show?"

"I'm hoping." While Tay watched my computer screen, and Archie watched her from his corner, I went upstairs and made us cappuccinos. We sipped our coffees and waited, and at 10:13 a message pinged into my inbox:

Hello, Mr. Claxton. I'm here now. Sorry I can't tell you who I am. But I promise to tell you the truth about what I know.

   I replied:

Okay. Fair enough. Start with the Claudia Borrego shooting. What did you see?

   What followed was a detailed account of what K209 saw that night, then this exchange:

Did you report this to the police?

Yes. Rupert Youngblood phoned it in to the cops for me. I was too freaked out to do that.

Did Rupert tell the police that the shooter used a silencer?

Yes, I think so. I told him about the silencer.

So, the shooter had a medium build, wore a ball cap and cowboy boots, and had a distinctive walk. Is that all you remember?

Yes. I think that's it.

Did you see a picture of the man arrested for the shooting in the paper? Was this the man you saw?

I saw the picture. Sorry. I'm not sure if it's him. I only saw the shooter from the back. I think I could recognize him if I saw him walking around. He has a macho strut like he's Mr. Cool or something.

Tay groaned and I said, "Crap. He can't ID Cardenas."

Okay. No problem. Now tell me about the Rupert Youngblood murder.

Tay and I put our heads together and read the account. Our attention was riveted, of course, by the disclosure that the shooter had worn a jacket with the Bridgetown Arsenal logo on the back.

Are you sure about the logo on the jacket?

Yes. Positive.

Did you report all this to the police?

I called 911 with a burner phone. I told them I was cutting through the parking lot and heard screams coming from the building. I said I didn't want to get involved. I didn't say anything about the other murder. My bad.

That's okay. You're doing a great job. Just to be clear: The man who shot Claudia has a distinctive walk you think you might recognize, but you did not see his face. And you did not get a good look at the other man who was present at the granary, but you think you could recognize his voice. Is this right?

Yes. There is something else. I watched the Arsenal for a while from a hiding place. I think I saw the shooter there once but I'm not sure. The other guy was there once, too. I'm sure I heard his voice.

Did you get a look at the other man?

No. Sorry. It was dark.

"Oh, man," I said to Tay, "I don't like that one bit."

I strongly advise you not to go near the Bridgetown Arsenal until this gets cleared up. And I urge you again to come forward. Your life may be in danger. Come to my office here at Caffeine Central and we'll talk about how to handle the police.

As soon as I hit the send button I wished I could have the message back. "Hope I didn't overplay my hand."

Sure enough. Tay and I sat staring at the computer for a long time, but no other messages came through. I said, "Damn it," and bounced a ballpoint pen off the office door across the room. Archie got up, looked at me with concern, and whimpered a couple of times. "Should have kept him talking."

Tay said, "Don't worry. I think you played it about as well as you could have. The kid's very cautious. Must have a pretty good reason for not giving a name. I have a feeling it's more than just the fear of being prosecuted for tagging."

"I agree. What else did you pick up?"

"Very bright, writes coherently, mid-teens, my

guess, fourteen to seventeen, maybe." She stopped here and gave me that sly smile. "And I think you're looking for a girl."

"*A girl?* How come?"

"Just the overall tone, Cal, and the line—'macho strut like he was Mr. Cool'—gives it away. And she's very observant, too, something teenage boys aren't known for. Trust me on this."

I paused for a couple of beats as her words sunk in. My mind flashed to Claire, my daughter, who shared some of the qualities I sensed in K209, and I felt a twinge of embarrassment mixed with shame. How could I have been so blind? "Of course, Tay. I think you're right—a smart, observant girl who's also athletic and gutsy as hell."

She nodded back. "That's what I think. What about her story?"

"Well, K209's not going to make a good witness in court, that's for sure. Recognizing someone by the way he walks or by his voice wouldn't hold much water in a court of law. So that's disappointing. But connecting the guy who shot Claudia to the Bridgetown Arsenal is huge. This thing's a big circle, and that damn gun shop's smack in the middle." I rubbed my ribs, which were still a little sore and discolored. "And I may have met the shooter, too."

Tay looked at me with surprise. *"You have?"*

I went on to describe my encounter with the one-boot cowboy in Claudia's apartment and to explain that K209's description might fit, although it had been too dark for me to recognize my attacker.

She gave me that one-sided smile. "I wondered

what happened to you. Anything else you haven't told me?"

I shook my head and smiled back. "No, partner. You know what I know now."

Her smile turned from sardonic to warm. "Okay, so if Cardenas is the shooter, then he must be somehow connected to the gun shop, right?"

"Yeah, but there's no evidence of that. Could be he's the *other* guy, the one who helped kill Young-blood."

"Why do you say that?"

"I'm having a hard time picturing Cardenas wearing a jacket with a logo on the back. Definitely not his style. The guy's into looking cool. And I don't think he was the one who tried to disembowel me. More likely he hired the man in the jacket to shoot Claudia and then went with him to beat the identity of K209 out of Rupert Youngblood. That is, if he's involved at all."

Tay shot me another half smile. "Still doubt that, huh?"

I shrugged. "I'd feel better if I could find a connection between him and what's going on at the Arsenal. Whatever the hell that is."

Tay nodded, then sighed deeply. "God, the thought of them torturing that poor man Youngblood. And to think he didn't tell them who the tagger is. What an act of heroism!"

I nodded. "You can understand why K209 doesn't want him forgotten. But what bothers me most of all is that she's still out there, and so is at least one of the killers. And the killers probably think she knows more than she really does."

Tay's eyes flared and she moved a hand to her mouth unconsciously. "Oh, my God, you're right, Cal. We've got to find her."

THIRTY-NINE

Kelly

KELLY LEFT THE library with her head down and her stomach tied in a knot. She had told Claxton everything she knew about both murders and answered all his questions. But apparently that wasn't enough, because he kept telling her to give herself up. *Can't he just go to the cops now and tell them that the dude, Cardenas, helped kill Rupert?* she asked herself. *Wouldn't that make it easy to catch the other guy, The Voice? What part of "I'm not giving you my name" did he not understand?*

And he tried to scare her, too. Was someone else still out there trying to find her? "Well, they haven't found me so far," she blurted out with enough volume that a young man passing on the street turned to look at her. But the truth was, she spoke with more bravado than she felt deep down.

It was getting late, but there was something else she needed to do. Kelly walked over to NW Everett, caught the number 44 bus at Fifth, and got off on Killingsworth in North Portland, a block from where she last saw Zook. The sky to the west had darkened to a purplish-gray like spoiled fruit, and she could smell rain in the air. The house where Sprague was squatting was dark by design. Squatters always made sure no light could get in or out of the windows in the rooms they used. The place was small, one story, and set back on the lot behind shin-high weeds and a couple of maples that had shed their leaves.

Kelly followed a pocked asphalt driveway to the rear of the house, took the back steps, and tried the door. It was open and warm, and the smell of urine stung her nostrils. She could see a dim light somewhere toward the front of the house. "Zook," she called out. "Zook, it's Kelly. Are you in there? Is anybody in there?"

She heard the floorboards creak and someone say something low and unintelligible. "Zook?" she called out again. She heard the muffled voice again. She wanted to turn around and get out of there but was determined to find Zook and make it right, or at least talk to him. She followed a darkened hallway past the kitchen on her left, which was stripped bare and littered with beer cans, pizza boxes, and fast-food wrappers. A door to a bathroom on her right was open, a hole in the floor marking where the toilet had been. She could smell sewer gases. Ahead on her left a light shown through the gap in a partially open door that probably led to the dining room.

"Zook. Are you in there? It's Kel."

She heard a noise, maybe chair legs scraping the floor. Somebody was in there.

Kelly opened the door and stepped in. Black garbage bags were taped on the windows, and an anemic propane lamp flickered in a corner, illuminating a couple of backpacks, rolled up sleeping bags, and a long skateboard propped against the wall. The longboard looked familiar. Johnny Sprague stood across

the room, partly in shadow. Kelly sucked a half breath
when she saw him and forced a smile. "Hey, Sprague.
Um, have you seen Zook?"

The corners of his mouth tilted up slightly. "He's
around here somewhere. Probably loaded, as usual."

Kelly felt a rush of relief, but it was cut short
when the door closed behind her. She spun around
and found herself face-to-face with Digger. "'S'up,
Kelly? Zook's, uh, sleeping it off upstairs. Maybe
Sprague and I can be of service."

Sprague laughed. "Yeah. There must be something
we can do for you, little girl."

"No, thanks. I, uh, just wanted to talk to him. Upstairs, huh?"

Sprague said, "Oh, he left strict orders for us not
to disturb him."

"Okay." Kelly took a step toward Digger, who remained standing in front of the door.

Digger's only movement was to cross his arms
at his chest. "What's your hurry, Kel? We got beer,
weed, you can shoot up on the house, anything you
want. You and me never had that party, you know."

"Move, Digger, I'm leaving."

"Oh, come on," he said, "you know you want to
party."

Anger and fear rose in Kelly in equal measure,
and she struggled to keep her voice from wavering.
"Get out of my way, please." She took another step,
felt a hand on her shoulder, and spun around. "Don't
touch me, Sprague."

"Whoa, the little girl's got a temper. That's such a
turn-on, isn't it, Digger?"

"Sure is," Digger said, as he wrapped his arms

around Kelly's waist and pulled her against his body. Kelly screamed and threw an elbow that caught Digger by surprise, hitting him flush on the chin. He cried out and loosened his grip just enough for her to spin free.

But Sprague grabbed her by both wrists before she could make it out the door. "Stop it," she screamed and kicked at him as he pulled her down and pinned her on the floor.

"Zook! Help me! Zoo—" Sprague clamped a big hand over her mouth and nose and suddenly Kelly could no longer breathe. Panic welled up in her, tears flooded her eyes, and she kept kicking with everything she had. But she was no match for Sprague, who was tearing at her clothes with his other hand.

Kelly's vision began to tunnel down, and her strength was nearly gone when she heard a door burst open somewhere in the distance.

"Get off her, Sprague." Zook's voice echoed down the tunnel. Then Sprague cried out, and she saw a blurry image as his head snapped back before his weight came off her. She lay there stunned, trying to breathe again. Digger cursed and when she looked up, he had locked Zook's arms to his sides from behind.

Sprague sprang to his feet. "Hold him, Digger." He punched Zook once, twice, in the face, hard. "Man, you really know how to kill a buzz," he said as he continued hitting him.

Kelly crawled on her hands and knees to the corner of the room, fumbled around until she found Digger's longboard, and got up on shaky legs. Sprague and Digger were focused on the beating they were giving Zook and didn't see Kelly coming.

"Look out!" Sprague cried. But it was too late. Kelly swung the skateboard like a baseball bat and caught Digger on the side of the head with the edge of the board. The blow made a thick, crunching noise. Digger screamed, dropped to the floor, and assumed a fetal position with both hands cradling his bleeding head. Suddenly finding himself free, Zook stepped toward a shocked-looking Sprague and hit him with a short, powerful right that flattened his nose and dropped him to the floor.

Zook scooped up his backpack and sleeping bag and took Kelly's hand. "Come on," he said. "Let's get out of here."

As they slipped out, Sprague had made it to his hands and knees and was mumbling something about his nose, which was bent to one side and dripping blood. Digger was still holding his head but had managed to sit up. By now Zook and Kelly were hurtling down the back steps and heard him yell out, "They're still looking for you! You're gonna regret this."

They headed for the bus stop on Killingsworth, walking fast and looking back often. Kelly had zipped up her jacket to hide her ripped blouse. Zook was dabbing a dirty handkerchief he'd extracted from his backpack on his split, swollen lip. Kelly stopped him under a street light and looked at the lip. "*Ew*, that looks bad, Zook. And your eye—it's all swollen and bloodshot. Can you see out of it?"

Zook nodded. "Yeah. I'm okay."

Kelly placed a hand on his shoulder, went up on her tiptoes, and kissed the side of his mouth that wasn't bloodied. "Thank you," she said and then blushed deep red.

Zook looked shocked for a moment, then tried to smile but grimaced in pain instead. "Well, that was the best move with a skateboard I've seen in a long time, Kel."

By the time they boarded the bus, Kelly had managed to pry out of Zook what caused him to suddenly drop out. He told the coaches at PSU that he had passed all the tests for his GED. Well, that wasn't quite true, and apparently they checked behind him at New Directions. So he was told he could no longer be on the practice squad. "All I ever wanted to do was play basketball," he told her, "but I'm not going to get a chance now."

Kelly said, "When you get your GED you can rejoin the team next year, right?"

Zook looked down to avoid her eyes and shook his head. "That's not happening, Kel. You know how hard the new GED test is, especially the math part. Hell, I couldn't even pass the old test, and it was a lot easier. You know how bad I suck at math."

"It's not that hard. I can teach you the math you need to know. Trust me."

He brought his eyes up and met hers, doing his best to hold back the tears. "Why did you come looking for me?"

Kelly looked away this time. "To, um, apologize for losing it the other day. I felt terrible about that."

"Yeah, well, you're wasting your time."

"No I'm not," she shot back.

The bus lurched to a stop and Zook stood up. "Look, Kelly. I'm not boyfriend material. Forget about me. I'm just a screw-up." And before Kelly could say another word Zook got off the bus.

Kelly sat there feeling like she'd just been slapped in the face. Then she cried all the way to her stop. It was only after she got off and was walking toward her apartment on the dark street that Digger's words came back to her... *They're still looking for you...*

Maybe that dude Claxton was right. Maybe she was in danger. She walked a little faster and glanced behind her as fear enveloped her shattered heart like a cold fog.

FORTY

Cal

Tay and I sat in my office for another hour or so, talking and watching my computer screen for another message from K209. But nothing came in. I sent a final message to her.

Please don't break communications with me. I will do what I can with this information, but I will need more help from you!

Tay said, "Are you going to involve the police in this?"

I shook my head. "Not at this juncture. I'd like to verify this, and I don't want to scare K209 away. She's obviously pretty damn good at staying below the radar."

Tay smiled. "I like the way you roll, Claxton. This is getting interesting."

I had to laugh. "Yeah, if you think walking a high wire without a net's interesting."

We were both starving by that time, so after feeding Archie and taking him for a quick walk, we headed across the river to Pambiche for Cuban food. I called Nando on the way, and he agreed to join us. We had some catching up to do.

Tay and I had just scored a table after a long wait when Nando made his entrance. As he worked his way through the room, it was clear his swagger was back. Before sitting down he took Tay's hand, bowed, and kissed it. "You look lovely as ever, Tayshia," he said, sitting down. To me he said, "It has been too long, my friend."

We ordered drinks and spent the time before our food arrived talking in generalities and studiously avoiding anything to do with Claudia Borrego. I broke the ice as we were finishing our entrees. "Uh, there's been a development, Nando."

He leveled his dark eyes at me with a look that said this better be good.

I unpacked the whole K209 story and then brought him up-to-date on the Brent Gunderson break-in, Bonilla's notebook, and how it all seemed to tie back to the Bridgetown Arsenal.

When I finished, Nando's shoulders fell some. He sopped up the last of his mojo sauce with a corn fritter and shook his head slowly. "It is unfortunate that this young tagger cannot identify Cardenas. You are positive of this?"

"She didn't rule it out," I said. Tay nodded her head in agreement. I knew better than to bring up my doubts about Cardenas being the shooter and was relieved when Tay was mute on the subject.

"So," Nando continued, "this changes nothing. The prosecution of Cardenas will go forward. The evidence is solid. As for this gun shop business and the deaths of Claudia's cousin, Manny Bonilla, and the homeless man, I have no real interest."

The whole thing went about the way I expected. I

did get Nando to agree to check with his sources to find out how the Portland Police Bureau was viewing the Rupert Youngblood murder. As we were saying our good nights outside the restaurant, Nando added, "You know, Calvin, perhaps you should let the authorities worry about all this. There is very little in this for you."

There never is, I said to myself, but to Nando I smiled and answered, "You've got a point. I'll give it some thought."

As he turned to leave, he gave me a look that let me know he understood I wasn't backing off. Good friends allow each other that kind of space.

Tay had hitched a ride from a friend to Old Town that morning, so I took her home, a nice little infill condo off MLK on SE Thirty-fifth Place. When she invited me in for a drink I said, "I need to, uh, get back." I didn't want to be alone with her. I didn't need the complication that I thought might follow.

She smiled and eyed me with her brown eyes. "Things still up in the air in Russia?"

"Uh, not really. It's pretty much over, but, you know, feelings linger."

Tay smiled, knowingly. "Yeah, I know all about that."

"She can't ever come back to the US legally. I've looked at every possibility. Anyway, I had to tell her, but she took it very well."

Tay nodded, took my hand in both of hers, and looked at me. Her eyes were warm and filled with the kind of understanding that comes from experience. She squeezed my hand softly. "I'm sorry to hear that, Cal." Then she hugged me and kissed me on the cheek. "Good night."

I turned and walked away, and I swear I could still feel the warmth of that kiss on my skin when I reached the car.

SUNDAY BROKE COLD and clear, the sky a ringing blue. Arch and I were up early and got in a good run, with the thought of the double cappuccino I would make upon my return providing strong incentive. I spent the morning catching up on emails and planning my week, which would include three client-packed days in my Dundee office. I also called my neighbor and accountant, Gertrude Johnson, to fess up that, in all the excitement, I'd forgotten to make my quarterly tax payments to the Feds and Oregon. "Jesus, Cal," Gertie said, "you were late last quarter, too. Get the checks in the mail tomorrow." Then she laughed. "Of course, at the rate you're going, you won't have much income to tax. I may have to recalculate your payments."

I swallowed. The threat of financial ruin was always out there for me, like a fogbank off the coast that could close in at any time. "That bad, huh?"

"You're spending too much time in Portland. Your receipts are way off. You better hope you get a holiday bump."

She was referring to the uptick in business I usually saw around the holidays, which were decidedly unjoyous for a lot of people. I told her I'd make the payments and was about to wrap up a situation here in Portland. Hope does spring eternal.

I also called a client of mine, a man named Hunter Barlow. I'd settled a lawsuit for him. Barlow had a forty-acre spread out in the Chehalem Valley, between Carlton and Yamhill, and he owned guns, lots of them. I figured he might be able to help me. He agreed to see me and we set a date at his place.

Around two that afternoon I got a call from Roz Jenkins. "Cal?" she began, "You coming to the rally this afternoon?"

"Wouldn't miss it, Roz."

"Good. Look for us up front. You can sit in the VIP section."

"Terrific. I'll see you there."

What every budding gun trust lawyer dreams of—VIP exposure at a gun rally.

FORTY-ONE

Cal

THE PRO-GUN RALLY was to be held on the river in the grassy bowl just south of the Hawthorne Bridge. To save time, I'd driven over and parked on SW Third. My plan was to catch the rally, then swing back to pick up Archie for a quick getaway to Dundee. The weather stayed clear that day, the walkway along the river jammed with Portlanders enjoying a sunbreak in the autumn weather. Just past the arching streams of the Salmon Fountain, a young, earnest-looking man handed me a flyer. I was early, so I sat down on a bench and studied it. The rally, I learned was spawned by a series of proposed ordinances aimed at tightening city gun laws. Lost or stolen firearms would have to be promptly reported, and handling firearms while intoxicated would be prohibited. *Huh*, I thought, *weren't these kinds of controls already in place?*

As I rejoined the crowd on the walkway, two young men passed me wearing camouflage and combat boots. Each carried a military-style rifle as casually as a loaf of bread. I'd seen photos of assault weapons being brandished in the rotunda of the Oregon State Capitol during a similar rally, so I knew it was somehow legal. But the sight was jarring, nonetheless, and people out walking that day said nothing and gave the men a wide berth.

A portable stage stood at the base of the bowl, the humpback outline of the Hawthorne Bridge and the brilliant blue band of the Willamette in the background. An American flag on the stage fluttered in the breeze, and a large white banner behind the stage proclaimed:

> *"The great object is that every man be armed...*
> *Every one who is able may have a gun."*
> Patrick Henry

The bowl gradually filled with people. I saw more weapons on open display, along with homemade signs supporting the Second Amendment and denouncing local and national politicians who were considered by the sign-bearers to be anti-gun. The media was out in force, as evidenced by a couple of TV trucks up on Naito Parkway and a helicopter hovering over the river. I worked my way over to the stage and spotted Roz Jenkins. She was being interviewed by a young TV reporter who looked familiar, although I couldn't name her or the network she worked for. I waited off to the side and watched the crowd. It didn't look like a big turnout, two, three hundred, tops, but, hey, this was Portland.

That's when I saw the bootmaker, Farnell Timmons. He was standing off to the side, about halfway up the slope, his arms laced across his chest, a ball cap pulled down firmly against the breeze. He was with six other men, two of whom brandished assault rifles. I recognized two in the group, the Mutt and Jeff pair I almost tangled with in the parking lot of that bar in Estacada. They came to stand with their pro-gun brothers and sisters in Portland, no doubt. They all wore stylish cowboy boots, I noted.

Roz finished her interview and joined me. She wore Timmons's boots, dark blue jeans, and her signature pearl button, long-sleeved cowgirl shirt. "Calvin," she said, breaking into a broad smile, "Glad you could make it." Then she hugged me.

"Not a bad turnout," I said.

"Yeah, it's looking pretty good. Who'da thought we could draw a crowd like this?" She laughed and shook her head. "Looks like the Second Amendment's alive and well, even in liberal Portland." Roz then introduced me to several people milling around the stage, all ranking members of an organization called the Oregon Friends of the Second Amendment. Roz, I recalled, was the president of OFSA.

At that point Roz's daughter and her husband, Arthur, walked up. When he saw me his jaw dropped for a moment, but he recovered and dutifully introduced his wife, Melanie. She was a large woman, like her mother, sporting a profusion of bright blond ringlets framing a round, fleshy face. She was apparently going for a Shirley Temple look. Roz said, perhaps a little defensively in light of Arthur's reaction, "I invited Cal to join us. He needs to see some good ol' American democracy up close and personal." If that made Arthur feel any better he didn't show it.

Just before the rally started, Jack Pfister appeared and offered his hand. "Claxton. Good to see you, buddy. And in the VIP section, no less."

Hail, hail, the gang's all here. I shook his hand and nodded. "Roz invited me."

He grimaced and said under his breath, "I hate all this apple pie and assault rifle crap. I have to be here. I represent the OFSA." He winked. "They're loaded, in more ways than one. The pay's great."

After a rousing a cappella rendition of the National Anthem by a high school girl and a long prayer led by a local evangelical minister, the meeting kicked off with a series of short speeches leading up to the introduction of Roz Jenkins. They didn't call her Rockin' Roz for nothing. When she took the stage the first thing she said was, "Good afternoon, Portland. Show me your guns!" The crowd thundered its approval as all manner of firearms were hoisted overhead. She raised both hands and smiled. "Folks, what you're feeling right now is what it feels like to be a truly free American." More hoots, calls, and wild applause. "You know, we've stopped them at the federal level, we've stopped them at the state level. Now—" she paused here as the audience roared "—now it's time to stop them at the municipal level right here in Portland. Are you with me?" The crowd went crazy.

She was funny, too. After explaining the thrust of the proposed city ordinances and how they were, in fact, a very slippery slope, she said, "Maybe we should take up a collection here so that we can buy us a couple of city councilmen before they're all gone. What do you say?"

By the time she finished talking she had the audience eating out of her hand. She exhorted everyone to attend the upcoming meeting in which the proposed ordinances were to be discussed and voted on.

"Lord knows," she said in conclusion, "we've got too many laws now that restrict our constitutional and God-given rights to own guns. We sure as hell don't need any more. See you at the city council meeting."

When the rally broke up, Roz was swallowed up by a throng of well-wishers, and Pfister was schmoozing with a couple of OFSA officers. I watched Arthur and Melanie leave and saw Timmons and his entourage heading down the slope toward them. Then a curious thing happened. It looked like Timmons was going to say something to Arthur, but then he abruptly veered off to the right and his entourage followed. Had Arthur warned them off with a look or a shake of his head? I couldn't be sure. Arthur and his wife vanished into the crowd, and I fell in behind Timmons, staying well back. All the way from Estacada just to attend a rally? I wondered about that. I didn't plan to follow them, but my curiosity was aroused.

Timmons's group headed down Naito and turned left at Salmon Street. At SW First, Mutt and Jeff and two others peeled off to the right to fetch a parked car, I assumed. Timmons and two others continued onto Third, turned left, and stopped at a big white truck with an extended cab. I was parked a block and a half the other way.

Damn, I thought, *it's worth a shot.* I broke into a dead run, jumped in my car, and took off. If they were headed back to Estacada, I figured, they would go up to Alder and take the Morrison Bridge to the I-5, in which case I would call this craziness off. But instead I caught sight of the truck as it turned onto Madison, which would take them over the Hawthorne Bridge in the direction of the Bridgetown Arsenal.

I decided to follow the truck.

When I got on the bridge, I swung into the left lane and gunned it. That's not saying a lot because my three-series BMW was a dozen years old. It shuddered a bit before responding, and I caught up with the truck just as it took a left onto SE Water Avenue. There was no traffic on Water, and I followed at what I hoped was a safe distance. It was clear we were headed toward the Arsenal. That's when I noticed the car behind me. "Whoops," I said aloud, "this could be a parade." I turned off at the next intersection but not before watching the white truck disappear behind the Arsenal. The second car slowed down as it passed the intersection where I'd turned off, then followed the truck behind the same building.

I headed back toward Caffeine Central, mulling over what just happened. The Arsenal was closed. What would a bootmaker from Estacada and six of his buddies be doing there on a Sunday evening? Maybe they had a special arrangement to use the range. Who knows? Had the second car noticed me? I didn't think so. I'd turned off, after all. But I didn't like the way it slowed down, as if taking a careful look or trying to read my license plate.

Then I thought of the confrontation back at that bar in Estacada. Timmons's two buddies, Mutt and Jeff, got a good look at my Beemer that night, and they were probably passengers in the second car.

"Shit."

FORTY-TWO

Kelly

RAIN SPATTERING ON Kelly's bedroom window brought her out of a deep, dreamless sleep. It was Sunday, the morning after the attempted rape. She lay there in bed listening to the rain and trying to untie the knot of her hopelessly tangled fears and emotions. She seethed with anger and frustration. Aside from the beating that she and Zook had administered, Sprague and Digger were going scot-free, a thought that enraged her. There were flashbacks of terror, too. What if Zook hadn't been there? What would have happened to her? Worse yet, she felt pangs of guilt for reasons she couldn't fathom, but she forced them down. *You did nothing to deserve that*, she told herself over and over again.

She withered in fear at the thought of Digger telling someone about her backpack. But he had no proof and probably wasn't sure, anyway. And maybe he was just saying that to scare her. He was such a bullshitter.

Then her heart would soar thinking of Zook's sudden appearance, like some knight in shining armor. But she winced each time her mind replayed the crack on the head she'd given Digger. He deserved it, but hitting someone like that still made her feel uneasy. It seemed like everywhere she turned she was confronted with violence, even by her own hand. Her life, it seemed, had taken another dark turn, like when her dad died.

But then she laughed almost uncontrollably when she thought of Sprague on his hands and knees, his nose sideways on his face like a Cubist painting she saw once. Then Zook's parting words on the bus would crash down on her, and she would descend back into darkness.

Kelly might have seesawed like this all day, but then she realized something—she had, in fact, accomplished what she set out to do. Zook was away from Sprague and Digger. They might try to get back at him, but she was sure he could take care of himself. And Digger was probably bluffing about giving her up to whoever was out there asking about her. So, all she had to do now was figure out a way to get Zook back into school and to teach him enough math to pass the GED. The romance thing would have to wait. *Men. They're so frustrating.*

Kelly found Veronica in the kitchen stirring a coffee and smoking a cigarette. She hadn't seen her since her big date with Larry. "How was the dinner party?"

Veronica smiled with more brightness than Kelly was used to seeing her project in the morning. "It was good. He's a nice guy."

Well, at least one of us is having some luck, she thought. "Does he have a job?"

"Yes," she answered, sounding more defensive than she probably intended. "He's a tow truck driver. Has been for a long time." Then she drew up her face in a look of genuine concern. "I saw your blouse in the laundry, Kel. It was ripped and looked like it had some blood spattered on it. What happened?"

Gross, Kelly thought, *Digger's blood*. She hadn't noticed it. She teetered on the brink of telling Veronica what happened, but thought better of it. She was afraid that if she started running her mouth she would wind up telling her everything. "Uh, there was a fight at the school, a couple of girls. I tried to break it up. Sorry."

Veronica's eyes narrowed. "Kelly, yesterday was Saturday. There was no school."

"Um, the fight was on the sidewalk outside school. We were just hanging out there."

Veronica looked unconvinced. "Who's we?"

"My friends and I."

Veronica sighed. "I wish I could meet some of those friends of yours."

Kelly eyed her carefully, trying to discern the degree of her seriousness. "I've kept them away like you told me. I tell them very little about my private life. My best friend knows your first name and that's about it. Fortunately, she's not the nosy type."

Veronica exhaled a plume of bluish smoke and ground out her cigarette. "I know it's hard, Kel, but we've got to be careful." She locked onto Kelly's eyes. "Look, things are starting to turn around for me. Keep your nose clean, okay?"

Good old Veronica, Kelly said to herself as she shook out the last flakes of cold cereal into a bowl. *It always winds up being about you.*

That afternoon Kelly went back to the library to get some homework done and check her Hide-My-Ass! email account. When she got out on the street, the fear of Digger's threat returned, although not in full force. After all, she told herself, it wasn't the first time he'd threatened her. Nevertheless, she felt jittery, and for the first time in her life the people around her in the street and on the bus seemed vaguely threatening. It was a weird, unwelcome feeling.

The cold, wet weather ensured a crowded library, and Kelly saw several students from the school. She felt a familiar pang of guilt knowing some of those kids would have no place to go that night. At least she had a roof over her head. When she was finally able to log on to her anonymous account, she found a single message from Claxton requesting her to keep in touch with him. She thought back over everything she told the lawyer one more time but couldn't think of anything else to add. She signed off the anonymous account without sending anything.

Kelly left the library feeling better, the specter of a threatening world vanquished, it seemed, by the simple act of doing her homework and the realization that she had done everything she could for Rupert, short of giving herself up. The rest would be up to the lawyer, Claxton, and the cops. She would talk to Kiyana the next day about Zook and how he rescued her, too. Maybe they could devise a plan to lure him back to school. What she wanted most of all was for her life to get back to normal. The thought made her laugh out loud. *Normal?* Normal was something she used to complain about.

The rain let up, and it was getting dark as she walked back to the bus stop. Even if she hadn't let her guard down she probably wouldn't have noticed the man following her.

FORTY-THREE

Cal

ON THE MONDAY following the Portland gun rally the
autumn weather took its gloves off and turned wet and
miserable. Back at the Aerie, I got up early, fed Arch,
let him out, then let him back in. He stood dutifully, if
unenthusiastically, lifting one paw at a time for me to
clean off the mud with a large towel I kept in a basket
next to the kitchen door. I made a double cappuccino
and stood watching the storm clouds churn above the
valley and worrying about the slant of the incoming
rain. The closer it came to horizontal the more likely
my bedroom window frame would leak from cracks
and fissures I'd been unable to seal despite the expen-
diture of vast amounts of caulk over the years. The
leaks, I was convinced, defied the laws of physics.

Arch and I piled in the car and drove through the
vineyards, now shed of their leaves, to my office in
Dundee. The grapes were harvested and a fine vintage
promised on account of the Indian summer the whole
region had enjoyed. I met with three paying clients
that morning and was tempted to call Gertie Johnson
and tell her that the rumors of my financial demise
were greatly exaggerated. At noon, I ate a quick lunch
at a Mexican grill at the south end of town, a lime-
green building with bright orange trim. It stood like

a reminder that, despite all the wine-induced gentrification, Dundee was still a proud blue-collar town with a sizable Hispanic population.

After lunch, I drove south out of town, took Highway 47 through Carlton, and turned into a narrow dirt lane marked by a single mailbox on a post. The mailbox had a number on it but no name. The lane cut through a thick line of mature sycamores that lay a quarter mile in and then curved to the left toward an immense, white Victorian farmhouse, an even bigger barn, a silo, and two wind turbines. I parked in the circular drive in front of the house, and Archie and I were greeted by two seriously upset pit bulls who stood barking at us below a sign on the porch that told us to beware of them. I knew the drill—don't get out of the car—and called Hunter Barlow on my cell phone. He popped out of the front door, waved at me, then opened a gate to a pen at the side of the porch and pointed inside. The dogs retreated to the pen, and he shut the gate.

Barlow was a tall man, lean with a full beard and a countenance that would lend itself well to high stakes poker. "Hello, Cal, welcome to the farm. It's been a while."

I rolled the back windows down for Arch and got out, a file folder in my hand. "Yes, it has. Good to see you, Hunter. Obedient dogs. Still leaving them out, I see." I'd handled an expensive lawsuit for him involving a FedEx driver severely bitten by one of his dogs.

He shrugged and looked a little sheepish. "I have an electronic eye down by the gate. I usually put them up when someone's on the way. Didn't hear you. Sorry about that. They're good boys."

A curious use of the word *good*, but I let it slide. We chatted a while on the porch, and just as I was going to bring up the purpose of my visit, he told me he had something to show me. I followed him around the house, through an apple orchard, and out into an open field, which sported a bank of solar panels at the far end. He stopped at what looked like a hatch on a submarine, took an electronic key out of his pocket and punched it. I heard a metallic click, and the cover popped up and slowly opened, exposing a vertical, corrugated steel tube with a sturdy ladder attached to the side. He allowed himself a thin smile tinged with pride. "Check this out."

I stepped up to the tube, looked down, then back at Barlow. I'd heard of doomsday shelters but never expected to see one. "Is this a shelter?"

He nodded. "Yep. Just put it in in August."

"Where did you get it?"

"Bought it off the 'net. Outfit in Texas. They brought it on a couple of eighteen wheelers. Come on, I'll show you around."

What good is a doomsday shelter if you can't show it off?

I followed him down into the shelter, navigating the ladder while carrying the file folder. The entry tube joined a larger horizontal tube that I learned was twelve feet in diameter, forty feet long, and buried twenty feet under the ground. A subfloor provided a flat walking surface, and storage space beneath the floor held a supply of food and water for Barlow, his wife, and three-year-old son.

"So, is this in case we get the 9.0 subduction earth-quake or something more Armageddon-like?" I asked.

Barlow seemed to think about the question for a moment. "Whichever comes first, I guess. I just believe in being prepared, Cal."

He led me from room to room, showing off running water, air filtration systems, a power grid that could be switched effortlessly from generator, to solar, to wind, even a forty-five-inch flat-screen TV. I wondered what kind of movies they would watch after Armageddon but didn't ask.

I knew Barlow would have a well-stocked armory, and he didn't disappoint. At the far end of the tube he showed me various rifles in racks on the wall, an assortment of holstered handguns hanging from pegs, and boxes of ammunition stacked in a corner below his and hers Kevlar bulletproof vests.

The pièce de résistance was a large weapon on a tripod sitting in the middle of the floor. I did a double take and said, "Is that a machine gun?"

The thin, prideful smile again. "Fifty caliber. Fully operational. Shoots like the hammers of hell."

"Is it legal?"

"Completely. I got it through a gun trust. I'm grandfathered in now. The Feds can't touch it, even if they change the regulations."

"Let me guess—Jack Pfister handled the gun trust for you."

"As a matter of fact he did. You know Pfister? He's a good man."

"Yeah, I know Jack." Then I added, "This is a good place to discuss why I came to see you." I opened the folder and showed him the drawings I'd photographed from Manny Bonilla's notebook. "What do you make of these?"

He extracted a pair of reading glasses from his shirt pocket, put them on, and leaned in. "Looks like my son drew them."

I chuckled. "I know. I'm just wondering if these make any sense to you or ring any bells. I think they may have been notes taken by a machinist."

"Hmm. These are various three-dimensional views of some kind of a trigger assembly. See, that curved arm is the actual trigger, and that oddly shaped element on top's the hammer. That little notch on the block's called the sear. It holds the hammer in place till the trigger's pulled. These sketches are of some kind of drop-in trigger."

"Drop-in trigger for what?"

Barlow studied the sketches for a long time before speaking. "Hard to say for sure, but judging from the design, it might be for a machine pistol or AR-15 assault rifle, probably the latter."

"What does a drop-in trigger do?"

"You take the existing trigger out and drop this one in, and it makes the rifle closer to an automatic, like a military M-16. You know, you can empty a big clip much quicker."

"Is that legal?"

He laughed. "Not likely. This looks pretty radical to me, like they're going for fully automatic capability. That would categorize it as a machine gun component, which is outlawed by the National Firearms Act."

"Would somebody be more likely to sell just the trigger assembly or an AR-15 that's been fully converted?"

"Either way, I suppose. If they were converting to sell rifles illegally, they would need straw buyers."

I raised my eyebrows, and he continued, "A straw buyer would buy the gun from a licensed dealer on behalf of the converter for a fee. The converter can then remove the serial number from the gun and drop the new trigger in. The straw buyer simply claims the gun was lost or stolen. Bingo, you have an untraceable, fully automatic AR-15 assault rifle, a real killing machine that's worth a lot on the black market."

"How much would one fetch?"

Barlow shrugged. "I don't know, maybe north of ten thousand."

I whistled. "Are the straw buyers required to report a lost or stolen gun?"

He frowned and shook his head. "No. Do you have to report a stolen wallet? But I just heard that the liberals in Portland are trying to change that, at least in the city."

Of course, I remembered that from the gun rally. I nodded but didn't comment. I didn't want to fan those flames with a true believer. We chatted some more, and as I was leaving I met Barlow's wife. When I told her I was impressed with the new shelter, she smiled weakly, and I saw a flicker of anxiety cross her face. It wasn't the reaction I expected, and judging from the stern look Barlow gave her, it wasn't the reaction he approved of.

Maybe you can be too prepared.

Barlow promised to call me if he thought of anything else, but I felt like he pretty much confirmed my suspicion—Manny Bonilla was probably asked to do few more things for the Jenkins family than drive Roz Jenkins around. I thought about talking to Truax, the ATF guy, but quickly thought better of it. All I had were some crude sketches, and bringing those up would require me to explain how they came into my possession. That was out, because it would put me crosswise with both him and Harmon Scott. And for all I knew they were working together by now.

I was making some headway and had a hunch that K209 knew more about this than she realized. If I could find her maybe I could bust this thing open.

FORTY-FOUR

Cal

THE FLURRY OF business at my law office was short-lived, and I found myself facing a light schedule in Dundee for the rest of that week. This was not comforting news, but it did make it easier for me to pack up and head back to Portland, where I planned to redouble my efforts to find K209 and figure out what I should do next vis-à-vis the cast of characters at the Bridgetown Arsenal.

Arch and I got back to Caffeine Central early Tuesday, and at midmorning I was surprised by another email from K209.

I left something out that might be important. Just before The Shooter killed Claudia Borrego she said to him, "Where is man—" or something like that. I don't know what man she was talking about. I hope this helps. Sorry about that!

I sat there for a moment before it hit me, and I had to take a deep breath before typing my response.

Could she have said, "Where is Manny?"

Yes. That could have been what she said. She didn't finish or I didn't hear it all because of the gunshots.

I thanked K209 and pleaded for her to come to Caffeine Central, but she went off-line once again.

I leaned back in my chair, laced my fingers behind my head, and reviewed the probable scenario. They must have lured Claudia out that night by using Manny as bait, probably forcing him to call to set up a rendezvous. She bit, because, as Tay explained, it was a family obligation. Manny got cold feet about something having to do with the Arsenal. Maybe he needed her help or money to get out of town. That would explain the pistol Gunderson found, too. Manny knew he was swimming with sharks. After they killed Claudia they tossed Manny off the Fremont Bridge. End of problem, except for one little detail—a young, fearless girl saw the shooting go down.

At noon Arch and I walked over to the art gallery where Picasso worked. He was with a customer, so we browsed the art on the walls, the best of which—at least in my opinion—had been painted by Picasso himself. I watched him as he discussed a painting with an attractive woman with a serious demeanor and, judging from her elegantly tailored suit and Prada handbag, serious money. He wore an open-necked shirt, so the tattoo of a coral snake on his neck was visible in keeping with the edgy nature of the gallery. Although it was difficult to tell which the woman was more interested in—the tattoo or the paintings—she picked out two of the latter and left after leaving shipping instructions to Scottsdale, Arizona.

"Buy you lunch?" I asked Picasso after he and

Archie had finished their ritual greeting. He agreed and we walked over to the Deschutes Brewery on NW Eleventh. I parked Arch outside and we took a table where he could see us. I filled Picasso in on the contact K209 had made with me and the apparent connection between Claudia Borrego's and Rupert Youngblood's murders. When I finished he shook his head. "I hadn't heard about Rupert. I'm getting out of touch, man. He was a legend over in Old Town. Always hung out at the Portland Rescue Mission. Used to do tai chi in the park. Everyone on the street over there trusted him, especially the younger kids."

I nodded. "He died protecting K209's identity. At least that's what K209 told me."

Picasso grimaced and shut his eyes for a moment. "Man, I'm glad you're still on this, Cal. Nando's fiancée, then Rupert. These guys need to go down."

And Manny Bonilla, I thought but didn't say. "Yeah, well, there's something else. K209's a girl, not a guy."

"I'll be damned. You sure?"

"Pretty sure. The language of the emails she sent me kind of gives her away. A female psychologist I'm working with picked up on it first. She's saying a fourteen- to seventeen-year-old female." I had to chuckle. "It wasn't my finest hour. Don't tell Claire. Anyway, this is new information. Does it help us find her?"

Picasso paused, absently tugged on his eyebrow ring, then sat up a little straighter. "The fact that she's a girl doesn't really help, but knowing she had a relationship with Rupert might. Rupert's territory was Old Town, around the Rescue Mission. The kid must hang out in the same neighborhood. She's probably not homeless, because homeless kids don't have climbing gear. But if she knows Rupert, she's definitely not well off, either. That would put her on the east side of the river. West side housing's too expensive. So, my guess is her draw across the river is most likely the alternative high school in Old Town." He looked a little embarrassed. "I told you I'd check that out, didn't I. I, uh, didn't get around to it."

"That's okay. Just give me a contact at the school, and I'll check it out myself. You've got art to sell."

Picasso called a case manager he knew at the New Directions Alternative School and arranged for me to meet with her later that same afternoon. Her name was Monica Sayles, and he told her I was trying to locate a student but didn't elaborate. After being buzzed in I found Sayles in a small, unadorned office on the second floor of the school. She was dressed casually in slacks, a ribbed cotton turtleneck, and jogging shoes, and her direct manner and level gaze told me she was all business. I introduced myself and she said, "It's nice to finally meet you Mr. Claxton. I hear good things about the work you're doing at Caffeine Central."

I shrugged, thanked her and explained the reason for my visit. When I finished, she said, "I thought the police arrested a man for that awful shooting?"

"They did, but there may be others involved who are still at large."

She made a face. "I see, but isn't this a matter for the police?"

I smiled. "Of course it is, but you know as well as I do that finding kids like this is not their strong suit."

She smiled in spite of herself. "There are probably

thirty to forty girls here at New Directions between the ages of fourteen and seventeen. I wouldn't know where to begin, Mr. Claxton."

"This girl's very athletic, smart, and knows something about stencil art. Does that narrow it down some?"

She didn't respond for several beats, and I could almost hear the wheels turning in her head. "Why is this so important to you?"

"Because I'm worried sick she's in danger."

She met my eyes, chewed her lip for a moment, and shook her head. "I'm sorry, Mr. Claxton. I wish I could help you, but my hands are tied. We have very strict confidentiality rules here. Even if I had a clue who it was, I couldn't tell you."

I told her I understood but left a card just in case she changed her mind. As I exited the building, I recognized a student out on the street, one of my clients. "Hi, Kiyana," I called out.

She turned and beamed a smile. The boots she wore made her even taller, and a hooded sweatshirt hid her dreadlocks. "Hey, Mr. Claxton."

I fell in stride with her. "I submitted your petition to the court. I'm waiting for a hearing date."

"All right! How long will that take?"

"Six to eight weeks." Then on a whim I added, "Listen, Kiyana, maybe you can help me. You must know a lot of kids at the school."

She looked at me, instantly wary. "Yeah…"

"I'm trying to find the tagger who uses the moniker K209."

She laughed. "You and everybody else, man."

"I know. I think K209 is a girl, and she probably

goes to school here." I stopped walking and turned to face her. "I'm looking for her because I think her life could be in danger. Can you think of any girls here who could pull off something like that?"

The smile on Kiyana's face froze for an instant, and her eyes got bigger. Then she smiled more broadly, but it looked a little forced. "K209's a girl? Is that cool or what?"

I nodded and met her eyes. "Can you help me, Kiyana?"

She broke eye contact and shuffled her feet. "I don't know, man. A lot of tough girls at New Directions could be doin' stuff like that. This tagger could get in a lot of trouble, too. Right?"

"Not necessarily," I added hastily and then explained that I would represent K209 if she came forward.

Kiyana looked out across Ninth Street and seemed to be lost in thought for a moment. "Sure, well, if I think of someone, I'll let you know." She forced another smile. "I gotta go to work now."

I watched her cross the street as frustration filled my chest like hot steam. Clearly she knew something but was unwilling to talk to me. I stifled an urge to run after her and demand some answers. That would backfire for sure. Kiyana wasn't the type to wilt under pressure. Just the opposite.

No, probably the best I could hope for is that Kiyana could somehow overcome the street code that says you never, ever tell The Man anything.

FORTY-FIVE

Kelly

THE MONDAY FOLLOWING Kelly's visit to the library passed uneventfully. On Tuesday it was nearly dark when Kelly stepped off the bus three blocks from her apartment. The street glistened with reflected light, although the rain had finally stopped. The audio components store was still closed and dark, but Kelly was cheered to see the apartment lights on the third floor. Veronica hadn't left for work yet.

The dog seemed to glare at her with his bug eyes when she let herself into the apartment. "It's me, you grump," Kelly said. "I live here, too, you know." Veronica was in the bathroom applying makeup. Kelly watched as she carefully outlined her eyes with mascara, her blond hair still in curlers. "How's Larry?"

Veronica smiled without taking her eyes off the mirror. "He's fine. We're going to a club tonight after I get off work. I, uh, left you some pizza."

After Veronica left, Kelly busied herself in the kitchen with dinner—a glass of milk, cold pizza, and a salad she made with some wilted iceberg lettuce and low-fat mayonnaise. Someday when she was on her own she promised herself she was going to learn to cook. Not fancy or anything, just healthy.

She'd just settled down with a book in the front

room when the mutt stood up with his ears pointing forward and whimpered. Kelly put the book down, went to the front door, and opened it softly. She heard a stair below the second floor landing groan, the familiar sound of someone on the staircase. Her spine began to tingle as she moved to the railing and looked down.

A man was coming up the stairs, his back to her, his shoulders dipping from side to side, arms swinging like a gun fighter. *She knew that walk.*

Everything froze for a moment—breath, heart, brain—then Kelly ducked back into the apartment, eased the door shut, slipped the dead bolt, and fastened the security chain. She ran to her room and locked the door, the mutt right behind her.

She grabbed her backpack and moved toward the window, then spun around and rummaged in the back of her closet until she found Rupert's gray box. She jammed the box in her pack and as she slid the window up heard two loud thumps, followed by the splintering of wood. She had one leg out the window when the mutt came up to her, ears down, tail between his legs, sheer terror in his buggy little eyes. "Okay," she said and scooped him up and stuffed him into her backpack. "But keep your mouth shut."

She practically slid down the copper drainpipe and when she hit the alley broke into a sprint. The dog whined softly from inside the half-zippered pack. *"Hush,"* Kelly told him in the harshest voice she could muster. He went silent.

She stopped at the building she called her refuge, looked back into the darkness of the alley, and listened for a moment. Nothing yet. The cornerstones were

damp and slippery, and she had a counterweight on
her back, which would make it even harder. How long
to summit? she asked herself. Two, maybe three minutes? She imagined Macho Dude's actions. Once he
broke down the bedroom door, he'd backtrack down
the stairs and go around the building. Then he'd have
to decide which way she went in the alley.

She just might make it.

She dried her hands on her sweatshirt, scraped the
bottom of each sneaker on a pant leg, and lifted off,
thinking of her dad. *Eyes on the goal, Kel*, he used
to tell her. *Never look down.*

The stone was slick, and the mutt hung like a dead
weight in her pack, making the going slower than she
hoped. But she quickly fell into a rhythm and with
every upward thrust of her right hand, then left, she
would drag her fingers across her sweatshirt to keep
them as dry as possible.

She paused halfway up, breathing hard from panic
more than effort, her breath condensing in thick
clouds around her face. The mutt whimpered softly
in the pack but didn't move. She pushed off again,
and, near the top, the mutt shifted, causing her to
lose a foothold. She hung there for a moment, spread-
eagle, her dangling left foot searching madly for the
seam between the cornerstones. She finally found it
and started up again, her heart pounding so hard it
almost masked the slap of boots on pavement coming in her direction from below.

Come on, she told herself, *you're almost there.
Don't blow it, Kelly.*

The footsteps got louder, and Kelly realized it
was too late. Macho Dude was almost below her.

She flattened herself to the cornerstones and froze, petrified that the hammering of her heart would give her away. She remained absolutely motionless as he passed below her.

Her worst nightmare from the night she witnessed the shooting was repeating itself. *People don't look up*, she told herself. *People do not look up.* She hung there for an eternity. But the footsteps faded, and she let herself breathe again before pulling onto the rooftop. She lay there for a while just sucking in the cold air and letting her pulse come back to something approaching normal. Then she sat up, took the mutt from her backpack, and did something she never ever did before—she hugged him.

Just moments later she heard the slapping footsteps in the alley again, coming back toward her this time. She glanced at the mutt, afraid he might decide to bark, but even more afraid of what he'd do if she tried to stop him. She looked at the dog, willing him to stay silent. To his everlasting credit, he just lay there panting, pleased, no doubt, to be out of the backpack. She moved to the low retaining wall and peeked over. Macho Dude was huffing and moving slower this time. She watched until he vanished into the darkness. She hugged the dog again and vowed that from then on she would call him Spencer, not "the mutt."

An hour later, Kelly stood in the shadows across and down the street from where Veronica worked. She'd been watching a good fifteen minutes and saw no sign of Macho Dude. It was probably safe, she decided. Kelly crossed the street and stood at the window until Veronica saw her. Kelly was holding

Spencer, who started squirming and making little whining sounds.

Veronica joined her on the sidewalk, her face filled with concern. "What's the matter, Kel? Is Spencer sick or something?"

Kelly handed Spencer to Veronica. "No. He's not sick." Then she looked her straight in the eye. "Listen, Veronica, you've got to leave Portland right now."

The concerned look dissolved into anger laced with fear. "Oh, no, Kel, what have you done?"

"I can't explain now, but you've got to leave." She held out a handful of bills. "Here's seven hundred dollars. Go to the bus station and take the next bus to Seattle. Go stay with your friend there."

"What do you mean? I can't do that. And where did you get that kind of money, anyway?"

"Just go. And whatever you do, don't go near the apartment."

Veronica's eyes flooded, and her face flushed red. "Oh, Kelly. How could you do this? I knew you'd screw things up for me."

Kelly thrust the money into Veronica's hand. "Just take this and go. I'll explain everything later. I promise."

Veronica snatched the money from Kelly's hand. "I'll go, but you need to understand something—I'm done trying to be your parent. It's over between us." Then she handed the dog back to Kelly and crossed her arms. "And take Spencer, too. I can't take him with me."

Spencer was as surprised as Kelly and tried to squirm out of her grasp. "But I can't—"

"Take him and get out of here. Good luck in foster

care. You're going to need it." Veronica snapped over her shoulder as she walked back into the restaurant.

Spencer whined a couple of times in protest and then seemed to relax. *"Sheeze,"* Kelly said, "just what I need. A pet." The dog didn't seem to mind when she put him in her backpack and started off…to where? It suddenly hit home that she had no place to go.

She crossed the street and stepped into the shadows of a building to mull it over. She knew if she went to the police, she'd end up in emergency foster care that very night. She'd been through that awful routine before. She could go across the river and find somewhere to sleep in Old Town, but Macho Dude would probably look for her there. She could go to Forest Park and sleep under a tree, but it was cold and wet and she had no gear. There was the all-night coffee shop farther up Sandy Boulevard, but he might look there, too.

Why not her refuge? It was four blocks from the apartment, but she felt like she could access it through the alley without too much risk. Besides, for all Macho Dude knew, Kelly had called the police about the break-in, so he wouldn't be hanging around there, would he?

She had no sooner scaled the building a second time when the sky opened up. Fortunately, the small enclosure housing the exit to the roof had an overhang that afforded some protection. She sat down, leaned against the wall, and unpacked the dog, who promptly jumped into her lap.

She was bone tired, but the events of the night flashed back in vivid detail—Macho Dude's unmistakable walk, the narrow escape, and the anger and disappointment in Veronica's eyes. The truth was, Kelly felt more shame than fear. Veronica was right, she admitted. She had really screwed things up for them. If she hadn't been out there tagging that night none of this would have happened.

Now Veronica was gone. Sure, the woman was selfish and self-absorbed. But she was also like a mom or a big sister, the closest thing to family that Kelly had. Kelly dropped her head in her hands, but no tears came, just a burning desire to somehow make things right.

Kelly tried to think about what she needed to do next, but she was too exhausted. Using her backpack as a pillow, she lay down, Spencer huddled on her chest, his warmth slowly seeping into her. She brought a hand up, stroked his back once, and fell fast asleep.

FORTY-SIX

Kelly

KELLY WOKE WITH a start at the sound of a siren down on Sandy Boulevard. She sat up, letting go of Spencer, who whimpered as he went over to the retaining wall and lifted his leg. The sun was below the horizon, marked by a narrow band of coppery gold light. It had stopped raining. She got up, stretched, and put the dog in the backpack. She needed to get back down now, in the cover of darkness.

Kelly was leery of being seen out on Sandy, so she cut over to Ankeny, and staying out of the streetlights, walked five blocks to a bakery she knew about. She was the first customer that morning, and the smell of fresh bread and cinnamon rolls caused her knees to nearly buckle. She ordered an egg and ham croissant and a cup of hot chocolate and paid with money from Rupert's gray box. She did the math in her head—she'd given the Rescue Mission two thousand dollars and Veronica seven hundred. That meant she had one hundred fifty-nine dollars left, or one hundred fifty-three and some change after breakfast.

She moved to a back table, and removed Spencer from the backpack. "Shhh," she told him as she pulled him into her lap. Then she teased the ham from the croissant and fed the dog, one small bite at a time.

"Ouch," she said after the first bite. "Don't you dare nip me, you little fart." He seemed to get the idea, and after he was fed and watered, sat quietly as Kelly ate her sandwich and drank her hot chocolate.

At the army surplus store on SE Grand, Kelly bought a cheap sleeping bag, plastic rain poncho, a small tarp, and a flashlight. At the Goodwill on SE Sixth, she found another hoodie like the one she had on and a second pair of jeans that fit her. She also bought a leash for the dog, a bowl to feed him with, and a small bag of kibbles at a market.

At the end of her shopping spree, Kelly had $64.37 left. But that was okay. She didn't plan on being homeless all that long. She had to find a way out of this mess and put her life back together. The sooner the better.

The sky was low and gray and laden with moisture, but the rain held back. She decided to walk the thirty some blocks to the county library on SE Cesar Chavez. It would be much safer than the one she'd been using in Old Town, where she was known to hang out. Spencer seemed relieved to be out of the backpack and trotted in front of her on the leash like a circus pony. She worried some the dog might give her away and hoped Macho Dude hadn't heard him as they made their escape. If that were the case, the dog would be good cover as was the hood on her sweatshirt that she vowed to keep up and tight at all times. Just another kid on the street with a backpack and a dog.

She was almost there when she realized she couldn't take the dog into the library. Maybe she could claim he was a service dog, but the thought only made her smile and shake her head. Spencer's lineage was unknown, but he definitely had some Chihuahua in him as evidenced by his short hair, sharp ears, and bulbous, liquid eyes. But the trouble was his features came together in a way that made him look more like a bat than a dog. What service could he provide besides making people laugh?

A thin young man with a dark beard stood near the steps of the library strumming an acoustic guitar and singing Dylan's *Idiot Wind*. A large white Malamud with pale blue eyes lay next to an open guitar case meant for contributions. By the time the man finished the song, Kelly knew she could trust the singer and his dog. She tossed a five dollar bill in the case. The man smiled and nodded. Kelly said, "Are you going to be here for a while?"

He looked up at the sky. "Long as it doesn't rain."

"Will you watch my dog? I need to use the computer in the library."

He agreed. Kelly tethered the leash, and Spencer lay down next to the Malamud like he'd known him forever. That dog was full of surprises.

The wait for a computer at the library in Southeast was shorter than what Kelly experienced across the river. She sat for a long time thinking of what to say, and when she finally got her turn sent an email to Cal Claxton.

Hello, Mr. Claxton. I saw the guy who shot Claudia Borrego yesterday. I am sure of it. Unless that guy in jail escaped or something, he didn't kill her! I wanted you to know this. I'm not sure what to do now.

Kelly chewed down the cuticles on both thumbs. Three or four minutes later a message came back.

Hi, K209. Thanks for contacting me with this important information! Anthony Cardenas is the man charged with the murder. He is still in jail. Where did you see this other man? Can you identify him? Did he see you?

She sat for a while trying to think how to respond. She was scared but knew instinctively that if she let him know that, he'd just up the pressure for her to reveal herself.

It doesn't matter where I saw him. It was him for sure. Nobody walks like that. Like some cowboy in a movie or something. I'm sorry but I ran before I got a look at his face. Dumb me. Maybe he's the partner of that guy in jail, Cardenas. A friend or something. This should be a big clue for finding him, right?

An email came right back.

Are you in a safe place? I know you must have good reasons for hiding your identity, but you are in terrible danger. Please come to my office or tell me where to meet you and I'll come immediately. I'm a lawyer. I can represent you and help make a deal that protects your interests. Please trust me and come in.

As Kelly read the message her eyes brimmed, and an urge go to Claxton surged through her, an urge so powerful that it took all her willpower to beat it back.

No, she told herself, *no, no, no.* Finally, she blinked the tears out of her eyes and started typing again.

Don't worry about me. I know how to take care of myself. Please just catch the killer, Mr. Claxton. He's a terrible man.

She would stay hidden for the time being and hope for the best. It was all she could think to do.

FORTY-SEVEN

Cal

Earlier that same morning

THE NEXT MORNING broke dark and cloudy. Arch and I took a quick run along the Willamette and returned for a call with a client from Dundee whose son had been arrested for stealing a dirt bike—an expensive one. When I finished up I called Roz Jenkins to tell her how impressed I was with her talk at the gun rally and to mention I planned to drop by the Arsenal that afternoon with my Glock for some target practice. "That's great, hon," she told me. "You be sure to pop in and say hello." My thought exactly.

It was somewhere around ten when the next batch of emails came in from K209 telling me about her encounter with the man she claimed shot Claudia, the man who was *not* Anthony Cardenas. Oh, man, I thought, this case just gets more and more dicey.

When it was clear that K209 had broken off communication, I leaned back in my chair and thought things through once again. Was it time to go to Harmon Scott and the PPB with what I had? I still didn't have proof positive the contact was genuine, and K209's new allegations rested once again on recognizing a man's walk. Damn, why hadn't she gotten a look at his face? I sure as hell didn't want to make a fool out of myself in front of Scott and the Portland Police Bureau, who were obviously invested in the arrest of Cardenas. On the other hand, the whole sequence had a ring of authenticity I simply couldn't ignore. Of course, if I went to the police K209 had vowed to "disappear." There was that, too.

I pushed myself away from my desk and got up. It felt like I was playing a big steelhead on an eight pound test leader. Pull up too hard and the line snaps. Let the fish take some line and you have a shot. I picked the latter.

There was one thing I didn't debate—I needed another set of eyes on the newest set of emails. I called Tay and plied her with the offer of another home-cooked meal. She readily accepted.

Early that afternoon I drove Nando to the airport. He was going to Cancún by way of Houston and then on to Cuba to visit his mother. "One can travel freely from Mexico to Cuba," he explained. "It is the best way for Americans to go to my country." He managed a smile and added, "I am not sure who is sadder about Claudia's passing, my mother or me."

Things had moved fast, and I hadn't even brought him up-to-date on the "Where is man—" utterance K209 heard Claudia make just before she was shot. It was a touchy subject, since it was the last thing his fiancée said before she died, and I proceeded cautiously. When I finished, he remained silent for a long time. Finally, he sighed deeply and said, "I suppose that is significant, although the young spray can vandal could have misheard what Claudia said, or worse yet, could be making this up for reasons you do not yet understand."

"That's possible, I suppose, but I doubt it. K209 seemed pretty sure of what she heard."

Nando laughed. "The word of some teenage delinquent who will not reveal her identity should be believed so readily?"

My turn to sigh. "Look, Nando, I don't think there's any doubt that Claudia was killed trying to protect Manny Bonilla, and that Bonilla was going to join some kind of illegal operation at the Arsenal that he decided to back out of." I took him through my logic, adding what I'd learned about the drop-in triggers from my survivalist contact. I also felt Bonilla's knowledge of Anthony Cardenas could have been used to set the gambler up. For example, he might have known where Cardenas kept the T-Bird, where the silencer had been planted. I left that part out, because proof of it died with Bonilla.

He listened without interrupting. "Okay. I commend you for being so persistent, Calvin. I would expect nothing less from you. But you still have not established a connection between all this and the killer, Anthony Cardenas, which for me is the bottom of the line."

"The connection's the silencer the cops found in his car."

His head tilted back slightly, and his eyebrows rose in surprise. "How do you know this?"

I shrugged. "My gut." It was the truth. I felt like the silencer was the key link between Cardenas and the Arsenal but had no idea how to prove it.

He smiled. "I see. Well, I need this week away

from Portland and all that has happened. When I return we will talk again. Perhaps by then you will have found this tagger who climbs buildings like a monkey."

I nodded, holding back the bombshell that, according to K209, Cardenas wasn't the man who shot Claudia. That news would have hemorrhaged him. Let my friend go to Cuba in peace, I decided. Hell, I didn't have any proof, anyway.

IT MUST HAVE been a good day for target shooting and weapon shopping because the Bridgetown Arsenal parking lot was nearly full when I pulled in. Maybe the gun rally had piqued new interest in the Portland citizenry. Who knows? I signed in with the sexy salesgirl, paid my fee, and made my way downrange to Lane 16, accompanied by the merry popping of firearms and the smell of freshly exploded gunpowder. I loaded the clip of my Glock, cranked the target out to fifty feet, and began squeezing off rounds just the way Roz Jenkins had taught me.

I was pleased with the reasonably tight pattern. I reloaded the gun, attached another target, and emptied another clip. This time I imagined pumping rounds into the man who'd shot Claudia Borrego and was now terrorizing a young girl who reminded me a lot of my own daughter. The pattern was tighter still, and I couldn't help but smile when I saw it was very close to what Roz's son-in-law, Arthur, had accomplished the last time I was here.

I finished up after firing off three more clips and felt a lot better. Shooting a high-powered handgun was cathartic, if nothing else. I told the salesgirl that

I wanted to see Roz Jenkins. She nodded, saying Roz had told her to buzz me in. I felt like an insider. Nothing like being known at your neighborhood gun range.

I took the stairs and leaned into the open doorway to her office. "Hello, there, Cal," she said. "How was the shooting today?"

I returned the smile. "Great. Tell Arthur I'm ready for a rematch."

We shared a good laugh at that and then chatted about the rally. Sensing I wasn't yet a true believer, I suppose, she told me again how ridiculous it was for a city to try to layer on additional gun restrictions. "My God," she said, "We've already got enough federal and state laws to choke a horse."

I said, "I read somewhere that the idea behind the requirement to report lost or stolen guns is to cut down on straw buyers." It wasn't a fib. I'd done some research on the topic of straw buyers after visiting the survivalist, Hunter Barlow.

"Oh, right, some guy being paid to buy a gun is gonna tell on himself. It's against the law to murder someone, too, but it happens every day, Cal."

I nodded and smiled with a kind of you-got-me look but said, "If someone wants to generate a volume of illegal weapons, aren't straw buyers the way to do it? I mean each purchase of a firearm has to be registered to someone, but once a gun is supposedly lost or stolen and the serial number ground off, that's the end of the trail, right?"

She smiled and gave me the look teachers reserve for slow students. "Of course, hon. Criminals use straw buyers all the time or just steal what they need.

Either way they're gonna arm themselves. Some stupid new law won't stop them."

Why bother with any laws? I thought but didn't say. "Do you keep an eye out for straw buyers in your operation, you know, people who make multiple purchases?"

"What, and invade their privacy? How do I tell the difference between a straw buyer and a collector? I say live and let live, Cal. The vast majority of people who buy guns are law-abiding citizens."

I nodded again and then asked about Arthur. "Oh, he's down in California looking at a possible new acquisition—a private gun club near Bakersfield," she told me.

"His gun collection's impressive. It must take real expertise to put something like that together."

She smiled with obvious pride. "Oh, he's an expert, all right. Designed our machine shop, too. There's nothing we can't fix on a gun in any of our shops. You know, we're so busy here that Arthur has put on a night shift."

"You don't say. That son-in-law of yours is a real entrepreneur."

Roz smiled, but it came out slightly strained. "Oh, he's that, all right." Her face clouded over, she sighed, and met my eyes. "I wish Raleigh were still alive."

"Raleigh?"

"My husband. The love of my life. He passed away eight years ago this December." She sighed again. "Sometimes I think Arthur's too ambitious. I, uh, worry we're growing too damn fast."

I nodded sympathetically. "Emulating Starbucks is a tall order."

She seemed to catch herself. "Well, I think he's trying to prove something. Arthur grew up poor as a church mouse. Went through Stanford on scholarships. His dream's to build something, uh, monumental, I guess you could say." She pushed out another smile and sat up a little straighter. "I've got a good man at the helm. And, besides, he treats my daughter like a princess."

We chatted some more, and then I left. As I walked to my car out in the parking lot, a familiar looking Chevy Silverado with an extended cab swung in and parked between me and my car. Farnell Timmons climbed out on the driver's side, opened the second door and extracted a leather rifle case. Two men who had gotten out on the passenger side came around the truck, each carrying rifle cases, as well. I recognized them as my friends Mutt and Jeff. I kept walking, and they turned in unison to face me, looking a little surprised.

I stopped in front of them. "Gentlemen. Out for a bit of target practice, I see. You've come to the right place."

Mutt and Jeff cradled their weapons as Timmons stepped forward. "Yep, the Arsenal's a fine facility." His eyes narrowed. "I'm surprised to see you here, Claxton. You don't strike me as the kind of man who appreciates a good gun range."

I held my briefcase up. "Oh, but I do. I've been brushing up with my Glock 17, you know, getting the cobwebs out."

Timmons pushed his lip up and nodded. "Impressive. Nice weapon, the seventeen." He showed a thin smile. "You always carry your gun in your briefcase?"

The comment caused Mutt and Jeff to snicker. He opened his coat revealing a chrome plated pistol resting in a hand-tooled shoulder holster. "You need to get yourself a decent holster for your Glock. Stop by the shop and I'll custom fit one for you."

I flashed an appreciative smile. "Well, thanks. I'll do that just as soon as I get my concealed carry permit." I tossed that last comment in just for effect. I really had no plans to start packing.

Timmons nodded, and the three of them headed for the Armory. Then he turned back and said, "Did the situation with that murdered woman get cleared up?"

"It sure did. Her ex-husband's in jail as we speak." I gave them another smile. "Happy ending."

Timmons gave me a thumbs-up. "Glad to hear it."

I stood there as they walked away, wondering why I got the nice guy treatment this time around. Maybe these guys were just less aggressive off their home turf. I wondered, too, why they were back at the Arsenal so soon after their previous visit. Was it just the sheer pleasure of blasting away with your bros or were there other, perhaps more compelling, reasons?

I watched for a macho strut, too, but realized I probably wouldn't know one if I saw it.

FORTY-EIGHT

Cal

I WAS IN the middle of cooking dinner that night when Tay arrived. After she finished making a big fuss over Archie—which he loved, of course—I poured her a chilled glass of Sancere and handed her a print-out of the latest exchange of emails between me and K209. As she read I busied myself with the meal, simple fare consisting of red snapper, sautéed fresh spinach with ginger, and Thai jasmine rice. I made a wine and lemon reduction sauce to give the fish a little extra snap.

When she finished reading the emails she stood up with the papers in her hand. "My God, Cal, if this is true, then Cardenas didn't do it. He didn't shoot Claudia."

I was wilting the spinach in a wok with fresh ginger and hot oil, the last step in the meal preparation. "The operative word is *if*. What do you think?"

"I believe her, Cal. The murder of Youngblood seems to dovetail into this narrative. Why would anyone make something like that up? Especially a teen who would have no apparent reason to carry out such an elaborate hoax."

I nodded as I set about plating our food. "I hear you. Still convinced she's a she?"

Tay glanced down at the printout. "More than ever. Those 'dumb me' and 'terrible man' comments are all girl." She smiled. "I'm sticking by my opinion."

I exhaled a long breath and shook my head. "I'm even more worried about her safety now. There's a lot she's not telling me, like where she saw the killer and how she avoided being seen, if she did. She's completely focused on staying anonymous." I set our plates down and poured myself some wine. "It could get her killed."

Tay winced at my words. "These street kids don't trust authority, Cal. She's probably been let down by so-called adults more times than we can count. That 'I can take care of myself' line broke my heart. I think she's really a very frightened young girl."

"Who has the skill and chutzpah to be painting a statement about global warming on a building fifty feet above a parking lot in Old Town at three in the morning," I added.

Tay nodded and smiled with some relief. "You're right. Let's hope she's resourceful enough to stay safe until we find her."

We ate my dinner, which was a big hit I might add, and continued to discuss the situation. I had half a pint of Ben and Jerry's pistachio ice cream stashed in the freezer. We shared it for desert while sitting on the threadbare couch below the window that looked out onto Couch Street.

Tay said, "Before I came in I was looking again at the graffiti K209 left on your building. I like her moniker—that K209 in black letters inside a red tri-angle looks pretty cool." She made a triangle by join-ing her opposing thumbs and index fingers and held it up. She looked at the shape she'd fashioned and paused for a moment. "You know, the triangle makes me think of a mountain, which kind of fits, don't you think? You know, she's a climber."

"Could be." I took a pen from my shirt pocket, sketched the moniker on the back of a magazine cover, and studied it for a moment. "Yeah, I think you're right, a mountain." I laid the pen down, and it accidentally covered the 09 portion of the moniker. An idea popped into my head. *"K2,"* I said. "Maybe that stands for the mountain in the Himalayas."

Tay leaned forward and studied what I'd drawn. I put my hand over the 09 for emphasis. When I took my hand away, she said, "Right. And maybe the 09 stands for the year 2009." Then she laughed. "Surely she didn't climb K2 in 2009. She was way too young."

"Maybe not her," I said as I got up and fetched my laptop. I tapped "K2 2009" into Google, and a series of articles popped up describing that particular year on what was termed the most dangerous mountain on earth. Tay and I scanned the articles. Not one climber summited that year. Several died trying. An American ski expedition managed to ski a fair portion of the mountain without killing anyone. I shuddered at the thought.

The only American climbing expedition that year ended in tragedy. One of the members was poised to summit when the freak collapse of an ice sheet swept him to his death. We jotted down his and the names of the other climbers, as well. We wound up with a total of nine names.

Tay leaned back and studied the ceiling for a few beats. "Now what?"

"If we're on the right track, she's probably using the moniker to commemorate something that happened on the mountain. Something someone did, probably a relative since she was so young."

"No one summited in 2009," Tay reminded me.

"True, but just going on an expedition to K2 is a big deal."

"Dying there would be a big deal, too."

I snapped my fingers and pointed at her. "Of course." I looked at our list. "The guy who died that year was named Donald Spence. Let's look at him first." I entered "Donald Spence obituary 2009" into the search engine. Four obits came up, but only one for a Spence who died while climbing the world's second highest mountain. His name was Donald Raymond Spence.

Tay squeezed my arm as she read the obit. "Cal, he's from Oregon."

I nodded, reading as fast as I could. The obituary said Spence had gone to high school in Albany, Oregon, and had attended the University of Oregon, although it didn't mention him graduating college. It talked about his love of climbing and his many exploits, including successfully summiting Everest, Nanga Parbat, and the Eiger, and included several quotes about his courage and character from fellow climbers. The obituary ended with this quote: "Mr. Spence was preceded in death by his wife, Kathleen, who died in 2000, and is survived by his daughter, Kelly Ann Spence, and his brother, Jerome T. Spence." There was no mention of where the surviving relatives lived.

Tay searched for Kathleen Spence's obituary using

her smartphone, while I ran the name Kelly Ann Spence through the online white pages. There was no obit and no Kelly Ann Spence living in Oregon. I tried Jerome T. Spence in the white pages next and got four hits, with one Jerome T. living in Spokane, Washington, and three east of the Mississippi.

I had the Spokane Jerome T. on the phone a couple of minutes later. "I'm an attorney trying to locate Donald Spence's daughter, Kelly Ann," I explained after introducing myself. "Are you her uncle?"

His voice became wary, which often happens when I use the A-word. "Uh, what do you want her for?"

"She's been named as a beneficiary in a will, and I'm trying to locate her," I lied. People respond best to happy news.

"Well, that's great, but I'm afraid I can't help you. Last time I saw Kelly was at my brother's funeral back in 2009. As far as I know, she's still in Portland, foster care, I think. I mean, she's what, sixteen?"

"Do you have an address or the name of the foster parents?"

"Nah. I don't." He paused, and I could hear him sigh. "I've been a lousy uncle, Mr. Claxton. When Don died on that goddamn mountain I was a raging alcoholic. No one was gonna trust me with her. Things are better now. Been sober for nearly two years."

I thanked Spence, punched off, and high-fived Tay. "All right! Kelly Ann Spence is sixteen, and she's probably living somewhere here in Portland with foster parents. I think we just might have something."

"I have some contacts at the Department of Human Services in Salem," Tay said. "I'll see if I can come up with the name of the foster parents tomorrow."

"Excellent. And I'm pretty sure I know where she's going to school and maybe even one of her friends." Tay looked at me, shocked. I told her about my visit to the New Directions Alternative School and my encounter with Kiyana Howard, who happened to be a client of mine. "You do your thing with DHS," I said. "I'm going back to the school tomorrow, first thing."

We weren't positive we had discovered K209's identity, but we sat there for a while anyway, basking in a sense of accomplishment. Tay and I sparked off each other, no doubt about it. There was something else buzzing in the air, too—a sense that our relationship had nudged up a notch or two. It was something that made me a little uncomfortable, and Tay, too, I sensed. I can't speak for her, but for my part, I was trying to keep my heart on high ground after what happened with Daina. The women I cared for, it seemed, had a habit of going away, and it never seemed to be my idea. Tay broke the awkwardness by stretching, popping up, and announcing she had an early day coming up and needed to get home.

Archie and I walked her out to her car. She hugged Arch and then turned and gave me a kind of knowing smile, like she knew something about us I didn't. She probably did. Her dark, gently curved lashes were like perfect nests for her brown eyes, which were soft and warm despite the harsh street light. She reached up with both hands, pulled my face to hers, and kissed me on the lips. The kiss lasted a little longer than a friendly peck's supposed to. I didn't mind. In fact, I suppressed an urge to kiss her for real.

"You're a good man, Cal Claxton," she said. "Talk to you tomorrow."

Coming from Tay Jefferson that was high praise. I walked away feeling rather good.

FORTY-NINE

Kelly

THE BIG MALAMUD and the little dog were still side by side when Kelly came out of the library. Spencer stood up when he saw her and wagged his tale. Kelly was shocked. With the exception of an occasional growl or bark, the dog had seldom even acknowledged her presence. It had started sprinkling, and the young musician was putting his guitar back in the case and pocketing his earnings. Aside from the five dollars Kelly left him, it didn't look like much. *I hope he has a real job*, she said to herself as she walked away with Spencer tugging on his leash.

She hadn't gone far when she remembered her job at Granite Works that morning. Phil Hanson is going to be pissed again, she told herself. Her first impulse was to take the bus to the gym and explain, but she quickly thought better of it. Macho Dude could be watching, although the only two people she'd told about the job were Kiyana and Zook. Better not to chance it.

The thought made her feel trapped, and she felt a stab of panic as she struggled to control her emotions. She couldn't even call Hanson, because her cell phone had gotten left behind. Her cell phone. She'd left it charging in the kitchen. Macho Dude probably found it. The thought was as revolting as it was frightening. Her phone was such a personal thing, like an extension of her hand. *Now that monster had it. What would he do with it?*

Kiyana Howard lived in a subsidized apartment with three other young women and an adult counselor on SE Thirty-first, just off Hawthorne Boulevard. Kelly headed in that direction. She hoped to catch Kiyana before her friend caught the TriMet bus that would take her across the river to school. No way was Kelly approaching the apartment, but she'd hung with her friend enough to know that there was a small park midway between it and the bus stop. She found a bench in the park, adjacent to a small fountain and facing the sidewalk leading to the stop. She sat down and waited.

Ten minutes went by, which seemed like hours. Kelly had almost given up when she saw her friend coming down the sidewalk. As she walked past, Kelly called out, "Hi, Ki."

Kiyana turned around with a puzzled look on her face as she strained to recognize the person enclosed in the black hoodie. She straightened up. "Is that you, baby girl?"

Kelly loosened her hood and smiled. "Yeah, it's me."

Kiyana smiled back. "I didn't recognize you with your hood up. Are you in hiding or something?"

"Have a seat. We need to talk."

Kiyana eyed the dog. "That's not the dog you're always complaining about, is it?" she said, sitting down next to Kelly. Spencer greeted her with a growl.

Kelly shushed him. "One and the same. Giving him a little exercise."

Kiyana leaned back and gave Kelly that streetwise look of hers. "Okay, what the hell's goin' on?"

Kelly exhaled a long breath, still unsure exactly how much to tell her friend. "Um, I'm in, uh, pretty deep shit. See, Digger told some people that it was my backpack the cops were asking about. Now those people are after me."

Kiyana looked genuinely horrified. "Sweet Jesus! That *was* you, then? I thought so. You've been holding out on me, Kel."

"Look, Ki, there's a lot I haven't told you about this. It's not because I don't consider you my best friend ever. I do." Kelly met her friend's eyes. "You know that."

Kiyana nodded, holding her gaze. "Yeah, but secrets aren't cool between friends. I want to help you."

"I know that. But these are terrible, terrible people. The less you know the better. I'm, uh, working with someone to fix this. I can't go home, but I've got a good place to hide, I—"

Kiyana's eyes got big. "You're working with Cal Claxton, aren't you? He came around school asking me if I knew anyone who might be that K-something tagger."

"What did you tell him?"

"Nothin'. He said the tagger might be in danger. He wasn't kidding, huh?"

Kelly exhaled another breath. "Look Ki, I came here to warn you. Don't tell anyone you've seen me or know anything about me, and watch your back. Don't trust anyone, and don't respond to any texts you get from me. They have my cell phone."

"What about Claxton?"

"I'll handle him, Ki. He says I can trust him, but he keeps bringing up the cops."

"No cops, huh?"

Kelly shook her head emphatically. "No cops. No way."

Kiyana nodded. She didn't know about Veronica's outstanding warrant, but she knew that people on the street often had reasons for not going to the police. It was a given where she came from. "You sure you're gonna be okay?"

"Yes. Don't worry about me. Have you seen Zook?"

"Yesterday. His lip's pretty messed up, but he looked good. Sober. He asked about you."

Kelly's heart fluttered for a moment, but she kept her expression in check. "Warn him, too. Don't tell him you saw me. Uh, just say you heard that Digger and Sprague might send someone after him. Now go. You're going to miss your bus."

The two friends hugged goodbye, which caused Spencer to growl again.

It was a half-decent day, so Kelly walked over to Division and took a bus heading east toward Mount Tabor Park. She got off at SE Sixtieth and ordered a grilled cheese sandwich and homemade tomato soup at a friendly little coffeehouse called Rain or Shine. They tolerated her dog and had a bookshelf full of books—mostly local authors—so she wound up spending the afternoon there reading.

She didn't head back until dusk, and by the time she reached her neighborhood it was dark. She moved carefully down the alleyway and felt a sharp sense of relief as she grasped the fingerholds on the cornerstones of her refuge. Those rough granite stones were a comfort, something solid and immutable in a life that had spun out of control. Her mind cleared, as it always did, as she began to climb.

She no sooner reached the top when it began to rain again, the kind of soft patter Portlanders hardly notice. The traffic sounds were muted down on Sandy Boulevard, and as the city lights began reflecting off the wet pavement, the cars looked to Kelly like boats on a river. She finally unrolled her sleeping bag under the eaves and climbed in. Spencer followed without hesitation.

As she drifted into sleep, she could feel his tiny, trip-hammer of a heart beating against her chest. *Don't give up*, it seemed to say. *Don't give up.*

FIFTY

Cal

AFTER TAY LEFT that night I was restless, so I poured myself some Rémy Martin, pulled my copy of Manny Bonilla's notebook out of my briefcase, and read through it again. Thanks to Hunter Barlow I was now pretty sure that Manny's crude sketches referred to trigger modifications that would render civilian assault rifles fully automatic. I Googled "drop in trigger," and a thicket of sites and advertisements came up offering the devices, mainly for modifying AR-15 rifles, the civilian version of a military assault rifle. I waded through enough of the texts to learn that most of what was out there didn't really allow weapons to fire in full automatic mode, and if the devices did they would run afoul of the National Firearms Act.

I held my glass up and swirled the amber liquid and watched the light dance through it for a while. Okay, I told myself, buying triggers on the open market would be a dead giveaway, and they didn't work all that well, anyway. Making your own would make sense on two counts—no one would know, and they could be designed to work efficiently. I took a sip and felt the soft burn of the Rémy as it found its way to my stomach. What would be the biggest market for guns like that? Probably south of the border. I immediately thought of the name Tay had given me—Javier Acedo, the local banger with cartel connections who'd met with Manny Bonilla in prison. Maybe Bonilla was the go-between to set up a deal. It made sense.

That line of thought brought me to ATF agent, Richie Truax. He was obviously all over this thing, and I could understand his not wanting me nosing around. While he was looking to bust a gun smuggling ring, I was trying to save a young girl and identify who had killed three innocent people, including my best friend's fiancée. If I talked to him now, I knew I'd be shut out of everything in a New York minute. I wasn't willing to let that happen.

I leafed through the photocopied pages again and stopped when I came to the weird entries I called the alphabet soup and looked at the first of them—

Oct. 23—two trucks/100 units.

ECA-25

MGC-30

BRC-45

Something was going to happen on that date, something important enough that Manny wrote it down. I sat there examining the combinations of letters for that entry, as well as the other three, for a long time but drew an absolute blank. Scrabble was never my long suit; just ask my daughter.

"Got any ideas, big boy?" I asked Archie, who had gotten up from his mat and was eyeing the door for his late-night walk. He looked back at me and whined softly a couple of times. That would be a no.

That night I dreamed about that shadowy young girl again, the one I couldn't decide was Claire or K209. This time she was marching with a sea of angry people, and every time I got close enough to recognize her, she would turn her back. The marchers carried weird looking weapons I somehow knew had been modified with drop-in triggers. They stretched to the horizon like the armies in a Hobbit movie.

I left a disgruntled Archie at Caffeine Central the next morning and got to the New Directions Alternative School around nine thirty. I knew from their website that they served a hot breakfast between eight and nine, and that the actual school didn't start until ten to accommodate kids, many of whom lacked dependable transportation. I got a coffee and stood across and down the street watching for Kiyana Howard. I'd decided she was my best bet for locating Kelly Spence. If I went to the case manager, Monica Sayles, with a name, I risked her going up the chain or worse yet, getting the police involved, which would screw up everything.

I saw Kiyana approaching the school at nine forty-five. How could I miss her? She walked with long, confident strides like she owned the city, not by fiat but by the force of her personality. She saw me crossing the street and stopped as if she were expecting me. "Got a minute, Kiyana?" She waited, her face deadpan. "Is there a student at the school named Kelly Spence?"

"Uh, yeah."

"Have you seen her lately?"

"No. She hasn't been around."

I stood there for a moment appraising her, my eyes focused on her face. She averted my gaze and looked down at the sidewalk. I said, "Listen, Kiyana. I don't have time to screw around here. If you know something, you need to tell me. Is she the tagger, K209?"

She shrugged. It wasn't a yes, but it wasn't a no, either.

"This girl's in grave danger, Kiyana. If the people who are looking for her find her before I do, she's going to die."

She looked up at me, her face clouded with uncertainty and concern. "I don't know anything."

I stepped forward and got right in her face. "Yes, you do, Kiyana. Do you want her death on your conscience? Do the right thing here."

She stepped back, and her eyes got moist. "She doesn't want the cops involved."

"I know that. I told her I'll represent her, that I'll do what I can."

The uncertainty drained away, and her eyes narrowed down. "You don't get it. She can't have the cops involved. And she doesn't trust you about that."

I huffed a breath of frustration. "Look, tell her I'll do everything in my power to shield her from the police. I'll find her a safe place. She can stay in the background while this is being cleared up. We'll find a way."

"She *has* a safe place."

"Right," I scoffed. "Where is it?"

"She wouldn't tell me. She said the less I know the better."

"Do you know where she lives?"

Kiyana hesitated, twisted one side of her mouth up, and shuffled her feet. "You mean it about the cops?"

"Yes, I mean it." I nodded in the direction of the school. "I can ask in there, but that might really blow her cover. And don't worry, I won't tell her where I got the information."

She looked relieved. "I've never been to her place, but it's across the river on Sandy, above a shop that sells audio stuff, used, I think. She's not staying there. She told me."

"That's okay. It's a place to start." I decided to press my luck. "Do you have a picture of her?"

She sighed with resignation. "I'll email you one of the two of us. I have your address. She has short hair now." She locked onto my eyes and held them. "Find her, Mr. Claxton. And remember, no cops."

I found the audio shop—Kleiman's Pre-Owned Stereo—on my phone and drove right to it. I figured I might not be the only one interested in the place, so I cruised by first, looking for a stakeout. Seeing none, I parked off Sandy three blocks down and walked past the place on the other side of the street, again looking for and seeing no sign of anyone hanging around.

The shop occupied the ground floor of a dilapidated three-story building. The shop was closed. A separate door and street number on the east side of the shop marked the apartment entry. I walked down two blocks, crossed the street and approached the building. I slipped into the outside door, which opened into a musty vestibule that had two keyed mailboxes, one each for the second and third floor apartments. No names were attached.

An inside door leading to the staircase was ajar,

so I let myself in, stopped, and listened. Nothing. I took the stairs to the second floor and knocked softly. The knock sounded hollow, like the apartment was empty. No one answered.

When I reached the third floor, my stomach took a sickening drop. "Oh, no." The front door was buckled in the middle and off its hinges. I stepped over it and went in. The place had been tossed. The door to a back bedroom had also been kicked in, and the only window in the room was wide-open. The back bedroom was Kelly's. I could tell by the framed pictures of Don Spence looking back at me from various mountain-tops, a poster of a group called the Black Keys, and high school textbooks and library books scattered on the floor. Judging from the authors—Camus, Austen, Angelou, among others—Kelly Spence was a serious reader. A laptop rested on the bed with its hard drive missing. I didn't see a cell phone. A roller suitcase sat empty in a closet stocked with clothes. A battered chest of drawers looked reasonably stocked, as well.

Nothing in the room hinted at Kelly's whereabouts, or so I thought at the time.

I looked out the window to the alleyway a good thirty feet below, then back at the smashed-in door. The only means of escape from the room had to be a galvanized downspout that ran along the corner of the building, adjacent to the window. I shook my head in disbelief and whistled softly. The conclusion seemed inescapable—Kelly got away using the downspout, a feat I wouldn't have attempted if the devil himself had been chasing me. And by the look of things, it had been a *very* close call.

I quickly looked through the rest of the apartment,

discovering only that Kelly had a roommate named Veronica Townsend, who had also left the place without packing. A small dog seemed to be missing, too.

I left the apartment untouched and let myself out of the building, clicking the inside door shut. As I was walking back to my car my cell chirped. "Cal? It's Tay. I checked at DHS. Kelly Spence was in foster care, but she ran away over two years ago. They have no records on her after that."

"Thanks. Look, Tay, can you get away for lunch, say at that little deli? We need to talk." She agreed.

Tay and I made a good team. Maybe she could help again, because I didn't have a clue what to do next.

FIFTY-ONE

Cal

IT WAS CROWDED and noisy in the deli, so Tay and I ordered sandwiches and coffees and retreated to my car. It was a cold, blustery day, so I started the engine to keep us warm. When I finished describing my encounter with Kiyana Howard and what I'd found at Kelly's apartment, I said, "So I'm torn here. I should probably go to the police right now. Her safety's my main concern."

"Well, she's evaded the police, the bad guys, and you so far. Maybe she's safer than you think."

I nodded. "I'd like to believe that."

"Are you exposed legally?"

I paused to consider that for a moment. "No, but I'm on the ragged edge." I chuckled. "That's nothing new. From a legal perspective, I still have no incontrovertible proof that Kelly Spence is K209. I'm just trying to verify that she's the witness she claims to be. No law against that. And remember, if Kelly decides to get amnesia, the cops can't touch her."

"Okay, so it's still about finding her, and that's probably the best way to protect her. She's somewhere where she has access to a computer. Using her own would be too risky, and it's stripped of its hard drive, anyway. She's not using her phone. That would be worse, and we would've seen a tag in the messages she sent. She could be using a tablet, I suppose."

"Not likely. She's living below the poverty line."

"Maybe this friend of hers, Kiyana, is secretly helping her, you know, providing a place to crash, a computer."

I shook that off. "I don't think so. The last thing Kiyana said to me was 'find her.' I think she meant it. She even sent me a picture of Kelly."

"Maybe Kelly's hiding out with her roommate somewhere. What's her name again?"

"Veronica Townsend." I nodded. "Could be. I tried a quick search for her but nothing came up. I need to talk to Kiyana to get more information. She didn't say anything about Kelly having a roommate."

The car went silent except for the whir of the heater fan. The windows were coated with a thin glaze of condensate, giving the outside world a kind of ghostly appearance. The clues for finding Kelly Spence seemed just as ephemeral.

Tay said, "Well, if I needed a computer I'd go to the public library."

I sat back in my seat. "Good thought. She had a ton of library books in her room. That would be a logical place for her to go and set up an anonymous account."

Tay nodded and was already busy pulling up a map of the Multnomah County Library locations on her cell phone. "Ugh. There are nineteen branches in the city."

I looked at the display. "The Central Library's just down from the school. She's too smart to use that one now that the shooter has figured out who she is."

"Right. And by the same logic, she wouldn't use

ones closest to her apartment, either." Tay rotated her phone for a landscape view. We both peered down at the tiny screen. "That would probably rule out the Albina, Hollywood, North Portland, and Gregory Heights branches," she said.

I nodded. "Yeah, and if we take out the branches at the outer edges of the city, that leaves what, four possibilities? Northwest, Holgate, Woodstock, and Belmont." I took a sip of my coffee, which had gone cold, but I hardly noticed. "By God, it's worth a shot."

TAY AND I cobbled together a plan, and then she went back to work and I went back to Caffeine Central. There was one small problem with the so-called plan—it assumed that Kelly would reestablish email contact, and that was not a given.

I took Archie out when I got back. He headed for the river, pulling at his leash. I stopped him at the Burnside Bridge. "Okay, big boy, we've got to turn around." He looked back over his shoulder with that baleful expression that always makes me feel guilty. He lived for his walks and runs with me. I tugged gently on the leash, and he just looked at me without budging. I sighed. "Look, I'll owe you, okay?" I tugged again and he turned and headed us back toward Caffeine Central. That dog of mine's a tough negotiator.

I had a briefcase of paperwork from Dundee and several phone calls to make, so I set to work at my desk, keeping one eye on the computer. At 12:06, the email I was hoping for came in.

Hello, Mr. Claxton. Have you made any progress in the case? I checked the newspapers today and

I didn't see anything. Please give me any news you have! I'm getting worried you won't catch the killer.

    I hurriedly typed a reply.

Hi, K209. Whatever you do, stay in a safe place. Don't take any chances. I don't have anything yet, but I'm waiting on some important news. Stay close to your computer and I'll be in touch. It may take a while, so sit tight.

    I signed off and bolted out of the office with Arch on my heels. I didn't want to take my dog with me, but what could I do? I owed him. I drove first to the Northwest Library, which was the branch of the Multnomah County Library System closest to me, and parked on Thurman Street. I pulled up the photo of Kiyana Howard and Kelly Spence that Kiyana had sent me and studied it one more time. The two friends were in front of the school, smiling back at the camera. Kelly was two or three inches shorter than Kiyana, with dark auburn hair, big, expressive eyes, and a couple of creases—not quite dimples—that bracketed a charming smile. She had a trim, broad-shouldered build that suggested athleticism. She wouldn't be hard to spot.

    One glance told me there wasn't a teenage girl in the computer section of the library, or any sign of one waiting for access. I hurried back to my car and headed over to the Naito Parkway and then across the Ross Island Bridge. I parked on SE Seventy-ninth and hurried into the Holgate Library. The trip took a little less than twenty minutes. Two of the computer stations were occupied by teenage girls, but I quickly ruled out both of them and left.

It took me another twenty minutes to eliminate the Woodstock Library.

I looked at my watch. It had been over an hour since I emailed Kelly. I wondered if she was still on-line. I hoped so. I backtracked to Cesar Chavez Boulevard and headed straight north.

The car in front of me took the last open space in front of the Belmont Library. I smacked the steering wheel. *"Damn it, that was mine!"* I had to drive another three blocks before I found a slot. As I hurried up the street I hardly noticed the kid with a backpack and small dog who passed me going the other way.

Every computer in the library was occupied, and there was no sign of Kelly. I did a quick tour of the rest of the library, but she wasn't there. I stood in the stacks, hands on hips, and thought about the fifteen other library branches out there.

I blew out a breath of frustration. *There's got to be a better way*, I told myself.

FIFTY-TWO

Kelly

Earlier that same day

KELLY FELT THE vibration first. Then a low, guttural sound that seemed to come from the bottom of a deep well. She spiraled up from sleep like a diver surfacing for air. *Spencer. Spencer is growling.* She lay there frozen, struggling to clear her head, which was partially covered by the sleeping bag. A light came on, and a hand gripped her shoulder and shook it. "Hey, what're you—"

Spencer burst out of the sleeping bag, barking furiously, fangs bared.

"Whoa, little critter! Calm down. I'm not gonna hurt you."

Kelly sat up, her chest constricted with terror. The shadowy figure of a man retreated, a flashlight in his hand. She grabbed the dog and pulled him to her chest, the light blinding her. Spencer struggled to get free, but Kelly held him tight with one hand, and put up the other to deflect the light beam.

The man lowered the beam so it wasn't shining directly in her eyes and kept his distance. "What in the world are you doing up here, child?"

Kelly sat there, too afraid to speak.

"Did somebody let you up here? I'm supposed to have the only key."

The dog growled and yapped another series of warnings. She hushed him. "I'm sorry, mister. I'll leave now. I don't want any trouble."

"How'd you get up here?" he insisted.

Without answering, Kelly climbed out of the bag and began to pack up. Spencer stood between her and the man, growling intermittently. She finished packing, clipped the dog's leash on, and followed the man through the exterior door and down the stairs. He was short and stocky with salt and pepper hair and walked with a slight limp. When they reached the third floor landing, he turned to face her, his eyes betraying a kindness he was trying hard not to show.

"You gonna tell me who let you up there?" he said. "I could lose my job for this."

"Sorry, mister. It won't happen again." She moved past him and started down the stairs. He moved aside reluctantly.

"Don't you have a place to sleep, child? It's cold and wet out there."

"I'll be okay, mister. Nobody let me in. You don't have to worry about your job."

"Oh, yeah?" he called down to her. "Then how did you get up there?"

"I climbed up," Kelly said over her shoulder.

"Sure you did. And I'm Michael Jackson."

When Kelly came out of the building she broke into a run. She didn't think the man would call the cops, but she wasn't taking any chances. It took a moment for the dog to react, but then he streaked out in front of her, his short little legs a blur. Dawn had broken, but the sun was blocked by a layer of low, thick clouds, and the streetlights were still on. When she got over to Ankeny Street she stopped in the shadows at the side of a building to catch her breath. The enormity of what had just happened crushed down on her like a huge weight. She slid down the wall, put her face in her hands, and squeezed her eyes tight to hold back the tears. Her refuge. Gone. The one place on the planet where she really felt safe. Gone. Everything was ruined. The tears came in a series of long, throbbing sobs. Spencer wagged his tail and whimpered softly. He tried to squeeze between Kelly's knees, but she wouldn't let him. "Go away," she hissed.

She suddenly felt exhausted, lacking the strength to hold it together any longer. It was too much. *And what did it matter anyway?* she asked herself. *Rupert was just a crazy old homeless man that nobody cared about. And your so-called family, what a joke. Veronica doesn't give a crap about you.* Kelly sat there and cried some more, but when she straightened her legs out, the dog jumped on her lap and began licking her face until he finally made her laugh. *Well*, she admitted, *there is Spencer. He needs a home.*

The bakery on Ankeny was warm and cozy, and as Kelly downed a hot chocolate she began to feel a little better. Spencer wolfed down the ham from the croissant like there was no tomorrow, but he didn't bite Kelly's fingers this time. When a stack of newspapers arrived, Kelly stood at the rack and read through one. No news about either the Claudia Borrego shooting or the beating death of Rupert Youngblood. She felt a sharp stab of disappointment. *What was taking them so long?*

It started pouring outside, so Kelly decided to have another hot chocolate and wait it out. The library was her next stop. She wanted to hear what Claxton had to say. She couldn't remember if the library opened at ten or noon on that particular day. Either way, she had time to kill. She needed a plan, anyway. She knew she could find a safe place to sleep that night. After all, she told herself, lots of kids sleep on the street every night in Portland. But at the same time she was tired and close to the breaking point.

A day, maybe two. If nothing breaks, she decided, *I'll give this thing up and go to Seattle. Surely Veronica will want Spencer back. Maybe she'll take me, too.*

THE RAIN FINALLY eased off as it usually does in Portland. Kelly arrived at the Belmont Library promptly at ten and groaned when she realized it wouldn't open until noon. She took the steps, sat down under the portico, and leaned against one of the pillars. She consoled herself that at least she would be the first in line for a computer. The young busker with the Malamud showed up not too long after that. Kelly sat out on the steps and listened as he practiced his Bob Dylan songs. Spencer took his spot next to the Malamud like he'd been doing it forever.

When the library finally opened, Kelly was the first in and first to sit down in front of a screen. She immediately logged in to her Hide My Ass! account and sent a message to Cal Claxton. He answered her right back. *Finally, some good news!* Or at least, Claxton said he was expecting to hear something, which she assumed was good news.

She sat there and watched her inbox, and as she

waited time slowed to a glacial pace. She fidgeted and squirmed in front of the screen, but nothing came back. *"Sheeze,"* she said when the computer timed out on her. An older man in a rumpled suit was next in line. Kelly said, "Can you give me another ten minutes?" He shook his head.

Kelly stomped out of the library, put a dollar bill in the guitar case, and leashed up the dog. She'd come back, but only after she walked off some nervous energy.

FIFTY-THREE

Cal

IT WASN'T UNTIL I was walking out of the Belmont Library that I thought of the little dog that passed me coming in. I think it was the big Malamud lying there that somehow jogged my memory about the dog paraphernalia I'd seen in Kelly's apartment. Maybe she had the dog in tow?

I hurried down the library steps and looked up Cesar Chavez Boulevard, trying to pull up the image of the kid I saw walking the dog. The sweatshirt hood was cinched up, so I had no impression of facial features, but the height and build were about right. The kid and the dog were out of sight, but I was intrigued enough to try to find them.

I jogged up to Yamhill and scanned both directions. No sign of them. The same for the next street up. My car was parked on Morrison, and when I reached it got in and continued the search. I must have driven around the area for ten or fifteen minutes before parking again, empty-handed. There were two possibilities—either the kid and the dog had ducked inside somewhere, for lunch maybe, or they'd gone into Laurelhurst Park, a nearby greenspace that covered multiple city blocks.

Archie squealed with delight when I let him out

of the back seat and leashed him up. "Come on, big boy, let's check out the park." He took off, practically dragging me. We entered the park at the southeast entrance and took a path that curved around to a huge duck pond with massive firs and hemlocks crowding the banks. We were halfway around the pond when I saw the kid sitting on a bench holding the little dog.

The bench was between the path and the water's edge, so Arch and I passed behind them. The small dog yapped a couple of times, but the kid, whose face was still obscured by the hoodie, just sat there looking out on the pond.

I stopped a little past the bench and said, "Hello, Kelly." The kid's head and shoulders made a quarter turn in my direction and then snapped back. Was it her or had the kid just reacted to my voice? "Kelly Spence," I repeated, "I'm Cal Claxton. I need to talk to you."

The kid rose abruptly and began striding away in the direction we'd come from without looking back. "You've got the wrong person, mister. Leave me alone."

It was the voice of a girl, I was sure of it. "Kelly, wait. If that's you, I can help you. You don't have to do this on your own. Just hear me out. Please." She stopped, her shoulders dropped, but she remained facing the other way. "Let's just sit down here and talk this over."

She turned slowly and faced me, her hoodie still drawn up tight. I was glad I had Archie with me, sensing his presence would reassure her. My dog had a way of doing that. She stood there for a while just looking at me. Finally she said in a low voice, "Will you let me leave after we talk?"

I would've done anything short of physical coercion to prevent her from taking off, but the truth was I couldn't really stop her.

"If you want to, yes. I'm not the police."

She came back to the bench and stood there. I approached with Archie leading the way. The little dog moved tentatively in front of Arch, lay down, and rolled over on his back, exposing his chest and belly. The act of submission was perfectly timed, serving to break the ice. I said, "This is Archie. What's his name?"

"Spencer." She looked at him, then back at me, showing a hint of a smile. "It's a stupid name for such an ugly dog." She sat down on the bench, and I joined her. The dogs arranged themselves in front of us like old friends. She loosened her hood but kept it up. Her eyes were pretty, blue like the McKenzie River. "How did you find me?"

I chuckled like it was nothing. "I know a computer hacker who eats anonymous websites for breakfast. I put two and two together, and here I am." It was a bald-faced lie and purposefully vague, but I hoped an allusion to technical wizardry would somehow satisfy her. I'd promised not to compromise Kiyana Howard.

She looked genuinely shocked. "He must be really good." To my relief, she left it at that, asking instead, "You said you were waiting for news about the murders. Did you hear anything?"

I couldn't lie this time. "I, uh, told you that so you would stay on your computer. That's how I found you."

She turned away from me. "That figures. So, you've got nothing, huh?"

"No, that's not true at all! Thanks to you, I've got a lot. What I need now is for you to take me back through everything you've seen, so I can put it all together. I'm close to cracking this thing, Kelly." That was a bit of an overstatement, but I did feel strongly that she knew more than she thought she did.

"I told you everything I know," she said while keeping her back to me. "Looks like it was a complete waste of time." She sighed deeply. "I should have known."

"Not at all," I shot back. "Look, are you hungry? Let's get you something to eat, and I'll get a coffee. Then we can go to my office and talk about this."

She turned around and looked me straight in the eye. Her gaze was unflinching and held an element of maturity beyond her years. "You're not going to call the cops? If you do, I'll say I don't know what you're talking about, I swear."

"Kelly, I get it about the cops, okay? Come on, let's go eat." I held my breath.

"Okay."

As we walked together out of the park, I felt an enormous sense of relief that this young girl was finally safe. At the same time, I was having a distinct dog-that-caught-the-cat moment.

What the hell do I do now?

FIFTY-FOUR

Kelly

AS SHE WALKED out of the park with Cal, Kelly struggled to make sense of her clashing emotions. On the one hand, it was good to finally share the burden with someone, and she felt a sense of relief that brought tears to her eyes and made her knees a little shaky. But on the other hand, she felt terrified at the prospect of becoming personally involved in a situation that held so much risk for her and Veronica. Here she was, getting ready to spill her guts to some lawyer. Okay, he had a good reputation in Old Town, and Kiyana liked him, but, hey, he was a *lawyer*, after all. Claxton knew her K209 secret now, too, and God knows who else. That made her sad for reasons she couldn't quite explain. There was something special about that moniker, a tribute to her dad, for sure, and a declaration that she didn't buy what she saw around her. She felt a sense of loss, like a chapter of her life coming to a close.

But there was something about this guy that made her want to trust him. He wasn't dressed like a lawyer—jeans, a thick wool sweater, and Merrill hiking boots—and he didn't look like one, either. He was big and broad with a shaggy mustache, long hair, and eyes that were friendly, but warned you not to bullshit him. There was his dog, too—the handsomest animal she'd ever seen, black with white and copper trim, and big without being threatening. And it was easy to tell that dog loved Claxton. *Dogs are excellent judges of character, aren't they?*

When they got to his car, a beat-up old BMW, she stood there for a moment, and Claxton gave her a look that told her he knew what she was going through. He let Archie in the back seat and got behind the wheel without saying anything. Kelly hesitated for a few moments and then went around to the passenger side and joined them.

THEY STOPPED AT a Pizzacato at Twenty-eighth and Burnside, where Kelly feasted on a gourmet pizza and an arugula salad. Claxton smiled, watching her eat, and she told him it was the best meal she'd had in forever. He suggested that instead of launching into the case, they take some time to get to know each other. Kelly learned that Cal—that's what he asked her to call him—was a bachelor who lived with his dog out in the wine country and that he also had a place above his office at Caffeine Central. He lit up when he began telling her about his daughter, a grad student at UC, Berkeley. It was pretty obvious that he loved her a lot. He told Kelly his wife had died, but he didn't talk about that. He laughed when Kelly asked if he had a girlfriend. He told her he didn't, but that there was a woman he was becoming interested in.

Kelly talked mainly about her dad, what a great mountaineer he was, and how they used to climb together. She told him about school, too, and how she was on track to graduate early. When Cal asked about her plans she said, "I'm going to college, and I want to be the youngest woman to climb the north face of the Eiger in Switzerland. It was Dad's favorite climb." She didn't mention Veronica, and Claxton didn't press her about her living arrangements.

They drove across the river to Old Town, where Kelly and her dog followed Claxton and his dog into the office at Caffeine Central. Spencer managed to appropriate a corner of Archie's mat, and soon both dogs were snoozing peacefully. Claxton came right to the point. "Look, Kelly, I got involved here because Claudia Borrego was the fiancée of a good friend of mine, and when I realized that K209 probably witnessed the shooting, I decided to find you, figuring the cops would have a problem locating a young tagger." Kelly smiled and nodded. "Then I found out from you that Rupert Youngblood was another victim, and there's even one more you don't know about— a young man named Manny Bonilla. There's also a man, who may very well be innocent, who's in jail for the shooting. As you can see the stakes are huge."

Kelly's smile faded, and her face grew wary. *Where is he going with this?*

"I promised you I'd do everything in my power to help you, and I will. But as an attorney in the state of Oregon, I took an oath to uphold the law." Claxton met her eyes and held them. "You've got to work with me here, Kelly. We can deal with the tagging misdemeanors you've committed. You've got tremendous leverage with the police because of what you know."

Kelly fought to maintain a brave front, but her lower lip trembled slightly. She dropped her eyes and studied the hardwood floor. *You should never have come here, you idiot.* The room fell completely silent.

After a long pause, Cal said softly, "Think about it, Kelly. It's the right thing to do."

A car passed outside on Couch, then another. Her dog made a little whining sound in his sleep. Kelly raised her eyes, sat back in her chair, and sighed. "It's not about the tags so much."

Claxton nodded like he knew that. "What is it then?"

"It's my dad's girlfriend, Veronica. She's in trouble."

"What kind of trouble?"

"She's wanted in California. Drugs, I think. She wouldn't tell me much about it. She's not using now."

"I can understa—"

"There's something else," Kelly interrupted. "I won't go back into foster care. I'll just run away again."

Claxton nodded, as if Kelly had just mentioned the weather or time of day. "Good," he said brightly. "We only have two problems." He asked her a bunch more questions, and they discussed them for a long time. He didn't bore in on what had happened to Kelly in foster care, but she made sure he got the picture.

Finally, Claxton said, "Tell you what. I'm a member of the California Bar. I'll represent Veronica down there if she'll agree to give herself up. Drug warrants are generally not a big deal, and what she's doing now is just making things worse. It's not fair to you, either." Kelly shifted in her seat but kept her eyes down.

Claxton went on. "I'll also agree to represent you in finding a good foster home, one that you are enthusiastic about instead of being in dread of. And if you want to go after your former foster parents, we'll look into that, too."

Kelly was stunned. It was as if Claxton, with the sweep of his hand, put to rest her darkest fears. But she was still wary. "Uh, what do I have to do?"

Claxton smiled. "It's simple. Tell the police everything you know."

"What about Veronica? She'll never agree."

"Let me handle that."

Kelly exhaled a long breath. "Okay, I'll do it but only if Veronica agrees, too."

"Good," Claxton said. "What's her number? I'll call her right now."

FIFTY-FIVE

Cal

I WAS RELIEVED when Kelly agreed to my proposition, although it was a deal that would make my accountant apoplectic. Running a pro bono case down in California could get expensive in a hurry. And I was a lot less confident that I could get Veronica to come forward than I'd let on. Kelly gave me Veronica's cell phone number, but when I called it no one answered, and I didn't leave a message.

I printed out all of Kelly's email messages, and we began to go back through them. I was particularly interested in what she'd seen at the Bridgetown Arsenal. When we got to that point in her narrative I said, "You say here that you watched the Arsenal for a while from a hiding place. Tell me more about that."

"Well, I wanted to see if I could spot Macho Dude. That's what I've been calling the guy who shot Claudia. Because of the jacket he wore with the eagle on it I figured he might be a customer or work at the Arsenal. I was too chicken to just walk in, but I noticed this building across the street just sitting there half built. I found a spot up on the fourth floor and watched from there. About the third or fourth time I was up there, these two panel trucks rolled in just as it was getting dark. A dude I thought was Macho

Dude got out of one the trucks, but it got dark before I could be absolutely sure."

"What were they doing?"

"They loaded up a bunch of boxes and took off."

"What kind of boxes?"

Kelly paused to think as she scratched Spencer behind his ears. "Just cardboard boxes, sort of square, not real big, but quite a few."

"Did the trucks have any markings on them?"

"Nope. They were plain white. Then the next day another truck got loaded up."

"Same kind of boxes?"

Kelly paused for a moment. "Uh, actually, that second day the boxes were bigger, rectangular. Anyway, I got up my nerve and walked over there and asked for directions. I didn't see Macho Dude, but this other dude drove up, got out, and said something to the guys loading the boxes. I recognized that voice. It was the man at the granary. I'd know that voice anywhere."

"Shipments," I said, more to myself than Kelly. "It has to be. When did you see this?" Kelly shrugged, so I got a calendar out and spread it on the desk in front of her. "What were the dates?"

"Uh, the first must have been a Thursday, so October twenty-third, and the second must have been on the twenty-fourth."

"You sure?"

"Yes, I'm sure. I remember that the first time was the day before the anniversary of Dad's accident on K2."

"Shipments," I said again with more emphasis. I jumped up and fished the copy of Manny Bonilla's

notebook out of my briefcase and opened it up to the page containing the alphabet soup. The first entry read:

> Oct. 23—two trucks/100 units.

> ECA-25

> MGC-30

> BRC-45

The second:
> Oct. 24—one truck. 45 mods-SDGC

The third:
> Nov. 19—two trucks/80

> ECGR-35

> RBRR-45

And the fourth:
> Nov. 23—one truck SDGC—40 mods.

I pulled up the Bridgetown Arsenal website, clicked on the *About Us* button, and read about the expanding empire that Roz Jenkins and Arthur Finley were building. Their business strategy was to buy existing gun shops and ranges and keep their original names to maintain local identities. So, their acquisition down in southern Oregon was called the Medford Gun Club, a venerable organization that had been around for decades. In northern California, it was the Red Bluff Rifle Range, which had been around for fifty years, and so it went on down to the Mexican border, fifteen gun shops and growing.

I sat there looking at the names of the shops when it popped. "*Of course*. MGC must stand for Medford Gun Club, RBRR for Red Bluff Rifle Range." I went through all the initials in Bonilla's entries and matched them up with businesses belonging to the Jenkins's family. I looked at Kelly. "I think what you saw was the load-up for a series of deliveries. My guess is that first day the 'units' were drop-in triggers made at the Arsenal to be delivered to gun shops along the I-5 corridor. The units might indicate how many triggers were delivered at each site, so 45 units at the Bakersfield Rifle Club, 20 units to the City of Angels Gun Range in L.A, and so on. Those units would be used to modify rifles acquired in the local area."

I glanced back down at the sheet. "The second and fourth entries are different." I looked at Kelly and spread my hands beyond the width of my shoulders. "You said the boxes were rectangular that second time. About like this? About the length of a rifle?"

She nodded.

"Okay, maybe the '45 mods' refer to 45 AR-15s modified at the Arsenal to be shipped to the San Diego Gun Club, which is probably the staging area for the entire smuggling operation into Mexico." I nodded slowly, awed by the implications. The potential scope of the operation was impressive. "Yeah, that might hang together."

Kelly looked back at me in complete bewilderment. "Is that good?"

I nodded again. "Maybe. If I'm right, then it should tell us when the next shipment goes out." I looked at the third entry in Bonilla's notebook, straining to read his terrible handwriting. I could hardly believe my eyes. "It looks like a shipment's going out *today*."

"Are you going to call the police?"

I shook my head. "No time for that."

No stranger to risk-taking, Kelly's face brightened. "I'll show you my hiding place and we can check them out, take photos or something." She described her perch and how to get there and ended by saying, "I think you could probably make the climb, Cal. It's not too hard."

Nothing like a vote of confidence. I leaned back in my chair and turned the situation over in my mind. "It would certainly confirm that I'm on the right track. And if this holds, there should be another shipment in a couple of days. That would be the one to bring the police in on."

Kelly continued to smile. "*Right*. And maybe Macho Dude will be there, too."

I picked up the phone and called Esperanza at Nando's office. "Do you have access to Nando's ghost hunter?" I asked her after we exchanged greetings. It was what he called his night vision camera. "I might need to borrow it this evening." Like any self-respecting PI, Nando had an array of eavesdropping devices, including a high-definition infrared camcorder.

"Of course I do," she told me. "Stop by before five and it's yours."

I thanked her and when I hung up, Kelly said,

"Yes!" and leaped out of her seat, spilling her dog and causing Archie to stand up in the corner and bark a couple of times. "How cool, man. I can't wait."

"If anyone tapes them, Kelly, it's going to be me all by my lonesome. You're not going anywhere near that place."

"But I—"

"Not going to happen, Kelly. Sorry."

While Kelly fumed in her seat, I called Veronica again but got no response. I would have to come back to that later that night. When Kelly went to the restroom, I called Tay. "I've got her," I said when she picked up and went on to sketch in some details, including the situation with Veronica and Kelly's fear of foster care. "Any chance you can get away?" I asked. "I need your help this afternoon."

"I'll be there around three," she told me.

I made Kelly go back over every detail of the layout at the Arsenal and even had her draw me a map. It looked feasable, and I was confident I could get in and out without being seen. I thought again about calling in Harmon Scott or Richie Truax but thought better of it. I'd promised to contact Veronica first, and besides, by the time I dealt with the police and ATF, this window of time would be closed.

It was worth a shot, I decided. What could go wrong?

FIFTY-SIX

Kelly

KELLY WAS TICKED off that Claxton wouldn't agree to let her go with him to the Arsenal. *Shoot, it was my idea*, she told herself. *This really sucks.* She was sitting there giving him the silent treatment when someone knocked on the door. Claxton got up, let a woman in, and introduced her. Kelly stuck out her hand, but Tay Jefferson gave her a big hug. "You had us worried, girl," she said, holding Kelly at arm's length. Tay was tall and stylish with the prettiest golden-brown eyes Kelly had ever seen. Kelly liked her instantly, and she figured Tay was the woman Claxton mentioned, the one he said he was becoming interested in.

They sat together in Claxton's office and went back through the story to bring Tay completely up to speed. It was clear he trusted this woman and had great respect for her. When they finished, Tay sighed heavily. "So, all this carnage for guns that shoot a little faster. Why am I not surprised? Is there any limit to this insanity?" Then to Kelly she said, "How did this shooter fellow find you anyway?"

The memory of the attempted rape sprang into Kelly's mind. She drew her mouth into a tight line and shook her head. "A guy named Digger recognized my backpack, figured I might be K209. He gave me up, for drugs or cash, or both."

Tay sighed again and looked at Claxton, raising an eyebrow. "Well, judging from the ruthlessness of these people, I'd say that boy Digger better watch his back."

Tay turned her attention back to Kelly. "I'm sorry about what happened to you in foster care. I don't blame you for not wanting to go back. And it's great that you've got Cal on your side, if you want to go after that disgusting creep who molested you." She chuckled and glanced at Claxton. "I wouldn't want to be in his shoes if Cal comes after him."

Kelly allowed herself the trace of a smile about something she rarely acknowledged, let alone talked about.

Tay said, "But you know, Kelly, there are a lot of good foster homes out there. You shouldn't let one experience, as horrible as it was, blind you to that fact."

The smile faded. "How do you know that?" Kelly shot back.

"I was raised in one, that's how. My single mom died when I was twelve. My brother and I were brought up by two of the sweetest people in the world." She paused. "Think about it, Kelly. That's all I'm saying."

Claxton left around four to pick up the IR camera and head over to the Bridgetown Arsenal. It was clear to Kelly that Tay Jefferson's job was to keep an eye on her in Claxton's absence. She loved Tay but didn't like the idea of being babysat one bit. She yearned to be out there in the action. After all, she knew the layout at the abandoned building much better than he did, and she could spot Macho Dude, too, if he showed up.

Kelly excused herself to use the restroom in the apartment upstairs. She tiptoed back down, slipped into the room behind the office, unlocked the backdoor, and let herself out. Once she was out on Couch Street she started running and didn't stop until she reached the bus stop on Burnside. The #33 screeched to a stop eight minutes later. With any luck, she might already be in position in her perch when Claxton showed up. She rode up near the front of the bus, focused on the task ahead, and tried hard not to think about Tay Jefferson's reaction to what she'd just done.

This is for Claudia and Rupert, she told herself.

FIFTY-SEVEN

Cal

I PARKED ON a side street, a good six blocks down from the Arsenal, and once more studied the map Kelly had drawn. Esperanza had checked me out on the IR camera, and I'd stashed it in a small daypack. I moved down Water Street cautiously, wearing black sweats, a down jacket, and a ball cap. When I reached the abandoned structure, I ducked off the sidewalk and watched the Arsenal across the street for several minutes. There were no cars in the portion of the parking lot I could see, and no one stirred on the loading dock, which ran along the north side of the building.

I began to feel a little silly. *What if I'm wrong? What if no one shows?*

I followed the chain-link fence skirting the structure around to the back of the property and scaled the fence. A steel skeleton of I-beams, cross ties and studs loomed up in front of me like a hollow Mt. Everest. I began to wonder what I'd gotten myself into. A few wall sections had been installed, mainly in the front, before the project went bust. This provided a modicum of cover, at least as viewed from the Arsenal. I still felt exposed as hell as I picked my way up through the center of the building, the route Kelly had suggested. The light was fading fast, and I was glad of it. I was also glad I'd worn my do-it-yourself Ninja suit. There was still the occasional car passing down on Water.

The steel was cold, unyielding and slippery, the going slow. When I reached the third floor, I hit a dead end and had to tightrope walk a narrow cross-beam until I found a way up at the back of the structure. *Easy, Kelly? You've got to be kidding.*

I finally made it to the fourth floor, worked my way to the front, and set up shop next to a gap in two wall sections that afforded a view of the Arsenal. It was getting dark, and nothing stirred across the street. I had the camera out and was futzing with the focus when I heard, "Hi, Cal." I snapped my head up so fast I almost fell off the beam. I squinted up into the low light. Kelly was stretched out on a beam looking down at me, a nervous smile on her face.

"Jesus, Kelly. What the hell are you doing here?"

She rolled off the beam and down a stud like a monkey down a palm tree. "I, uh, thought you could use some help, Cal, you know, spotting Macho Dude." Her look became defiant. "This is my fight, too, you know."

I rolled my eyes. "Now I know why you remind me of my daughter. You don't listen to me. Come on, we're out of here. I'll bet Tay's beside herself." I pulled my cell phone out and turned it on. Tay had sent a text saying Kelly had taken off. I texted back that I'd found her and not to worry.

Kelly was looking out the gap toward the Arsenal. She turned back to me, her eyes wide with excitement. "Well, if we leave now we're going to miss the show. They just pulled in."

I looked out. Two white vans were visible, just barely, in the near darkness. A group of men, three or four, stood next to the vans. I could see the red dots of smoldering cigarettes. I exhaled sharply. "Okay, sit tight, damn it."

I picked up the camcorder and zoomed in. Their images seemed so close it startled me. I felt a twinge of excitement as I immediately picked out two familiar faces in the cluster—the Mutt and Jeff duo I'd encountered in Estacada. Then a bright light bloomed at the edge of my field of vision. I panned over and voilà, Arthur walked through a door onto the dock and then closed it. He stood on the dock, said something to the men, and then went back inside. I handed Kelly the camera. "Tell me if you recognize anyone."

She put the camera to her eye. "They're going to have to walk around if you want me to pick out Macho Dude."

"I know. Be patient. They're smoking now. They'll get to work in a minute."

An eternity passed. Finally, she said, "Oh, they're moving now, up the stairs, one by one. Perfect." Another interminable pause. She handed the camera back to me and frowned. "Sorry. I, uh, don't think he's there, Cal. Those guys walk like normal dudes."

"Okay. It's early. He might still show up." I shot a lot of footage of the vans being loaded and periodically handed the camera back to Kelly, but she didn't see the swaggering walk we were both hoping for. I wondered if it was possible to be so certain about the way someone walked, but Kelly seemed so confident. And I reminded myself that she had recognized the shooter's walk at her apartment, and that had surely saved her life.

The filming wasn't a complete bust, though. I now had direct proof Arthur was tied into this thing, and some nice cameos of the men loading the vans. Of course, I had no direct evidence that they were loading modified AR-15 assault rifles, but I was now pretty damn confident that they were, that I had broken Bonilla's code.

When both vans finally pulled out I said, "Let's get out of here." I followed Kelly back down through the building and did everything she did, except I did it a lot slower and with my heart in my mouth. Climbing down, it turns out, is a lot harder than climbing up.

We hurried to my car, which was up on Taylor in a section unlit by street lights. I was opening the door when I heard a voice behind us. "Well, well, if it isn't the country lawyer."

I spun around as a man emerged out of the shadows from across the street and walked up to us. It was Farnell Timmons, and the chrome plated pistol leveled at Kelly and me shown in the low light. Kelly sucked a startled breath. I said, "What do you want, Timmons?"

He held his free hand up. "Hush, Claxton. Let me enjoy the moment. You brought the little tagger with you. What a perfect surprise. Just call me lucky." He settled his eyes on Kelly and made what might pass for a smile in the reptile world. "Did you jump out of that window or what? I thought I'd never catch you, and lookie here."

Kelly took a step back and bumped into the car. I said, "You got this wrong, Farnell. She—"

He brought the gun up, aiming it at my face. "Shut
the hell up, Claxton. Now, take that backpack off and
hand it to me, *very* slowly." I did what he told me.
With the gun leveled on us, he deftly unzipped the top
of the pack and looked in. "A camera. Imagine that."
He zipped the top and slipped his free arm through
a strap on the pack and said, "Come on, we're gonna
walk back to the Arsenal just like folks out for an
evening stroll."

Not one car passed us on Water Street on our way
back, and I had no doubt he would have shot us both
had I tried anything. Better to wait for an opening, I
decided, as I swung between cursing myself for getting Kelly into this and wondering how in the hell
Timmons knew where I'd parked. Halfway there,
Timmons said, "That was you that night in Borrego's
apartment, wasn't it."

"Yeah, that was me."

"Well, you owe me a boot, asshole."

"Sorry. The cops have it, and it's got your DNA
all over it."

He laughed, a sharp bark ringing with anger. "I'm
not in that fascist database. Never been arrested. At
least there's some privacy left in this police state. And
I gotta tell you, Claxton, I'm real sorry I didn't spill
your guts that night."

Farnell took us in through the loading dock into a
warehouse. Arthur was over in one corner writing at
a small desk in a pool of light. He looked up, laid his
pen down, and came over to us, an anxious look on
his face. "What the hell, Farnell?"

"Found these two in the neighborhood. The little one's the tagger I've been looking for. Claxton here—"

"I know Claxton," Arthur said. He appraised me with colorless eyes. "What's going on, Cal?"

I shrugged. "Nothing. People know we're here. Let us go now, and there won't be any trouble." Lame, I know, but it was the only thing I could think to say. We were screwed, and I knew it.

Farnell tossed Arthur the daypack. "Check this out."

Arthur removed the map Kelly had drawn for me first, studied it for a moment, then took out the camcorder and examined it with the air of someone familiar with electronic gadgets. He switched it on, rewound it, and put it to his eye. The warehouse fell silent. He lowered it and looked at Farnell. "He taped the load-up tonight." Then to me he said, his voice almost pleading, "I knew you were up to something, Claxton." He clenched his jaw and glared at me as a vein popped out on his neck like a small purple snake. "Why couldn't you just mind your own damn business?"

"This is a good thing, Arthur," Timmons said. "We got the only witness now, and Claxton knows too damn much, anyway."

Arthur turned and shot Timmons a look. "Yeah, well, this isn't what I signed up for. This was supposed to be a business deal."

Farnell glared back at him. "You're up to your ears in this, and you know it. I shot her, but whose idea was it to plant the silencer and frame her ex-husband? Deal with it."

Just as I started to speak the door leading into the

warehouse from the main building swung open, and Roz Jenkins walked in. She stopped when she saw the gun in Farnell's hand pointing at Kelly and me. She looked from Farnell to Arthur and wrinkled her brow. "What the hell's going on here?"

Arthur's face went bloodless, his look a study in pure anguish. "*Jesus Christ*, Roz, what are you doing here?"

"Never mind what *I'm* doing." She walked up to Farnell. "Lower that gun, Farnell. *Right now.*"

Farnell had lost his air of confidence. He retreated a half step, looked at her, then back at me. "Sorry, Roz, no can do. We caught these two breaking in, and we're just taking care of business. Best you run along now. We'll handle this."

Arthur turned to her, his eyes pleading. "Yes, Roz. Just—"

"*Shut up*, Arthur," Roz cut in. Then she eyed me with a puzzled look. "Is this true, Cal?"

I was torn. If I told Roz the truth, I was probably dooming her, too, but she was our only hope, slim as it was. I said, "Of course not, Roz. They've been trafficking illegal weapons out of your stores. They think we witnessed a murder, and they're getting ready to kill us."

Kelly's knees buckled a little at my words, but she followed my lead, "That's true." She pointed at Timmons. "I saw him shoot an innocent woman."

Roz's eyes enlarged in utter disbelief, not at our statements, but at what was unfolding in front of her. She placed a hand on Farnell's arm. "Lower your weapon," she said in a voice ringing with the authority of someone used to getting her way. Farnell snarled in response and slapped her across the face with the back of his free hand, a sharp, stinging blow that reverberated through the room.

Roz staggered back, and I saw my chance to rush Farnell, but he read me perfectly. He extended his arm, pointing the gun at Kelly. "Don't do it, Claxton."

Roz looked at Arthur, a hand to her reddening cheek, a fierce glare in her eyes. *Do something, Arthur, for God's sake.*

Arthur looked at Timmons in horror, then back at Roz like a cornered animal. There was a pause, and all eyes in the room shifted to him. "Roz, I'm sorry about this. Tell Melanie I love her." As he said that, Kelly's map slipped from his grasp. Arthur went to one knee and extended a hand as if to retrieve it. His other hand brushed his pant leg, and then his arm extended and pointed at Timmons. I saw a momentary metallic glint and so did Farnell, but not soon enough.

Pop. A dark red flower the size of a dime bloomed between Farnell's eyes, and he dropped like a column of ash with a look of pure astonishment on his face.

Arthur turned his hand around, and I saw the derringer. *Pop.* He fell over backward, not caring in the least that his head hit the concrete floor first.

FIFTY-EIGHT

Cal

THE MURDER-SUICIDE at the Bridgetown Arsenal made the national news, and the bigger story was the break-up of a highly organized gun trafficking and money laundering scheme aimed at supplying military grade assault rifles to the drug cartels as well as criminal elements and gangs north of the border. ATF Special Agent Richie Truax announced that the entire chain of gun shops owned by The Jenkins family had been shut down and numerous arrests made. With the help of Kelly's and my video work, these included four arrests in Estacada, among them, my old friends, Mutt and Jeff.

Truax explained to the media that the murder victim, Farnell Timmons, had headed up a large network of "straw buyers," who were responsible for supplying the AR-15 rifles, which were purchased locally and through the Internet. The weapons were then modified at the Bridgetown Arsenal using a novel, low cost "drop-in" trigger. The trigger assembly was designed by the suicide victim, Arthur Finley, a self-taught weapons expert. Finley was the mastermind behind the scheme, which was in the process of being replicated across the entire chain of gun shops owned by his mother-in-law, Rosalind Jenkins. Jack Pfister, an attorney for the Jenkins family, stated that Mrs. Jenkins and her daughter, Finley's wife Melanie Finley, had no prior knowledge of the illicit operation and intended to fully cooperate with the ongoing ATF investigation.

In a separate but parallel effort, the Portland Police Bureau was mopping up its part in the case, as well. Based on Kelly's and my sworn statements to Harmon Scott and his partner, Aaron Ludlow, the case against Anthony Cardenas was being "reexamined." Prosecuting attorneys are never quick to drop charges, because it makes them look bad and invites lawsuits. But they would have no choice in this case.

On the plus side, Scott and Ludlow were poised to close two cases—the murders of Claudia Borrego and Rupert Youngblood. The Youngblood case had been up in the air until a DNA sample from skin found beneath his fingernails matched Timmons's DNA, which, incidentally, also matched DNA taken from the cowboy boot I'd wound up with that night in Claudia's apartment.

All indications were that Timmons killed Manny Bonilla, too, but with Timmons's death, there was a good chance that case might never be closed.

It was also assumed that Arthur Finley was the second man Kelly saw with Timmons at the granary the night Rupert was killed, the man she dubbed "The Voice." That subject came up in a second interview, which involved both Kelly and me. As promised, I had already taken care of the concerns about her K209 tagging exploits. The Portland Police Bureau agreed not to press charges in exchange for her full cooperation, as I knew they would.

When Scott asked Kelly if she recognized Arthur's voice during the confrontation at the Arsenal, she glanced over at me. I had already asked her that question and knew the answer. I nodded for her to go ahead. "Um, I don't remember noticing anything at the time, but I was so freaked out that I might have missed it. When I think back, it's like everyone's voice sounded the same to me that night. I'm sorry."

I said, "That's okay, Kelly. It's understandable. I was as freaked out as you were." I looked at Scott. "I hope you guys will continue to hold Kelly's identity in the strictest confidence."

"She's a minor," Scott answered. "We do that as a matter of course. We got her out of there in a hurry. Nobody knows about her, not even ATF."

"I know. You've done a great job. But you know as well as I do that word gets around. I don't want to see her name pop up somewhere."

Ludlow said, "You think there's another perp out there?"

I smiled. "One thought did cross my mind." I reminded them that Jack Pfister had met with Bonilla several times at Sheridan. "Maybe Pfister was doing more than mentoring there. Maybe he was setting up the cartel business with Javier Acedo by way of Bonilla."

Ludlow nodded, and Scott shot me a knowing smile and said, "Yeah, we agree. He's worth looking at."

Kelly was declared a ward of the state, but I convinced a judge to grant Tay Jefferson temporary custody of her until a suitable foster home could be found. Tay volunteered to do this, which suited Kelly just fine. She had become fond of Tay and seemed, if not enthusiastic, then at least resigned to reentering foster care.

As for Veronica, I finally got a hold of her, but she hung up on me before I could get ten words out. I'm hoping she'll come to her senses and turn herself in. Kelly was inconsolable when she heard, and Tay and I have been trying to get her to see that it wasn't her fault, that Veronica had made her own choices.

When Nando returned from Cuba, I had him over for dinner. I'd called him in Cuba with the news, so he was aware of the broad outlines of what had gone down at the Arsenal that night. Nando was always hard to cook for because of his fondness for Caribbean style food and my decided lack of skill in that particular cuisine. Undaunted, I made a skillet full of blackened red snapper, a pot of black beans, and an avocado and tomato salad with a lime vinaigrette dressing from a recipe I found online.

We ate with gusto and drank cold Taberna, a Cuban beer my friend brought. I watched for signs of his mood, and he seemed fairly sanguine. Perhaps the visit with his mother in Cuba had helped him cope with Claudia's death. I hoped so.

We discussed the whole case in great detail. I went over what happened in the warehouse at the Arsenal at least twice, but he couldn't get enough of the details. At one point, he took a swig of beer, swallowed, and said, "So this man, Arthur, took a gun smaller than his hand and shot Claudia's killer right between the eyes. The killer dropped, wondering what had happened to him." He smiled, and it was clear he was storing away a mental picture he could revisit and savor.

"That's right. He had a holster strapped to his ankle. The guy collected guns. I saw a derringer like that one on his office wall. He was an expert marksman, too. I know. I saw him shoot. But dropping Timmons at fifteen feet with that little thing took unbelievable skill."

Nando raised his bottle. "I will put some flowers on Arthur Finley's grave. And the young spray can vandal," he continued. "She witnessed this and then the man turning the gun on himself?"

I nodded. "Kelly. Her name's Kelly Spence. If it hadn't been for her, Farnell Timmons would probably still be out there. She risked her life trying to find Timmons."

"I am not understanding it, Calvin. How could a child of sixteen be so courageous?"

"She was outraged at what she saw, Nando, and she knew Timmons had killed not only Claudia but a homeless man that she loved. Kelly stands out, but I can tell you there are lots of kids out there on the street trying to get by, kids with plenty of courage."

He nodded solemnly. "Is she all right now?"

"She's pretty traumatized from all she's been through, but Tay Jefferson's working with her on a daily basis. Kelly's a very tough young lady."

Nando drank some beer and sighed. "I suppose I should feel bad about Anthony Cardenas's false arrest, but I do not."

I nodded. "He made his own bed, trying to buy an alibi."

Nando's eyes narrowed down. "Yes, and he threatened my Claudia. Do not forget that."

"Yeah, he had motive, but they never put him at

the crime scene. It was a crap case. I think he would have beaten it."

We talked and philosophized until the beer was gone, and by that time, I could hardly hold my eyes open. I walked him down to the first floor entry and extended my hand. "I'm glad you're back, Nando."

He took my hand, pulled me to him, and gave me a bear hug that nearly crushed my chest. Nando was not the hugging type, and the move left me speechless. Then he fixed me with his big, dark eyes. "Calvin. Thank you once again. I will not forget this. Ever." He smiled. "And as for the young tagger, Kelly Spence, I shall have to think of a suitable way to express my appreciation. Good night, my friend."

I watched as he faded into the misting night, a big hulk of a man with an even bigger heart.

FIFTY-NINE

Kelly

FROM THE OUTSIDE, at least, Kelly's life was back to something resembling what it used to look like. She was back at New Directions. Her absence was no big deal, because the school's a drop-in center, meaning kids come and go, and the studies are all individualized and self-paced. She got her job back at Granite Works, too. Claxton had stopped by the gym to talk to Phil Hanson, and that was that. He never told her what he said to Hanson.

But things were far from back to normal for Kelly. The school seemed different somehow, almost alien. A bunch of street kids like her worrying about what some poet was trying to say, how to solve an algebra equation, or how the government worked. It all seemed so trivial now, not trivial as much as irrelevant. The real world, the adult world, wasn't waiting out there with open arms for kids who did their homework. It was a cruel place, a place where people died suddenly and violently at the hands of people who looked so, so *ordinary. And the guns! My God, was the world becoming an armed camp?* she asked herself time and again. Would every man, woman, and child need a gun for protection? It seemed so, but she hoped not. She never wanted to see another gun in her life.

Kelly yearned to find her old self, the K209 tagger who'd been out there putting the adult world on notice that things weren't right, the fighter who'd stood up for what she believed in. She wanted that back but despaired that it was gone forever, that her spirit had bled out like the people she'd seen die. Tay Jefferson warned her that she might have dark thoughts like this.

"You've been through a terrible shock, Kelly. Remember, the whole world isn't like this. There are good people out there and reasons to be optimistic."

Optimistic? Are you kidding me?

After school that first day back, Kelly and Kiyana walked over to O'Bryant Square to talk. The sky was a dazzling blue as if to compensate for the previous week of rain and grayness, and a young woman with flowing red hair stood in the Square playing a mandolin and singing. The two friends were dancing around a touchy subject. At least Kiyana thought it was touchy. "So, we're good, then, about me ratting you out to Claxton?" Kiyana finally said.

Kelly smiled a little impishly. "Yeah, we're good. I just wanted you to squirm a little. I know you talked to him because you were worried about me."

"Worried? I was petrified that those bastards would catch up with you, and so was Claxton. I had to trust somebody, baby girl."

"Speaking of bastards, have you seen Digger?"

"Nope. Nobody has. The dude disappeared."

"Zook?"

Kiyana smiled. "I was wondering when you'd get

around to him. I haven't seen him, but I heard he admitted himself at DePaul. Detox, in-patient treatment, the whole nine yards."

Kelly smiled, and a small bubble of hope rose up in her. "Oh, that's wonderful, Ki. That's great news."

KELLY WALKED OVER to Caffeine Central after Kiyana left for work. Cal was waiting for her, and they immediately left in Cal's car for the Portland Police Bureau building over on SW Salmon Street. Kelly knew the building well. She'd tagged it with a big, red, middle finger one night, one of her finer accomplishments. She felt a little tug of pride, and maybe a little bit of her fighting spirit returned as they approached the imposing building.

They signed in and were escorted up to the Homicide Division, where Scott and Ludlow were waiting. Scott told them to sit and handed Kelly a bottle of water. "Here," he said with a slight smile. "I know you kids can't go more than a few minutes without one of these." He sat down and grew more serious. "So here's what we're going to do, Kelly. We've spliced together audio excerpts from Jack Pfister's interview, and then had seven other people speak the same lines. We're going to play them back for you, one at a time. We want to know if any of the voices sound like the one you heard that night at the granary and then again in the parking lot of the Arsenal. Are we clear?"

Kelly nodded, and Claxton said, "It's like a lineup, but voices instead of people."

"Right," Ludlow chimed in. "We can't hang our hat on this, but if you can pick him out we'll sure as hell look at Pfister a lot harder."

They led Kelly into an interview room where a tape recorder was set up with a pair of headphones. "All set, Kelly?" Scott asked. She nodded and swallowed as her stomach clinched up. She had to get this. She didn't want to let them down, and most of all she wanted to nail The Voice, the other man who'd beaten Rupert to death.

Scott placed the headphones over her ears and switched on the tape recorder. Kelly hunkered down, closed her eyes, and listened with all the concentration she could summon. It wasn't even close. None of the voices sounded the least bit familiar to her. *Who am I kidding?* she asked herself after she took the headphones off and admitted defeat. *Why did I think I could do this? How embarrassing!*

Kelly must have apologized ten times to Scott and Ludlow, but they seemed to take it all in stride. "You gave it your best shot, Kelly," Scott told her. "We appreciate you coming in." She could tell he really meant it. Not a bad guy, that cop.

When they got out in the hall, Ludlow said with the first smile she ever saw on his face, "I gotta ask you one thing, Kelly. How in the hell did you get up on this building to paint that finger?"

Kelly looked at Cal, who had started to laugh, then back at Ludlow. "Trade secret," she said, absolutely dead pan.

When they came out of the building, Cal said, "It's a beautiful day. Let's walk over to the fountain and decompress. It's one of my favorite spots."

"Mine, too," Kelly said, although at the moment she felt like she'd just let the entire world down.

They sat there for a while just watching the breeze

lift spray off the streams that converged into a seething column at the center of the fountain. Claxton said nothing, as if he were waiting for her to speak. Finally she said, "Bummer. I was sure I could've picked him out, Cal."

Cal shrugged. "Well, that's a lot to ask, you know. What did you hear at the granary, all of ten or fifteen words?"

Kelly thought back on that night, how those words seemed to sear themselves into her brain for reasons she couldn't really explain. "Yeah, but I heard the same voice again at the Arsenal, don't forget. I'm sure of that."

Cal nodded. They both fell silent and watched a toddler venture to the perimeter of the fountain, then dash back to her mother over and over. Finally, Cal asked the question on both their minds. "So you think it's not Pfister, or is it that too much time has passed and your memory's blurred a little?"

Kelly's nose began to burn, her eyes filled, and she struggled to hold the tears back. "I don't know, Cal. I just don't know." A sigh drained from her chest. "But I wish this thing would end."

Cal put an arm around her and pulled her to him. She began to cry. "Hey, it's okay," he said. "You're not in this alone anymore, Kelly. We'll find this guy, I promise."

Promises were not on the list of things Kelly took stock in, but she knew this guy Claxton meant what he said. He was as stubborn as she was.

SIXTY

Cal

WHEN WE GOT to the car after leaving the fountain, I said to Kelly, "Claudia Borrego's fiancé wants to meet you. Are you okay with that?" She told me she was, so we drove over to Nando's PI office in Lents. Esperanza sprang up from her desk when we walked in. "Oh, Cal, this must be Kelly." She came around and hugged her. "Nando has told me so much about you." Kelly smiled back politely, seemingly taken aback by another exuberant greeting. Esperanza took Kelly's hand. "Come with me. Nando's dying to meet you." She looked at me and winked. "You can come, too, Cal."

She led Kelly into Nando's office, and I followed. The big man came around his desk, bowed deeply, and said, "Such a pleasure to meet you, Kelly," and kissed her hand. Kelly didn't know what to do, but her face did—it blushed three shades of red. We chatted, keeping the banter light, with Nando doing most of the talking, and Kelly sitting there absolutely mesmerized by my flamboyant friend. It wasn't until we got up to leave that Nando took the conversation in a serious direction. He said, "I am sorry for the violence you witnessed and for the loss of your friend, Rupert Youngblood. He was courageous beyond mea-

sure, but your courage surpassed even his in risking
your life to bring those monsters to justice. It is an
honor to meet you, Kelly. I am forever in your debt."

Modest to a fault, Kelly blushed all over again and
thanked him.

As I filed past Nando he handed me an envelope
and said in a low voice, "Here, Calvin, Kelly needs a
college fund and this will act as seed money." I took
the envelope only to find that Esperanza had an envelope for me as well, a much larger one.

"You asked for a background report on Farnell
Timmons a while back," she said. "I know he's dead
now, but here it is. I forgot to give it to you in all the
excitement. Sorry, Cal."

When we got to the car, I handed Kelly the smaller
envelope, not knowing what Nando had given her.
She opened it and removed a light-green check and
stared at it in bug-eyed amazement. "Cal, I think this
is a check for ten thousand dollars." She handed me
the check.

Yep, four zeros.

Nando was the tightest person with a buck I ever
knew, but there you go. I drove off feeling very proud
of my friend.

I HAD DINNER with Tay and Kelly that night. It turned
into a celebration of Kelly's new college fund, and
both Tay and I took heart at Kelly's buoyant spirits.

When I got back to Caffeine Central, Archie would
not make eye contact with me, a sign that he was thoroughly pissed off. "Hey, big guy," I told him, "I'm
sorry but I had a lot on my plate today. Don't worry,
I'll take you all the way down to the river just as soon

as I feed you." It's always a good idea to apologize to your dog when you screw up.

When I went to bed that night, I couldn't shut my brain down. I kept coming back to this crazy case and wondering what in the hell I'd missed. There was a loose end somewhere, a big one, and a threatening one. Finally, I swung out of bed at one thirty or so, put on slippers and a thick terry robe, and padded down the short hall to the kitchen table.

I poured myself a glass of Rémy, sat down, and opened up the report on Farnell Timmons. It was probably old news, but it was the only thing I hadn't scrutinized up one side and down the other. Like anything prepared by Esperanza, the report was thorough and well documented. It covered Timmons's education, where he'd lived, where he'd worked, his marriages, credit reports, anything newsworthy about him, and so on. I began to slog through the report, noting first that he had no criminal record, which is what he'd told me that night as he herded Kelly and me back to the Arsenal.

I must have been five or six pages into the report when I stopped reading and moved my face closer to the page, as if that would somehow verify what I was seeing. I leaned back in my chair, then came forward and whacked the table hard with the ball of my fist. Archie sprang to his feet and began barking wildly.

"Of course!" I shouted. "That's it. It has to be."

SIXTY-ONE

Cal

I STAYED UP late that night planning a way forward, then got up early the next morning and took Archie for a brisk run. The good weather was holding, and the walkway along the west side of the river was jammed with Portlanders starved for sunshine. At a little past nine I walked into Harmon Scott's office. He looked up from a desk covered with papers and frowned. "Uh oh, why do I have this feeling I'm not going to like this, Claxton?"

I sat down and showed him what I had and laid out my proposal in detail. He countered with a barrage of questions, all of which I answered. I finished up by saying, "This will work, Harmon, I know it."

Scott took off his glasses and polished them on his shirtsleeve, his forehead lashed with deep furrows. "Goddamn it, I thought this was going to be a quiet day." He exhaled a long breath. "This is touchy stuff, you know. Stings always are. I'll have to sell it up the line."

I nodded my understanding but felt a little anxious. Scott bought my plan, but would his more politically attuned higher-ups give us a green light? I had my doubts.

I met Picasso at a little before eleven as he was

opening up his gallery. I had a double cappuccino in one hand and handed him a green tea with the other. He took the tea and smiled. "My favorite hot drink. This must be serious business, Cal. Come on in."

We went inside, and I told him what I needed. When I finished he stroked his chin a couple of times and nodded. "That's definitely in my wheelhouse. I'll need some good samples to work from."

"No problem with the samples. How long will it take you?"

"One page? A day or two to practice and one day to make the document."

"Good," I told him. "Stand by. I'll be in touch."

Next, I drove across the Hawthorne Bridge to the Bridgetown Arsenal. The parking lot was deserted except for a single, extended cab Ram pickup. Roz Jenkins got out of the cab when I drove up. "Hello, Cal," she said, taking my offered hand. She gave me a strong grip and a strong smile, but I could see a tinge of sadness in her eyes. "I figured we could meet here since I have to go through some files today, anyway. The cops and ATF have finally finished with the building."

"How bad a hit are you going to take?" I asked.

"Oh, I'm gonna lose everything I put into this business." Her gaze shifted to something past me and became wistful. "It's not the money so much. Hell, I still got plenty. I wanted to build something I could be proud of, you know?" I nodded and she snapped her gaze back to me. "Well, come on, let's hear what you have to say." I followed her through the showroom, which echoed with emptiness. She waved a hand. "Confiscated. Everything."

"Even the Thompson submachine gun?"

"Oh, yeah. ATF took Arthur's complete gun collection, just like that. Jack Pfister's trying to get our personal items back, but he told us not to hold our breath."

"How is Jack?"

"Oh, he's fine, but he's feeling a lot of heat. He thinks he's a suspect in this deal."

"What do you think?"

"Jack? No way."

I followed her up to her office, noting that she was no longer wearing her Timmons boots. Her office was bare, the drawers of the filing cabinets open with a few folders left here and there. When I finished explaining what I had in mind, she leaned back in her chair with a kind of dazed look on her face. "Well, I'll be damned to hell. You think he'll actually buy it?"

I looked her straight in the eye. "Yes, I do, Roz. If anyone can pull this off, it's you."

Later that afternoon, ATF Special Agent Richie Truax dropped by my office at my request. He surprised me with a bottle of Springbank single malt Scotch. When I thanked him he said, "Least I could do, Cal." He laughed, "You're a meddlesome bastard, but we couldn't have taken that operation down without your help." We huddled for a while, and before he left Tay and Kelly dropped in, and I introduced them.

My ducks were now in a row.

SIXTY-TWO

Cal

SCOTT MUST HAVE done a good selling job, because three days later we got the green light to set the plan in motion. I said "we," but that wasn't quite true. With the exception of some coaching of Roz Jenkins and liaison with Picasso, the Portland brass decreed I was not to be involved. Scott told me it had to do with liability, but we both knew it was about who was going to get the credit.

In any case, I was pissed. I wanted to be there.

It was another six days before the sting actually went down. Tay, Kelly, and I sat in my office at Caffeine Central that day anxiously awaiting for a call from Roz Jenkins with news. At two fifty-eight that afternoon the call came in. I listened and then turned to Kelly and Tay, *"They got him!"* Over the din of the two of them dancing around like crazy people, I invited Roz to join us for a celebration.

Roz arrived later that evening bearing a cold bottle of Dom Pérignon. "I thought we could toast that bastard's demise and hoist one for Arthur, too." She hugged Kelly, and after I introduced her to Tay, said, "You should have seen the look on that ATF agent's face when the cops moved in. Couldn't have happened to a nicer guy."

I said, "I knew you could sell it, Roz. Were you nervous?"

"Well, maybe a little when we made the exchange. He gave me a briefcase with the money. I looked it over, hundreds and fifties just like I'd asked for, lots of them. I gave him the letter. I figured if he was going to try something that would be the time. But the cops had him covered six ways to Sunday, he just didn't know it." She patted the side of the blazer she wore and smiled. "I was packing, too."

I poured a round of champagne—just a taste for Kelly—and after a toast, Roz sat down and said, "I only got bits and pieces of this story, Cal. How did you figure it was Truax?"

I chuckled. "I was totally focused on Jack Pfister because of his relationship with Manny Bonilla. But one thing bothered me about Truax—he always showed up to talk to me alone, which seemed a little off. But I didn't think too much about that until I read a background report on Farnell Timmons. Turns out he was an outstanding football player in high school and wound up being recruited by the University of Southern California in the eighties, although he never became a starter. Well, that's the same team Richie Truax played on during the same four years. I knew that because Truax was a big star during that period. So I had a connection. I figured Truax could have recruited Timmons to set up the straw buyers and provide drivers from around that part of rural Oregon. And this could explain how Timmons knew Kelly and I were at the Arsenal that night, something that baffled me. After all, Truax had followed me on a couple of occasions. Why not that night?

"There was another loose end," I continued. "If I assumed Jack Pfister wasn't involved, then how did the deal with the cartels get set up? I thought all along that Manny was used as a conduit to Javier Acedo inside Sheridan." I glanced over at Tay. "Tay helped me with that."

She shrugged. "All I did was remind Cal that Manny was gay, that he could have been seeing Acedo for more, uh, personal reasons. An ATF agent like Truax would be capable of setting up the deal without Bonilla's help, or even Acedo's help for that matter." Tay looked at Roz. "So Manny Bonilla showed up at the Arsenal for a legitimate job as your driver, Roz."

"Right," I said. "And Arthur knew from Jack Pfister that Manny was an excellent mechanic, someone he could use in the expanding production of the drop-in triggers. So, he turned him with the promise of easy money. I mean, why not? The guy was an ex-felon, and the work would have been right up his alley."

"Then Manny tells his case manager, Claudia Borrego, what he's gotten himself into, and she convinces him to pull away," Tay added. "But by then he knows too much, and when he tries to back out—" she dropped her eyes "—well, we know the rest."

Anguish washed over Roz's face and she shook her head. "God, I have such mixed feelings about Arthur."

I glanced at Kelly. "The man's a hero in my book. He wound up doing the right thing."

Roz showed a wisp of a smile and nodded. "Thank you, Cal. You're right, I suppose, but he was such a damn fool. For Arthur it was all about money and ego. He wanted his goddamn little triggers in all those AR-15s. He obviously didn't care one wit where the guns wound up, as long as they made money, which he turned around and plowed back into the legit business." She looked at me, her smile laced with bitterness. "The Starbucks of shooting ranges. That's all he could think about, you know? Hell, we were doing fine. We didn't need those damn triggers. Now he's dead and so's the business. Like I said, what a damn fool."

The room fell silent. Finally, Tay said to Roz, "How is your daughter holding up?"

Roz exhaled a deep sigh. "Oh, the shock and the humiliation have taken their toll, but Melanie's a strong woman. The only saving grace is that Arthur's last act saved lives, including mine. She'll get through this." She took a sip of champagne and forced a smile. "Tell me how you handled bringing the police in, Cal. That must've been ticklish."

"I figured my chances of selling the idea to the Portland Police Bureau were fifty-fifty at best. Anyway, I took what I had at that point to Harmon Scott and managed to convince him to let Kelly have a shot at recognizing Truax's voice. Then I invited Truax to my office and arranged to have Kelly drop in. Scott and his partner, Ludlow, were upstairs watching the video feed from a hidden camera."

Roz looked at Kelly. "What did you think when you heard Truax speak?"

Kelly's eyes got big, and she brought a hand to her mouth. "Oh, my God, I just about fainted, but there was no doubt in my mind." She looked at me with a mock glare. "He just had Tay and me walk in. He didn't warn me or anything."

I raised my hands in defense. "Scott and Ludlow

insisted on that. We had to be certain, and telling her in advance would have compromised the test." I winked at Kelly. "Anyway, I knew she could handle it."

Roz slapped her knee and laughed.

Tay joined the laughter and turned to Kelly. She lost a lot of color and had this look like she just swallowed a bad clam or something. I was afraid Truax might suspect something, but he didn't. When Truax left, Kelly turned to Cal and me and said, "That's him! That's The Voice. I'm positive."

Roz said, "Oh, I want to see that video, but it still wasn't enough, right?"

"Right," I said. "Not even close for an arrest. But Kelly was so confident that she convinced Scott and Ludlow, and they sold the sting up the Portland Police Bureau chain of command. The case was dicey, because it crossed jurisdictional lines. We needed a solid story to go after an ATF agent."

Roz nodded. "That's where your artist friend comes in. He did one hell of a job on that letter. Truax never questioned the authenticity of the thing."

"Yeah, well, Picasso's as good as they come," I said. "I knew Truax wouldn't have time to authenticate it, anyway." I looked at Roz. "How did that first phone contact go?"

Roz sipped some champagne and settled back in her chair. "Oh, that went well, thanks to your coaching. I told Truax that Melanie knew everything that he and Arthur were up to, but when the killings started, she became afraid for Arthur's life. I said she had him write a letter stating that the whole gun running scheme was Truax's idea, and that Truax was making sure things ran unimpeded by the ATF. The letter also stated that Farnell Timmons had told him Truax was directly involved in the murder of a homeless man, Rupert Youngblood, at a granary in Portland. The idea was that if anything happened to Arthur, the letter would go to the police."

"Mentioning the Youngblood murder was key," I chimed in. "As far as Truax knew, the only two people who could put him at the scene were Timmons and Arthur, and they were both dead. So I figured the letter would look like the genuine article to him." I turned and smiled at Kelly. "But he was wrong. There was another witness."

Roz raised her glass to Kelly before continuing. "Anyway, I told Truax I didn't personally care if he beat a homeless man to death, but I thought the cops and the ATF might. I said that Melanie and I thought it was only fair that since he tanked the family business he should buy the letter back. After all, he must have a lot of cash stashed away."

"But Truax wasn't sold. He said, 'If Arthur supposedly wrote this letter for protection, why the hell didn't he threaten me with it?' I laughed out loud at that and told him, 'You know Arthur, for Christ's sake. He was too damn chicken to confront you. Melanie must have asked him a dozen times to man up and tell you about the letter.' That seemed to do it. Truax paused on the line for a while, then said he wanted to see the note. The rest was easy."

Tay raised her glass and said, "Bravo, Roz," and Kelly and I followed suit. Then Tay said, "One thing I've been wondering about—how did Arthur and Truax get together in the first place?"

I shrugged, but Roz managed a laugh. "Funny you should ask. About eighteen months ago, Arthur told me he was playing with a trigger design he wasn't sure was legal. I told him to check it out with the ATF. I didn't want any trouble with the Feds. I was pulling back from the day-to-day operations then, so I didn't give it another thought." She looked at me somewhat apologetically. "I didn't think of this until I was driving over here, Cal."

"So, the ATF agent that showed up was Truax?" I said.

She nodded. "Yep. That's the way I figure it. The bastard saw the potential for illegal sales and pointed it out to Arthur." She shook her head emphatically. "No way it happened the other way around. Arthur wouldn't have suggested something like that to an ATF agent. He didn't have the balls for it."

AFTER ROZ SAID her goodbyes, Tay, Kelly, and I gathered up Archie and Spencer and took a long walk along the river. The reflection of the city in the river shimmered in a gentle breeze, and the cars up on the Marquam Bridge looked like a chorus line of fireflies. Kelly was full of energy and went dashing up and down the greenspace with the dogs leading the way, barking and straining at their leashes. She laughed and shouted, acting like, well, a happy sixteen-year-old girl. It was good to see that.

Tay and I continued walking, not saying much, both lost in our thoughts. I felt at peace for the first time in a long time. I set out to simply help a friend find his fiancée's killer and bring a young tagger in from the cold, and look what happened. Looking back, it felt a lot like turning over a rock only to find way more snakes than I expected. But at least some bad actors were off the board and fewer automatic weapons would fall into the hands of the wrong people. Was I trying to bail the ocean with a thimble? Perhaps, but from where I sit, that's the human condition. Do what you can. Make a difference in the small space around you. That's as close to a philosophy as I can get.

We stopped to gaze at the spectral lights that decorated the Morrison Bridge. Tay took my hand, gently squeezed it, and said, "I'm glad I met you, Cal Claxton. I think we make a pretty good team."

"I couldn't agree more," I told her. Then I stopped, took her in my arms and kissed her. For real this time.

Kelly laughed and called out to us, "Hey, you guys, knock that off or get a room."

SIXTY-THREE

Cal

Six months later

Spring in Oregon is more than anything else a celebration of light. After months of bullying by a gray, joyless cloud cover, the sun begins to assert itself again with more than just token gestures. Not that the rain isn't appreciated here. Without its abundance Oregon simply wouldn't be the place that it is, and we Oregonians get that. But the sun, the light in spring— ah, that's a welcome treat.

From my deck at the Aerie it seemed like you could see forever down the Willamette Valley, which stretched to the south between the Cascades and the Coastal Range, a patchwork quilt of greens, golds, and ochres. Closer in, a few hawks circled over the vineyards, where just a few moments earlier a bald eagle had graced us with a fly-by that allowed a clear view of its snow white cap and fierce yellow beak.

Tay, Kelly, and Nando had joined me for a cookout to celebrate the approval by DHS of Tay as Kelly's foster mom just the day before. I was busy barbecuing corn in the husk and a slab of Chinook salmon on a moist cedar plank, while Tay chopped veggies for a salad she was building. She was fascinated with cooking and had quickly mastered the handful of kitchen tricks I knew.

Nando was bringing us all up to date on Richie Truax's legal situation. "So, the man is looking at enough federal gun charges to keep him in jail the rest of his life."

"Was anyone else in the ATF involved in the gun running?" I asked. It was something I hadn't heard anything about.

Nando shook his head. "No. What I am told is that Truax acted as a lone wolf when he set up the illegal operation with Arthur Finley. He had transferred up from San Diego, so he had a thorough knowledge of cartel activities and border security operations."

"Motive?" I asked. The truth was, I knew very little about this man who had disgraced a proud law enforcement agency.

Nando opened his hands. "The usual—a penchant for expensive toys, speedboats, sports cars, fast women, all of which require money. Lots of it." He waved a hand dismissively. "But jail time is the least of Truax's worries. I just learned his attempt to plea bargain the Rupert Youngblood murder to second degree was turned down by the DA. They're charging him with aggravated murder, which carries a mandatory death penalty. I am relieved. I thought they might let the bag of scum plea down."

"Why would they do that?" Kelly snapped. "I mean, he bought back a letter claiming he killed Rupert."

"That was a bit problematic for the prosecution," I chimed in. "Truax could claim he paid Roz Jenkins for the letter to cover up his involvement in the gun running, that he had nothing to do with the murder."

"But I identified his voice as the one I heard at the granary," Kelly protested.

"True, and that put him at the scene," I said, "but the defense would have come after you with a vengeance. The case against him was solid, but prosecutors are a worrying bunch and look for ways to avoid expensive trials." I looked at Nando. "So what swung it?"

"Farnell Timmons," Nando said. "Truax was scrupulously careful in hiding his involvement in the scheme, but two straw buyers gave sworn statements that Timmons had bragged to them about the Youngblood murder and Truax's direct participation in it." Nando looked at me and smiled. "They were the two you referred to as Mutt and Jeff, I believe."

"So much for honor among thieves," Tay quipped. She sat on the deck, propped against the railing with Archie on one side of her and Spencer on the other. Her relationship with Kelly had blossomed, and it was an easy decision for DHS to sanction the foster care arrangement. They were both ecstatic with the outcome, although I had a feeling it would take some adjusting. An independent, headstrong kid used to the freedom of the streets and a tough, no-nonsense woman who had never experienced the exquisite joys of parenting. It promised to be interesting.

As promised, I took a look at going after the foster parent who had molested Kelly, but it turned out the man had died of a massive stroke six months prior. Frankly, I was relieved and I believe Kelly was, too. Call it poetic justice.

Zook was back from rehab, and the basketball was back on his hip. He passed all his GED exams except math, and if Kelly gets him over the hump and he stays clean he has a shot at a basketball scholarship at PSU for next season. Kiyana is finishing up at New Directions, as well. The hearing to win her emancipation from her parents was a slam dunk. The judge remarked what a pleasure it was to see such a fine, independent young woman. She's applying for a paying internship at Intel and using me as a reference. I think she'll get it.

I never did get to talk to Veronica. Her cell number was no longer active. Kelly still held out hope that Veronica would get in touch, that she would decide to stop running. It was clear that she still loved her dad's girlfriend. Such are the workings of a pure heart.

As for me, I'm trying to spend more time in Dundee these days to get my law practice back to a paying proposition. Well, that and getting ready for a float trip on the Deschutes River to catch the upcoming salmon fly hatch. It promises to be a dandy. Claire is coming up from Berkeley to join me on the trip this year. I can't wait for her to meet Tay. I think they're going to like each other.

* * * * *

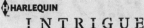

Get 2 Free Books,
Plus 2 Free Gifts—
just for trying the Reader Service!

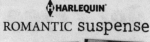

Get 2 Free Books,
Plus 2 Free Gifts—
just for trying the Reader Service!

WORLDWIDE LIBRARY®

Get 2 Free Books,
Plus 2 Free Gifts —
just for trying the Reader Service!